MetEoR

In thE

MadHousE

With a foreword by **MARIANNE FORREST**

Leon Forrest

Edited and with introductions by **John G. Cawelti** *and* **Merle Drown**

■■■ TRIQUARTERLY BOOKS
■■■ NORTHWESTERN UNIVERSITY PRESS
EVANSTON, ILLINOIS

TriQuarterly Books
Northwestern University Press
Evanston, Illinois 60208-4210

Printed in the United States of America
10 9 8 7 6 5 4 3 2 1

ISBN 0-8101-5114-6

Library of Congress Cataloging-in-Publication Data
Forrest, Leon.
    Meteor in the madhouse / Leon Forrest ; with a foreword by Marianne Forrest ; edited and with introductions by John G. Cawelti and Merle Drown.
        p.   cm.
    ISBN 0-8101-5114-6 (alk. paper)
    1. Forest County (Imaginary place)—Fiction. 2. Afro-American civil rights workers—Fiction. 3. Afro-American authors—Fiction. 4. Male friendship—Fiction. 5. Mentally ill—fiction. I. Title.
    PS3556.O738 M48 2000
    813'.54—dc21   00–012338

The paper used in this publication meets the minimum requirements of the American National Standard for Information Sciences—Permanence of Paper for Printed Library Materials, ANSI Z39.48-1984.

For my dear wife, MARIANNE

Contents

Foreword

Marianne Forrest

I met Leon in the spring of 1970. Our first conversations centered on his ambition to write a great American novel. We both lived in Hyde Park, an area that surrounds the University of Chicago. Over coffee we discussed the writings of Ralph Ellison, Richard Wright, and F. Scott Fitzgerald. He introduced me to his many friends, who joined in these discussions. I don't know of anyone who enjoyed the company of others more than Leon did.

A compassionate man, Leon allowed for human frailties, finding good in those people that some in the community spoke of as rascals. This compassion lives in his portraits of the sometimes unfortunate characters in his fiction.

I was a divorcée and perfectly content with my work and my own friends and family. I had vowed to myself that I would not marry again. However, I fell shamelessly in love with this man, and when he asked me to marry him, I said yes.

As the years passed, Leon's passion for the written word increased. He also had a generous respect for the oral tradition, which he integrated into his work. Although he wrote few personal letters, he kept friendships that spanned decades, often communicating by telephone. The artist Richard Hunt and the renowned composer T. J. Anderson were the recipients of many of Leon's late-night calls. The three of them were a happy trio. Once, at Richard's summer home, they tape-recorded their ideas on the differences in artistic expression in their respective fields.

Leon wrote plays, poems, librettos, and essays and published four novels. He left behind reams of unpublished work, including the manuscript that made up the five novellas of *Meteor in the Madhouse*.

John Cawelti and Merle Drown—the two men I chose to edit these novellas—were Leon's friends for more than thirty years. John has followed Leon's work since the 1960s. He edited a very accurate critique of Leon's novels: *Leon Forrest: Introduction and Interpretations*, published by Bowling Green State University. Merle read almost everything Leon wrote, both published and unpublished. In the days before my husband's death, Merle came from his home in New Hampshire to spend time with him. They discussed the outline of Leon's work-in-progress, the novellas that make up this book. Several times when Leon refused to eat and the nurse could not persuade him, it was Merle who fed him.

Two weeks afer Merle left, when Leon became too weak to use the word processor, he dictated the last two pages of the final novella, *The Meteor in the Madhouse*, to me. In those long-ago, sun-filled days in Hyde Park, Leon had told me that he would write as long as he lived. He did.

Editors'
Introduction

Thoughts on
Meteor in the Madhouse

John G. Cawelti

> Surely there, the ever high-flying Sugar-Groove will settle not so much
> in harmony with the stars but rather dazzle the Heavens with a most
> inventive light, which down the light-years of memory will be rekindled
> by newly illuminating beacons of lyrical light of the mind and soul. New
> bards will find new dazzling searchlights, and even lighthouses within the
> spirit of the forever shape-shifting Sugar-Groove.
>
> *Divine Days*

One might think that after completing a major novel of 1,135 pages
the author might feel himself emptied out, but Leon Forrest's fictional
imagination, his extraordinary capacity to reinvent his life into a dazzling
galaxy of stories, continued to pour forth material. In the wake of *Divine
Days*, Forrest began an even more ambitious project, a group of novellas
that he hoped would be a culmination of his life's work and of the
fictional world of Forest County that he had created in his four previous
novels. Unfortunately, the devastating illness that brought about his
tragically early death at the age of sixty prevented him from carrying
out his immense project as he had first envisioned it. Nevertheless, he
continued heroically to work on *Meteor in the Madhouse*, and shortly
before his death he felt that he had brought a unified work to completion,
albeit on a smaller scale than he had originally intended.

Merle Drown and I were both longtime friends of Leon Forrest, and we met him around the same time, though in different ways. Merle was a fellow writer and resident of the wondrous Avon, a wild, multicultural boardinghouse just across the Midway from the University of Chicago. I was a young instructor at the University of Chicago, brought together with Leon by my friend and colleague Perrin Lowrey, in whose classes Leon had studied Faulkner and many other things. Our friendships did not actually overlap until Leon's death, which Merle describes so movingly in his introductory essay. That both of us knew Leon so long without knowing each other is perhaps symbolic of the many different circles of people who orbited the remarkable figure of Leon Forrest.

When Marianne Forrest asked us to assist with the editing of Leon's manuscript, Merle and I found that we were able to work together and to arrive at the necessary decisions quite easily. Indeed, we discovered that the sense we had of Leon's intentions and style was remarkably congruent, another testimony, I think, to the great power and spirit of the man and the writer. The work here presented is in every respect that of Leon Forrest. As editors we have corrected obvious mistakes and smoothed over a few elisions and apparent gaps in the manuscript. In the process, we have added nothing of significance and in some cases have left minor breaks and inconsistencies rather than trying to invent something to fill them. We were greatly aided in this process by Marianne, who helped us decipher things we could not read and who has read and approved our final edit. The design and virtually all of the words are those of Leon himself.

In this introduction I will discuss some of the central characteristics and artistic accomplishments of *Meteor in the Madhouse*. Though most of the book seems easier to interpret than some of the more difficult passages of Forrest's early work, it is still true that a good knowledge of Forrest's imagined world and its characters make many things clear that might otherwise be somewhat hazy for the reader. To aid the reader, we have added an appendix with more detailed commentary and interpretation of the individual novellas, as well as a genealogy clarifying the relationship among the characters.

Meteor in the Madhouse is made up of five interconnected novellas framed by an account of what turns out to be the last days in the life of Joubert Antoine Jones, the character whose narrative of a crucial week in his young manhood is the basis of *Divine Days*. But *Meteor in the Madhouse* also looks back to characters and episodes from Forrest's first three novels, the Nathaniel Witherspoon trilogy of *There Is a Tree More Ancient Than Eden* (1973), *The Bloodworth Orphans* (1977), and *Two Wings to Veil My Face* (1983). Thus *Meteor in the Madhouse* displays the major worlds of Forest County. Much of it centers on the mature Joubert Jones but it also traverses the richly comic world of his youth as represented in *Divine Days*. The fourth novella, *To the Magical Memory of Rain*, revisits the surrealist world of archetypal myth that played such an important role in *The Bloodworth Orphans*. The final novella, *By Dawn's Early Light: The Meteor in the Madhouse*, echoes both in story and in style the lyrical and tragic consciousness of Forrest's first novel. However, though reminiscent of earlier work, *Meteor in the Madhouse* also presents new elements and new potentialities that make one deeply regret that Forrest's death did not permit him to explore these literary realms further.

Meteor in the Madhouse's structural form can best be explained with a musical analogy. The influence of jazz, blues, and gospel music on Forrest's work has been often commented on both by himself and by others, but Forrest also loved classical music, and the structure of *Meteor in the Madhouse* rather resembles that of one of the late Beethoven quartets, whether intentionally or unintentionally we do not know. Like a Beethoven quartet, the work is framed by two long and complex movements, with a number of shorter, more lyrical, and dancelike movements in between. *Lucasta Jones, in Solitude: Lives Left in Her Wake* and *By Dawn's Early Light: The Meteor in the Madhouse* are the complex sonata forms of Forrest's "symphony," and they state and develop many of the same characters and themes. *Live! At Fountain's House of the Dead* and *All Floundering Oratorio of Souls* are briefer, more witty and satirical, in the manner of scherzos. The moody and lyrical *To the Magical Memory of Rain* is the adagio of *Meteor in the Madhouse*, a passage of deeply beautiful mystery, very different in tone from the novellas that precede and follow it. While there is a narrative and expository framework in *Meteor in the Madhouse*, the power of these musiclike structures in the work is very important to its ultimate effect.

Another key, musiclike pattern in *Meteor in the Madhouse* is Forrest's use of contrasting themes in the form of characters who symbolize different aspects of African American culture but who together represent the richness, the complexity, and the ambiguities of that culture.

The most important relationship of this sort is that of Joubert Jones, the narrator, with his adoptive kinsman and fellow writer, the poet Leonard Foster. Leonard was a political agitator and civil rights protester in the 1960s, became a madman in the 1970s, developed a cultish following as a preacher in the 1980s, and ended his life as a drug addict in 1992. Leonard represents an alternate life for Joubert and a symbol of the cost that the struggle for freedom and equality has sometimes demanded of gifted young African Americans. In some ways, Joubert feels guilty that to save his own art he has resisted the temptation to plunge into the political struggle. Now he wishes he could save Leonard, but it turns out to be too late. Ironically, Joubert himself becomes a victim of the chaotic violence of African American culture, as if to show that he could only escape temporarily from this fate.

The relationship of Joubert and Leonard also reflects the interplay in Forrest's work of his two successive major protagonists, Nathaniel Witherspoon and Joubert Jones. These narrative creations represent in turn two aspects of Forrest's own character: the young, embattled journalist struggling to make some room for his artistic interests in a world that is more concerned with politics and economics and the later distinguished university professor and novelist that Forrest would become. In a way, Joubert and Leonard represent conflicting worlds with different demands and perceptions, yet both are interlocking aspects of the African American experience.

Such intersecting worlds appear from the beginning of the first novella, *Lucasta Jones, in Solitude*. Here, the central character, Lucasta, is a pivotal figure linking the worlds of Joubert Jones and of Nathaniel Witherspoon, protagonist of Forrest's first three novels. Lucasta was the birth mother of Nathaniel Witherspoon's father, Arthur, and therefore Nathaniel's actual grandmother, though he never knew her. She is also Joubert Jones's great aunt, the sister of his beloved Grinny Gram Gussie, a wonderful character whose hilarious banter with her husband and Joubert is a central feature of the novella. At one time, Forrest apparently thought of creating a story in which Joubert and Nathaniel, his two alter egos, or reinvented autobiographies, would meet and become involved in some way. He did not carry out this project, but as we have seen, the character of Joubert's deeply disturbed kinsman, Leonard Foster, does stand in, to some extent, for Nathaniel.

As *Meteor in the Madhouse* continues, Joubert's complicated life and his memories cross many cultural and spiritual boundaries. The striking contrast between the two sisters, Lucasta and Gussie Jones, provides an example. Lucasta is the embodiment of the blues tradition. Gifted as a dancer, she is so sexually magnetic that the young Joubert has some of his first erotic fantasies about her, but she is unable to hold a man for very long. Lucasta's life is one of perpetual loss—of children and lovers— a veritable text for her idol Billie Holiday, some of whose problems Lucasta also experiences.

Gussie Jones, on the other hand, is a comic figure of solidity and sense. She has lived her whole life with one man, Joubert's grandfather Forester Jones, who idolizes her and humorously puts up with her benevolent tyranny. Gussie represents the solid peasant tradition of the southern Negro transplanted to the urban North but never loses the "grit and mother wit" that made it possible for her to endure and triumph over almost anything. Lucasta is a source of artistic and erotic imaginings for Joubert, but Gussie is the solid basis of his sense of morality and responsibility.

Many other symbolic characters and their worlds intersect in the course of the novellas: the strange double world of Fountain's House of the Dead, funeral home by day and brothel by night; the realms of the university—represented by the aspiring intellectual Shep Bottomly— and Eloise's Night Light Lounge, with its gallery of characters like the "terrible tonnage," McGovern McNabb; the romantic fantasies of a young, middle-class black woman such as Desirée Dobbs and the terribly seductive and destructive world of drugs. Among other things, *Meteor in the Madhouse* is, like much of Forrest's later work, a vivid portrayal of the great diversity of urban African American life.

This intersection of characters and worlds also involves some of Forrest's major themes, developed here with a richness and compression that go beyond the exuberant expansion of *Divine Days*, among them the struggle to make "a way out of no way," the flow of reinvention and re-creation, the dialectic of Protestant and Catholic spiritual visions, the ambiguous interplay between art and protest, the perennial quest for resurrection and redemption, and, ultimately, the struggle between the forces of life and of death. All of these themes come into play in Forrest's narrative, which sees life in both comic and tragic terms and finds a richly creative balance between order and chaos.

Leon Forrest's
Final Journey

Merle Drown

In October 1997, I drove to Chicago to spend a week with my dying friend, Leon Forrest. Though cancer had laid waste to his body, Leon still held on to his keen mind and rich spirit. During the day, he needed frequent breaks from conversation, and while he rested and dozed, I sat in his living room and read the manuscript we have called *Meteor in the Madhouse*. Although Leon had told me, "You see, Merle, I can't go on like this," pointing to the weakened body that would not even support him to walk to the bathroom on his own, he talked about his manuscript energetically and grew enthusiastic with the prospect of completing it. One morning when I arrived at his apartment, he had moved into his study to work on one of the novellas. And on that afternoon he sat in the living room to receive company. "I have taken up my bed and walked," he said, in recognition of the miracle.

We discussed small glitches that I'd noted in reading his manuscript, but we also talked about the larger issues of the work: its structure, the recurring themes that he treated so wisely, and the newer—and, to my taste, stronger—force of his narrator, Joubert Jones.

Already in his masterwork, *Divine Days*, Leon had moved his narrator to a more active position in the plot and away from the contemplative collector of stories, Nathaniel Witherspoon, of his earlier novels. In the novellas of *Meteor in the Madhouse*, however, Leon brings his wit and wisdom to play much more directly and with more direct reference to autobiographical elements. He himself recognized this new direction in his fiction and delighted in it.

I was overjoyed to see this development. For me and for most of Leon's friends, he was the wisest person we had ever known. He was also among the funniest, his sense of humor resonating with and enhanced by his tragic knowledge and his hopeful faith. Now this force would be added to his already powerful tools of language, observation, and theme.

We talked about the wonderful stories he had made of the characters who'd lived at the Avon, a seedy apartment house just over "the line" from the University of Chicago, in the ghetto, so appropriate for Leon's whole-mouth approach to life—the street, learning, art, and the constant sense of struggle; he had an appetite and appreciation for it all. The old Jewish woman who ran the Avon catered to "artists, musicians, and writers and students," and it was there, in the brief time I shared Leon's room in the midsixties, that I met the originals for the Deep Brown Study Eggheads and the wonderful Purvis Cream. In those days we crossed the Midway to eat at International House, the University of Chicago's building for international students, where we could eat cheaply and associate with that great range of people he came to write about.

I told Leon that in this manuscript he had gone beyond the narrator he'd once described as "shy and unassertive," a hat-in-hand character, smart and wise but without the author's power and sense of humor. Already in *Divine Days*, Joubert Jones had emerged as a bolder character, far more active in his own narrative. In *Meteor in the Madhouse* he emerges as a force unto himself.

Leon had also come to have confidence in a more direct presentation of his own autobiographical material, albeit fused with his fiery musical language and shaped by his ever-constant thematic concerns.

Both these changes have merged in the novellas we call *Meteor in the Madhouse* and give Leon's work a new territory and a new power with which to explore that territory.

Although Leon and I reminisced about the originals of the Deep Brown Study Eggheads, Mrs. Titlebaum (whose voice he could still imitate perfectly) and Purvis Cream, the smooth-as-silk and absolutely likable young man who pursued his music while women pursued— and supported—him, these novellas are not merely memoirs. They are neither sentimental nor nostalgic, for Leon has enriched them with his mighty themes, themes that I think are all the clearer for a new approach.

Around Leon's work looms a frame of suffering. As he wrote these novellas, Leon knew he was dying. He was often in pain, from the disease itself as well as from the treatments. (And even in his pain he could appreciate that irony!) Cancer visited wretched indignities upon him. A proud man, a man who stood up to the tallest of the tall, Leon faced a tragic struggle in trying to complete the work while at the same time accepting his death and seeking the light and grace he hoped would follow.

As he had once inscribed in a book for me, he still followed his belief that "All God's children got wings."

You see that fearful struggle played out in the final section of *Meteor in the Madhouse*, where light becomes the dominant metaphor.

He and I had often used boxing metaphors, both because we were fight fans, with a particular fondness for Ray Robinson and Mohammed Ali, but also because we enjoyed our own sense of struggle, training, and the rigors of the "writing ring." In his wonderful, funny portrait of the female boxer Martha Hopper, Leon again delves into boxing to find the strength and range of human experience that fired his narratives.

Sadly, at the end he was thin, barely able to stand, nearly unrecognizable. When I told him he looked as though he'd gone fifteen rounds with both Ali and Smoking Joe Frazier, he smiled and shook his head. Then, in that voice he had so often amused us with, the voice with the wonderful power of mimicry so evident in these novellas with amazing dialogues, solos, and arias, he said, "Oh, maybe not fifteen rounds, Merle, but a good twelve. And I've got a demon cut-man."

A major difference between *Meteor in the Madhouse* and Leon's other fiction is the absence of any figure greater than the narrator. Even in *Divine Days*, Sugar-Groove, a larger-than-life character based on the Staggerlee of legend, towers above Joubert. As does the powerful and evil W. A. D. Ford. But in *Meteor in the Madhouse*, Joubert is, as Leon was fond of saying, "at the height of his powers."

But in his memories of youth and childhood, the Joubert of *Meteor in the Madhouse* is not overshadowed by the great panoply of characters he creates, from Granny Gram Gussie to his father, from Leonard Foster to Hopkins Golightly.

With his art, Leon has set his point-of-view character free to soar through the lives of these powerful figures who embody the themes about which he cared so much.

Always, of course, Leon embraced the dynamic of opposites: blues and opera, black and white, male and female—and his favorite, daring and cunning. What he admired most was the wisdom to know when to choose which.

The recurring figure of Hopkins Golightly in *Meteor in the Madhouse* is a case in point. Often Leon and I had discussed the character of Shorty, the elevator man in Richard Wright's *Black Boy*, who let white men kick his butt for a quarter because "Quarters is scarce and my ass is tough." When Joubert first sees Hopkins Golightly, he is taunting white men to throw balls to dunk him at Riverview Amusement Park, but he refuses to "blacken up" and is fired. His pragmatism has its limits, and he asserts his pride (and his self) by playing "The Battle Hymn of the Republic" in protest.

Throughout his life, Hopkins Golightly reinvents himself to take advantage of each fad and to hustle a buck. But when Joubert requests—and challenges him—to play "The Battle Hymn of the Republic" at a blues club, he does so, recapturing the spirit of personal protest he had shown years before at the amusement park and also saving Joubert from the wrath of the customers, ironically a group of young white men.

Leon often treated his themes both comically and tragically. In struggles over love, for instance, he has the warm couple Forester and Gussie Jones, with their earthy humor, contrast to Lucasta Jones, who loses her lover to another woman and to death.

In one theme, however, he brooked no contradictions—the soul's search for authenticity. Whether in Hopkins Golighty's refusal to "blacken up" or in Joubert's struggles as an artist, the soul is not to be trifled with. Increasingly, as this work develops, the problems of evil focus on "people born without a soul." The idea first introduced by mad poet Leonard Foster takes hold in the characters of W. A. D. Ford and the evil drug dealer Reign. Foster accuses Joubert of losing his soul, but Joubert—and the reader—know this to be false.

People in Leon's fiction find themselves overwhelmed by all sorts of forces: love, lust, alcohol, drugs, violence, even hats (as the usually wise Forester and Gussie Jones illustrate), but most of these characters are "lost-found," capable of learning, discovering, finding not only solace but joy in a thousand wondrous things.

Leon had great faith in learning. Many times he told how his mother had used false rent receipts so that he could attend a better high school. (It's no coincidence that his nickname there was "Doc," for his learning and his intelligence.) Throughout his works, his narrators seek wisdom and knowledge at the knees of aunts and grandmothers, in the barbershops of Latin-speaking, Shakespeare-quoting barbers, and from great figures like Sugar-Groove.

And certainly we see teaching in *Meteor in the Madhouse*. Think of Georgia C. J. Glover's taking the white boxer Martha Hopper under her wing. "By me getting this baby into prizefighting, I probably saved her from getting killed." This example also embodies the reversals Leon so loved—a woman fighter, a black training a white, wisdom coming from the black woman, brashness from the white one. And he treated these not as ironic but as a natural part of the landscape for those who have eyes to see. Learning, in Leon's fiction, always means getting beyond your own experiences and expectations.

Joubert gives his niece Phillipa high praise for her devotion and innovation in teaching the starving (in so many ways) children of the city streets. Where but from Joubert has she learned to combine love with wisdom so that she can put a gun to the head of a gang leader to prevent him from enslaving her ghetto students?

Often when Leon and I would sit in a Hyde Park watering hole, his own younger cousins and nieces would come to him for advice on everything from mad, spurned lovers to sad, failing parents. Never did he refuse to teach, and always he taught with the patience and humility of a master in full possession of his powers.

And this is the Joubert we see in *Meteor in the Madhouse*.

Oh, but teaching is not all. There is joy. Joy foremost in music, music of all sorts, from opera to Jose Feliciano's "California Dreaming," Mahalia Jackson to Hopkins Golightly wailing the gutbucket blues out of "The Battle Hymn of the Republic." And joy in Leon's remarkable humor—the humor of satire in Joubert's portrayal of the Deep Brown Study Eggheads, the humor of the dozens in the roasting of McGovern McNabb, the social humor of the late-night cab ride to the university. *Meteor in the Madhouse* is the funniest of Leon's works and shows his wonderful comic sense, his mimicry, and the puncturing, deflating insights his friends enjoyed so often and miss so much. Even in his final illness, he would slip into an Indian or Jamaican accent to regale us with a funny story about his doctor, his nurse, the two men who argued about how to treat him when he had fallen on the sidewalk, revealing, once again, his deep and wide appreciation of the great tribe of lost-found children.

And there is excellence and achievement, but whereas in his previous fiction excellence was always in the hands and minds of others—whether the master nineteenth-century black magician who could make a dead pig speak at the whites' dinner table or the wise and cultured barbers of *Divine Days*—in *Meteor in the Madhouse* Joubert himself carries the blessing of excellence. The awards and recognition given his plays certify his achievements.

But Leon could still tug on his own coattails and does so in the figure of Leonard Foster (surely the alter ego of Leon Forrest, for Leon was careful and cunning in naming his characters). Leonard Foster, who was shot in the South during his fight for social justice, sought purity and truth. He accuses Joubert of neglecting the struggle for freedom and equality for the frivolous pursuit of art. He judges Joubert to be guilty of seeking truth through the lies of literature, for turning the serious suffering of the streets into entertainment and profit, and for working only for his own selfish purposes. Although Joubert ponders these accusations and prays for Leonard and weeps at his wasteful death, he does not accept the Little Dreamer's characterization of his life or his art.

It is in Joubert's assertion of his self—his soul—that I find a firm new direction in Leon's fiction. Although *Divine Days* began this new direction, *Meteor in the Madhouse* is already a long way into the journey.

Sadly it was to be Leon's final journey. Even at the end, however, he made his dying into art, telling lies to tell the truth.

On the last page of *Meteor in the Madhouse*, Joubert indeed sails "out to other voices and other democratic chambers and other spheres into the distances of time." He goes with the Creator's bold command ("Let there be light") and with the believer's humble hope ("Let there be light") and dies, yet is whole—holy—and complete.

MetEoR

In thE

MadHousE

Lucasta Jones, in Solitude: Lives Left in Her Wake

....

NOVEMBER COTTON FLOWER

Boll-weevil's coming, and the winter's cold,
Made cotton-stalks look rusty, seasons old,
And cotton, scarce as any southern snow,
Was vanishing; the branch, so pinched and slow,
Failed in its function as the autumn rake;
Drought fighting soil had caused the soil to take
All water from the streams; dead birds were found
In wells a hundred feet below the ground—
Such was the season when the flower bloomed.
Old folks were startled, and it soon assumed
Significance. Superstition saw
Something it had never seen before:
Brown eyes that loved without a trace of fear,
Beauty so sudden for that time of year.

Jean Toomer, Cane

But now, seeing her sitting in the corner with her frightened eyes and a finger placed on her lips, maybe we accepted the fact that she'd had a childhood, once, that once she'd had a touch that was sensitive to the anticipatory coolness of the rain, and that she always carried an unexpected shadow in profile to her body.

Gabriel García Márquez,
"Bitterness for Three Sleepwalkers"

Exhausted from the lecture circuit and seminars for what appeared to be all of the would-be playwrights in the Midwest, I now found myself tossing and turning (and trying to avoid contemplating the extensive schedule of "required duties" I had slated for this new dawning November day). Now I ever so gradually found sleep in this last third of the bumpy bus ride homeward, after an Appalachian mother and child departed. Scores of students had wanted to take seminars or three-day tutorials with "Joubert Antoine Jones, one of this nation's most profound and *successful* playwrights," so the publicity ran. The "successful playwrights" (not particularly true in terms of money in the coffers) probably hooked most of the kids bent on immediate, overnight success. My kinsman, the poet Leonard Foster, and I never had such sudden, overnight plots. Dreams? Yes.

Yet even as I am engaged by sleep, and lured by that mistress of death, I tried to sketch out a jumbled sequence and time space for the events and chores before me. For you see I am obsessed with the relationship of order to chaos. To view the body of a dear and remarkable former student, murdered by her lover. . . . I had an important engagement set with some actors for later that afternoon to sit in on a performance of a scene I had worked up to a trial-and-see stage for my new play-in-progress. . . . To mail off the packet of mainly unpublished poems to the lesbian magazine, written by my deceased "aunt" through marriage,

Lucinda Hickles. . . . To get a much-needed haircut at that barbershop named for its original owner (Oscar) Williemain, who was murdered by three black punks while parking his car, adjacent to his Park Manor residence, in 1982.

I also had to visit the bank to do my banking and to check on the status of Leonard Foster's account. Of *this* money, what can I say, a mysterious stranger had set the "gift" in motion, and in so doing had laid claim to Leonard Foster's soul in some eerie, even enigmatic manner. In my soul I could hear the voice of the deceased Lucasta Jones, humming to Lady Day singing "In My Solitude" in some distant sphere. A visit to my grandmother's apartment for the final stages in getting her boxed up and moved to a nursing home. And then back out to the university—even though I was on leave—in order to meet with graduate students.

I had delighted when the big-butt bulging woman in the tight-fitting orange and green pantsuit, with the yelling baby daughter, had finally departed, with all of her bags and baggage, too. She hailed from Kentucky, had a thick Appalachian accent; her hair done up in elaborate cornrows. Brown-skinned baby named Tabby, in dire need of a diaper change for the last thirty miles. The stench still reeking in my nostrils.

So now, finally, I can get some sleep. I thought with disgust of the dominant buttocks of this woman, *all* of which had commanded three-fifths of the double-seat arrangement (designed on a principle of separate, but equal), when suddenly I discovered that in the crevices of the seat, mother and babe had left a tiny teething ring, within the seam, which falsely separated the lived-out sections. I had crushed it when I had turned to the left to nestle myself into a better sleeping posture. Carry this Tabby through the toy fair? Shit. Yet hadn't I selected this mode of transportation to get back to the feel and texture of the people, their voices, moods, etc.? Just then an older memory invaded my dream: that of a coffin being carried down the steps at Fountain's House of the Dead Funeral Home.

Despite my many successful ventures into the world of the theater, the honors and prizes, I have maintained certain attributes and qualities of my early adulthood (which for good or ill have only expanded over the years). I've always liked to play jokes on myself and friends, and most often these pranks backfire on me. Since I've known many of the most famous people in the cultural spheres of our country, either directly or indirectly, I have great fondness for doing imitations of their voices. (Recently, I was completely miffed, then delighted, to uncover a detailed story of how my voice and eccentricities are imitated by my present and former students.) I am obsessed with hearing voices, and they often take over my life and mind, trying to follow out their directives. Down the years I've gained some power of attorney, as it were, over their ensnaring authority.

I realize that my penchant for donning masks of all kinds has roundly nourished this underground industry. States of lostness seem to characterize my wayward searching searchlight condition; while driving, walking, and talking I easily get lost, as if my Maker had said, at some point: "Brother-Bear: get lost!" and that I would have to get lost within the blue-blackness of my shattered condition, in order to inch my way to a crevice of spiritual Light. Ah but there I go: sounding off and overstating that which many people handle quietly and inwardly.

As a young courting man, I read every female palm I could get my hands on, as a social entrée into the dark. Read their palms, but never my own. Read everybody's mind, but my own remained neglected. Although I tend to be a rather observant man, I would go to a party or public encounter; again and again I would miss out on the main cultural issue of the evening, or the central core of gossip spewed forth in the dark of brightly lighted corners. Trying to find a spiritual wholeness amid my haplessness. Talk about not seeing the forest for the trees.

I have become obsessed with old things, old antiques (probably from a legacy and linkage with my aunt Eloise or Granny Gram Gussie). For example, take this 1963 Lincoln Continental I've been driving around since when. The kids at school go howling about and the jokes around Professor Joubert are legion, off and on campus. Still, only in a university setting could you uphold such motor sporting behavior. So, here I am, a relic, so is my car. Now the darn thing has grown to become something of an iron icon. My black friends in the Negro bourgeoisie are embarrassed by the prominence this relic plays in my life. My white friends smile and laugh how well integration really does work, despite the enraged voices calling for Black Power, which heralded the late 1960s and early 1970s.

Soon I was in the depths of sleep and dreaming of another late November, when I had left the old apartment where my grandmother

Gussie Jones (referred to as Granny Gram Gussie in my earliest memories) resided with her husband, Forester Jones, and then drove through the slum neighborhood to the University Hospital to visit that wretched man Leonard Foster in the psychiatric ward. The journalist, my aunt Eloise—knowing that this was one of my days to see Granny Gram Gussie and Grandpa Forester—had called ahead, leaving instructions for me to cover an ongoing scene of chaos, right on their block, in which a rather noted poet was flipping her wig and threatening to commit suicide.

Chapter 1

Now that I had moved away from the home of my dear aunt Eloise (the celebrated columnist for the *Forrest County Dispatch*) I had vigorously embarked on evolving an epic idea for a verse play, in the grand manner.

On March 1, 1966, I had moved into Mrs. Myrtle Titlebaum's teeming apartment building: home for wayward souls, foreign spirits, nearly domesticated university students, oddball artists, off-the-wall musicians, raggedy-ribboned writers; small-time has-beens, would-be politicians who claimed now to be nationalists; fellow travelers who sold grave plots by dawn's early light; obese lunatics with thin portfolios. There were eternal lovers with soggy armpits who were always setting up doomed love affairs (for their lovers) slated as springboards for their own career ambitions. There were high-minded Marxists predicting the imminent financial collapse of the United States, *any day now,* who despised the Jehovah's Witnesses (and their predictions), who in turn loathed the Roman Catholics in and out of the building under Mrs. Titlebaum's ownership.

There were several black nationalists awaiting the impending advent of an imperial African messiah, who could and would arrive upon the White House lawn (take over the Rose Garden) in a black, green, and red chariot (to match his cape) at high noon with a staff of angelic officers armed to the grinding of teeth, their rifles at the ready. There were several of their ilk who believed in a Jewish conspiracy. Despite the affable Mrs. Titlebaum's largess of spirit, they swore that this elderly Jewish woman "was a front for a huge, though mysterious cartel."

I observed at least three dropout Muslims, fiercely disillusioned with Elijah's direction of the Nation, and continuing their grief over the murder of Malcolm X; as if the assassination had occurred just yesterday, at the Audubon.

There was a steady flow of exchange students with "revolutionary agendas" for their return home (even as they had been away from "home" seven to ten years), where they planned to take over CIA-spawned governments.

Then there were those identity-crackled African Americans, searching in twelve different tormented-air circles for an ideal core soul source: intellectual babes of toyland, ever pulling after and pinching for elusive and high-bouncing balloons, which, when punctured, did actually explode an odorless gas, guaranteeing death to the reasoning portion of the brain, as these rhetoricians mongered on, sucking up large gasps of the heavily polluted air of their own creation. (I later came to give them titles, born out of their self-assumed designation.)

I had written a significant segment culled from Sugar-Groove's saga, initially in the form of a journal, and then converted the log into a complete play about this fabulous courtier, bon vivant, and spiritual uncle/father. In November 1968, the play was "performed" in a reader's-style theater at a playhouse on East Sixty-seventh Street. There had been about seventy-five people present at the "reading and rendering" of this play (with a working title of "How Can You Destroy What We Created?"). My aunt Eloise had sent out many invitations and to some degree the size of our audience was a response to her call. Normally the Playwright's Workshop drew only twenty people, in addition to the twelve of us enrolled in the course. Each month a play was presented in a reader's-style theater to the students and a public audience.

Aunt Eloise had been in attendance (though not Hickles, her husband). "I'll review your endeavor, Baby-Bear, but you'll get no once-over-go-lightly-cream-puffs from Auntie," she had said, winking those fiercely competitive gray eyes at her nephew and stepson. Eloise Hickles wrote a complete review of the play (a lengthy critique) as if it were to be published for the *Dispatch*. Her unpublished, though formally written review—actually mailed to me at the Avon—both hailed my potential and castigated "this playwright, concerning the very real structural defects of his play." Throughout her review she referred to me as "this man, Antoine Jones." She went on to proclaim: "Antoine Jones takes on and attempts to take over, then explore native grounds common to Richard Wright and William Faulkner. In many ways Antoine Jones goes beyond these two modern masters of the southern Agony. However, these writers were novelists not playwrights, and Antoine Jones has yet to master the craft of drama, which calls for a certain kind of immediate yet smoldering electricity between players and audience. He is most definitely a young playwright on the way up, still in the process of learning stagecraft-savvy, and surrendering to the demanding and selfish taskmistress of theatrical discipline." The critique was nine double-spaced pages. I read it twenty-one times. She never referred to me by my full name, Joubert Antoine Jones, in the review.

Another journalist in attendance for the public reading was Washburne Withers. I had been most anxious to hear the opinion of this reporter, who worked for Jacob A. Gooselaw's weekly newspaper, *Spearhead*. Gooselaw had been beseeching me to write for his paper ever since I returned from the army in February 1966. I was seriously contemplating how I might incorporate a few hours at Gooselaw's weekly *Spearhead* into my own fairly tight schedule. Gooselaw's paper was far more progressive than the *Forrest County Dispatch*. The second attraction was the possibility of working not only with that wily Marxist Gooselaw but with Washburne Withers. The talented Withers wrote straight news and some features for *Spearhead* on a part-time basis.

Withers had recently been hired as the first black reporter to write for one of the main downtown dailies. His first feature story had been published the week before the presentation of my play; the piece was on the local legend Ma Fay Barker, a social activist originally from Kansas City, Kansas. It was a fine story about this woman, whom I had met through Aunt Eloise. Ma Fay Barker was very much aware of certain jazz movements and currents of the territorial jazz bands. She stayed on the periphery of the various movements and dealt with individuals in crisis. I admired Withers's controlled, thoughtful savvy, his burnished intelligence, and the devotion to his craft that shone through his probing news stories.

At the reception for my play, with a glass of white wine in my right hand and my manuscript in the left, I recalled turning away exactly at *what* the venomous Angel St. Clair poured into my left ear. She was one of twelve students in the Playwright's Workshop. Her play was being presented in January. She was *proclaiming*, just now, in a razor of a whisper: "I didn't come here, Joubert Antoine Jones, to hear nor preview any of your chauvinist shit. Not going to be conquered by you Bear hound-dog you, by no stretch of my imagination am I going to be diminished, as a very intelligent African woman, by this old wive's-down-home-nigger-woman honky bastard poison."

I moved away from the stalking black feminist's shock waves to the porches of my ear, in order now to drift over to where Withers had stood, at the other end of the room, but it was at this very moment that the ruggedly handsome, tall, medium-dark-brown-skinned reporter suddenly vanished out into the November rain, his bare head buried now beneath the hood of his raincoat, his shoulders huddled.

Then I observed the lean and mean Angel St. Clair stalk out of the reception on a pair of wicked high heels—the black leotards protecting those shapely legs of a stallion from the nasty November weather—as she whipped a lengthy, purple scarf about her shoulders.

The new sophisticated lady, without silk stockings, and a jagged-edged razor for a tongue: the new armies of the night. Duke's lady no place to be somebody here. I thought of the Satin Doll, out of the not-too-far-removed past, which was the place where a clique of white gangsters in Forrest County frequented and picked up black women. No Negro males were allowed entry into this place, as audience. Only black musicians (males) were allowed onstage. Somewhat akin to the Cotton Club in New York, yet quite different. Black musicians— white audience. Ripped off Duke's title but the song goes on. Same old tune.

Not ever getting the quote from Blake exactly right, Angel St. Clair, as always, paraphrased in class: "The wrath of tigers is more useful than the horses of instruction," no matter the situation, or the setting. What had probably most pissed the Angel was the central dramatic story of my play.

Read aloud over three weekends in November at the Sixty-seventh Street Theater, my play "How Can You Destroy What We Created?"

was culled out of a confrontation between Sugar-Groove and his white father when the lad of fourteen discovered pictures of his scantily clad mother, Sarah-Belle, stuck up in the Bible of his white father, Wilfred Bloodworth. Taken perhaps twenty years earlier, at some remote part of a beach, these photographs revealed Sarah-Belle to the youth's awakening eyes.

Sarah-Belle had died in childbirth. William Bloodworth (later known as Sugar-Groove) had only heard descriptions of his beautiful mother. Old man Bloodworth had come to despise the lad, because Sarah-Belle had elected to give her Negro baby's life dominion over Bloodworth's bodily passions, possession and power over her existence. Because of his mysterious tie to Sarah-Belle, Wilfred Bloodworth felt something for the son, akin to outrage and pity, filial tenderness and jealousy, racial arrogance, and also a measure of affection not previously gauged.

On this particular occasion, when the white man returned to his magnificent library, in Forrest County, he and the youth he sired by Sarah-Belle fought over the meaning of those photographs (as much mythic as real). Mainly each fought to own the photos (to actually repossess the woman in the photos as his very own, as if she would step out, life size, and reveal herself at any moment).

The enraged older man gets the better of the physical struggle and is about to crash a chair over his son's head, when suddenly they both became aware of a presence in the room. The window was elevated and the cracked library door flew open on this Mississippi night. Sarah-Belle's spirit was suddenly heard to faintly aggrieve, in a declarative spirit: "How can you destroy what we created?" The voice seems to have floated through the room under some sheer, nearly invisible veil. (Young Sugar-Groove of course had never heard this voice.) Both man and boy were charged and shocked by the presence of the voice. This confrontation came to a momentary close.

As the adult Sugar-Groove informed me in Williemain's Barbershop, his furor at Bloodworth remained alive. He revealed the dream of castration wherein he severely punished Bloodworth for what he believed to be the sexual exploitation of Sarah-Belle, on the very night of the battle with the man who sired him.

Raised as he was by his aunt and uncle, Sugar-Groove's overview of the relationship came to be more muted and complex with the flow of reflection carried down through the years with this obsessive memory. Eventually the play was given a major mounting, in Forest County; it forms one of the cornerstones of my reputation as a playwright. This play garnered several prizes and it was nominated for a Pulitzer Prize. The honors, the awards, the visiting professorships, all stem from this well-saluted and often-produced play. My most recent visit to the internet revealed that some twenty dissertations had analyzed aspects and scenes from this two-act play.

At this time, I had a second life's commandment, too, concerning the existence, care, and keeping of my eccentric kinsman Leonard Foster.

■ ■ ■ ■ ■

Now that I was back home, at the Avon, I finally got around to telephoning Shirley Polyneices. She immediately vaulted into the living torment and anguish that dwelling under the same roof with Leonard Foster meant. He had been leaving suicide notes in the basement, but now he was situated in the psychiatric ward of the University Hospital. Then she insisted on reading a long poem, word for word, that Leonard had recently written. I was instructed to take the poem down, word for word, in longhand. Shirley's voice was full of lament and torment.

"Joubert, you and I had two literature courses together, at Brighton High—in case you've forgotten—but I do remember how good you were at interpreting shit. So, apply your imagination to this crazy poem as written by this riddled-brain nigger of mine, and your crazy cousin.

"You, with your oddball self *ain't* crazy, you just daffy to get away without being committed by the skin of your Adam's apple. But then all the dead people *ain't* at Memphis Raven-Snow's Funeral Home. Still and all, you'll probably tell us—mainly me—more about your cousin, from your knowledge of him, direct from this poem. And certainly more than any of these white-boy psychiatrists here at this university, which is internationally known for its crackpots and crack-ups. Hell—far as they are concerned we are all a bunch of crazy niggers. I sure heard enough of that kind of shitty interpretation behind prison gates, down South, marching to try to free up this lousy country of ours, too. Leonard was arrested far more than I was. I got slammed away in the honky-hearted jailhouse. But Joubert, you with your daffy, crafty, and cunning ass can lay in the cut no doubt and conjure up some profound shit about layers going down in this sappy but sweet splib of mine."

Wound-licking in its monstrous, self-inflicted loves, then suddenly called away from its mission, it still slouches and snores with the mayhem-ecstasy, under its belly, astride its reverie nightmare-genius (pale-horse) in the bottom of a ship, whose destiny is Eternity . . . to take me back through space in time to Mississippi . . . to Forrest County . . . take the blood of the lamb and strike upon the door posts and the lentils. . . . And when I see the blood, I'll pass you over and I'll take you in. . . . Must I go back to that, too? But oh, how can there be blood on my hands before I Arrive?

The monster-bloated spirit rebukes the God-willed mission and the innocent ship is moored in Disaster made wretched by the sea's brooding, Raging monster, smoking with avarice, industry, Bondage, Miscegenation, and torment. . . . Take this Swine from out of mine eyes. . . . Clothe me in my Right mind. Let the devil depart me . . . afflicted With every folly and suffering Known and Unknown Unto mankind and worthy only to the bodies of swine . . . tumbling down to the sea . . . in its hallowed be thy name talons. . . . Who knows not itself its face to the horrors of the wind, I ride out like the wind in the breath of those Hounds after the vixen transformed stag. . . . Lucasta Jones, hail woman full of denied grace, The Lord is with you.

Oh vamping vixen, in the shape of an hourglass with the face of a November leaf—pouring dread from her spider's web of a hair net; but he awakes on high and hard to find a haunting bloodstained cloak has grown about his shoulders; a tarnished Crown, ingeniously fashioned of rusty, Bloodstained, blood-pounded nails, shells, beads, Scraps of iron (with a bulging round of paper in the band) . . . sits tentatively upon his swollen head. Wretched pair of whispering, wounded wings blossoming nails sits upon its side, primed for Golgotha's ride up the Stations. Primed to wakefulness, the driftwood bestial body (as if God Touched) now sacrifices only itself to whatever Spouts and smokes out there upon Creation's Shape changing sea's face: a prologue and a Reality too abhorred and awesome for Remembrance wakefulness, forgetfulness, nostalgia, or mere fear. Is there blood on my hands? How dare you! . . . Keening, tumbling, turning, and tobogganing, In a feverish dance-swim, vaulting delirium, the bottomed-out of this tribulation; engulfed, Sanctimonious monster is bloody with slime-puke And the buds of an entangling, savage miracle. He is of the sea monster's body and soul. (But I found out too late.) Keening . . . Eden's fruit foul in its haughty, Fly-shrouded breath; God's tears touch time. The color-shifting rainbow's wings; he is the Dangling requiem for Gomer, and the spirit Auctioned. (Oh the withering away of the Soul.) Yet too much for mere monster to devour, the Angled monster knows not of its catch.

"Well, give me two days, Shirley. But I promise to stop by the hospital tomorrow, after I leave my grandparents."

"Now you figure all that shit out. Leonard asks for you constantly, Joubert. Please don't fail me, nor especially your cousin."

Poor little Leonard Foster, for though I loved him, I also loathed his innocence. But why didn't I tell him earlier since none of them would tell him, for so long a time, so that when it did come down upon him it snapped something deep within, something deep and fragile, as a branch caught up in an electrical storm. Broken bones blasted before he decided to burn all bridges and start anew, deep down in the Southland. Trying to free his people, in search of his own people. Something else, too, had taken possession of Leonard's soul, a literary magazine.

Leonard's name for this "quarterly" was *The Dark Tower.* I had never cared for the name of the magazine. However, Leonard insisted upon the title and he was bankrolling the enterprise.

Another intertwining branch connecting Leonard and me was a shared memory behind the meaning of a mysterious funeral we had attended as lads, at Fountain's House of the Dead Funeral Home. Nearly every time we talked at length, each of us ended up re-creating his own special memory of the original event, adding to and subtracting from it as we went along. Probably more than anything else, we debated over what was the true identity of the *funeralized* man who was never eulogized. There were no programs made available to describe his life, nor were there biographical sketches made known to the public. Years later I came to refer to this man (with the influence of the Muslims so prevalent in Forest County) as Mr. Double X, the mystery man. In fact, I remained uncertain as to the identity, even the gender, of this person.

Why had Granny Gram Gussie and Grandpa Forester insisted that we bear witness by attending this funeral, this odd spectacle, with them? And yet over the years, they, each in his or her own way, had let slip bits of information on the man or woman inside the handsome bronzed casket. Not strange enough? Then what of the following factor: there were no grieving relatives there to send this personage on their way?

The organist did play "The Death of a Princess" over and over again, in a most eerie tone, as I remembered it. And this led me to think that the person on the inside was female, but all of the references my grandparents made to the gender of the dead body implied that it was a male inside this casket, which was not adorned with flowers on the outside. Apparently the "house" organist did not know the song from memory since he kept a close reference to the sheet music before him. How could anyone know that this was the song requested? Who had placed the request? Had a relative of the deceased filed a petition that this song be played, at the last minute? Besides the four of us, there were a few outsiders—five or six? Leonard and I usually ended up arguing over the body count of the living presence at the funeral. Lucasta Jones arrived late. However, it was the mysterious man who sat in the second row all through the service whose presence really shook us up.

Since the events were so vivid in my memory, I had thought on several occasions of trying to write a play about what had happened, or didn't happen, at "the funeral"; however, I was thrown for a loop, because what in fact had happened? Would this qualify for the theater of the absurd? Talk about waiting for Godot! Where was the garbage can?

Leonard always felt that I was too lavish in my storytelling ("too flowery" was his phraseology, and particularly about this saga). Yet I thought now that this would be exactly the story I would bring up in my recall, in order to sweep Leonard out of his deadly doldrums. Well, I could try anyway. I'd stay away from the Freedom Movement days, because, after all, he had Shirley for those shared and shell-shocking memories. The war stories from the battlefront would only bring on more mental pain.

All of this would fit into a routine of our dialogues over the years. Leonard was always telling people how I was forever and a day setting him up and using the materials from our conversations as the seeds for play conflicts. My ambitions to be a playwright are certainly not beyond this manipulation. If it were not this kind of thinking, would we, after all, have the Socratic dialogues in our possession?

Before I drove to the hospital that late morning, I headed out south.

Now I was moving ahead in Aunt Eloise's old green 1963 Lincoln Continental, on my way to grandmother's house.

But I could also sense some impending chaos, mainly because of the enormous barking of a dog's voice beyond relief (which, as it turned out, was Marvella's brutal-voiced canine). A forest of children was scattered about as I started to tool down the block where Granny Gram Gussie lived, and some of them greeted my old car with rocks, or pebbles, then darted off to the sides of the adjacent buildings.

There was indeed a stand-off taking place, between the police and some woman whose outline I could make out on the top floor (I thought I recognized her immediately), threatening to blow out her brains with the gun she moved back and forth into and out of her mouth. My God, I howled, it was indeed Marvella, the crazed poet, who headed up a singing group (composed of lesbians) at one time.

As I came into the front-door vestibule of the building where my grandparents lived, I recognized three attendants from Memphis Raven-Snow's Funeral Home moving a sheet-covered corpse to the elevated rear door of the mortuary's pickup Caddy for deceased bodies, five buildings down to the left of where Forester and Gussie Jones lived.

Marvella—dressed in a red, green, and black wraparound African headpiece and a bright blue dress (as far as I could see) continued to curse out the power structure and their ancestry, with particular stress upon the cop's lack of a biological tree. Granny Gram Gussie ushered me in nimbly, as if she was prepared now to impart some great family secret. I got my notebook out and took general notes as they spoke. Also, I turned on my tape recorder.

GUSSIE JONES: Yeah, Brother-Bear, that's her all right (your old girlfriend, I guess, leastwise your aunt Eloise thinks so) high up there on the third floor. And high on God knows what. Screaming, hollering, and threatening to kill off half the block, say nothing of what she's prime to do to herself.

FORESTER JONES: When Marvella don't have that gun loaded into her mouth, like she's reared to make book on threats, if sane people don't surrender up to her foolishness craziness. And not be harmed by her death (now ain't that a killer)—and with the trigger pressed with her own fingertips, gun in her mouth. . . . Sure asking a lot of pity out of people.

GUSSIE JONES: Baby-Bear, you better call your aunt down at the paper

to find out what she want reported on. . . . While you in the field, as
they say!

JOUBERT JONES: I'll do that right away.

How did Aunt Eloise know that I was coming—? Oh, that's right,
she knew the four days of the month I set aside to visit with my
grandparents. In fact, knowing Aunt Eloise, she probably had those
days marked down somewhere. But what was this about Marvella being
an old girlfriend, offered by Aunt Eloise and picked up by Granny Gram
Gussie? I came up front to hear what was going down. This was wild,
like a carnival.

GUSSIE JONES: Why, this very morning, Joubert, Marvella just crept
her old heavy sweeping broom up to our very step. Trying to beautify
the whole street, she proclaimed, like she was one of these saleswomen
on television. Had the nerve to come all up in my face, with the *bad*
news for five dollars, like she was egging for old man Grimm's grieving
widow woman. This here was tax for a block drive, all right, since the
city wasn't giving the kind of service we need. Alderman never to be
found until a week before the election, when you might see a precinct
captain, if you lucky, if you catch policy. Cops so glad somebody doing
something halfway dishonest, and her cleaning up, too. *They* cleaning
up, too, from the drug dealers, so *this* makes their business area look
so much better over in those lots across the way . . . and old runaway
houses now used as drug centers but not for cleaning people up; but
for funeralizing addicts' mainline.

JOUBERT JONES: Of course you didn't give her any of your money!

GUSSIE JONES: Course not. That's my money that Forester worked hard
for (and spending change to play my little policy gig).

FORESTER JONES: Better-never-ever. That's the kind of distortion tax
the Blackstones try to take from good citizens, who owns businesses
paying off. Marvella's bootlegging into that kind of money.

GUSSIE JONES: Showed up with good faith and five singles come
tumbling out of her pockets. Marvella talking about she wants the
neighbors to put up five dollars for the month, or whatever they can
"cough up" for *her* services and flowers for "this wonderful dead man
who up and died, late last night." A special bouquet of flowers for the

grieving widow of Fletcher Grimm. So we "getting a sweetheart deal for chipping in," and her street-sweeping only come to two dollars and fifty cents. (Probably going send along some packs of dandelions, tied up with raggedy shoestrings.)

FORESTER JONES: President Nixon would like that. Must be some of those cocoa-leaf flowers Marvella hiding her reefer and coke behind. Why, that gal knowed old man Fletcher Grimm 'bout well as she knowed Jack the Ripper.

GUSSIE JONES: Man ain't hardly de-nounced dead yet. Joubert, you see Memphis Raven-Snow's workers taking Grimm's body out, just as you was ringing the bell? I almost thought it was them looking for Grimm's body, not you (also 'nouncing yourself not as grandson but reporter). You going off so many directions, wonder you can keep up with yourself, and your head spinning off your neck. Marvella gone off, went off, too, about eleven o'clock. Broom in one hand, dog on a leash (if that's got true hold of him) in the other one. *Nerve* stirred up in her backbone—cancel out her skull bone—to believe she could do any spin on the pigeon drop on us, over here. She ain't living in Hyde Park. Here your Grandpa and I been living in Forest County too long to forget to remember. I believe to my soul Marvella got a grudgeful heart; she mindless to a windstorm.

FORESTER JONES: Lawd, listen to that dog ever roar. He shameless and smart, too. (Like his mistress.) Sounds like we drifted over to the lions' part of the zoo. Yeah, Joubert, like your grandma say, nerve of Marvella trying to work up a drowsy-eyed pigeon drop on us old settlers, like we was scrubs, just off the train this week, with yesterday's news of jobs for Negroes inside our grips from the *Forest County Dispatch*, up out the ole country—Forrest County, Mississippi. Then, of-a-sudden, Marvella flipping her wig. Just snapped off at the nape.

GUSSIE JONES: Like green beans. I said to Marvella, plain and simple: "Look, I ain't got nothing in this house what belongs to you. Now I do have some mustards, string beans, and my emerald-colored green hat I wore to Easter services; and you can't have none of it."

Now down the street, as if in a caravan, came ABC and WGN, with CBS trailing far behind. Kids were leaping about trying to run after the television trucks, in awe and glory.

FORESTER JONES: I tell you, Joubert, that gal's ripe with rascality. Courting destruction and death.

I continued my efforts to jot down a few observations gleaned from the intelligence of their words. But this really sounded like a feature story to me. TV cameramen, reporters, nearly all white, were out on the street immediately and started a long process of milling around, talking with the cops and the growing throng of kids and adults; some from the print media wrote in their notepads from these interviews.

JOUBERT JONES: Have you noticed? Granny Gram Gussie? Grandpa Forester? Have you seen any pattern or way she acts regularly? Or, I should say irregularly acts.

FORESTER JONES: Yeah, acts-out irregular. Been living over in her Great-mother's building for the last three months and each day stirs up a new mess of scorched potatoes meant to be scalloped.

GUSSIE JONES: Forester, don't serve nothing on my grandson's plate he *can't* put in the newspapers under his very own name and get hisself carried off from the job, as writing for crazy folks, like Marvella going for crazy. She playing crazy, not going crazy.

FORESTER JONES: That great ole gun Marvella keep poking in her mouth don't look too much like a play gun to me. Must think she's got a turtle's lease on life, and a shell to duck inside, 'case the gun goes off.

GUSSIE JONES: Tell it true, Marvella not crazy. She's mentally. 'Spectable people can't play crazy; keep up their reputation. Marvella could get away with anything—till she moved around here. We got people over here chuck her mess of scorched and mashed potatoes out. Know they scorched without calling city hall. She's just plain mentally. Sure 'nough ain't crazy. Play crazy like those actors do in some of Joubert's plays.

JOUBERT JONES: Sometimes I think my actors were already crazy and then just learned to play crazy once they are on the stage, in order to keep some parts of their sanity, on the outside world!

Granny Gram Gussie now excused herself and went to the bathroom. So Grandpa Forester directed his words to me.

FORESTER JONES: Won't hardly be talking about Marvella without talking crazy talk; be talking about a double Marvella and Almighty

God ain't hardly made no double-Marvella's. Couldn't happen in one family: too much to bear. But you see what they doing these days is this: they calls in the whole family to bear witness. Something like a church service. The whole family together and sit down to study this all out what went wrong. Map it all out, but your wonderful grandmother got the whole world already mapped out in her mind. She, of course, who knows all, sees all, and hears all is the primary mother of all wisdom. That's why they don't need no doctor. . . . Just call on Gussie Jones. She already the Anchor Lady, before she's moved up the ladder, from street reporter. Cronkite don't have nothing to fret over, she's already Boss-lady-Gussie.

Immediately now, when Granny Gram Gussie returned, Grandpa Forester "chord-changed" moods, directions, and diction.

FORESTER JONES: Yeah, Joubert, there that Marvella was running the scales. Out there on Monday skipping rope double Dutch with the young'uns.

GUSSIE JONES: Now Marvella cussing out her dog. People will you look! Claim the cops and TV camera folks can't hardly hear her for Zelda's barking mouth.

FORESTER JONES: Cussing those same kids and her dog out, like a sailor on shore leave on Tuesday. Sun-up Wednesday, Marvella's sweeping down the complete street, like she's running for precinct captain, or dogcatcher. For Thursday she's passing out leaflets against cruelty to small, lost children (while she's chasing kids with that dog on a leash in the other hand). Some of the adults might take a leaflet but can't worry too much 'bout small, lost children when they might lose their hands to Zelda's teeth. Next thing we know Marvella hooking off some mens into her grandmother's building on Friday. High noon on Saturday, that really got it. There she was, in the middle of the block, mounted up to the top rung of a nine-foot ladder reading out that crazy poem of hers, or crazy poems to the crowd. (Trying to get money for that. Just like she's up there now, trying to make people believe in her.) Up there on that fourth floor, claiming she's going to do away with herself if folks don't dance to her fiddler's jam. If Marvella really went on and shot off that gun, she'd put herself out of misery . . . and—

GUSSIE JONES: Keep us from spending a lot of tax money calling cops. Rid this community of one less crazy junkie. Yeah, I know what you 'bout to say, Mr. Forester Jones, but wait a devilish minute. 'Sposing Joubert went off and put that part of what you just said in the *Dispatch;* just think how that would look? They'd be sending the white coats 'round here, not after Marvella but after Baby-Bear Jones, and for his auntie Miss Eloise for letting it get in the *Dispatch*, anywhere other than the funny papers, and B. O. Plenty. What you up to Forester? Writing advice column for lost/found fools, byline: *Sir Forester Jones.* Lawd, today, will you people listen to her dog baying at Marvella, every time her mistress put that gun into her mouth.

FORESTER JONES: Bear-man, when your grandma gets going ain't no way in Heaven you can hold her fast, 'cause she's off into so many directions, like she's got a new lease on life, what's going to outlast the owner of this land.

GUSSIE JONES: Now Forester, would you *could* tell Joubert? I'm going to tell you what you and especially *you* could tell him. Sunday Marvella's day for snoring: just alaboring in her sleep, sawing down a forest of trees and ladders. Now look what's happening, she commencing up to recite that long poem of hers. People will you look! Wonder will she charge?

FORESTER JONES: She got nerve 'nough to charge that black cop trying to bring her back down into the world of the sane. She got that gun *and* Zelda to back her up. Crowd sure ain't with the cops.

GUSSIE JONES: Yeah, where she can really go all the way crazy. But Joubert, now she reciting that poem, you, with your proper education, might could give the straight of that poem or wild, crazy poems that she loves to read. Some is clear as rain-struck windowpane on a stormy day. Far as me and Forester concerned, her poems plain-outright-nuthouse Tinley Park poems. Marvella what they call *educated fool.* Laying up crazy and playacting crazy.

Now all of Granny Gram Gussie's attention went to rendering an interpretation of what we were seeing before our very own eyes: a high-priced anchor woman on television at a tennis match, for example, and your own television is getting a perfectly good reception and there is not a cloud in the sky over Forest Hills. Grandpa Forester (who had won some minor distinctions for his efforts of bravery while facing enemy fire in the military and decided it was best to stay down in his foxhole) then whispered out the side of his mouth to me.

FORESTER JONES: I'm a natural-born fool if I could ever get a word on high up to her highness in this house.

GUSSIE JONES: Lawd, do you see what I see? Marvella has directed that dog of hers up the steps and now she got Zelda at the window barking in her behalf to cops, firemen, NBC, and you name it.

FORESTER JONES: 'Course now, Gussie, our Joubert here may be going use this stuff to make him a new play. Like the hangman figures, keep putting some meat on those bones. Driest of bones seem able to live down in the bowels of Forest County. Joubert, you know I'm always saying you don't have to worry none 'bout keeping your "stuff fresh." Just let up the shade, take off the leash, lift up the window, and let the foul air in! "What a formula for living," as they say on Educational TV—if you can stand the breathing!

GUSSIE JONES: Baby-Bear, tell me what all this means, in your words, what she means by that poem. Don't use Marvella's words, 'cause that'll only confuse me.

FORESTER JONES: Gussie, just 'cause Joubert spent what folks back in the old country used to call a "right heap of time heaving hay in the sun" don't mean he can 'splain Marvella's poems. Probably couldn't make heads or tails of Leonard Foster's poems. As for me, I just stick with—"Only God can make a tree," and let it go at that. Period.

GUSSIE JONES: Leonard Foster never had no turn! Lucasta don't either.

FORESTER JONES: College don't give people no turn. Don't always turn them down, or around, either. If it was the case, Joubert, you could turn some fools out of nuthouses (jails, too) down the road to colleges. Tell me how lots of those high professors in great colleges is stone crazy. Bear-man, you ought to know, as many colleges and universities you been studying, inside out. Forester Jones doesn't know, since I ain't never been inside of a high school, less it was to clean up the place. Grade school, either. But now Gussie, be fair. Lucasta did have turn, and plenty of it, too, at her ironing, her dancing, and her way of remembering things.

GUSSIE JONES: Nanny should have turned out those low-life men in her life. Sure didn't have no turn when it come to men. Lucasta had the looks to turn the house lights down. Marvella ain't got no candlelight safe in the storeroom.

FORESTER JONES: Does make me think back to poor Lucasta, though. You know that boy, Leonard Foster, puts me in the mind of Lucasta—of poor Nanny—in ways I never thought till now. But that woman should have turned down her lamp to off—not down low.

GUSSIE JONES: People! will you'all look, CBS has finally arrived! I wonder did they send along Mr. Cronkite! Where's my makeup? People, WALTER!

I watched her hobble back into the house to garner up her makeup kit. Grandpa Forester, her husband of fifty years, shook his head sadly. Then I heard him say, softly:

FORESTER JONES: Still hung over 'bout some white man, after all these years.

JOUBERT JONES: Oh, Grandpa, don't feel moaning-low-blue. Much of the country has a crush on Walter Cronkite, and the other half looks to him as our first father, these days.

FORESTER JONES: He wasn't at my mama's table. [Shouting out to his wife, I heard the old man call.] Gussie, you sure you ain't related to Marvella? Distant cousin, or something, twice removed?

GUSSIE JONES: What did you say about Marvella's distant cousin?

FORESTER JONES: Nothing! Now you see, Joubert, I'm what you call a wise fool, without wisdom. But watch this. You know Cronkite on national news, woman. He'd be captured in Vietnam before he'd be caught on the South Side of Forest County, buying him some Royal Ribs from Leon's. Even if your Walter liked Marvella's poems. Maybe you oughta write him, send him one or two of her poems, see what he thinks 'bout them. Wait a second, don't do that, because they might send the FBI to visit us. Why Miss Gussie, you all gussied up!

Granny Gram Gussie reemerged, looking twenty years younger—in the face, with the aid of Max Factor and several other kinds of makeup "known only to womankind," Grandpa Forester often reflected.

GUSSIE JONES: Well, Forester, you right for once in your life. Cronkite is national, no reason to fly out here. Talking about that devilish Marvella got me mindless, too. Po-lice blocking off the streets. Tell me Marvella famous once. Baby-Bear, did your aunt Eloise ever know anything 'bout her? I know how Eloise kept a lookout on all famous folks. Used to read her column 'fore my eyesight went poorly on me.

FORESTER JONES: Before they put her down, Marvella held up a whole singing group.

GUSSIE JONES: Yeah, and she 'bout ready to sing again, too, with all this attention.

JOUBERT JONES: Why, yes, Marvella was, once upon a time, fairly famous. She was a lead singer in an all-girl lesbian group.

FORESTER JONES: This won't change your grandma much, she'll still have to play reporter—like she was the anchor lady and we deaf, dumb, and blind fools.

GUSSIE JONES: Surprise she ever let anybody sing. Probably tried to sing everybody's part.

FORESTER JONES: Seen her on television once, but she changed her 'pearance so much. Joubert, did you see that time they arrested Marvella and she threw a blond wig in the judge's face? Kinda sad, too. She got a good learning, they say. You told us that yourself, Bear-man. Only thing I can make out clear from that crazy poem of hers: crackers back down home, now they truly like filthy ice water with they craziness?

GUSSIE JONES: They so dirty, son, you'll never know. Never have to know.

FORESTER JONES: He better soon-up-this-morning learn, then. Leonard learned some of it. Just how many times was he shot down in the Deep South?

JOUBERT JONES: Oh no, I certainly know her story all right. How the powerful whites ran her groom-to-be (while Paul was driving his truck down a rain-sleeked road, with important papers in his cab)—ran him off the road.

GUSSIE JONES: Broke his neck at the wheel. That plain 'nough.

JOUBERT JONES: But what wasn't plain (maybe) was the fact that Marvella came to blame some of her closest friends (mine, too) who should have warned Paul about the coming plot against his life.

FORESTER JONES: Cracked up the cords in the chile's heart, got Marvella to aching in a rainstorm, morning, noon, and night. And speaking of down, back home. Fact of the business is, we thought there is something we needed to talk to you about, Joubert . . . to unfold and finish off. Pull your coat about. Some ole money business what still ties us to the ole Country of Forrest County. We'll never be free from that.

GUSSIE JONES: But we ain't never got free from the old land, and those what super-ruled it. How the Old South came to play even here in Forest County.

FORESTER JONES: Though flee from it we tried . . . lying down crazy, too, with nobody in that coffin but sawdust that came off from where they planed it.

I now thought of another way in which they were still tied to the old country, too. For Grandpa and Grandma Jones had started up a garden in the rear of this house, where they had re-created some of what they lived by down in Forrest County. Growing tomatoes, cucumbers, collards, squash, mustard greens (and tulips, too), the old couple had inspired some of the neighbors, with varying degrees of success, to grow up their own patches of self-help vegetable gardens.

FORESTER JONES: Yeah Bear-man, to talk with you 'bout how we come by this very old house, that hardly nobody wants today.

GUSSIE JONES: Not in this neighborhood, Baby-Bear.

FORESTER JONES: Less it be some whites, who might want to return to rule, lease property, and recapture this land, like they forefathers robbed off the Indians, and right here where we sitting and Marvella raising so much hell. And put them Indians on a leash, like dogs in a kennel, and *us* in cages.

GUSSIE JONES: Yes, recapture this house. This part of Forrest County, leading back down to the lake and the downtown area.

FORESTER JONES: And Bear-man, they'll be back down to they work sooner than you could say—Jackie Robinson!

GUSSIE JONES: Love drive the sane—insane; forget how to tell a clock the time. But Brother-Bear, pity her as we might, hollering and screaming up there, Marvella's still mentally. I had to see that with my Nanny-sister, Lucasta, even though she wasn't crazy-crazy, she was sure lame, and lost when it came to dealing with the wrong men she was crazy 'bout. This here I'm telling you, don't spring up from no grudgeful heart.

FORESTER JONES: Awful to see how our young people (with the learning, the commencing, the breaks) . . . the ones who might and could lead us to something better, they often be 'zactly the ones going 'round and 'round in circles like horses on a carousel, merry-go-round.

GUSSIE JONES: Others, educated fools, I'm trying to learn you about. These days some high on horse, too. Riding for a sure fall; and ain't never visited no carnival. Don't do the kind of clowning anybody clothed in their right mind pay good money to see.

FORESTER JONES: Some of 'em high in the saddle, just like upstairs. Well, I ain't had but three grades of learning and one grade of bad hair, and now all these strands is divorced me to patches of baldness; but I got some meat on my head; mother wit all 'bout; five changes of underwear for work.

GUSSIE JONES: Ride-before-the-Pride before the Fall, too?

FORESTER JONES: And my sweet Miz Honey-du-Melon Gussie at my side. Keep my mouth cleared of curse words, and away from breathing bad whiskey, and my nose away from good-smelling perfume, from the wrong direction!

GUSSIE JONES: Wish you'd keep off every form of tobacco. Clouds your brain. Keeps my house in a stogie and a stink. But Forester don't run the streets, whore hop, gamble, and never liquored away his life; ain't no pickled joker to face cards. Don't love to chase down no fast cars, and wouldn't know how to get to Sportsman Park if you gave him a map to go by.

Down the street a wedding party was trying to get assembled, but their way was blocked because of the saw-stall horses, and the limo to pick up the bride couldn't get through the TV trucks. Cronkite, of course, never arrived.

I thought I might try what little binding memory tie I had invested with Marvella. In a situation that had occurred years before, when the poetess had visited Eloise's Night Light Lounge looking for Milton Beefeater Barnes, she had stalked down my friend, who seemed mentally stewed out at times, in a cruel attempt to link him up to the outrages of her history (through a harsh rendering up of her long poem).

Marvella "indicted" Beefeater and her own sister for not warning her groom-to-be that the forces of white supremacy were tailing her beloved Paul, to drive him off the road and kill him, as the civil rights militant sought to deliver newspapers and messages to another location within Forrest County.

Back in 1966, the scenario at the Night Light Lounge had twisted brutal, comic, and bizarre turns, with taunts and threats going down at every level. But now my problem was this: Marvella, with her memory and imagination, might well remember that late afternoon (when she ended up flipping over backwards one of the Terribleness Tops), and she probably would connect me with Beefeater Barnes, as compatriot and as one involved in the evil design against her lover, Paul, even though, at the time, I was living in Forest County, here in the North. I could get fired upon without warning, but I decided to take my chances.

First of all, I called over one of the officers, whose face was familiar to me from down at the *Forest County Dispatch* (where he had a part-time gig as a night watchman). I told him the situation and explained that if he supplied me with a bulletproof chest protector, I would see if I could talk Marvella down. He was leaning against a light post, with a toothpick in his mouth. The officer appeared delighted to have someone come forward and offer his services, "resolve the stalemate and bring sanity to the situation." However, before giving his approval, he needed to talk this offer "over with his superior."

But soon the police sergeant went into the trunk of his squad car (outside the sight of Marvella) and gave me a packaged chest protector. Explaining my plan to a trembling Granny Gram Gussie, I hurried into the Jones's bathroom, stripped off my jacket and shirt, and donned this protective shield. When the policeman had handed it over to me, he had also supplied me with a large helmet liner, in case Marvella started really to go for bad. Well, she was bad enough.

Now I was back down the steps and making direct contact with Marvella. I began to call up to her and (dangerously so) attempted to stir up some memory of me within her, and fostered up my admiration for her singing. But immediately she was cursing me out, too . . . "a toadstool of the state . . . a nigger toady, at that."

Then I reminded Marvella of the newspaper columns my aunt Eloise had written about her performances at Ravinia and other places. I recalled for Marvella my bylines, about her performances (my voice shouting out with surprising, newfound authority) when she sang with the all-female group. She is beginning to remember all right, I thought, but she had to tease me a little bit more. . . . And of course the night she flipped Fat, of the Terribleness Tops, at the Night Light Lounge, as she continued her efforts to force a confession out of Beefeater, was actually a pleasant memory in Marvella's imagination, I suddenly realized. Yet there was the reality of that damn gun. When all of a sudden, without warning, Marvella picked up this weaponry and with greased-lightning speed, or so it seemed to me, damned if she didn't fire it off just above my head as she cried out:

"Nigger, if you believe in me so much, then how come you had to bring that helmet liner out here? Down there at your feet? You think I'm some space cadet?" I was down on my knees, shaking all over. The crowd and the cops had all run for shelter. I felt like the biggest fool on the planet, yet I had to go ahead and act in order to keep her from acting out! (Somewhere in my mind, it occurred to me, you had an opportunity to keep one person from committing suicide, what are you going to do about this threatening soul?)

Meantime, Marvella was screaming and hollering and cursing and having a great time, at my expense. The police sergeant I had initially spoken with now leapfrogged his way over to me to proclaim that perhaps we had "better call this phase of the action off."

Now Marvella was screaming: "Weren't you the one who coined the phrase 'the dark-town dykes,' while you praised my singing group?" But she said this last with salty humor. I had, of course, never written anything of the kind.

"Hell yes, I remember you and your aunt. Maybe we can conjure up something." Marvella actually appeared to then consult with her wild Doberman, Zelda, about what her next step must be. When Marvella came back, she made her proposition known to me.

Marvella wanted me to represent her before the authorities, and force . . . imagine this . . . *force* Milton Beefeater Barnes to participate in a news conference concerning the events down in Forrest County that I have just spelled out. Marvella and I (with three reporters) would "interrogate" Beefeater for approximately an hour, and at the end, "We all should know just how guilty Beefeater, my sister, and her lover, really were . . . still are." I promised, of course, that I would do all that I could to locate Beefeater, and with a telephone call into Aunt Eloise, I was able to establish that the editorial offices of the *Forest County Dispatch* would be an excellent place to hold the press conference, especially when (and if) we discovered Beefeater at one of his several haunts and havens.

As a lean and attractive brunette interviewed me for CBS, the lethal Zelda almost tore off her blue dress with a huge bite aimed initially at the reporter's microphone, when Marvella and she passed my way.

I despised the notoriety that I could envision happening around this situation and found Aunt Eloise's green Lincoln Continental, a perfect car to get lost in traffic for the simple reason that it was the last car I would be expected to be driving as a would-be intellectual. I had told this reporter that I was motoring to Riccardo's in a purple Vega to have a drink, after I settled things at the Grand Crossing police station. Apparently a dozen reporters from various facets of the media showed up there looking for me, later that evening.

Later, Marvella was released on bond money provided by Aunt Eloise with the pledge that the columnist do a major weekend feature story, page one, for the *Dispatch*, centered on the poetess's perceived plight. That night (after I ducked out and spent much of the afternoon with Leonard Foster and Shirley Polyneices) there was some footage on the major television channels showing me in heated discussion with Marvella (who adored publicity). I was also shown being interviewed by the CBS reporter Scottie Barksdale. Aunt Eloise proclaimed in her column, the next day: "A Star Is Born!" in reference to my "heroic action."

On the strength of my TV appearance, I immediately received a job interview as a reporter for one of the downtown dailies. The very same paper had turned down my petition for a job interview when I got out of the Army (and on three other occasions over the next five years, starting in 1966, despite the growing quality of my news clips, which were nearly ninety in number). Washburne Withers had just started working for this paper's main competition.

■ ■ ■ ■ ■

As I was leaving, Granny Gram Gussie placed a sheaf of letters and effects of Leonard's in a large garbage bag, along with this admonishment: "It's up to you now, to see what you can do to save that boy from the harm stewing up in his head. A real crazy. You see Joubert, Leonard's *mentally*."

"It's gone far beyond even your idea of *mentally*, Granny Gram Gussie." Out on the streets, the cops were calling to get this strange woman into the police car and down to the station (and off their backs). Marvella was chanting, fuming, chiming, and generally speaking in other unknown and perhaps even unutterable tongues. I could hear her too plainly just to my left.

The squad car followed us at a safe but secure distance. I kept thinking as we rode down to the police station, why does it appear to be my fate that chaos will always follow my best-mapped plans? After Marvella was finally released to her mother (who indeed did have some money), and she reimbursed my aunt Eloise, I headed out to the hospital. Now my problem was, how would I duck the reporters?

Aunt Eloise had said, earlier in the week, "Baby-Bear, you've got to have some dominion over the life of that wayward Leonard. Kinsman or no. For some peculiar reason that I can't articulate, the fate of Leonard Foster may well be in your hands." And I almost said, "*But my fate is not in your hands*, Auntie dear."

And Shirley Polyneices, Leonard's girlfriend, and my classmate at Brighton High School, had called this morning, once again—had beseeched me: "Get over there, J.J. See if you can lift Leonard out of himself. Help me uplift my baby. If anybody can rustle Leonard out of his doldrums—well, it's worse than simply doldrums. His bed is surrounded by professionals; but I'm telling you Bear-man, there is a devil creeping up the bed of this man of mine, and about to take him away from here, and it's something these white people don't know nothing about (although they have conjured up most of it upon us, in this world). No, I know you have never heard me talk this way before, beside my protests in the Movement. But this shit is way out. So, maybe you can uncork within him—through your humor, wit, and comedy— some shared memory? And it may well be the catalyst he needs. A jump start. All I know is that Leonard loves you in his own crazy way." Then

I asked, "Shirley, do you really believe he loves anybody, or anything except a vague vision of his own quest and mission?"

Then there was the deep fondness and love I held for Lucasta Jones, Leonard's "mothering" one, and my aunt. But I also realized this man needed professional help that I could not render. There was an ever-weaving web of consciousness around Lucasta, which echoed with her heartbreaking loss of Leonard Foster and his father (later from Tucson's shadow, too). But all of this was connected in my imagination about her to the saga of Lucasta's only babe, stripped from her bed, by the hands of the powerful judge.

Seated now in the parking lot of the hospital, I thought out loud that a quick visit to the bundled-up sheaf of letters on the passenger's side (culled from Leonard's sojourn into the South and his Civil Rights Movement days) might provide a skeleton key into the mysterious files of Foster's curious quandaries. Some of the papers I had looked at before, others were new to my eyes, and left off with Granny Gram Gussie, by Leonard, for safekeeping. But what about the sources of the money in his bank account? Was there anything here that might explain or reveal this?

I struggled to find some answers in the "Running Log Summation of (Racial) Incidents" that Leonard Foster chronicled as editor of the *Freedom House Bulletin*, called *Spirit of the Movement*, or in letters or postcards relating his experiences "forged in the belly of belligerence," as Leonard had referred to the agony of the struggle in the South. Yet even these letters of state, so often wrought with pain to a point of becoming Leonard's epistles, were fundamentally public matters, and the soul of this poet remained somewhat enigmatic. I would have to remember *not* to bring up the late-morning experience about Marvella, because Shirley Polyneices most definitely knew all about the singer of wild songs. They had met a few times (that I was aware of) during the heady days of the Movement. Any mention of the crazy incident might throw Shirley, or me, off track. Though God knows what track or course our conversation might take. Anyway, she would see enough on the local news this evening. But what would happen if the television people did successfully trace me down? I'd have to handle this situation. Perhaps I'd read aloud from one of my scenes culled from the new work-in-progress. My ambitious aunt would be proud of that, albeit an example of unbridled, excessive behavior, which she also feared in me.

I sat there mulling over these effects for half an hour, as one might hover over a dead man's last will and testament, or his face, a foot away from his bier, trying to get some answers in his countenance in repose. The deceased was momentarily frozen, as it were, in time, and might offer some answers to the meaning of his existence—and therefore keys into our living.

There must be some assemblage of keys to unlock the turbulent soul of Leonard Foster, whose poetry seemed ever to elude the mesh of the curious chaos with his mind and spirit.

I believed there was something challenging and compelling behind the basis of the bank account I held jointly with Leonard (which formed a mysterious yet real weight at the core of his soul). "Shrouded in a crepe coffin of yesterdays, where worms rejuvenate themselves upon our bodies. And we have only Yorick's skull to oddly humor us." Those were lines taken from one of Galloway Wheeler's send-ups and rambling riffs on deeply guarded secrets. My barber, Mr. Galloway Wheeler, celebrant of William Shakespeare.

Well, the money was definitely Leonard Foster's. Where did the initial thirty-three thousand dollars come from? Who had bankrolled Leonard Foster? And thereby directly drawing me into the loop of this jumbled, riddled man's complex fate, I heard my soul cry out. Yet could the holding of a mere bank account drive one to the brink of madness? Perhaps the driving sources behind the money formed a powerful piston in the wheel within a wheel of Leonard's whirling dervish of a soul.

Now surreal fragments appeared in my dreams, of those times when I had picked up my kinsman at the train station or the bus terminal. We drove to the bank and Leonard Foster would enter the edifice (but not to participate in the actual withdrawal ceremony of extracting one hundred fifty dollars or so, necessary to send back down to Forrest County or elsewhere, in order to free one of the civil rights workers from jail).

Leonard had legally signed over to me what he termed "powers extraordinary" and had actually given to me the authority to make withdrawals, so that he did not and would not ever actually add to, nor extract from, "*our*" savings account any of the money that was his. "But what of interest?" I asked. His answer was: "Never touched my hands to blood money." He would often say this to me in a cluster, whispered and hoarse. Was Leonard clairvoyant?

Then there was Leonard's actual viewing of the cash dollars in my hands, or the paper upon which the numbers were printed out onto a piece of white paper, in order to spring from jail certain freedom fighters. The paper transformed now at the Forest County Trust and Loan Bank—another cage—turned into an instrumentality called a cashier's check, "paid to the order of Forrest County, Mississippi" (and other places), in order to liberate.

Out of Leonard's eyes, it all seemed too magical and horrible for him to look upon this white paper with the black print on it for very long. Or, this money would go to the struggling organizations within the Freedom Movement. Small sums, or shares, for sure. But why the elaborate scheme, which involved me (and during the time I was in the Army, even Aunt Eloise)? So much for what "blood" money symbolized as a freeing agency in Leonard's imagination.

"Leonard for labyrinth," I laughed aloud, as I now turned down the car window and set out for the hospital.

Ah, but the incarcerated was released through the mysterious money of a man who was chained to a deeper imprisonment, it suddenly occurred to me. Or, how many times had Leonard himself been hurled into jail during the struggle and had I sent this money south to liberate Leonard and his compatriots from the prison cells? How much did Shirley Polyneices know of the financial sources that Leonard held in his possession? I wondered whether Leonard Foster had wanted to keep all of this secret, because he wished to repress "any and all" appearances of what he himself, oddly enough, expressed as "signs of culpability . . . or vulnerability." What was behind these vague terms?

There had been the issue of Leonard Foster's signature on the checks. He took care of that matter by coming up with a pseudonym, the Little Dreamer (the same signature note with which he used to sign off on his poems). Then, Leonard talked me into the handling of the bank account, by walking me through the processing of withdrawals from the account. Much of the process was simpleminded, but I allowed for Leonard to have some dominion over his day and this deed. I found myself constantly saying, "But Leonard, do you really want to do this?

Give me this kind of authority?" But then money never meant anything to Leonard Foster.

There was the question of taking a small sum from "our" account to bankroll our magazine, *The Dark Tower*. As much as this enterprise meant to him, Leonard was never sanguine about the idea of using the funds for such a lofty purpose.

■ ■ ■ ■ ■

Now, as I walked up the steps to the hospital, I pictured myself describing certain events that we had both experienced (gathered up by Granny Gram Gussie's eccentric ways) so that I might bring the former "freedom fighter" (as I liked to call the Little Dreamer) out of at least a primary stage of some psychological stew. Leonard was something of a shell-shocked veteran of the Freedom Movement. How many times jailed? How many times abused? And knocked in the head with sticks and stones and rifle butts and then shot down in the streets (twice) and left for dead in the alleys and backwoods of the South. Once at the door of a Klansman.

Leonard needed much more than what I could give him.

Even though we were in sharp conflict over most public and private matters, we were somewhat unified by an interest in literature. Our magazine had ultimately gone under. After debating with him, on several occasions, he had finally directed me to release funds from "our" account, to help in the production costs of our literary enterprise. Aunt Eloise had put up an initial two hundred fifty dollars to help defray costs. Twelve issues of *The Dark Tower* appeared before the enterprise did indeed go down dead.

■ ■ ■ ■ ■

At last I obtained clearance from the quite officious hospital desk sergeant, decked out in his handsome, neatly starched, deep blue uniform. He was a towering, shrill-voiced, medium-dark-brown-skinned Jamaican, with a name tag that read: JEFFCOAT PADDINGTON. He was particularly difficult on those "unqualified persons seeking visitors' privileges into our psychiatry ward."

I didn't help the situation with my inability to explain what "exactly, precisely your blood relationship is to this man in question." Paddington queried in heavily accented British tones, with little of the Islander's mythical-musical tongue coming alive to delight the ear.

It was my student-at-large status with the university I was attending (as evidenced by my ID card) that won me admission into the hospital proper and down the labyrinth of steps. I may show out, or use my powers for lying (which on occasion border on the magical), as an evolving, working playwright; but I don't ever seem very keen or quick when it comes to lying on the spot. My problem/gift for hearing voices overrules me, time and again, and I simply can't get my lie straight. On the other hand, I suspect the nuances and complexities of black American families were baffling to this Islander. How I was not a relative of Leonard's and yet more than kin, in his extended family, presented a web that Mr. Paddington probably found as yet another one of the "mysteries of American Negro life." So, after I plucked down my university ID card, and we fell back on the basics of institutional authority, Paddington said, as if designing a sentence,

"We Jamaicans have great respect for education, and the high standards your institution places upon intellectual attainment and values fits well within our schemata." I started to give him a military salute, or a round of applause: Chairman of the Board of Operations.

Guided through a maze of arrows pointing and tracking the pathfinder everywhere and nowhere, I found myself brooding over "Yes, and what indeed are the specifics of this kinship?" Leonard is "part cousin," older/younger brother for starters, and yet none of the above. Ah, the extended branches of the Negro's complex family-fate.

For twenty minutes I wandered about the hospital halls in a distracted state, partially looking for *Ward C. J. Psychiatry*, yet mulling over the complicated heritage of my father's side of the family, which in a circuitous manner it held within the driftwood story of Leonard's outer saga and how he—the Little Dreamer—had been *reborn* into the Jones family.

GUSSIE JONES was born on the Dahomey Plantation, Forrest County, Mississippi, in 1900. She had a fling with, and a baby by, Curlew Bloodworth, a white man. Born in 1917, the baby was named Jerry Jones. Heading north out of Forrest County (in order to avoid the ravages of the 1927 flood and accompanied by the ten-year-old Jerry), Gussie Jones and her black lover, Forester Jones, were married in Memphis, Tennessee.

Years before she accepted Jesus Christ as her Savior, Gussie Jones had spent a year in that city with a dance troupe. When a threatening lover had not only put a gun to Gussie's head—but then fired it off to the side of her temple—she quit Bailey Birdsong and his dance troupe and returned to Forrest County and rekindled her love life with Forester Jones. Forester Jones and Gussie had met while picking cotton on the Dahomey Plantation.

PRIAM BLOODWORTH had helped them get out of Forrest County by giving Forester and Gussie not only travel money but also enough to tide them over for a brief time, once they arrived in Forest County. Time and again, Forester Jones was proud to show Leonard Foster and me the by-now-yellowed journal he had kept, which revealed "every dollar, quarter, dime, and nickel I sent off to that white man Priam Bloodworth . . . to pay him off down to the last dollars and cents—here's my black hand to Gawd—Gussie and me owed him out for our freedom to be. The year, date of the month, time of the hour, too, I sent it out to Priam Bloodworth. . . . No banknotes, nothing but cold hard cash," and echoed in that old Negro voice of pounding pride.

FORESTER JONES worked his way up with the Pennsylvania Railroad, first as a shoe-shine boy, janitor, then as a redcap, in Forest County. At one time he took care of a building in the neighborhood, as the janitor in order to pick up a few extra dollars to secure their old age. Later, Grandpa Forester worked at a hotel recently "turned over" to Negroes, in the late 1940s, for six months, where he "truly saw some sights and heard some sounds—fit for wild stallions, and those inside wild sporting houses—way, way out West."

My parents, JERRY JONES and AGNES TOBIAS, were married in 1936. Born in 1920, and five years the junior of her sister, Eloise, Agnes Tobias was killed in an airplane crash in 1940; I was three when she died. Three years after the death of my mother, my father married my mother's sister, ELOISE TOBIAS, the newspaper columnist. (Roderick Tobias, Eloise's alcoholic uncle, lived with us, intermittently, when he wasn't off passing for white.)

My father was killed in an automobile accident, in late 1949. He worked on the Santa Fe Railroad until his death.

LUCASTA JONES (sister of Gussie Jones) was born in 1890, on the Dahomey Plantation. She started her way north, in 1902, arriving in Forest County in 1903.

"Ah, the dance provides Lucasta with a revival of the spirit—away from her workaday world of preparing dead bodies. Her body, now so lyrical, then so furious. What man could ever pin her down perfectly! Better to dream your father was Pegasus, and you were born to ramble, plunge, and plunder," T. C. Larkin had written in a book he paid to have published, complete with reproductions of his pen and ink sketches, in which he attempted to arrest the motions of Lucasta Jones, from the flight of dance to the printed page.

Larkin had approached a patron about funding this project, but the response had been negative. So he published a limited number of issues with a very small press, complete with his notes and observations. By the early 1920s, T. C. Larkin had become quite involved with photography and he had taken a few motion pictures of Lucasta, even though she was thirty by then. Some of those surviving pieces of film footage reveal the innovation and dexterity with which Lucasta moved in her celebratory approach to the dance.

"She was a spitfire on the dance floor," according to Granny Gram Gussie. Even as a kid I believed many of the powerful accolades hurled at her feet. However, I yearned to add my own as I grew up, and I still do. For when I watched Cuz Lucasta's dancing (decades away from her prime) in the front part of the house, as a child, I'd peer at my aunt through the length of the room out of the darkness into the light she cast out of the shadows of her movements.

It was a dancing body changed out of liquids, and wondrous as blood and wine transformed out of simple water, I remember thinking as a child, not far removed from my first Holy Communion. I longed to write this down, touched obviously by the wine at the priest's lips. I also soon discovered that I had some strange crush on Cuz Lucasta, when I watched her dance, in and out of the shadows, during the early hours, after midnight, even as I despised her partner. In the world of that beacon, I found myself loving Lucasta by a different light. Something of a miracle to watch her and to see what she did with her motions inside of her body.

And from the pen and ink sketches and the few feet of motion-picture film footage that I observed, I came to see (in the mid-1950s) how she deployed her handkerchief as she slipped away from the beseeching, bewitching, and beguiling Lucifer's haunts. Her thrusts, wing and buck, were magical as individual pursuers curried favor with Lady Lucasta in the shimmering dress, up three inches above her knees. Despite the poor quality of the film, this was the pattern of light my imagination fastened on during these years, recombined with my actual memories of her, when as a small boy I drifted off into the shadows of the apartment to watch Lucasta dance, and dared to look upon that which I was not supposed to see. Her very hem twanged and whistled with wickedly alluring flames and sparks. "A whirling spitfire." Granny Gram Gussie used this term, in mockery and, now I realize, jealousy.

But I was coming out of some of this by the time of the announced wedding, in November. Still loathing her lover, Tucson, even more as a groom for Lucasta, and yet drawn to the memories of his dancing pattern. What a team they made on the dance floor, as one or two of the folks whispered and I believed by the light of my own eyes. Otherwise, they were not well matched for each other, as the old folks used to say, always arguing and fighting, with Cuz Lucasta winning the arguments and Tucson winning the brawls.

■ ■ ■ ■ ■

On her way north from Forrest County, Mississippi, Lucasta Jones stopped off, initially in Memphis, where she worked for the original Memphis Raven-Snow's Funeral Home. At Raven-Snow's she washed down dead bodies and developed her skill at pressing out shrouds and ironing shirts. Lucasta contacted Memphis Raven-Snow (Jr.) when she got to Forest County and went to work for him doing the same work at his funeral home as she did for his father. Lucasta was "body washer and wardrobe mistress for the dead," from the age of twelve.

When Lucasta Jones first arrived in Forest County, she often worked with a troupe of dancers. When she worked, she was the outstanding member of the troupe. Lucasta staked out a role equivalent to a contemporary shake dancer, within the troupe, emerging out of the chorus line at the climax of the act in order to do an erotic self-choreographed piece, which lasted about twenty minutes.

At this time there appeared in Forest County (back in the States from Paris, where he had been taking art lessons) one T. C. Larkin. He was greatly interested in making something artful yet different out of the world of talent and entertainment that abounded in Negro life "everywhere I go." Larkin had a natural gift for quick sketch portraits. In fact, this dark-skinned, handsome, self-confident native of New Orleans often supported himself by doing quick portraits in pen and ink on the streets and in bars throughout cities in this country and in Europe, where he wandered, drifted, landed, or emerged out of the water. Larkin was also adept at painting watercolors. He had shown enough talent and capacity for hard, serious work that he won support from two private patrons, so that he might study art in Paris. Larkin took studio courses and private instructions during the two years he was in Paris, before returning to the United States and coming to Forest County.

Larkin started doing sketches of the troupe Lucasta danced with, but soon after his arrival, he began to draw in his large sketchbook "the enchanting, brilliant, bizarre, deeply erotic, and moving twenty-minute-solo dancer—this, Lucasta Jones's performance." Larkin attempted to gather upon his sketchpads every gesture, motion, and movement that went into Lucasta's artwork. What Larkin was attempting at this time was to convey on paper what was also a potentiality already being tried out in film: recording motion on the silver screen.

It was indirectly through the mortician Memphis Raven-Snow, Jr., that Lucasta met Judge Jericho Witherspoon: a reddish, fair-skinned Negro (a runaway slave) and the first African American judge in the state. For Raven-Snow informed the judge about this semiprivate club where Lucasta danced and he extolled her dancing.

Lucasta Jones had a baby by this legendary figure, on April 4, 1905. I learned of this through several conversations with Cuz Lucasta. This babe was named Arthur, by Judge Witherspoon, "because the name rings with authority, and then of course there is the legend of King Arthur's Round Table," the ancient judge explained to the babe's teenage mother. Lucasta had thought his words so beautiful that she told him to write those words down. "For a time, I thought that he, this High Judge, was going to lift me up and be my educator by his hand and his high-flowin' words," she said.

Convinced that Lucasta Jones was far too young, too wild, and ill prepared to care for his *male* babe, Judge Witherspoon virtually "stole Arthur by night" and "took him to his wife, Sweetie Reed, to raise up." Devastated by all of this rupture and dislocation of her life, Lucasta informed me:

"It was promised and pledged to me, by this High Judge, how I, me, Lucasta Jones, would be 'lowed to see my baby every once'n while. Then after the age of two, he would be returned to me. But that I could not raise him up proper. I was kind of wild—it's true. So? I needed my baby! Lucasta wanted her baby. 'Sides, Gussie and Forester would have helped me raise up the babe. Turning him back over to me at two would mean those dearest infant years to be cut away from him. Would have been dead to me. By then he would turn away from my breast, my eyes, my laugh, my voice. I would have been dead to Arthur.

" 'Cause you see, Joubert, I went along with it like a fool. 'Cause I thought I was a hip fool, could outsmart the smartest. . . . Sure 'nough could outdance the dancingest. Thought Gussie and Forester would stand up for me, but from the start they said nothing. The way they were so quiet and silent was to say maybe baby Arthur be better off with this Sweetie woman, who had such a grand reputation for helping up people to stand on their own two legs. What could I do? The High Judge was too powerful and my own family fell down on me when I needed strength to lift me up, so I could hold my baby's body fast to my breast. Lift 'lil Arthur to the titty he needed, to suck from my milk of life to his heart, near where he could hear my true heart dream breathed." Sometimes when Lucasta spoke these words, or their variant to me, clusters of tears formed in her reddened eyes, where she had been weeping the night before. At other times, she called it all the hard bulletins of life's tragic news, in a voice similar to a blues singer, without accompaniment, reciting her litany before she sings the words on the stage.

In her subterfuge of playing out the hip fool, Lucasta did find ways in order to see the babe. Judge Witherspoon never did intend to return the toddler of two to the arms of his mother. The judge did give Lucasta a brief allowance, in order to purchase her silence. "Chump change" was what her main lover, Tucson, later called it.

Lucasta decided to do the judge's shirts for free during the babe's first year, feeling certain that this *free ironing* would "lay a claim on his heart," and he would bring "my baby, Arthur, to see me, when he picked up his bundle of freshly washed and ironed shirts . . . that the baby Arthur would be bundled up beneath his arms in the baby basket." On a few occasions this scene actually took place.

Lucasta told me that when she had to administer to the dead bodies of babies at Memphis Raven-Snow's, the procedures always sent her into what could only be proclaimed as a state of madness: their bibs, shrouds, aprons, dresses, or whatever the family brought over for the presentation of the body, any of these materials kept her in tears. These tasks of preparation always brought her back from a state of daydreaming. Some mourners might leave a few nickels and dimes for her in a saucer, near a wee casket, in respect for the work of this invisible body-preparer, even as she apparently did a highly commendable job in making the dead bodies of babies appear as life forms, before the eyes of the infants' kin. "But I couldn't think of other than the baby Arthur, who Judge Witherspoon slipped out of my bed. So, if they liked what I did for their babies, I could only think of how I would have dolled up my 'lil Arthur so . . . in suits to live in."

Finally, because of her anger over Judge Witherspoon's "backhanded" treatment (and as a way of getting at him through Memphis Raven-Snow, who had after all, made the introductions), Lucasta quit working for that mortician. "Out-of-spite unemployment," she confessed to me. Over the years, I came to pity Lucasta's plight and the awful circumstances that always seemed to befall her. Pity Cuz Lucasta all the more because it appeared to me that both sister Gussie and her brother-in-law, Forester, were so harsh in their judgments of this beguiling, sweet, generous woman, who always took up more personal time with me than any of the rest. Lucasta always spoke to me as a near confidant.

As I grew older (surely by the time I reached puberty), I came to pity Cuz Lucasta for the wrongheaded decisions that she made. For example, once she left Memphis Raven-Snow, she soon gained employment at Fountain's House of the Dead, an establishment of rickety reputation within the community. She did the same kind of work there that she had for Memphis Raven-Snow. However, now Lucasta Jones was pressed into a greater variety of other services for half the salary she had received by her former employer. She divulged this to me rather reluctantly.

Judge Witherspoon thought Lucasta was a loose, lost woman and something of a numbskull, from what I could glean out of overheard conversations of Gussie and Forester Jones. When I tried to probe Aunt Eloise about what she might have known of Lucasta's plight, my journalist aunt spoke in several voices, either knowing or fearing to reveal too much. Then she scoffed, "Well, I'm not as old as you make me out to be. Your aunt Lucasta is a lot older than your aunt Eloise." On several occasions as I headed into my teens, when I brought up the topic of Cuz Lucasta, Aunt Eloise said, "Joubert, your fondness for Lucasta fascinates and disturbs me. But is it all just prologue for a larger enchantment with the Perilous, Tragic Woman, who lives on the brink of existence, the slippery slopes; who hovers over the foggy bottom? I hope you will not be fated to embrace women of this sort as you come into your questing young manhood. Let's put it this way, Baby-Bear, Lucasta squandered (and continues to squander) her beauty, to a point of floppish insolvency."

Taking in money from her washing and ironing, Lucasta tried to raise Leonard Foster on an off-and-on basis from 1939 to 1946. She saw herself as something of a "grandmother" figure, she confided to me, even after Luke Foster "left Leonard and me and vanished out of this world with a chorus girl." Lucasta kept her records of Bessie Smith and Billie Holiday playing all the time.

I came to think of Leonard Foster as an older cousin (he was three years my senior). Down the years, I found myself captured by several memory fragments of Leonard Foster's uniqueness. But there was especially that one, observed at the Easter-egg hunt. I saw then that there was something buried within that suggested that he either had eyes in the back of his head or that Leonard Foster was "born knowing." How out of a pack of flying gym shoes, this Leonard Foster had emerged, two feet from the sack, and artfully scooped up the three dyed eggs hidden from view, beneath the first-base bag. Then he flew off into the distance (with the eggs in his pouch of a pocket), as if vaulted into motion, high-riding just above the saddle seat of a motorcycle. Later this fragment drove me to speculate that one day this Leonard Foster would find his own pot of gold.

Lucasta Jones was my aunt on my father's side. She was referred to, by me and other family members, as Cuz Lu, or Cuz Lucasta, because of the sweet, childlike affection she projected. "That Cuz Lu always seems like a foolish teen about many things—particularly men. Always going off on blind dates, with men who live in the dark, or those whose steps are cloaked in a garb ill-colored ill, but appealing to some taste for the wanton, in that blind woman," Aunt Eloise said. My grandmother, Lucasta's sister, often referred to her as "Nanny."

Granny Gram Gussie seemed to see her as a "semiwhore" and "living in sin," expressed in pig latin to Forester Jones. Leonard Foster came to think of Lucasta as his mother, and Granny Gram Gussie as his grandmother.

Cuz Lu, I had learned (or realized, too) had lived with various men and ended up taking care of various children, of "other women's babies." But she harbored a deep need to raise a child by her hand, in order to replace that "one who was snatched" from her. Lucasta (and indeed other family members as well) "took" to one of these children, in particular. The boy's name was Leonard Foster and he was born in 1934. His father, Roland Luke Foster, turned away the "slave name of Bloodworth to take one of my own creations, *Foster*, rather than the nonbinding illegal and bastardizing name of Emmett Bloodworth, the last of that clan (Klan, too) of brothers," he told Forester Jones, many times, and Grandpa repeated these words to me on several occasions.

Lucasta had known Roland Luke on the Dahomey Plantation. I once overheard her tell her sister, Gussie, "He was the one what first plucked my cherry." This man's actual date of birth (who preferred to be called *Luke Foster* or even *Jude Foster*, and that it be said in one breath, if possible, I gleaned from Granny Gram Gussie) was unknown to all.

As far as I knew, Cuz Lu had three great heartbreaks in her life. Baby Arthur was taken from her by the father, Judge Jericho Witherspoon. Leonard Foster was stripped from her, when Luke Foster's relatives back in Forrest County, Mississippi (working in combination with Gussie and Forester), devised a scheme of sending the boy back south to go to a Negro Catholic school. This institution was operated by a group of defiant, wily, radically progressive white nuns, referred to by the local whites as the "nigger nuns." These women were determined to give blacks a first-rate education in the primary grades.

The third tragedy of her life involved Lucasta's tremendous love (also lust, I came to see through my own eyes and the mixture of the two) for a man by the name of Tucson, whom I remembered vividly. They were "set to be married," Cuz Lu said.

I would always recall that stormy November day as I sat in a corner, playing solitaire before the rain-drenched windowpane in her apartment, while she ironed Tucson's clothing and some of her own. Cuz Lu was listening to the voice of Billie Holiday on her record player. Then, the telephone rang. I heard a spirit-shattering voice come unearthed out of my aunt's body and soul.

Now I reflected that Lucasta Jones was a fixture and an adornment of eccentricity and rarely taken seriously by her family. And so, as I grew up, I often thought aloud how Lucasta Jones symbolized those who always claim that life never allows them a moment to call their own, as something of a measure to go up against, most ironically so, in this industrial eye of the storm. The ruthless claim on God's turf! Her stubborn streak (which worked against her in so many ways) actually provided Lucasta Jones with an inner power of living her life, as she willed it to be in certain ways. But because she was driven by a willful force to have a life of her own set apart, she was particularly vulnerable to the devastations of human existence. Her religious philosophy (such as it was) came in the form of a placard she kept in her apartment: LET NOT YOUR HEART BE TROUBLED. Below this wording was a picture of Jesus with the sheep welcomed back into the flock by the shepherd. So, she held out some hope that at the last hour she might represent the lost sheep, who are returned to the flock. She surely did not live this way. Cuz Lu claimed no formal institutions as her own.

If she went to church at all, it was on rare occasions with Granny Gram Gussie and Grandpa Forester for the Christmas service, or perhaps she might get one of her men to buy her an Easter outfit, which she would wear to church. To complement her rich, medium-dark-brown complexion, Lucasta preferred to dress in green, gold, or pink. Until the advent of Tucson in her life, the idea of marriage hadn't apparently crossed her mind. And this possibility came late in their relationship. They had lived together for three years before the double announcement came: first the voice from the other end of the telephone that day in November, and then later, Lucasta Jones's discovery of his real intentions. In her freewheeling style, Cuz Lu never played by the rules, if she could help it.

Though she spent most of her days in Forest County (she died in 1966), Lucasta Jones was a Southerner down and through her body and soul to the dancing soles of her feet. There was a lazy streak, some felt, about Cuz Lu. Once she fell for someone, it was "all over with," as the saying goes, whether it was her man or her devotion to her ironing (to which she did indeed give all of her powers of thought and talent).

She was always being written off, at best, as capricious. However, Lucasta was capable of being loyal, even as she was dismissed as someone inconstant by the family, in general, and by Granny Gram Gussie, in particular.

A certain bigotry always set in when one thought of Lucasta Jones. Judgment went out of the window. We loved her, we loved her not, all in the same sour-bread breath.

There was rarely any keening sensitivity allowed, no attempt at proper assessment of her character, when it came to measuring the spiritual weight of Lucasta Jones on a truly balanced scale. Lame, inadequate, impotent decisions were immediately affixed upon her frame. A scarlet cross of purple ice was often placed about her neck. When Lucasta "fell into the room," immediately conclusions were reached!

Often, Lucasta Jones arose by dawn's early light, normally to put in a fairly long day at her washing board and at her ironing. She usually bedded down early to do exactly what, with whom, God Almighty knew. Or, for months on end nobody's body, I mused, as she reclined in her narrow bed. I came to reflect, in my childhood, that Cuz Lu's waywardness was lubricated by her obstinate, even modest nature. All of this helped form some of the odd poetic tributaries of Lucasta's soul.

You probably could break and bruise her spirit before you could bend her will into the service of your resolve. Yet there had been the dominating presence of this man, Tucson, in her life. In general Lucasta maintained a kind of a distance from life, which she interpreted as her own self-possessed leveraged authority. But when Lucasta Jones was proven terribly wrong, she retreated into some small corner of her soul, deeply wounded, pinched off, pushed aside, and embarrassed to the nerves in her toes. *There* she was a pitiable soul. But out of the doldrums of despair, there in her dungeon of desolation, Lucasta allowed the music to creep in: the voices of Bessie and mainly that of Lady Day's singing "Good Morning Heartache, here we go again."

There were few forces other than these formidable ones to nourish her spirit, such was the condition of Lucasta after the telephone call came crashing through about Tucson, and the well-founded rumor of his future plans. Subsequently, Lucasta stopped her payments on her life insurance policy.

Her butcher's paper bundle of laundry in a newspaper outer wrapping knew the touch of Lucasta Jones, now transformed and handed back to the customer at the door. The small change flowed into her lean, medium-brown hand. Coins flowed into her strawberry-colored handkerchief, through a slot in the floor, and landed in a scorched cooking pot below. Sometimes when she took Leonard, or me, or both of us to the picture show, at the Joe Louis movie house, she extracted the fare from this same strawberry-colored handkerchief, given to her by Luke Foster. Or if Cuz Lu ran low on quarters, she would unfold a few nickels and dimes from the left leg of her Burnished Georgia Brown stockings, where the garter was located, which meant that she had to raise her dress and expose her undergarments. . . . "Close your eyes, boys," she'd say. Leonard would always become very embarrassed. I would pretend as if I had my eyes completely closed, but they were not. Even then at seven or eight, I came to realize the great shapeliness of her gams.

I was embarrassed about noticing my aunt's legs, but I didn't stop peeking whenever she needed to call on her reserve funds.

Chapter 2

In a small area leading to Leonard's room sat the attractive Shirley Polyneices, who immediately leaped up, tears streaking down her fair-skinned face. I found Shirley's perfume quite enchanting as she whispered in my ear:

"Joubert, dearest, my lover needs to be restored. You're vital to his mental state. Bear-man, maybe it ain't scientific, but it's *real*. Restored (not redeemed and all that jazz) out of his past; even if that utterance comes out of the voice of a liar. You can unpack the old stories without tearing the tissues of his fragile soul. I've known you since high school. You were always a great storyteller, with the potential of being a great liar. Now use your gift to help spring my baby back into my arms."

Shirley wore a tight-fitting blue suit, which played off her sizzling shape.

"Shirley, I never thought of myself as a form of some healing agent. I'm at my best when I'm writing for the stage; outside of that I'm as blank as the next person. Still, I want to be helpful."

"You can be. . . . You should be. Besides, Joubert, you're somehow or other kin to Leonard. Let me see if he is still asleep. If he still is, you can try some of your stories out on me, what you're going to say to awaken him out of it all." Now Shirley dodged into the room, found that Leonard was asleep, returned, and said, "This side of paradise! Tell me though, what had you planned to run past him, and what did you plot to reveal to him about the old days (which weren't always all that good for Leonard)? We want to awaken him into a happy frame of mind, not shock him down into a deeper pit of the doldrums."

"I don't think Leonard has ever recovered from the nightmare phases of the Movement."

"Oh, agreed. Agreed."

"Though his family history is deeply involved with the tunnels of his turmoil."

"So, before you get too deep, Joubert, what are you going to reveal?"

I had to stand up. There was only one chair provided in the small briefing area (used for a moment away from the immediate presence of the patient, or no doubt where the physicians might consult with family). Shirley sat perfectly still, her delightful legs crossed in a self-tantalizing manner.

"Shirley, one highlight that constantly comes back to me, as out of a dream, was when Granny Gram Gussie Jones would do a magic trick, rivaling something one might see at the carnival sideshow, at Riverview. Before supper, Granny Gram Gussie would take the complete set of teeth out of her wrinkled mask of a falling face, place them on an empty salad plate, and then commence to say grace; one step connected to the next in some mysterious, seminal ceremony, as it were. Now, she was turned to *Grinny* Gram Gussie in my imagination, Shirley, but not in Leonard's. This was not something Leonard could face without putting on a face."

"Already we've got a problem of what we can include, how much of it, and how much you dare not include. We want to awaken Leonard out of the doldrums, but we don't want to shock him out of his wits." But I could see Shirley was intrigued somewhat by the beginnings of my memory.

"You're repeating yourself," I scoffed. But then she changed up on me.

"What did you think of that poem I read to you over the telephone?" In attempting to amplify my memory, with the immediacy of the words upon the printed page, Shirley fished the poem out of her small, purple handbag and handed it to me. I allowed my eyes to flicker over the two and a half pages rather quickly, and gave a rather rambling reflection.

"Leaving aside your voice and inserting Leonard's voice, his words, and this poem did reflect some broader purposes of thought and intellectual character. Then there is all of this palaver about monsters and swine in Leonard's vision. Savagery, devouring sea. Middle Passage in here, too. Some Job. Some Yeats. Leonard always did admire him. Leonard was always given to much verbiage in his poetry, a quality he despised in the works of others. 'Too much fat,' he'd wildly proclaim, as he edited down the poetry section of our little magazine. Yet during his daily conversations, Leonard's contemplations were usually expressed more in terms of a lament, not a howl."

"Well, that was a big help. You must be a smash in a classroom, baby."

"But Shirley, since you've called on me for special services, then let me be the judge. Gag law for the gag writer, eh?"

"Continue where you left off with Granny's gums."

"There was tiny, but oh my, light-skinned *Grinny* Gram Gussie offering over the steaming evening meal, which made her appear as a sour-soggy old sea-salt, jawboning on the curd with Mr. Death himself. She was that serious looking. And Grandpa Forester, tall, deeply black in complexion, reared back, seemingly miles away in a deep fog, yet a presence created (if not actually visible), cast by the smoke he exhaled from puffing upon either cigar, cigarette, or pipe, which was not quite cleared away, despite the fact that he had stopped smoking at least half an hour before the meal was started. But the smoky presence gave a smoke signal testimonial to his identity, without him saying a word or giving Granny Gram Gussie a word of back talk, which was probably wise, given the power of that tiny woman's authority in that household!"

"You mean to tell me this Grandpa Forester needed all of that smoking to live with his Gussie," said the fair-skinned Shirley Polyneices, a blush coming across her face.

"Shirley, you've hit upon yet another feature of their most engaging soap opera of a marriage. To screen Gussie out I might say. Your Leonard would bend over his food with great seriousness as Grinny Gram Gussie's prayers for this meal flew up to God. (This usually took about seven minutes because her offering up always was original and improvisational.) And Shirley, it was all I could do to maintain a straight face, between looking at those teeth, hearing the gummy gum—sounding of words to Almighty God from out of the fallen mask of a face; then I took a peek at Leonard's face. . . ."

"Yes, and what pray tell was it like?"

"Oh, stony-to-stoic. Even at a child's age."

"Oh, that Leonard was something else around the corner and off the wall from way back when. Then there was that Catholic influence, of the beloved 'nigger' nuns."

"That was later. The nuns came to liberate, but really enchained. Shirley, when the spectacle occurred that first time and ever after, Granny Gram Gussie seemed ancient for a spell, as one dead in mummy cloth; I imagined the ghostly appearance of Granny Gram Gussie's face after it evolved into the wrath of old age.

"But Shirley, as far back as I can remember, this ritual commenced on that strange, late afternoon, on into the early evening of November, when we were all to go to eerie Fountain's House of the Dead for the funeralizing of a mysterious man (or woman) I had never heard of. First funeral I ever attended, and I remember everything that happened clearly. My mother's funeral is also buried there in my mind and soul, but I was only three at the time and recall the memorial in fits and starts.

"Yes, Shirley, I knew Leonard's would-be stepmother, Lucasta Jones, had worked here, but what were the reasons for going to Fountain's? And to this funeral? The mystery person's funeral. Intrigued as I was by it—and so surely had been and was Leonard—I could never figure it out, nor could Leonard, for that matter, or, if he knew, he never told me."

"What was the funeral like—like any other?"

"It was wild, yet muted! Original, anyway, for its absences."

"Maybe that's the place you should start up with Leonard," Shirley said, smiling slyly. Shirley went back into Leonard's room to see if he was still asleep. Soon she was back.

"Still snoring; odd repose on his face, twilight zone no less. But go on with your story. This is new stuff to me about Leonard. Granny Gram Gussie is always spoken about with such respect; this Lucasta Jones is often spoken about with so many visions of awe. I kind of wondered sometimes about the truth behind those masks—especially when he started leaving those suicide notes scattered around the basement."

"Shirley, I am thinking back to your questions about the face Leonard projected. It was more than just stoic and stony. For one thing, Leonard never had much of a sense of humor. He was usually dour and doleful."

"See, that's what I'm talking about. That's where you come in. Your stories shine light on his general sourness. Build up on what he remembers and you too can riff and expand on things from out of the past."

"In the long ago, at those evening meals, Leonard Foster would put on a face, as if to protect himself from what his eyes were viewing. Those dark, sorrowful eyes of his kept sweeping from the dentures to the mouth of his grandkin, with disbelief, as the words warbled forth from out of the long tongue prayer of blessing and from the shape-shifting mouth of Granny Gram Gussie. Because you see, Shirley, apparently the actual absence of teeth forced her to even project and prosecute (and yes, persecute, too, not only the food before her but to pursue the listening world with her particular brand of wit and venom). It all had something to do with the jaw muscles, the boy in me observed at the time.

"Granny Gram Gussie would go into the bathroom with those double sets of dentures, rinse them off, and soon return looking twenty years younger. (Blessed now of course with rouge and lipstick and a touch of eye makeup.) We then would eat. Shirley, I had been about ready to crack up each and every time it happened, starting that November late afternoon. Grandpa Forester closed his eyes through the whole ritual."

"But tell me about Leonard's family. His other family, he was so vague about this. How can you get to know a man, when he keeps so much of his life hidden?" Shirley asked.

"Ah, so now I see it all before, too. You really hope that this exercise will shed light on hidden places for the lover of Leonard Foster, as well."

I figured I'd answer Shirley directly, not merely for the pure sake of exploration but also as a way to prod her on later and get her to respond to the following query:

How did Leonard Foster get the money he had in the bank and that he "handled" so judiciously for the Freedom Movement? How much did Shirley know about how *this* came to be placed in Leonard's bank account in the first place? So, I simply started off by saying:

"Shirley, it was only through overhearing (eavesdropping, really) that I found out about Leonard Foster's other family. Granny Gram Gussie and Grandpa Forester were reflecting over the numbers they were going to play, in the Clearinghouse book, on that November morning before the funeral. Because the old man had dreamed about somebody faintly mysterious, named Roland Luke Foster."

"This was Leonard's biological uncle? Right? On his father's side," Shirley said. I simply shook my head in the negative.

However, Shirley rushed forward in a spirit of declaration rather than in the voice of one simply raising a question:

"But now where . . . maybe you know, Joubert, and maybe you don't. Since we are laying out a lot on the table, where did he get the money, directly or indirectly? The grapevine rattled the word along that small sums out of Leonard's bank account contributed to getting Movement people out of prison. Was there money from this Roland Luke Foster lingering about?"

"Shirley, no. Simply put, as best I know, Luke Foster didn't have a crying quarter or a weeping buffalo in his pockets before and when he split the scene on Lucasta. But now you're getting me ahead of my story. Well, I should close out your question, too. Yes I did know more than just a little about the existence of the money, in fact I got involved in dispensing some of the funds, at Leonard's behest. But I am without clues as to the genesis of Leonard's bank account, this I pledge to you. I swear, though I've tried, time and again, to find out the sources of this money, the roots of it."

"I'll accept this for the time being. But go on with your story."

"Shirley, Granny Gram Gussie was looking up the Dead in Aunt Jenny's *Dream Book*. But Grandpa Forester was getting the physical disappearance of one Roland Luke Foster all mixed up with death and the real funeral of the person they were going to view that evening: that seemed to be the bone of Granny Gram Gussie's contentiousness just then. In her imagination, one was real and one was false.

" 'But how do you know Roland Luke Foster is dead?' she had asked. 'Dead to his own!' Grandpa Forester swiftly, though softly, had replied. So Granny Gram Gussie elected to look up the subject of the Dead and Funerals, in the *Dream Book of Life and Death*, as if she didn't know any of this despite her constant play in the numbers racket."

Because I had started to speak so softly (as if psychologically releasing heated, though national, secrets), Shirley Polyneices motioned that we should go outside, just twenty-five feet from where we were sitting. This allowed her space and air to light up a cigarette. Then I was saying:

"Granny Gram Gussie placed the name of Roland Luke Foster on a piece of paper in indelible ink and dropped it into a solution, and if the name disappeared immediately, the person in question was dead. Shirley, this was an old-time ritual. If left there overnight and the coloring in the water rose, turned gray, then the person was more alive than dead; or, 'physically alive and spiritually dead, most likely,' as Granny Gram Gussie said."

Shirley broke in. "What if it turns any other color?"

"If blackened and it turns to a crisp, the soul is dead. If white? The soul is alive."

"Oh, no! Here we go again."

"Granny Gram Gussie went on and on about all of this, and finally Grandpa Forester declared, 'Shit. I'm just gonna play *dead* flat out and see what tomorrow brings down. Not lay down dead. What's that number, Gussie?'

" 'Probably 3-6-9—the shit row,' she said, in an offhanded but mocking manner.

" 'You getting too sharp with your back-talk-teeth, and your front fangs steady keep your butt in trouble.'

" 'Death might have your number, too,' she asserted, in a wickedly coquettish voice. (I can tell you this, Shirley, but not Leonard Foster.) Encounters of this kind sometimes led Grandpa Forester to refer to Gussie as 'Cussie,' underneath his breath, and Lord knows behind her back.

"Grandpa did play the numbers that day. And we were led to believe that he won a big sum of money. For a long time I believed that the nest egg in Leonard's bank account came from these winnings. So did Leonard. Of course, we boys, at the time of the funeral and the great good fortune, didn't know the exact sum of his winnings, but we did suspect that it was large and mysterious. Now, Shirley, tell me, and tell me truthfully, how much were you aware or unaware of this account? Maybe since we involved in this exchange, you can be as open to me as I am to you . . . with you."

"Well, frankly, Joubert, you haven't told me shit about what you knew or didn't know. You went as far with me as you wanted to go, period. I did know about the account, but vaguely, vaguely. People did whisper that I knew more than I ever did. But you know how Leonard enjoyed keeping his business to himself. It was a wall you couldn't crack with a wrecking ball. Not just this money business but the whole man. Another side over the wall, you break through one with luck, here is another behind a delightful garden of discoveries, only to come up short, once again, because here's yet another garden wall. Wreck it down. Or try, and you might destroy some of the flowers in the garden. Oh, I'm getting beyond my own powers. Leonard keeps Foster hidden away in the dark chambers of his soul, you might say," Shirley reflected as she drifted off, behind a cloud of smoke, which momentarily masked her face away from me.

And then Leonard's tormented face arose before me, out of a bouquet of flowers, amid the suicide notes, his letters and postcards, his bills from shotgun wounds attendant to his honorable and quite daring efforts in the Freedom Movement down South. His courage on the firing line. And behind this I heard the words pour up out of me from Ezekiel: "Then said he unto me, Son of Man, hast thou seen what the ancients of the house of Israel do in the dark, every man in the chambers of his imagery."

"Oh, Joubert, I know all roads lead back to Leonard, but go back to this Roland Luke Foster, maybe that'll give me a little relief?" Shirley said, fighting away the tears. "Oh Bear-man, you can't know what it means to stand by and see the person you love struck down in some form of illness, that's unanswerable and if it's something as hideous as this . . . coming to believe, or at least anguish over the fact that maybe it's something you have done to drive him to think of suicide . . . and for him to write his intentions down on small bits of balled-up paper, hurled into corners of the basement where the mice and rats run over Leonard's expressed wishes to end his life.

"The *Dream Book*, the dead man, the ritual of burning the name, all of that was intriguing. This was relieving, if not uplifting. Now I'm sounding off, as if I need the tonic I called you to deliver to Leonard."

Then I started riffing about Leonard's shortness of stature and particularly the heroes that he had written about in his poetry, who were all examples of the Napoleonic personality. Small or diminutive in stature were all three of the men Leonard Foster wrote about so lovingly, or he would imitate their characteristics and gestures, incorporate their attributes, from time to time. One of the trio was a famous writer, who also happened to be gay; another was a journalist, who ran for Congress and finally won; the third was a madcap poet-playwright, who thought of himself as a would-be revolutionary. He was always changing his name, his game, and his ideological claim. Jeremiah Brinkman, Gilbert Stubblefield, and Learned Jackman were the names of these gentlemen, in the order in which the three above appeared in Leonard's mind-set, and their eccentricities dripped off into Leonard's psychological system of transforming values. For a long time, Leonard lived out of the values he saw reflected in their sense of life.

I came to believe that Leonard possessed a soul of larger potential than the others, but their sheer power of personality overwhelmed him into surrender before the altar places where he (Leonard) worshiped, with their other fans. The cult of personality fashioned around his heroes shook Leonard up terribly, even as my poet kinsman had done his part to celebrate the lives of these famous or well-known public figures. Each in his own way—without knowing it—had made Leonard feel his inadequacy so deeply, so sharply, so crudely, that he found an ironic cave-shelter inside these men, who all had their own enormous insecurities. There was Leonard, swimming in the tides of their lost-found souls. Lost souls to be sure, but capable of using their lostness for their own salvation artistically, or employing the idea and the reality of group oppression, with the concept of their outlaw heroism as the metaphorical bridge to their audience.

From time to time, Leonard did work for Gilbert Stubblefield and "the crusading newspaper" that he published on a weekly basis. And Gilbert Stubblefield kicked his ass and ran him errand-boy raggedy. At this time, Leonard wanted so to be "something more than simply a poet." He thought writing for a newspaper (as indeed he had written for the civil rights paper, in the South) would free him up for a major contribution, and that by working in the shadow of Stubblefield, he would learn, firsthand, the craft of journalism. But he fell in love with Gilbert's sensational species of charisma, and ended up writing poetry about Stubblefield. And so I continued a kind of summation of the three to Shirley.

Now I heard myself weeping aloud to Shirley, and to my personal surprise.

"Shirley, probably Leonard was more talented than these fellows (or as talented), but they charmed him away from developing his inner soul for writing. Then, too, for Leonard, these were issues of spiritual-ideological gestation, brooding and brewing. Beneath this was the Freedom Movement, in which he was arrested countless times and shot down three times, but Shirley, you know all of this. Oh, Leonard, you were also, you are also my hero, you enacted the life, dared to live out the life; I only dared enter from afar. Marched with my tin drum on the periphery, in my own good time and cadence, and beneath the shirts of a certain safety.

"So Leonard, if you have cracked up like a recently released prisoner, or like those we think of as shell-shocked souls from Vietnam, then let me pray for your soul. You will be saved and not destroyed; not destroyed, yet defeated."

Shirley was shocked to hear these words come pouring out of my heart. But we were outside and it was getting chilly, and besides, Leonard didn't know about my sentiments. As we drifted back inside, I heard myself pray out loud but within my own heart. After all these months of missed obligations . . . yet stay still my heart for the poor bastard who will open his eyes and attempt to awaken to the light of the phantasmagorical. Shirley has called me here to come to your bedside to take what's here, some remnant of yourself, and help change it through those things between us, out of the repository of memory. Something salvageable, where it is rich, strange, and mainly comic or humorous. But since I've been called to be "out of the species of Rumpelstiltskin," I'll demand a certain price. Price? Yes, to find out if I can from Leonard (if he knows), who was the Daddy Warbucks who unleashed the pot of gold in the bank?

Why was it that even as I had hoped to awaken Leonard Foster, my kinsman, by comic tonic and humorous light, I found myself lusting after his old lady, sitting there before me, surely flirting with me, with those wicked hip moves of her figure as God is my witness. *Turn it over to me, baby, and I'll tickle old Leonard to death.* Shirley Polyneices, so sweet, so cold, so fair. So fair that they used to call her the Snow Queen in the Movement. If I fell upon her, a splinter of ice would end up in my veins. I'd become a pain-filled junkie forever and ever, world without end, amen. But when I spoke of Granny Gram Gussie, why was it that I also thought of *Grinny* Granny, out of Brier Rabbit's tall tales, and the pot-boiling incident involving Granny Wolf? Fighting off tears of joy, laughter, and mocking borne out of the responsibility to memory and irresponsibility conceived out of just plain old love and lust . . . then in my tears I remembered back to a time when I had the mumps and Leonard had read to me with such care from the funnies: *Terry and the Pirates, Popeye, Dick Tracy, Batman,* and my favorite, *Mandrake, the Magician* (and of course the beautiful Narda). Also, *Wonderwoman* and *Superman.* (I guess I had grown up thinking I might be something of a Clark Kent; then where was Lois?) But even back then I found myself equating a portion of Leonard's reading and heavy presence with that of B. O. Plenty. For in all truth, you had to force Leonard to take a bath. He read those comic strips with great patience and exactness, all of which added greatly to the humor of the experience, if you are hunkered down with mumps, a comic-looking condition if there ever was one. Oh, big brother that I never had. He spooned them out in completely the wrong voice, and diction. Comedy also remained untapped by his didactic voice. Leonard was always looking for a moral.

Yes, and while he was rendering up those comic strips to me, wasn't Leonard often thinking of how he himself had been abandoned by his primal parents (as he often termed them, and where he had picked this up I don't know)? When tears ran down Leonard's face, didn't his driftwood parents come to mind, behind the mask? Were not the stories behind the comics unleashing something else in Leonard's imagination and surely not within the confines of the drawing slot and print spread out before him? And yet upon reflection, even the funny papers could make Leonard weep, too. Was it not true that the demonic W. A. D. Ford had traveled and studied in the East (after leaving Heidelberg) under various and sundry Bhagwan types?

I then elected to tell Shirley what I thought she should know. She was shocked or surprised at every turn in this story. For although Shirley had marched in the South, during the Freedom Struggle, registered voters, and faced down some tough situations, she actually knew little about the complexity of Negro-American relationships (relations, too) with white individuals from the South, nor was she particularly alert to class stratifications amongst African Americans. In fairness to Shirley, I must hasten to report that I learned much of the Roland Luke Foster story indirectly from my grandparents' whispering lips.

Roland Luke Foster, a mulatto offspring of the Bloodworth family, had so despised the vile, volatile, racist image of the Bloodworth clan, that rather than retain the odious name of Bloodworth, he had changed his name to *Foster.*

Believing that to *foster* something was to push it further along, to encourage its growth, yes and even to father-it-along, he changed his name from Bloodworth to Roland Luke Foster. Grandpa Forester laughed at every recall of this story, which he himself varied from time to time in the retelling, as he had that day in November (while Leonard was out on an errand), and we were all going to the funeral for the stranger. Rarely had I heard him deliver up so many words, in the presence of Granny Gram Gussie. Rarer still did she allow for him to recite any remembrance of his own, or to slide in with some sort of corrective dissenting riff.

"Now, Gussie," Grandpa Foster said, "I looked up that word in the dictionary Joubert always leaves here, when he stays over, for his lessons and homework. Made some discoveries, myself, too, 'bout this *word* 'foster.' (Goin' always be just Roland Luke, or even Roland Juke to me, as he was in the beginnin' time.)"

Reciting now from the notes he had taken from my dictionary, I heard him declare: "Affording, or sharing or nurturing, or parental care, though not necessarily related to blood kin, or legal ties." Then he said from a deep-barrel place within his soul, "So, what I wants to know is this: how did taking on a new name (and disdaining the peckerwood pappy's shame of the plantation his family come out of) *improve* Roland Luke's actions, *foster* them, too, towards his Negro/black own? His black kin? Kith, too? He still Roland Juke, far as my thoughts go down. Yeah, though it may be hard to swallow as a pint of Joyful Heavenly White-Lightning Whiskey out of the Civil War, guaranteed to take you out of this world backwards."

I'm certain that they didn't see me standing near the doorway. A strange look had already emerged across his wife's face. Grandpa Forester suddenly withdrew into an old familiar shelter shaped out of silence.

Years later, Grandpa Forester picked up the story. I was doing the driving and I brought it up. He said, as if he had only stopped midway in his dialogue, a decade earlier, for a short breather, on that day of the funeral, "Yeah, Joubert, he still Roland Luke, Roland Juke, to tell the truth. 'Cause he lived out them juke joints, far as I'm thinkin'. Run off from his duty to that boy same as them count-no-account unlegal bound peckerwood mens used to do, down in Mississippi, goddamn! Worse, too, 'cause at least a few of 'em built homes for their Nigra mistresses. Worse than all that, too, 'cause you see Leonard's pappy not only knew better, by blood and breedin' and his self-claim 'bout how he was a better man than the peckerwood what sired him. He *Fostered* all right. Fostered himself up a lie."

Then Grandpa Forester was silent for a moment. Measuring how much he wanted to reveal even to me, perhaps especially me. But freed from the authority of his light-skinned wife, Gussie (momentarily), he took a deep draw on his pipe and went down a little bit deeper: "Probably Luke-Juke Bloodworth closer to the truth-in-mirror picture."

Then this in a whisper: "Well, all I can say is most of these colored women who had babies by white men . . . you see, Joubert, before I came up here to Forest County, I used to be a delivery man, right early in the morning. I seen over a course of time scores of white men heading out from their creeps at colored women's places." Then he looked over at me to see if he detected any blushing. After all, my grandmother was there. "How come they used to say back down home: two people what ruled the South—white man, colored woman?"

"But you were about to also say—something else, too."

"Well, yeah, these kinds of colored women, what had babies by these white men, *you*, meaning, as a Negro man, you, or especially men like *me* couldn't tell 'em anything. Never-ever."

Then I recognized what had happened to him that day, years earlier, and why the dialogue had ceased between Roland and Grandpa Forester (who of course was not my grandfather by blood, even though I thought of him as my very own). The blood connection to my white grandfather was relatively meaningless, in terms of personal remembrance and love; yet it was surely cast there in my features and the mix of my complexion . . . but so what? How many times had I heard Grandpa Forester say, "Oh how these yallars stick together." Believing, too, that my generation would crack this code and send it flying off into the dust.

Yet not only had Grandpa Forester married a light-skinned woman (who else could he marry to challenge white authority, even as he knuckled under to the symbolism of white beauty?) who lorded it over him with the power of her color throughout their relationship. So, sitting there now, I did not go into all of this with the fair-skinned Shirley Polyneices because I didn't quite know how she would take to all of this. In a personal way, I mean, even as she had marched for Black Freedom and led the way against White Supremacy.

■ ■ ■ ■ ■

Grandpa Forester smoked three kinds of tobacco (all of the time, over the course of a day into night), perhaps to give his mouth a spirit and heated life, in order to make his tongue fire-licking. Most often all of this was denied him, in his wife's presence, though she stood no more than four-foot-eight, and he was nearly six-foot-four in his bare feet, which rarely had the pleasure of actually touching the linoleum naked, because usually Granny Gram Gussie had him running errands from first light to lights out. No wonder that man smokes three kinds of tobacco (even unto this day). It was but a wonder if he can find the time to not simply smoke but discover the few seconds necessary to set fire to the weed, pipe, or cigarette, I wondered aloud. As for drinking? Never. Both of his parents were alcoholic, it seems.

Now I was revealing to Shirley, "Yet the family kept Lucasta away from Leonard Foster, allowing him to be 'with her in seasonal shifts.' Viewing Lucasta as wild and wayward half of the time, and lovable, tender, bighearted, and foolish with the wrong kind of men the other part of the time. Always like an adolescent, in mind, body, and soul, and therefore improper to raise the boy, on a full-time basis.

"You see, Shirley, this wasn't the first time Lucasta had lost a child because of the judgment of another, because of what was perceived as her immeasurable lack of character."

Shirley immediately prodded me about this statement, and I went on to tell of Lucasta's relationship to Judge Witherspoon and the baby Lucasta had for him. I could see that she had great identification with Lucasta Jones.

"Shirley, much of Lucasta's energy became consumed by her talent for ironing, or by her many affairs. High above her workplace a placard read: LET NOT YOUR HEART BE TROUBLED."

"In the South I came to know women like this Lucasta, and came to feel a profound longing to awaken this branch of the sisterhood. I don't know how effective I was, but I was sure out there trying. To move them past the ironing board and their dependence on some form of the service plate."

"In our growing up years, Shirley, Leonard and I had often spoken of his dreams for both parents. His mother, Lucasta, screaming for his father and him chasing after both of them, begging for them to recapture the thousands of days and nights they had left behind, by backing and retracing time."

While Shirley was off in the bathroom, I found myself doting on a central saga in the misfortunes of Lucasta Jones. Something about Shirley's identification with Lucasta and her own surprising talents for the dance unleashed a certain confidence to speak more intimately when she returned. Indeed, I remembered how Shirley became the star performer at the Senior Varieties show performed at our high school and the surprise it had engendered in us all. Stole the show, as it were, so that it was equally startling when the news of her entry into the Civil Rights Movement came shuddering through the grapevine. What or who had turned her life around? According to the grapevine, a fiery young minister out of the Civil Rights Movement had visited her campus with the truth of the bestiality visited upon blacks. This of course was Leonard Foster, who spoke of the repression in the South and the North. Shirley "fell" for him at her all-Negro campus when he spoke out concerning the injustices there and then suddenly returned to the struggle. Soon she followed this minister/poet and became caught up in his mission.

Chapter 3

I will always remember that day—a heavy rain at the window—November, the month of Lucasta's birth. Tucson was to marry Lucasta; then the telephone rang.

The first time I saw Cuz Lucasta come alive in the music's merriment with madness (where she alone held dominion) was when she danced with Tucson.

Wondrous and magical, sweeping and reviving to her, to him, as I recollected it all now from my adult space in time. A slumbering swan now come alive to a lyrical, pyramid glide of a lava-licked meteor, in new space, new time. Etched upon my consciousness, the scores of times I saw her dance with him, with other men, or by herself, it appeared to me how Lucasta had tangled with pure lightning in her limbs and the fortune to lose, but not to die out, and was now pulsating the purloined pleasure of that experience that had rendered her speechless, touched as it had been by the singing, swooping, swinging torments of her blood.

"THAT VERY NOVEMBER DAY the tragic event occurred," I told Shirley, "Lucasta Jones was hovering over her ironing board, pressing out the left-hand corner of Tucson's drawers. She found herself repeating his favorite line, 'Let not your heart be troubled,' amid her normal daytime dreaming, concerning that one who was 'bone of my bone, flesh of my flesh,' as Lucasta now commenced to turn her humming into another voice that would surely advance soon into singing the blues, I thought, as I played solitaire in the corner and she occasionally glanced up at the window and into the growing splashes of rain in the eye of the gathering storm.

"Now ironing out his shirts, as she so often did, over and over again, Shirley, as if to get them beyond perfection this time, while on tiptoe, tried to look out into the street three stories below, despite the gathering rain, to capture a glance of Tucson's tilted, light blue Stacey Adams hat. How futile and foolish for Tucson, who in his pride would never have submitted to a trickle of the November rain, unless his body was guarded by a huge umbrella. But her mind would always be frozen in a sprocket of time when her Tucson came tipping around the corner; even if the dripping rain did a solo dance off the brim fashioned by his hand, so often a stingy-brim manner.

"Meantime, the intensity of the rain was gathering up its whipping straps with a furor, which boded forget all about the bridal gown, look to the wind in the rain. At least that's the way Granny Gram Gussie expressed it later to me, as she had told Forester that same afternoon, when he called from his job, on the afternoon break, in order to check on the passage of his beloved's day.

"When I would look up from my game of solitaire, which I did more and more (because now, Shirley, the considerable rain made me think I'd better move away from this window, or be face-to-face with thundering and lightning), I could also see what was captured in the face of Cuz Lucasta, for I had come to recognize the glow cast there by thoughts of Tucson, dozens of times. She had told me that this day was special in another way: for this was the same date when 'the judge taken my baby.' Then she said, 'But this day is to be a celebrating day.' It seemed apparent to me now that Tucson turned Lucasta's heart into a carousel. That time we went out to Riverview Park, I had seen some of this soaring of spirit within the often low-key temperature of Lucasta.

"Lucasta let her left hand reach behind her back and bathe her fingertips in the cool water of the basin on the nightstand. Now the humming moved her voice to singing a blues not unfamiliar to my ears:

He threads my needle
Creams my wheat

Heats my heater
Chops my meat

My man is such a handy man. . . .

"Lucasta often enough called Tucson *T*, with such temperature in the pronouncement: holding on to that *T* for such a long note, that could start off hotter than the trickle down to an aching icicle.

"Tucson had set Lucasta up in this tiny apartment (out of the dwelling basement) in early November. On this day, Lucasta was beside herself. Giddy, Lucasta forewarned me, as it were, once again, 'Tucson 'bout to spring the big question,' in a voice that would remind one of a teenager.

"But their dancing together was something else again. I found myself meditating over this, down the years. Not only Lucasta's but Tucson's twanging body—down to his way of inching, worming his way up to her royal rump of plenty."

Hunted after the form Lucasta set alive before his eyes, hands, whispering fingertips, this ace of hearts was sky high. Prancing, stuttering his not-quite-naked form: Lucasta's *Tooo-Song*.

Lucasta flinging to paradise on spiked high heels; his hands cupped under her royal rump. Each limb was an awakened wing now stretched beyond expectation and existence, reaching, crackling of bones so that only Lucasta knew light; and they, the believers, in her transforming powers, knew only the shadow and shades, the angles, the near glances, the trances, the fury flings, the riff-drifts that she turned out the night into light, this lyrical Lucasta.

Her long fingers flicking and sprinkling and anointing his fury charge; yet keeping her winging warrior just at bay, with the sweat pouring down his skull bone, up his backbone. Lucasta revealing to all how seasons are changed. Uncoiling her body beyond cycles within the expanse of her imagination with her back up, her stud horse, her rabbit's foot, her perilous boa constrictor, so close and yet so far away; yet colder than ice, full of steel and velvet. Unfurling, unfolding her body like a long-gone flag, uncoiling so that she appeared upon a daredevil's high-wire act in the air, her body a magician's, weaving a web out of that raspberry handkerchief that Tucson had given her, his one gift, to cast a spell upon him; she kept it knotted up, too, as one trying to keep fire on a string. She hung in space and solitude. And the feather, the stuffed teddy bears. *No good man, ever since the earth began.* But what a great time it had been to be taken to see and hear the great Lady Day, at the Regal, by Lucasta and Tucson. He could, when he would, think of everything under the stars. And then the telephone alarmed me away from the game of solitaire (knocked off the cards), even as my imagination was caught up to me with the memory dance of Lucasta and Tucson, now that he turned her heart into a carousel.

The first time I ever went anyplace with Tucson and Cuz Lucasta was out to Riverview Park, and in general we did have a good time at that famous amusement grounds, until we drifted over to the other side, where baseballs were thrown at taunting black men in cages. Lucasta had heard that one of these men was an old friend from her Memphis days, when on her way up to Forest County. His name was Hopkins Golightly.

Later, my father and my uncle, the body and fender man, often took me out to Riverview and to the grounds where the black men hung in cages. For years I was to follow phases of Hopkins Golightly's variety of jobs, from a certain distance. Recalling him always made me think not only of Golightly but of the others in cages as they slung off, draped on, or hung over slanted, oval-shaped bench boards, which formed uneasy resting perches, in the nine-by-nine-foot cages, suspended in time, as it were, at Riverview Park.

Now, the thick slanted boards were attached to two pulleys made of shipyard rope and extended from the ceiling of the black men's confinement, so that they—when seated—often used the planks as swings, lowering or elevating their positions as they gleefully swung back and forth, letting out wild screams of merriment, taunts, and crackling laughter at the crowd of whites, who devoured this theater body and soul and spewed it back with venom, and the flight of baseballs to match. None of the men were more tauntingly inventive than Cuz Lucasta's friend Hopkins Golightly, a heavyset, medium-light-brown-skinned man, slightly under six feet tall.

Each black man was dressed in prisoner's garb (and during the nine times my father and uncle took me over to the other side, Hopkins often added jungle-colored regalia to his cell and his outfit). The men made leering faces, tossed off lighthearted jeers, occasionally projected moderate, one-butt shuffles at the gathered crowd standing below on the green grass; 99 percent of their numbers were whites. These spectators were separated by gravel from the elevated black men in cages. A restraining bar circumvented this immediate area. In front of each cage there was a deal table of baseballs, sold by white men in red, white, and blue uniforms—three balls for twenty-five cents.

This audience of spectators was composed mainly of young white men, with their wives or girlfriends at their sides. They clung to these men, with awe, fear, and wonder in their eyes over the ensuing spectacle (only stepping aside to get out of the way of their men, momentarily, so that the guys could limber up their pitching arms and fire away at the caged black targets). The game was called Tank Boys, or Cage Tank. The white men would hurl battered-looking baseballs at a rounded target marker (embossed with a leer-black minstrel face) that projected about eighteen inches from the cage, upon a bronzed stick; it recalled for me, as I grew older and reflected upon this memory time and again, the long arm of the law.

Dangling his rabbit's foot in his right hand constantly (that first time I saw the spectacle), Tucson appeared to relish the antics of the black men; but my father was deeply upset by this clowning performance. He always wanted to analyze the participation of these men who performed in this manner, *and* he wanted me to fiercely question the theater before my eyes, from every standpoint. The face within the target reminded my father of an "imitation of life" . . . or of some of the pictures of captured Negro slaves in barracoons. Sometimes he used terms such as "heresy" and "racial sellout." My uncle seemed less aroused and only saw Hopkins and the others as men trying to make a living, "best way they can, Jerry." But if Daddy felt this intensity, why did he constantly take me back again and again to the scene of the crime, as it were? I often wondered.

Powerful fluorescent lights gave sufficient illumination to this staged show of vaudeville-cum-picnic, but no more than what one might expect from a night game of Double-A baseball. Each time my father, uncle, and I went over to the other side of the park, it was a perfect night. Clusters of stars, a moon of undaunted beauty, a lovely temperature characterized the remains of the evening.

Now, if the hurling spectator was on target, the platform flooring in the cage would immediately collapse from beneath the black man, as a trapdoor suddenly shot open. Then a howl of approval would soar from the crowd. The hurlers, confined to the restraining area, where the black-and-blue battered-looking baseballs were purchased, meant that they were winging from the sixty-foot distance of a pitcher's mound. The center and "most-desirable core of the target," as advertised by the carny men, was at "the throat, mouth, eyes, and head" of the black minstrel face inset upon the marker. Certain white men would aim not at the target but at the dark men behind the bars, for their fondest, wildest pitches . . . this despite the probability that the balls would not sail through the bars.

The black men in cages were expected to lightly taunt the spectators into greater furor for trying to knock them off of their seesaw slants and perches; and if this didn't work, spew jokes and rough one-liners at them. Daddy said something to the effect that the idea of black men playing Sambo and taunting and deriding white men to knock them down fed into the highest forms of the white man's idea of black arrogance and stupidity and the Caucasian notion of racial superiority, particularly ironic amid the truth of the black man's actual situation in this country, "where we are getting derailed, each and every day."

I was often asked to give my various opinions of the spectacle before my eyes. Sometimes when I thought of these men behind bars, I thought of the grasshoppers bottled up in mason jars, with twelve ice pick holes punctured into the top of the rusty tin cover. I thought of the blades of grass I had stalked within these jars and how the grasshoppers would intertwine and intertwine about the threadlike foliage, even as the black men spun about the ropes in their cells. Almost from the beginning, I was intrigued by the spectacle and I also found it quite loathsome. After a time, I came to call the place of this spectacle on the other side of the intriguing amusement park *Lucifer's Heights.*

It seemed to me, as I grew up a bit and reflected upon the scene, that long before the men were bottomed out—by the hurled baseballs—into the tub of water, they apparently were washed out in a luckless sea of fortune to be imprisoned behind cages. Fall, winter, or spring, I could not get that forging scene out of my mind much of the time. Hardly a day went by that I didn't think about it. What did it all mean? Hopkins Golightly was always at the center of it all. I often saw his visage in my dreams and even in my nightmares, getting dashed down by hurlers on target, down into the water tubs below; or verbally slicing after the white men, and coupling this with some clever moves, tough gestures, and gutsy words. Yet to my embarrassment as well, the blacks (and particularly Hopkins Golightly) went about their scripted routines with ebullience.

I was taken to view the carnival spectacle perhaps nine times. Analogues for my life and lessons were drawn. I was uncertain—in this phase of my childhood—as to the deeper reasons why we should keep coming back here, each time, when there were so many wonderful rides and games to pursue. It was akin on one level, in my imagination, to the repetition with which one endlessly practiced a particular piano piece for a recital.

Each time we returned home, Daddy would ask me what new views and lessons and even *interpretations* could I offer about the meaning of the scene. "Use your God-given imagination," he challenged. Daddy rarely included God in his speeches or statements. And I wondered what punctured dreams had led these black men in cages to this work? Couldn't they uncover some other form of a hustle for survival? And why was it unfailingly true that the Negro men in these cages—except for Hopkins Golightly—were very dark in complexion? This scene at the Riverview Amusement Park allowed Daddy to reveal the sagas of the minstrel shows of the nineteenth and twentieth centuries, even down to Al Jolson, whose blackface routine I had seen as a small child.

It was there before the cages that I heard drop from the lips of white men—for the first time in my life—the not infrequent spittle-streaked cries of "Nigger," and the hoots and howls of "Knock these niggers on their butts," or, as if to prod themselves to lower resolve, "Wash those niggers out!"

It was the last time that we went over to the other side at Riverview, yet the memories come flooding back again. First of all we discovered that Hopkins Golightly was no longer employed behind the cage—he had been recently fired. Then all of a sudden, we heard someone letting out a wail of a wolfing howl of the blues upon a harmonica. This sound was cutting up from the rear of the picnic area.

Now with a picnic basket on his left arm, dressed down to the nines, in a soft, summer blue-brown suit, and doing a blues with the harmonica at his lips (held in his right hand), was that nonesuch man Hopkins Golightly, and the crying-howling-wailing of his riffing was pitched to certain lines of "The Battle Hymn of the Republic" at the exact place where the lyrics of the song proclaim:

In the beauty of the lilies Christ was
    born across the sea,
With a glory in his bosom that
    transfigures you and me;
As he died to make men holy, let us
    die to make men free!
While God is marching on.

Hopkins Golightly played that refrain over many times, with wonderful wildness, wickedness, invention, but without a core center to its being. We sang the song in school, but nothing like this! (I had no idea of this talent. Cuz Lucasta had said Golightly had played blues down in Memphis, in the long ago.)

Finally, Golightly was arrested and taken away in handcuffs, his picnic basket (possessing a loaf of bread, a bottle of white wine, and three catfish) was hurled into a wire-basket garbage container, along with his glistening silver harmonica. For you see, Hopkins Golightly had been barred from the grounds of Riverview.

We later discovered that Golightly had been fired because he had not been willing to "blacken up" his complexion for this caged act.

Now as the attendants ushered Shirley and me into Leonard's room, I could make out the mumbling, the murmurings, the bitter broken glass cuttings of words, and then the actual high tenor voice of the poet (oh so crossed with outer diversity and inner torment, as the sacred over the secular crucifix is forged), often revealed through one of his many letters from the battle fronts of the Old South; on occasion, Leonard would send along one of his wild poems, for my consideration—and "Should we include this effort in the next issue of *The Dark Tower?*"

We had maintained an off-and-on correspondence during these years. Foster's poetic diction and his formal writing (when he addressed any individual) was so very different from any species of talk, formal or informal, that happened out of the mouth of Leonard Foster, it seemed to me, until you got him going, or heated up. Did Leonard also hear voices, too? I could smell faint offshoots of the mixed brand of smoking tobacco I had given him years before, the dying embers in Leonard's pipe as Shirley now nervously grabbed my right arm and we entered the room assigned to Foster.

Live!
At Fountain's
House of
the Dead

....

Gaunt Leonard Foster, in his string-tie hospital gown, appeared as a sort of acolyte on a mission of mercy for the despised and the loathed. With his "otherworldly" eyes gone sour on the things of this life, my eyes beheld him for the first time in well over a year.

Leonard's nose was quite keen, as if he was always sniffing out stenches, odors, and foul vapors. The wee and strangely shaped mouth appeared as if shaped by a sculptor employing an instrument somewhat akin to a buttonhook. His lips were clay-looking and not fondly memorable, and even spiteful; he was surely bent on sitting out all things, visible and invisible, into the troubled river of despair, that his inner eyes beheld.

The grade of his hair was referred to on another day (before the advent of the Afro) as "nappy-good." He had during the late 1960s evolved and cultivated an elaborate, voluminous, defiant Afro. Now Leonard wore a hairstyle that was closely cut to his skull. This fashion greatly reduced the African influence, which with his high, arching, sharp nose, led to a kind of Arab view of his countenance.

Leonard's light brown eyes, which appeared so soured and tired at their recesses, were actually quite intelligent, though more exhausted than ever. And in the old days, you often thought he was onto the currents of conversations at a much higher level than reality bore out. Yet in truth, Leonard was probably far behind the ongoing dialogue of the scene—not because of dullness but rather for the ease with which the flight of his imagination could take him off to unknown vistas.

Always the kind of youth and young man who never did well on formal learning examinations, Leonard discovered (and so did I) that these intellectual surveys often failed to plumb even the surface of his intelligence. Therefore, Leonard came across as one not quite up to snuff, or gone to seed before he had bloomed, fully, as it were. Or, that he was really out in space, gazing somewhere, tracing the shape of the Milky Way, I once observed in my defense of Leonard to Shirley Polyneices.

The effect of his goatee had added much personality to Leonard's razor-thin face. Shirley had encouraged the growth of this goatee, and since I had last seen Leonard, the poet had cultivated the style with great care. At that time (because he was not naturally hairy) there was just a whisk of a mustache. (He had no doubt worn a piece to give a certain visible support to his goatee for a few months, before the goatee finally sprouted into being.)

However, the goatee helped to make him look like one of his heroes—the diminutive Haile Selassie.

Leonard's teeth were amazingly clean, given his devotion to his pipe; they were rodentlike in their size and sharpness. Over the years, the constant grinding and nibbling sounds emitted from his mouth made me think of one who is always chewing up something that he found distasteful, but must be masticated in order for the nourishment process to occur.

Leonard's complexion was honey brown, and it was smooth and virtually unblemished. His face had rarely encountered a razor. Leonard's babyish complexion was one of the main features of attraction that women found so alluring. Many others found his complexion too smooth, too honey brown perfect. But for the most part, girls were abundant in their hands-on feel for the poet. Leonard would never concede to give them a tumble down the darkness of his private staircase. "She wants you for your body, asshole," I screamed at him concerning one of the young ladies, who found Leonard's appeal adorable. Then he said, "Zenobia needs to check out her mind. Besides, her head's still fried." Despite his declared admiration for the Afro (and even during the time he was wearing one), none of the straight-haired women he dated dared an attempt to cultivate their version of the Afro style.

In the days before Leonard became fairly well known in civil rights circles, he had enjoyed wearing "good clothing"; however, he usually purchased his garments from "good" resale shops in the suburbs. There he would buy nice suits or sports jackets. He dressed like a professor he had deeply admired at this point in his life, even to a point of imitating this professor's walk and style of argumentation. Leonard found abhorrent the tenure process, and said that it was a "guarantee for the survival of dead wood." Leonard Foster was always quite natty and neat in his appearance—even "clean," as the street dudes used to say.

Now I remembered Leonard saying to Shirley and me, "All right then, if it is your will, Joubert Antoine go back to the beginning time, that late afternoon in November, when Granny Gram Gussie (and no *Grinny*, either) first commenced to take her uppers and lowers out—and then back. Yes, we were amazed. But *your* presence initiated the devilment, and our rascality. Drifting attention away from her blessing and the meal steaming before our very eyes. (And smoke, too, from Grandpa Forester's pipe.)

"My attempt was to keep from laughing out loud, not because I wanted to, but because, Shirley, I was always a fool to follow the lead out of Joubert Jones's mouth—even though he is five years my junior—because I truly believed that following you, trailing after you would lead me out of the shadowy valley of wilderness of bastardy, and into the long night of suffering and sacrifice . . . and maybe, *just* maybe into the light of another day. You were the light of Lucasta's eyes; *you* of course know that. . . . Must I go back to that, too? And because of, and despite all things, it is true that blood is thicker than water."

Now Leonard Foster was taking down what he announced as his second pill of the morning. "One of the pills he *had* to take," Shirley whispered to me, "to keep his turbulent spirit from overflowing"—that was the way he had explained this pill to her.

"Ah, but Leonard, in the late night, just before bed, and lights out, and those false teeth missing in action and Grinny Gram Gussie—."

"Joubert Antoine! Granny Gram Gussie!" Leonard corrected with great sobriety.

Now I couldn't subdue my turbulent spirits of memory (as if spun out of a blustery November afternoon).

"Yes, and Leonard Foster, she would be seen sucking her breath up one moment, then exploding bad air behind the Reaper's back in the next sprocket frame (as she finally convinced the Angel of Death to extend her credit lines, one more once, by taking a few weeks off some scoundrel's hide, back down in the remembered past of Forrest County) of the time out of mind. Sucking out into the eternal darkness. Her ears full of cobwebs (though Granny Gram Gussie could hear all manner of things visible and invisible to the naked inner ear), thereby producing yet another mask, or ruse. In her head going from reddish yellow to high yellow to baby bitched-slobbering; balloon-collapsing to wrinkled-up explosive funny papers sailing towards the swooping up stock-shock fireplace. . . . Maybe the colony of the teenie weenies, too, which she read to us on occasion."

Shirley gave me a nerve-racked look, as if to say, You are getting away from my directive to you.

"Nostalgia is about to take you over. I warned you, Joubert Antoine (ha, ha), you sentimental slob," she whispered in my ear, full of fervor, and passionate liquids.

"Joubert, there you were off to the races in your rambling. How do you actually ever know these things to be absolute, good, and gospel-like true? You were always a gifted liar: an honorable outlaw, with a switchblade for a tongue. Do you still hear voices and do they still act on your unconscious mind? If so, perhaps it is *you* who should be in this bed, and I allowed free passage down the streets of Forest County. Although, on occasion some of your tall tales were not too far from the mark (you probably employed them against the very funny-paper characters you borrow for your plays); yet you have no problems telling out-of-school lies on your very own grandmother, if it promotes your career of prevaricator-cum-picnic, when it suits up with one of your evil set designs."

"Granny Gram Gussie's gingerbread was outrageously precious to the palate—."

"Never had much of an opportunity to reside on *your* plate, Brer Bear," Leonard mused.

Now an amused, happier look crossed Shirley's face. It seemed as if

I was beginning to process her directives and enact them, too. This cut me some slack, so I said:

"Precious that is . . . until the moment Granny Gram Gussie would dash those front two horse shows of teeth (with the golden horsemen, as sentinels at extreme stage left and extreme stage right) into the especially prepared sweet-water solution of the mason jar, which was also loaded down by the power of this mysterious compound of a pill. Stocked with untold wonders and apparently forced her teeth to jabber, if not to talk in tongues."

"There was and no doubt still is—something magical about that woman . . . our dearly beloved Granny Gram Gussie. And when have you last laid your eyes on her? And Grandpa Forester, as well?" Leonard asked, avoiding my most recent reflections.

"An hour ago. And she asked several times for an immediate report on your progress, just before I left and just after a whole wild circus event occurred, *sponsored* and performed by none other than Marvella Gooseberry herself. . . . I can't go into all of the phases of her stylized carnival-one-woman-show-out, but let it suffice to say, Marvella damn near brought the whole neighborhood down into fits of chaos, just at the apron of my grandparents' home. Anyway, you'll get to see it all on the five o'clock news."

Shirley's eyes went wild with anticipation and Leonard's were darkened in deepest sorrow. They both, of course, knew Marvella and her saga.

"But shortly before I arrived, Granny Gram Gussie was boxing up some of her old, new hats. Shirley, she must have some seventy-five of these plumages and plucked out of the pocket of poor old Grandpa Forester, who loves his Gussie's millinery expeditions—mad-ly."

"Oh," said Leonard, in a voice that pleaded that ignorance is indeed bliss.

"But Leonard, then you and I go peer into the hollow-would-be thy name darkness and rediscover—."

"With your irreverent tongue, Joubert Antoine, going off like a bell clapper in hell. For if I recollect plainly, it was always you who led the way," he gingerly said.

Shirley now appeared to fall back on a let-the-boys-be-boys attitude for the moment; and at least Leonard appeared energized.

"Joubert, we rediscovered the two sets of purely white miracles spangling forth and projecting out of the blackness of the darkness in that room: her glowing teeth, and that foot-long, foot-wide crucifix on Granny Gram Gussie's dark wall. Illuminated three times its actual length by the light of day. And those upper and lower pearl pure—."

■ ■ ■ ■ ■

"Twenty-nine point five," he whispered to me, with measured authority, as if answering a question not raised. At first I wondered whether the "point five," wasn't part of some higher arithmetic, or even of fractions, perhaps, or equations. Maybe outside of his brain power at this point. Until it occurred to me: more messages from Leonard's zany zones. For example, once upon a time, Leonard had warned me to not let the girls, try though they might, plant a kiss on my cheeks. Kid stuff was embraced with admonishment scheduled for the perils of a "poison kiss," touched from the lips of an evil fairy queen. In this case, Leonard was actually counting—or trying to recall the number of steps down the staircase—with some precision.

"Shirley," I cried out, "they were carrying that coffin down those steps with such dancer's grace, rocking from side to side, each step of the staircase giving up its own cry in a wheezing voice ('Because the cargo of life can carry a deadly freight, even when stripped of its weight and woe down to the skeleton,' Granny Gram Gussie had declared, explaining everything and nothing at all, even as she thought she was giving overt reasons why the high arching steps creaked and wheezed not only with the swaying bodies of the pallbearers but something about the dead life of the old body inside that coffin). I didn't think of all of this at the time, but I came to interpret Granny Gram Gussie down in the years, in this *way*."

"Off the wall and sliding down the years and off the mark," mumbled Leonard.

"It made some sense to me, though, even in my child's mind, at the time. Because you see I had overheard Grandpa Forester say that 'Fountain's had been something of a bawdy house, as the white folks call 'em, once upon a time.' Then, Leonard, you asked, 'What exactly is a bawdy house, Grandpa Forester?' And sure enough, when the old man revealed a set of definitions of not only what a bawdy house was but a few of the actions that went down in a true bawdy house, *you*, Leonard, raced out of the house and sat weeping furiously out on the stoop. I guess those so-called nigger nuns who taught you had cut you to the well, good and deep."

Shirley howled out loud. Then, feigning a wand of calm to her soul: "Joubert, you bastard you. You really do still have a flash of Rumplestiltskin within your soul."

Leonard just sat there rocking back and forth with anger, yet not un-amused, since the conversation had turned back to him, albeit perversely. Then he mumbled something about me "knowing . . . or, should know with a mountain of evidence concerning life in a bawdy house, since your auntie's grandkin, the Creole Madam, had a whole street named after her down there in New Orleans."

"But don't just stop there, Joubert. What did your Grandpa say? How did he define it?"

"Well, Shirley, something to the effect that it was a place where once upon a time, 'a whole lot of shaking went down, . . . order to the night . . . killing floor-trimming and mind-blinding . . . jelly-roll do-ings and dealings went up and down unto the rising sun . . . all around the world . . . ain't fairy tale time. . . . Women's grinding their lives away . . . bacon burning up and coffee grinding away.' I just remember phrases like that. But I had it all mixed up in my head, so that when we started off for the funeral at Fountain's, I simply asked, 'Grandpa, is this kinda like a funhouse carnival, once upon a time—where we are going?' "

Now, Leonard seemed to take this as an evil plot-of-a-put-down on my part, before his beloved Shirley.

"Shirley, I told you this Joubert would put me down, before he picked me up. Always was his method and his madness."

"Look, Leonard, you asked—practically beseeched me to get Joubert here. You can't expect him to lie all of the time to keep you entertained. Maybe that's the mistake I've made in our relation—." I spotted a perfect place for me to break in and back to my story.

"But the pallbearers were also moving with great care, ceremony even, as if the casket were really a vessel and inside they were carrying precious cargo, as the geography and history books described in school. But who was on the inside of that coffin? And for that matter, was he really dead? Because you see, my aunt Eloise was always talking about people being buried alive and waking up from the dead, when really alive in their coffins, back down in New Orleans. Or, she talked about body snatchers, too." Even at the age of seven, I was made aware, through my aunt Eloise, of how dead bodies were often counted on the voters scroll for election purposes. Shirley Polyneices had an uncle who worked for the Machine.

I was shaking Leonard Foster out of his doldrums, using Shirley Polyneices for audience, but the price might be my friendship/fellowship with him.

"And Shirley, Lawd today if Thurston Fountain didn't look like Mr. Death corseted down and wearing a pair of deep-flame-colored and reddish-purple long johns, poured over his body from Satan's cauldron in Bee-Luther-hatchee, by the very hand of hurled-out-of-heaven Lucifer himself.

"Shirley, he was probably six foot, six inches, in height and weighed in at no more than one hundred fifty pounds soaking wet, black and blue and bare-butt bold, these bandages and tissue plates for biceps—he wore before the world—about his bony-macaroni body; wore a neat, black bow tie, sharply executed and rancid-looking white shirt. Thurston Fountain *wore* a gaunt set of high, brown cheekbones. Like one of those mannequins in shop windows along that great street called State Street. It got me to wondering, over the years, whether his real face was covered over by the mask he wore before the world.

"A mechanical man, whose body now appeared to be strapped together by tissue paper, hospital gauze, white tape, catgut, bandages, ironing cords, sinews, and cartilage, but by no visible means of support from suspenders or straps any system of muscular manifestations discernible to the naked eye, that it. . . ."

Shirley Polyneices was laughing with wicked mirth; Leonard Foster was beginning to melt down from his frozen-faced essence.

"You see, Shirley, my kinsman's problem has always been that he truly believes if you tell a lie strong enough, the devil will take it over and provide you with some sort of a weird truth," Leonard said. Then, looking directly at me in the eye, he said: "And as for you, old man. Tell us when was the last time you went to confession—you lying wonder."

Then Leonard fell back onto his pillow and started laughing aloud in rungs and rungs of chuckles and weeping.

■ ■ ■ ■ ■

"Mr. Skeleton-Skeffington Thurston Fountain took tick-tock-tick mining steps, Shirley, even as he appeared to shake forward, as much as he actually moved side-angle-side. I thought that he was going to unravel out of his bandages. Because, you see, he appeared as 'one who was woven into existence, a breath before the baseline bottom of zero was formed,' as Galloway Wheeler, the barber, once said of the perverse and fabled mortician. Shirley, Mr. Galloway Wheeler was our authority on Shakespeare, but one of our customers at my aunt Eloise's bar, the Night Light Lounge, Talcum Tommie, proclaimed him as the 'minister of Shakespeare.'

"Why, Leonard, you remember how Granny Gram Gussie said, 'That child-man-child sure 'nough could use him some righteous fatback and some butter beans to boot. Why, he's skeleton-bone-bare-born. Seem like he's trying to take on the form of the peoples he buries, after the worms got hold of 'em for three months.'" Shirley found great hilarity in this storehouse, but Leonard appeared now to find disgust in the extent of the tale, as some species of excess, which always frightened the poet within the Little Dreamer.

"Why, Shirley, that man was unworthy of a soup-bone special for a hound dog kennel of lost-found canines, alley mongrels, and beastly bitches. But Fountain's sheer lack of frameable parts had actually led Granny Gram Gussie to one of her famous inner dialogues, which resounded through the house: 'Why, that child-man sure 'nough could use him some righteous fatbacks.' Then another voice: 'But he's a skeleton bone . . . could help to soup up a seasoned bone. . . . Why, what you talking about girl, his whole body gets lost in a stir-about of a decent pot of soup.' Then another voice: 'Don't let onto no starving dogs when he's 'bout, they'll forget all 'bout what they done buried if they get a sniff of his ribs and a whiff of his short ribs protruding in that purple jacket.' Then another: 'What you talking about—no decent thoughtful dog going to leave a buried-a-home-away-from-home bone—for some stray dog to dig up—*for that*,' pointing to an imaginary Thurston."

Then Leonard Foster said, "Shirley, an organist (wearing those blind man's dark shades) accompanied their actual promenade down, down, down those steps, too."

"You're right," I said. "And do I ever know a story about him."

"His presence and playing must be weighed into the equation," Leonard said in a wry, high-pitched voice.

"Playing something oddly mournful, as I remember."

"Yes. It was 'The Death of a Princess,'" Leonard Foster said with total authority; the Indian-head pipe tilted at a perfect ninety-degree angle. I had given this pipe to Leonard as a gift, when I returned from a trip to London, where I had gone to review a group of plays. Also, the odd mixture of tobacco, Hummingbird's Wings, was a gift from me to Leonard.

"He was playing with great gnashing of teeth, off to the side of the room. But I was never certain about the actual condition of that man's sight," Leonard said with much seriousness.

"Leonard, Shirley, once Grandpa Forester told me how that very same organist had been playing so many weddings and funeral gigs stacked on top of each other, week after week, night after night, in order to make ends meet. Got drunk on elderberry wine, 'in order to keep his head straight.' Showed up for this wedding where there was also a high, vaulting staircase, but with his dark shades on, and none can perceive how he is so extremely high on the spirits plucked from the grape. So, when the bride steps off, instead of this organist swinging into a full-blown version of 'Here Comes the Bride,' this wine-headed, overworked, sapsucker blasts off the wall and ceiling with 'Amazing Grace,' and played in a jazz-blaze, like Wild Bill Davis was at the keyboard." Shirley almost fell on Leonard's bed laughing. Leonard simply shook his head, as if to say, *Well, yet another lie*, the pipe almost falling out of his mouth.

Using his pipe as a teacher's pointer, Leonard said, almost in a streak of nostalgia of his own, "Joubert studied lying from way back when, Shirley. Get a group of neighbor kids together. Used to send me off to round them up. Throw up a sheet from ceiling to the floor in the garage, then a chair and a little old rickety desk he found in a garbage heap, all

Joubert would need. Soon he was playacting and tossing off all kinds of characters out of lying tongue. Profane ones, cool ones, church people. I'd go off and throw up at the end of the alley—time and again. Joubert was talented—then and now. But to me, after a time it was disgusting. Disgusted something in me. Joubert, you disgusted something in me. Shirley, meantime I was turning to Almighty God. But I didn't find humor in much of what you were putting down, Joubert, then. Not even now.

"Shirley, he was just too free. That's what I know now. You were too free. Granny Gram Gussie said you sniffed like a dog after too many odd, wanton, and willful situations. How you'd lose your soul, after a time, Joubert Antoine Jones. Lost it to the stage, I guess you'd say; you lost your heart to the stage. But I would say, Joubert—my little brother—that you sold your soul to the devil."

I was jarred for a few moments. I said nothing. Tried to revamp my artillery. Then I came back with: "Granny Gram Gussie often said that Forester's downfall to sinful sniffing came about when he started doing janitorial work around at the once-upon-a-time-high-powered hotel, but now was 'going back down into its falling-away days; located where Sodom meets Gomorrah. Where all kinds of dirty doings and foul deeds went down, from way up the steps.' But Shirley, Granny Gram Gussie was always attempting to cut Leonard and me off from firsthand experience, from spinning out of her control. Tried to cut off Grandpa Forester, too. Almost did. Using always the idea that there was sinning going on, and that we were sniffing after it. She always wanted to bind up the lives of the men in her life away from any forms of the secular experience. Grandpa Forester himself had commenced to calling it not by its true name but by his own made-up name, the Doo-Doo-Drop Inn."

Leonard said, quite severely: "And Granny Gram Gussie was no doubt right. After all, the whites turned it into a Sodom and Gomorrah."

We were all silent for a moment. Finally, Leonard said: "Ah, that winding staircase and yet Grandpa Forester said that 'Fountain's House of the Dead could only account for two bodies per week on its best weeks of the months, so that there must have been other activities going down.' "

He held the pipe (which of course he didn't light) in his hand and then to his lower lip exactly as Grandpa Forester did, I observed. Soon Leonard grew sleepy. The pipe appeared heavy in his mouth; it tumbled to the sheets, turned over, and a few ashes fell on the bed clothing. Shirley Polyneices cleaned away the ashes and placed the pipe in an ashtray on the hospital nightstand.

As I accompanied Shirley outside—she craved a cigarette—I could not get over my virtual shock and anger with Leonard's curdling remarks against my freedom of spirit, manifested at such a young age.

"Shirley, wasn't this painful and ugly that Leonard Foster, of all people, who fought so hard in the Movement for our freedom, could talk like that . . . would dare speak of someone being too free?"

"Joubert, I thought you recognized this *sorry* streak in Leonard long ago. Leonard is very conservative; he's been fighting it all of his life, I guess. And there is something else operating here, too. Leonard's deeply envious of you because of your free spirit; you seem able to get away with it, personally and publicly."

"In a strange way, Shirley, I recognize the strangled dangling man within Leonard's soul. The abandoned boy in our presence. Maybe he said it to ignite an argument. Pull me away from my comedian's role over his soul."

At her behest I soon found myself explaining about not only Leonard's smoking of a pipe but how his style of holding it in came from the molding lips of Grandpa Forester. She let out a howl.

"Tell me more about this Grandpa Forester, Joubert. He seems to be a trip up a different river. Leonard never talks about family in any meaningful way, though he seems absolutely obsessed with his lost family and his lost condition. . . . Then down he goes into the pits. I want him to free himself up, but to do it . . . he has to go down there . . . dig down there, where it is stark and dark and full of despair. Anguish, too. Anyway, Fountain's story already seems wild enough. Unleashed some release, some humor, some solace. I don't know what I expected. Too much." Then she was drifting off into an unsettlement of her own. I said: "Shirley, as a feminist, you should have great pity for Grandpa Forester! He is a man who has lived under a repressive regime for years. Seriously, though, don't lead a picket in front of their apartment. He just loves the oppressor, the queen of his life—Gussie Jones. For example, he's purchased over seventy-five hats for her that I know of. Took an extra job to help buy 'em. That's the phase of the Doo-Doo-Drop Inn saga."

"Then maybe I should talk with Miz Gussie. The woman who could shape up any man vaguely tied to Leonard (and you, too) is worth seeing and learning from. But the hats—now that's something else again."

"Well, a lot got hidden behind those hats. For one thing the extra job also allowed Grandpa Forester some time away from beneath Granny Gram Gussie's direct controls; and the job he got cleaning up the hotel allowed him some wild experiences."

I told Shirley how Grandpa Forester remembered some crazy happenings at the Doo-Doo-Drop Inn, which also contained a terrific bar and restaurant service.

When I stayed over at their apartment, I had often placed my ear firmly to the wall at a certain spot, and I could hear the rich sulfur baritone of Grandpa Forester's tale rather clearly; then Granny Gram Gussie's laughter (sometimes a harking-howl); soon the switching off of the lights. I recalled a fragment of one of those stories for Shirley, just now.

"Shirley, there was this white man who came in every three months or so carrying two sacks of luggage. He'd take a seat, order a Bloody Mary, survey thoroughly and coldly the available ladies at the bar. Then he'd go upstairs to the suite he had let. Soon, a call from his room would reach the bartender, and Mr. Johnny-Come-Lately-Come-Lately would let it be known, through a most vivid set of descriptions, the particular lady he wanted to share the performance with him for most of the rest of the evening—" But before I could finish the story the nurse was beckoning us, indicating that Leonard Foster had awakened and that he was asking for Shirley and me.

"Once Mr. Johnny-Come-Lately-Come-Lately was spotted entering the circular bar, and seen retiring to his suite, *each* of the ladies of a certain inclining (Grandpa Forester reported from beneath the sheets) hoped that when the telephone behind the bar rang out, she would be the lucky party designated to make the evening romping-right for the mysterious stranger, Johnny-Come-Lately-Come-Lately." And as Shirley blushed and was about to burst with feminist anger, I explained:

"For you see, Shirley, the call never rang out for sexual purposes but rather for a form of 'room service.' Once inside the room, the lady of his choice would then be made aware that her John was about to unveil the first stages of a floor show of his own; her job-on-the-john was simply to be a good audience.

"Taking out gorgeous gown after gown, and trying each one on with great ceremony, Mr. Johnny-Come-Lately-Come-Lately, as the girls called him, proceeded to put on one helluvan extended fashion show. Tossing off each gown down upon his bed (with what must have been considerable derision, if I interpret Grandpa Forester's meaning) he asked his lady-in-waiting only to stir his drinks and serve the snacks sent up by the hotel, during the moments of respite from the fierce and frantic ordeal, the wear and tear of presentation. The Lady of the Evening would also, most definitely, be expected to comment with great appreciation upon not only the mysterious stranger's choice of gowns but mainly how beautiful he looked in them.

"After the floor show was finally completed, Mr. Johnny-Come-Lately-Come-Lately would then meet the woman's dollar request for 'services rendered' immediately—and he would give her the gowns reproachfully hurled upon the bed. Then he would quickly split the scene. He was a Southerner.

"One of the problems for the lady in question would be this: how did you, or could you, keep a straight face while watching Mr. Johnny-Come-Lately-Come-Lately don each gown, with all of the seriousness in the world—and then how could you come up with words inventive enough to show appreciation for his appearance 'enshrouded' in each gown, because you see, Shirley, according to Grandpa Forester, every girl reported how hideous he looked, like a cadaver, in each gown worn in the floor show.

"On three occasions, Grandpa Forester said that one of the mysterious stranger's more popular ladies sold off her finery to Thurston Fountain. Fountain used these fabulous gowns to enshroud dead members of the underground gay world, who, while keeping their real lives hidden, wanted to be buried in the kinds of gowns they often wore at secret, effete parties, where true body and soul were revealed. Thusly I came to believe for a time that the man *funeralized* that time at Fountain's, when Leonard and I were kids, was in fact a part of this underground gay community."

Despite what Shirley had asked me to do, just now it was revealed to me that I should shed the comedian's role in my attempt to awaken Leonard from the doldrums. There were several routes to his soul. We had been involved in marches and protests within Forest County. Perhaps the recall from one of these times would show the way.

When Shirley and I returned to his room, we found a reflective Leonard Foster placing a bookmark in Augustine's *Confessions:* the wholesome memories of vigor and social engagement always connected up with a spiritual force in *my* kinsman's imagination, whenever he read those meditations. I soon found my tongue:

"Leonard, do you sometimes think back to how we led our first march, then slipped into the basement and uncovered firsthand the odious situation?"

"Ah, yes, you are recalling the days of protesting the old Red Rooster." His spirit seemed immediately enhanced. "Before the crowd of protestors, I ended my speech by saying: 'I know of the sardine's relationship to the whale.' Apparently you liked the metaphor, as a poet and protestor."

"Shirley, you were protesting in the South at the time. But Leonard, remember how in the basement washroom of the Red Rooster, those lily-whites plucked (so plucked of their souls as they were) and shaved down those strung-up hens, like one scaling down a fish?" Immediately, Leonard's face commenced to color in a new glow.

"Bastards injected those dead chickens with a booster shot: from a diviner's red-hot rod," I said. Shirley seemed quite intrigued.

"Yes, Shirley, we were there. Bearing witness to the light of their evil deeds. They doused those birds in a sleek Max Factor brew they secretly called Boss Sauce. These white folks will steal anything—lightning out of gingerbread included—even and especially our idiom, and then turn it against us."

"Brushed pink and red tint to improve the body complexion of those old chickens. ('Operation Bird Renewal' took twenty seconds per bird.) Up the street some black brother 'be beating his drum,' so-oh-so secure in his newfound blackness, unsuspecting of what was going down in that basement and what might be winging down his stomach the next night.

"They went about their mock trade with fealty . . . a wave of the red flag flung in our faces . . . a bloody shirt (their white wash-wand) high above our newly blackened reality.

"Or Shirley, they'd present the Slum Standard: ground horse meat, round up into loaves of leavings to pump pressure. And we thought this tragic health loss part of our Black Yankee Cross in Forest County."

"And so we organized and pumped up pressure; cleaned out their swinish operation: 'Clear out, or Go Down, Dead.' Soon we realized Red Rooster was not about to change. But Shirley, we were organized and for once we were together, here in Forest County. *And* we didn't lose our humanity. Joubert, tell her about our scheme to bring the Red Rooster down. Our successful scheme—Stage I."

"We slipped into the basement, after closing hours. I had the latest Kodak. We watched and we waited for those liverless swine to arrive. Shirley, I'm telling you we got to work early. No C.P. time. They had their tubs of water, solution, Boss Sauce, and their hypodermic needles, pitchfork ready. Had some hillbilly music going loud and long. So, we just kept our cool. Leonard and I took turns snapping off those pictures, from as many angles as we could get, without them seeing us. They couldn't hear the three of us, Leonard, W.A.D., and myself, because of the hillbilly music, and they couldn't see us because the odor of that Boss Sauce was so foul that they wore hoods over their heads, with eye sockets opened in the cloth, so that they could tunnel in on what they were doing but with no peripheral vision. Boss Sauce was so foul we took turns snapping those pictures—then we'd dart outside for a three-minute breather.

"My aunt Eloise, the journalist, finally got the *Forest County Dispatch* to run those pictures, but she had to do much haranguing and threatening down at the *Dispatch* editorial offices, even to a point of proclaiming she would take these pictures down to the *Tribune*, if they didn't run these very clear shots—full indictment of the Red Rooster operation. Shirley, soon after the story ran in the *Dispatch* under *my* byline, with that devastating photo spread, the red flag atop the Red Rooster flew no more!"

All through my recall of this saga of the Red Rooster rout, Leonard Foster had been applauding and even egging me on. But now as I was ending this segment of the story, the spirit and mind-set of Leonard took a different turn of brooding and anger concerning "the failures of our day." And he started speaking out, in the midstream of a series of thoughts, unleashed now because of the current of the memory of the protest; and yet, I thought, he sounded as if he were speaking from a bully pulpit out of a voice previously locked away in the underground of his personality and soul.

"You may be royally pissed concerning our latest faddish direction, only have to raise our clenched fist to prove brotherly affiliation. (Like presenting a rattler before the beige, black, and blue face of a screaming toddler.) Bonded in blood and by Blood bonded, bleeding the Blood white and blind. Bucket of Blood Brothers in need of a blood transfusion in the emergency ward. Bloodstained patches hatched everywhere. Bloodcurdling gang proliferation everywhere, full of bloodletting linkage, everywhere, our children going up, growing up, and up for grabs everywhere. Going nowhere fast. Except to link up with a black street royalty, exploitation cast. Our Bucket of Blood Brothers full of profound Black Consciousness—rip-off style. Oh, how you feast off Lost/Found starving for crumbs of bread."

And now the startled Shirley and I watched and listened as Leonard arose from his bed and continued, as indeed before an audience, his arms raised aloft, his eyes—otherworldly; his voice accusatory, shrill, and getting louder and louder:

"Love? Our lost-found tribe of twelve times twelve. For the profit of your fat-cat soul. Oh-so-brilliantly tapping doom down the fire escape. Masked in blackface, you roll, extol, toll, rap, and escape. Rape the breath out of the Blood. Draped out in mourning sleeves of crepe-scape-goat, you escape any known or unknown length of width, or height of previously honored scroll of measuring tape. Punk ideologue politicos, hustlers of misfortune, squander money like cheap wine. Praise these ruinous punks without design; as prodigal sons, or dudes down on their luck. That's shit! You parade yourselves off as a royal guard of righteousness, as a political vanguard; but I know your slum name: mortified in the streets paved by your horrors. 'Then went the devils out of the man and entered in the swine.' Depart the remnant, you've lost our spiritual spine, stripping pockets of aged ladies, by any means necessary, at any time."

Soon three medics tried to return a howling, trembling, spitting, cursing, unraveling Leonard Foster back to bed: we were asked to leave the room, just as Leonard started screaming for "Mama Lucasta," over and over again. We attempted to restrain the medics, beseeching them to free up Leonard, but they would not hear of it. One of their number had sounded an alarm.

A new rush of medics came charging past us into the room of the wretch, in order "to administer their form of science, solace, and sedation," Shirley now whispered in an eerie voice to me, then she added, "Frankly, I sometimes get worried, Joubert—these bastards might try to work a lobotomy on Leonard. Part of the reason why I called you, to help me protect him from them."

I promised Shirley that I would return the next day, if she thought I might be of help. But the comedian's role seemed less satisfying. Over the years, so often out of Leonard's beleaguered states would tumble the spirit of confusion.

■ ■ ■ ■ ■

Just as I was coming out of the hospital, I almost collided with the social servant and one-woman-activist Ma Fay Barker. She had been visiting the sick and destitute at the hospital and was on her way home. The bus stop was just adjacent to the parking lot. We chatted briefly. I had covered some of her activities for reform of the women's prison system. She accepted my offer for a ride home, and as we headed towards the lot, who should we come upon but Washburne Withers, the journalist. An immediate kind of warmth was evidenced by Ma Fay Barker's response to the tall, handsome, medium-dark-brown-skinned reporter, who possessed such a deeply resonant, confident voice.

Conveying her trust of Withers to me as she introduced us, Ma Fay Barker seemed to glow all the more with Withers's presence. Once again I was drawn to this man, whose tough-minded, artful byline stories had often commanded my attention. Now that Withers had been hired by the *Forest County Daily Sun* (as their first black reporter), Ma Fay Barker proudly declared, "He is still keeping his allegiance to the community alive, through part-time work with *Spearhead*, and Gooselaw's undiminished torch for the truth." Well, that was us all over again, always giving the eloquence of a valedictory, when only a simple introduction was called for. Or, where there might be one or more people complimented, a virtual hothouse of round-robin accolades would go blooming and booming, I mused, when only a few simple words sprinkled over the greeting ritual would have established sufficient communication. But no, this was only the beginning of Ma Fay's full-blown pronouncement. For soon she was giving one Joubert Antoine Jones an equally expansive introduction, surely beyond anything he had achieved (or would ever accomplish, I laughed). No wonder Aunt Eloise often spoke in such a royal manner about this woman, her unfailing courtesies, right along with her valor for social and group uplift.

Shaking hands with me in one of the new forms of solidarity—in which you needed a manual-of-arms chart to get it exactly right—Washburne Withers smiled broadly. He had a wide, thick mustache and glistening teeth, with glints of gold and silver fillings in the rear of his mouth. Now he ever so clearly and softly whispered on the light breeze of the afternoon air:

"Brother Joubert, man, don't let this wonderful lady take you to another zone about me (there's nothing to me but what you see). Now I like what Jacob stands for, truly, but I need the extra bread for my kids' ever-expanding shoe sizes, even more."

"Glad to hear you are still working with Gooselaw; he's been after me to do work for his paper. Now that I know you are staying on, maybe I'll take him up on the offer. From what I've seen of your articles, I know I could learn a great deal from you about the craft, Washburne."

I had wanted to thank this man Washburne Withers for the keen review he had written about my work-in-progress created out of the life of Sugar-Groove, and presented in a reader's-style theater performance. In a room of forty people, Washburne had sat in the rear of the small theater; appeared to be taking constant observations on his note pad; said nothing during intermission. And at the end of the performance he had immediately disappeared. The review had not been without criticism, but even there, his insights had been useful and perceptive. So that the last time I had seen Washburne was that night on a late, eerie, dank November evening. Now I looked up into the man's large luminous eyes, which were set quite wide apart (and overlooked by heavy eyebrows). His observing manner went from innocent and beguiling to penetrating, which bordered on the cunning. Here was a man who has not missed much, and what he has missed, he's willing to indulge himself to learn.

But this occasion didn't seem quite the proper place, and I had been lost for words. Stirred by Ma Fay's words, we vowed to get together, soon, over a drink. Soon I had them both cracking up over what had happened to me earlier in the morning, outside my grandparents' house with Marvella's confrontation with the police, and my involvement, in which I tried to bring order into the chaotic scene. "So, be sure to look for me on the evening news. I hope I didn't end up playing the fool." It also occurred to me, as we parted, why didn't Withers bring up the subject of the play, since Ma Fay Barker went on and on about my potential as a playwright?

As we drove away from the hospital, some of the reasons why such an elaborate form of ritual often characterized the kinds of introductions that Ma Fay Barker had just made occurred to me. Scrapping traditional one- or two-line openers, Ma Fay (and others) wanted to turn these occasions into ceremonial events in order to bring two or more individuals into a higher state of solidarity, for there were so many levels at which we were virtually estranged from each other, through class, money, ideology, politics, religion, color, South/North, and, in Forest County, Southsider versus Westsider, professional versus peasant, more and more male versus female. So that Ma Fay Barker (with her elaborate introduction of Washburne Withers and myself), I speculated, wanted not only to vault over these differences but also to seal up the many obvious estrangements between us, because she no doubt felt there was much we both could contribute to each other and to the group. In this sense, I thought that Ma Fay Barker was in the tradition of the race woman. Her introduction wasn't intended as a way of bridging differences at all, but rather it was offered as a way of suggesting that the next time you meet, you'll have many territories to operate from, discuss, and interpret (because of her minibiographies), but you will be meeting and hovering over these ideas, principalities of thought, without the pettiness of turf confrontations of animosity over inner-group prejudices and educational gaps, which so mock us with a plague of ill-blood brooding into vitriolic hostility. Nor were the introductions so charged with a romantic overview that the utterances melted the manhood of each into mushy compliment, and trimmed away the blubber and bullshit of these young men. And yet that often was the case, I observed, concerning these pulpitlike validations of reference presented by solidarity forgers of all kinds.

No doubt Ma Fay Barker realized that these inner-group distances would never be canceled out, even as the solidarity increased, I projected, but rather that they would no longer stand in the way of bridge building, and staunch-hearted deliberations. At least this was some of what I came to believe that the new sensibility was attempting to establish, or cultivate, as exemplified by Ma Fay Barker's elaborate introductions, that went on for about three minutes for each man; yet both also had been more than a little embarrassed by the largeness of it all, and uttered by an oracle of a woman in whose shadow neither one of us younger men felt worthy to walk. It was a way, too, I observed, of passing historical connections in the here and the now. . . . "Well, it'll take more than complex handshakes to bring us together; I was never hailed nor well met," I exclaimed out loud as I turned on the car radio.

Just then, I thought that it would be good to discuss my ideas for the epic play I was working on, with Washburne Withers. This contact with Withers would also add to my reasons, albeit calculated, for doing some part-time reporting for Gooselaw.

We were driving out of the hospital gates and over the radio came the voice of Billie Holiday singing "God Bless the Child" and "Gloomy Sunday" in a special tribute to Lady Day over public radio. As I drove to Ma Fay Barker's apartment in the near slums (ever so close to the great university), we passed Timmy's Tap. Soon we were not far from the old Avon, where I lived.

Jessie Fay Battle Barker (they often called her Death Row Life Guard) was born in Texas. Her father was a horse breaker and worked in rodeos; her mother ran a saloon. Her maternal grandfather owned three blocks of real estate. It suddenly appealed to my imagination that Ma Fay's total name—Jessie Ma Fay Battle Barker—sounded like the handle of an outlaw heroine, spun from tall tales out of the Old Wild West. She was a hefty, bitter wood—colored woman (with a large mole on her left temple, just above her eye, which looked, at least to me, like the last traces of knotty string from a cowboy's eye patch). Given her heritage and her activist history, it seemed to me that Ma Fay carried within her a steely resolve, and a two-hearted river of soul, along with individualism, which was at once the colors of the blues and then church-tower gray. Even though the aged, huge black Bible was never (apparently) out of her reach, nor a reference from the good book never far from the spirituality of her mental file, Ma Fay Barker was full of moxie, street wisdom, and musings concerning the vicissitudes of the human predicament.

Observing Ma Fay Barker at rallies and on panels, before and after I went into the Army, I felt that I could attest to the fact that when Ma Fay Barker gets extremely angry, she immediately becomes very quiet, contemplative, and often turns to a muted deliverance of a sermonette, as she had at the jailhouse a few minutes ago, when Bettye Burnside had parodied the words of the Death Row Life Guard's Redeemer. She was a harmonized blend of granduncle and grandaunt, and I had seen her transform the lightning rod of rage into a symphony of marching feet, as Dr. King had once said of Ma Fay Barker.

Probably for most people, Ma Fay Barker is a volume of contradicting lifestyles come home to roost in one woman. She had witnessed three lynchings in her life (Uncle Buckholder, her father's baby brother; her first lover; and her first cousin on her mother's side, Willis Wardell Washington). No doubt some of her cry for justice was forged by these eye-witnessed, soul-tormenting memories, I thought, as I listened to this woman speak in such a matter-of-fact voice.

Jessie Fay was raised in West Helena, Arkansas, where she saw her first lynching at the age of five—the hanging of her Uncle T. D. Buckholder. The next week she received the first of several personal branding-iron experiences. She was struck down with a life-debilitating crisis, when she was paralyzed, from her shoulders to her knees. For the next forty years, she was either in a wheelchair or on crutches.

She still depends heavily on a cane for deliverance to and fro, and up and down the steep steps and along the corridors of jails. She is all right negotiating these steps until you attempt to help her, I acknowledged to myself. Ma Fay spurns all support. And she'll tell you or inform you that you "should turn all of that energy over to finding someone who truly needs support and affirmation; it's the best way to keep away self-pity from your doorstep and your instep."

Just now Ma Fay Barker was recalling how her family soon moved to Kansas City, Kansas, home of so many great jazz men, black cowboys, and an ethos of "bold-faced bodacity amongst blacks, and certain women generally," she says, laughing in a private kind of whisper. I can't help but notice how Ma Fay's speech is much more idiomatic now, and secular, too, since we left the prison; and since she has been removed from the presence of Bettye Burnside. Her formative memories were defined out of that tension between the lynching heart of the South, the crippling paralysis, saloon songs, her conversion, her wonderful father with his abundant appetite for life. Then there was the legendary story of her great-grandfather, who had been a slave and lived to be well over one hundred years old. He was proud to proclaim that he had not only "repossessed" the property, where once he had been held in bondage, he had eventually turned over the major portion of this land for the erection of the first Negro school in the area.

Tall, handsome, and jet black in complexion, Great-grandfather Barker, Ma Fay Barker reported, "never called any white man mister. Great-grand fought segregation and racial despair in the most uncompromising ways: kept his rifle at the ready, encouraged the local Negro attempts to vote. I can remember when I was a little girl, he would line up over one hundred blacks to try to get the vote, election after election. Occasionally we would get a handful through. But he kept that rifle loaded near his bed, fearing that the powerful whites in collusion with the Klan and the government would take back the freedom the Negroes supposedly had and return us to Slavery, just as the corruption of white power had taken our freedom from us after the Reconstruction, and returned our people to a system of political exploitation, intimidation, and constant fear for their lives. So you can get the picture, Joubert, I am sure, of a man living out a paradox; raging for the power of the ballot (even though so few of our own got through) and keeping his rifle clean, loaded, and near his bedside. . . . And he always warned other Negroes to do the same thing. And even though he was a tremendous individualist, Great-grandpa never held to high-and-mighty, me-first notions (yet he was the model of the high and mighty to me). For actually he was extolling group effort in the importance of sticking together. Staying on guard with each other, for each other. I remember, for example, how he kept what he called a 'royal guard' of black men with shotguns hidden in an old farmhouse across from where our folks were lined up to vote, in case there was some attempt by the whites to attack the blacks trying to get to the ballot. His breadth of purpose and manliness nourished all around the county. And there wasn't a time when this old farmer—who eventually gave up much of his land for the education of his people—didn't give away vegetables, fruits, cattle, chickens for the local down-and-out Negroes. So, for me, he was a freedom fighter, long before I ever met Dr. King and any of the other modern-day heroes and heroines." With tears welling in her eyes, Ma Fay Barker still remembered a tree house this grand old man had built for her in his eightieth year. That July she was struck down by paralysis.

I could now see why Ma Fay Barker had made so much over Washburne Withers, viewing him, no doubt (or at least what he appeared to stand for), in the light of a connection with her great-grandfather.

Mainly recalling lifeline-affirming men, elevating her upon their shoulders, and up to ladders to dream upon, and into tree houses. The memories of these men linked the generations, from Jessie Fay Battle Barker's paternal great-grandfather—who was called Battle-Barker by the local Negroes, in both awe and affection—to her grandfather, whom she referred to as a "poet, singer, storyteller, and one of the first of the teachers on the plot of land his daddy had turned over for the school . . . a magical man who taught the local blacks the importance of rotation of crops, the importance of basic mathematics, and the beauty of the sound of language inside of words." Then there was the "lean, tough-heartiness of my own father." Soon Ma Fay Barker was talking about the baby uncle who was lynched, who had introduced her to the silent movies; hunting and fishing; mountain climbing and horseback riding and cabinetmaking; and "some parts of electrical wiring available to his imagination at the time, Joubert." This maternal uncle had been particularly dear to her, because her own mother had died giving birth to Fay, and he had worshiped his sister and told his niece wonderful stories of his sister; her beauty, her intelligence, and her "spiritual zeal."

Although she didn't go into it directly, I gleaned the idea that Ma Fay's father, Armstead Barker, had somewhat broken with the land-bound, community-lodged ways of his father and grandfather. Ma Fay was still most alive when recollecting her father's stories of breaking horses and working on track-lining gangs. Psychologically wrecked after her baby uncle's lynching, she had gone to live with her maternal grandfather for a time out in the Southwest. The crippled child found some spiritual healing in the loving household of this grandkin, and his adoring young wife. Ma Fay was also the beneficiary of a whole arsenal of southwestern frontier lore, from her maternal grandfather, Wiggins Longstreet, whose father was a Hopi Indian. Grandpa Longstreet delighted her with stories (and examples, too) of the Antelope and Snake Dances. From him came sagas of *Bleeding Kansas*, from the standpoint of the Negro people.

Struck down at the age of twelve by paralysis, Fay Barker was converted to the Gospel of Jesus Christ while in a wheelchair, at a rally where a "female first cousin of mine, on my mother's side (who was a minister of the Word), was trying to seduce me, had also taken me there, beneath the campground circus tent, for divine healing, in total sincerity of purpose; so that the questions of blood and outrageousness, incest and spiritual honesty, do indeed get all mixed up, Joubert. But you see, son, it all must be presented forth in the spirit of balance, yet oddity, and misshape and mishap, leading us indirectly into the soul of all things invisible. Just at the border where visible creation stops short before the bars of total injustice. Now don't quote me there in that last part of your article."

The form this healer took was that "of a man named Hal Freefriend, an albino, who was tattooed from his shoulders to his knees; an idolatry from his previous condition of devilment," she said in a deep whisper of her tenor voice. Hal Freefriend didn't heal Jessie Fay, his praying over her and pouring of anointing oils did seem to "touch my lame limbs in a wondrous manner," and she said just now how "I did feel Jesus Christ stirring throughout the dead parts of my body. But, Joubert, it was upon this occasion that I truly did find Jesus Christ. My great-grandfather Barker shunned the Word of the Lord (probably because of the racist interpretation of that Word that had been handed along to him), but his son, the poet, had been a part-time preacher, and so I had picked up some Christian visions early in my life. But without any women directly in my path, directing me, this faith-potential lay fallow."

Now I found myself gradually taken up by Ma Fay's words of faith, coupled with the fact that she so believed in the power of giving as the form of her redemption. It was a coupling she had come to see initially through what she had gleaned from her great-grandfather's view of service to his people, through sharing what he had recombined with Christian faith. "The old man in his way was very spiritual," she said, in a different voice, which was, it struck me, sad, and deeply contemplative.

Inspired by her family story, and what appeared to be her inner strength, I asked Ma Fay if I could conclude the interview the following week, and if I could get her opinion on something that still troubled me deeply. My question concerned Imani. And why she had committed suicide, over and above the obvious reasons. Ma Fay Barker had known of the talented painter; had met her on several social occasions. I knew of the cruel encounter session; but what other forces might Ma Barker, as a woman of faith, recognize, that I, as a man without any strong rock of faith, have missed? Then I proceeded to give Ma Fay all of the particulars about the suicide that she perhaps was not aware of.

To my surprise, Ma Fay declined to give any answer; rather she said she would pray over the matter, study the saga, and what I had added to the story, and call me when she "received the answer." Except for the last part of her rejoinder, she had sounded like an attorney, expressing some reluctance about taking on a case for the damned. When I concluded the interview the next week, perhaps she might be willing to cast some light on the suicide. Or, I thought, as I arrived at her house, did Ma Fay see my questioning her on this matter as nonprofessional? It certainly didn't have anything to do with her life. And yet Ma Fay was known for such broad-ranging concerns, such humanity, it was hard to think that she would have excluded this question about the suicide from her purview.

As I watched her move slowly but steadily on her cane towards her small bungalow, I found myself still unsettled about Ma Fay's abrupt silence about Imani; when it suddenly occurred to me: how vastly limited was the female role in Ma Fay's early years. Were the two matters connected in her imagination?

All
Floundering
Oratorio
of Souls

■■■■■■■■■■■■■■■■■■■■■■■■■■■■■■■■■■■■

Chapter 1

Whenever I would come home to the Avon at night or early in the morning, I would always hear the classical FM radio station playing (next door to my small domicile) as I placed the key in the door. In this room resided one of the strangest of the odd fellows in our building characterized by eccentricities. There were broken-down artists, college dropouts with eternal plans of returning to school, while they worked at the post office or for drugstore chains. I had dropped out of college seven times. There were others from the Third World (mainly African countries, recently independent) who were waiting for their stipends to flow, so that they could live on a meager student budget; but the waiting was in vain. They knew it, and the ever-patient Mrs. Titlebaum knew the truth of the situation, too. Some of their number soon turned to driving a cab, but they most often did not return to school. We were viewed as not only eternal dropouts but also as eternal dropout student-scholars as well, in an almost European manner or way of life. The IOU box I kept under my bed was plentiful with receipts. It was filling as fast as the IOU box we kept at Aunt Eloise's Night Light Lounge.

There were a few whites that worked at the post office who saw themselves as stalwarts of standards, but were not beseeched by the "assaults of a new kind of nonesuch worker, whose productivity sucked." These white supervisors—who had not advanced in the last ten years—were now going through the middle stages, midlife crises, too, of whispering and bemoaning the decline, at the post office, of "our good colored help," of full- or half-time employees. The potential pool of "good colored help" was taking advantage of the jobs made available for blacks by the breakthroughs in the Civil Rights Movement; and to the post office on a weekly basis came riffraff, irresponsible, driftwood, backwater country blacks, who could and would "scare the devil out of Satan if confronted on a dark road," one white guy, who himself bore a remarkable resemblance to Senator James Eastland, was overheard saying to one of his colleagues as they emerged out of the toilet together. Had they been showering together?

Then there were what I called the Deep Brown Study Eggheads, whose voices whistled like boiling pots about to crack as they essayed to articulate every word on racial deceit, racism, white supremacy, Black Uplift, Garveyism, with a withering, spitspieling shine of final word erudition, in order to ground into the dust forevermore their opponent's "argument." But then the next day, these blacks were back at their posts, ready for a brand-new argument, refreshed and full of zest.

And as often as not, these African American brothers were not proponents of anything so high-minded as a counterargument; but rather, they were only a tenth of a degree to the left or to the right of one debating team's stalwart position, which might best be articulated by the simple, trite proverb "I'd rather be right than be president." No matter, the three would hold forth at the drop of a hat into the ring. The main thing I learned soon after moving into the Avon was to avoid running into one of the three "learned-hand," high-powered rhetoricians-turned-magicians, when you were particularly busy . . . or not busy at all. Each represented a species of the liar.

And to get out of their clutches (for they stood right by the outer door, hungry for prey) you had to come up with some outrageous lie, a falsehood that could challenge their high-flying expansiveness over the Problem. Upon the seventh escape-hatch lie, which centered on my needing to hail a taxi because I was to meet Haile Selassie at the airport for a one-on-one interview with the *Forest County Dispatch* (which of course was dumb), because the three erudite eggheads revered Selassie. Now, Selassie really was a catch to net, or as they put it, to "engage in a fleeting moment of argumentation." So, from then on, when tripped up by one of the three, I would say: "Look my man, my grandmother was just devoured by a fox and my real name is Brer Bear; can you dig it? I'm splitting the scene before the bastard boils her soul for lunch."

Holding themselves erect with their hands folded forth as if in prayer (beseeching the heavens for a prey for their net of argumentation), they could hold forth for hours on end. I remember time and again going off to work for a newspaper assignment at 8:30 A.M., and returning for a quick bowl of self-stylized gumbo at 1:00, only to find one of three experts on the Problem holding forth with the highest erudition possible, "on planet earth, which was available only to a select few talented types of black men, as we hurled towards the end of this grievous century."

Their style of speech combined those of Churchill, Benjamin Mayes, Adlai Stevenson, the "And God Loves You" passion of Fulton J. Sheen, and the high-arching preacher argumentation of Mordecai Johnson. "Ignoramus" was one of their favorite terms to apply to any lost soul whom they caught on a given morning, afternoon, evening, or night. For in all truth, you were something of a fool if you fell victim to their "engagement in argumentation."

The highlight of their net-catching work was to capture any of the half a dozen whites who still lived in the Avon and ensnarl them in an encounter over the Problem, which long ago had become invisible, when engaged and grounded by the furor of their earsplitting rhetoric. And of course, as I soon learned, you also had to be quite gingerly in your motions and movements out of the firing line of the spittle that flung forth from their mouths as they attempted to articulate the highest zenith of verbal high jinks; as they tried to take you up one mountain to the next, you were forced to step aside from a rain of spittle.

And there were writers of various levels of ambition, talented but toothless alto and tenor saxophonists, one male opera singer, long past his prime, who gave occasional voice lessons to students with "immeasurable potentiality." There were, of course, politicians (who had never held actual offices) who had now gone from dogcatcher to precinct captain, and were now turning gray in their new-spun nationalism in the heat of the night, even as they maintained their old political contacts with the machine, their soft jobs downtown, and their help to bring out the vote on election day. These remarkable few were not held up at the Avon, because they had lost a lot of their social power through recent divorces. Their problem now was to decide in exactly what form they would reenter Forest County's social and political life. Called jive-fed by the true black nationalists, these wayward party hacks never argued with the old-time Garveyites of a bygone era who lived off slender pensions from jobs as redcaps or railroad waiters. There were at least three former Black Muslims who lived very close to the fish bone and now practiced a most severe form of Sunni Muslim faith. And there were Africans, mainly Nigerians, who would put up with the nondebate encounters with the three Deep Brown Study Eggheads long enough, if it all seemed to lead to a meeting with some nonnationalist female flesh. The Africans had their own private white stock.

Along with the Islanders, these Africans were most looked up to and down against by the three eggheads, I discovered to my great surprise, disgust, and instruction. None were more damned as ignoramus, nor accentuated as genius, than the Africans and the Islanders by the eggheads. Then, there were several "chaps" who were always in the process of planning and plotting a trip to the "motherland." Describing the continent of Africa as a "huge pork chop" in an attempt to attract African Americans, these motherland dudes and their dolls had allured a fledgling black magazine in a "deal" in which the new monthly rag, called *Black Star Line*, would foot the bill for these black American operators, as long as the seven bright young people of various hues pledged to send back stories on life in Africa. I had learned through Aunt Eloise that *Black Star Line* was actually bankrolled by a right-wing group of white fundamental Christians with deep investments in South Africa and Israel.

But the chap who lived next to me, Shep Bottomly, tuned out most of the political palaver as "incorrect." He held pridefully and fiercely to his faith in the Marxist-Leninist gospel of wealth, devoured his classical music as he chain-smoked his Pall Malls, and read the great Russian writers, particularly Dostoevsky and sometimes Tolstoy, in the original.

I had first met Shep Bottomly (an African American graduate student, majoring in Slavic languages) at International House. Shep was seated in the rear of the cafeteria all alone reading *Crime and Punishment* in Russian, sipping his English tea, and smoking one of his eternally present Pall Malls. It was four o'clock in the afternoon. Despise the English "island race" as he said he did, Shep Bottomly always kept fast to the ideal of four o'clock tea time; a habit he had picked up, he said in a most disdainful voice, from his sometimes sweetheart Mary Frances Essault, the Australian. At our first encounter, Shep and I got into a long and protracted discussion over Dostoevsky's character Svidrigailov.

Shep Bottomly keep wads of news clips (in his back pockets along with his red handkerchief) stripped from national and international newspapers, all of which pinpointed the imprecise but real decline of the American economy, or the erosion of this nation's dominance in the geopolitical movements of this world in the very immediate future. The political system of the Soviet Union held a celestial place in Bottomly's heart and soul. I preferred to talk with Bottomly about Dostoevsky (and even from the beginning of our friendship, Shep was very helpful in mastering pronunciations of the characters in Dostoevsky and Tolstoy). But Dostoevsky's *Notes from Underground* brought on terror in Shep's vision; the Crystal Palace remained a sharp moment of abject encounter in the mind and soul of Shep Bottomly, who saw himself as a student of economics, as well.

No woman could domesticate this wayward Marxist, often shabbily attired, Bottomly. (Though many sought this dubious honor.) Shep had the makings of a handsome man. Of a light-olive-skinned complexion and a distinguished-looking countenance (as a young DuBois, perhaps), he always appeared as one prepared for a painter's portrait of his proud profile (a little like one of his heroes, Emiliano Zapata, too), or the sculpture's rendering of his head in bronze.

I often reflected that the painter Imani would have loved this man Shep Bottomly and immediately would have proclaimed him as a "lost child of African genius," and proclaimed him as yet another one of her lost-now-found brothers, meantime wanting also to make love to him. And, of course, Imani would have wanted, greatly, to paint his face as "sacred" and "holy." He, in turn, I speculated, would have made mincemeat out of her before she ran into that hideous encounter group, which marked the beginning of her ending. Imani had thought she was at the birth of a new day not only in her life but in the life of the race.

After twenty years of marriage, Shep's father had suddenly left the mother and taken up with a much younger woman, a Mexican beauty who was his graduate student, in the small college where Bottomly, Sr., taught economics.

Shep's mother soon used her contacts in volunteer work to land a position as head of the city's arts center, at a time when the community was going through a pattern of racial and ethnic change. The Jews on the board—who had been her friends, and supported Sarah Jewel Bottomly as new head of the arts center—had ultimately turned on her, so expounded Shep Bottomly. Although it sounded to me as if the Jews (and what there was of a tiny liberal white presence) had been fundamental in Bottomly's mother getting the job in the first place, I could never get Shep to open up to this phase of Sarah Jewel's political rise at the arts center. "How the fuck do you know? You're a Forest County shit head, and you probably believe that the sun rises and sets over some political deal between the Irish mayor and the rest of the ethnics, in every place this side of Paradise," Shep Bottomly had screamed at me one night. For he despised the Jews for "turning on" his mother, and Shep believed that the Jews held the reins of power in the Party, as well. No matter how much he believed in the democratic openness of the group, over several bourbons Shep would weep in his cup about the power of the Jews over his life. Yet, as far as I could tell (with the exception of Mary Frances Essault), nearly all of Shep's girlfriends down the years had been Jews. "We speak the same language," he would say rather heatedly, showing his mighty profile, smugness, and disdain for the very contradictions that marked his life.

In his growing up years, Dr. W. E. B. DuBois and Monroe Trotter were among the many intellectuals who had visited the Bottomly home. Shep recalled the specifics of these visits again and again. And in sharply defending the mother in the ruptured marriage, Shep liked to point to the picture of himself as a boy of perhaps ten years, looking up with great reverence at the deeply reflective face of Dr. DuBois. In the background and standing above the great intellectual and her boy was the handsome Sarah Jewel Bottomly. Shep Bottomly kept this picture on his dresser next to pictures of Marx and Lenin.

The presence of these intellectuals in his life was as much a contribution to the Bottomly home life from the mother's powerful mind
as it was from the fount of his father's contacts, Shep assured me. Yet
it was because of the college and the contacts the family had through
the superbly well educated father and his many (unpublished) theories
on economics that many intellectuals were drawn to the Bottomly
home. Once there, it was the exquisitely trained Frau Bottomly (with
her German and French education) who became the darling of the
intellectuals. Sarah Jewel had been involved with feminist causes all
of her life.

In the marital breach, Shep had sided with his mother, and he saw
his father as a renegade, both as a husband (father, too) as well as quite
a reactionary economist. That the old man had taken up with "a fiery
Mexican bitch" only added to the insult Shep felt was for his mother's
plight. Shep didn't weigh into his evaluation his mother's own personal
development after the divorce. This process of her becoming fascinated
me; for in some ways, I identified the life career of Sarah Jewel with
that of my own aunt Eloise. The public career of Bottomly's mother
started to take off the very year she sought and won the divorce from
Shep's father. I observed how Shep was only fundamentally interested
in rehashing the story of the "Mexican bitch," the fact that his father
had forsaken his mother, and ultimately the ways in which her friends
and supporters at the arts center had abandoned his mother, particularly
the Jews.

The father's fortunes never tumbled, but he was never promoted to
full professor, either, and remained for the duration of his stay at the
small college as an associate professor with tenure. As the only Negro
professor at the junior college, he had suffered many racial slings, and
he believed, according to Shep, that the chair of his department and
the dean of the College of Arts and Letters (who remained dean for
fourteen years) had used the divorce as an excuse to mask their racist
reasons for not promoting him. This was particularly vivid in their
imaginations when "the old man ran off with the Mexican broad," a
relationship Shep despised, even as he "loathed the college for cutting
the old bastard down because of this fucked-up affair." Shep hated the
politics of these men's economics; the sheer reactionary stain of them,

and because, "You see, Joubert, when publication was denied him in liberal journals, then he was lured into right-wing camps." Shep hoped he'd put his head in an oven the way a Negro scholar did up in New England when his dissertation was denied, although seven years later the same man's findings were hailed as breakthrough research.

Shep Bottomly lived intimately with the reign of chaos in his room. At any moment, in a given conversation, in which, say, the latest shift in the hemline was being discussed, Shep Bottomly would immediately pull out a clipping from the rancid wad of newspaper items he sliced from the newspapers with his keen-edged, six-inch razor, which he could slip out from his back pocket with street-slick deftness. When Shep would start slicing up scores of newspapers that he kept (the *Manchester Guardian*, the *Wall Street Journal*, or the *New York Times*, to name but a few), he would go after his avocation with cunning zeal and a stealth for reversal of the intended meaning of a given article. He was not opposed to the use of scissors for these operations on the newspapers. I observed that high, proud nose of Shep's actually sniff at the bait for what could be pitched for a catch of international rascality, with the fervor of a fisherman casting out his lines.

There sat Shep Bottomly, the one-man-clipping-agency, in a rocking chair, endlessly rocking, pinching at his broad and shaggy mustache, pondering and pouring over his disaster clippings, all of which projected the decline or predicted the fall of the nation's financial or moral structure, if you reversed the meaning of the scribe's intention, or you plunged the reporter's data into the swill of Marxist-Leninist theory.

Oftentimes, I would come upon Shep—with his door ajar and the FM radio station tuned low—holding forth concerning the decline and fall of Western Civilization in general and the United States in particular—and surrounded by two or more of his satellites. Adorned with the large old shawl his mother had given him about his shoulders, Shep would be in the throes of giving a lecture on the relationship of the nation's moral decline, caused by the upsurge of the hemline, the political bankruptcy of our national life spun out of hegemony, and the wasting away of our moral treasure in foreign wars, and the ever-constant drip of our economic fortunes.

Then, he would go rambling away to reveal how all of this was interconnected to imperialism, the assassination of JFK, and the repression of Third World government. And to support his theories, he would hand over yet another clipping for his satellites to read, see, and immediately agree with his position. And as satellites and friends listened to Shep (I considered myself not a satellite but a friend), with music of Beethoven or Mozart going on, Shep laid praise of revelation and revolution at the feet of Father Marx and the Savior Lenin, with *Das Capital* representing the Holy Scripture with the good cheer of one hailing the advent of Christmastide. At every conceivable turn in the room, Shep Bottomly's library cell of a chamber was littered with newspapers from many sources.

Shep Bottomly was a man who always convinced himself of the rightness of those causes that he believed in with a religious fervor. Recalling a powerful swimmer who set out to span the lengths of the sea, he had depths of expansive faith in his powers to plumb and probe the currents of the most stormy tides, then ascend to the heights of his intellectual diving board with truth renewed and awash in his hands, and where he could be seen standing nude with a book of theory from either Marx or Lenin in his hands held aloft.

To begin with, Shep Bottomly did not argue with just anyone. He was highly selective and prejudiced about those he engaged in the log-rolling combat of ideas. Women were rarely entertained in this privileged position worthy of an opponent (though he did have one or two female satellites). Yet I knew him to be attracted to intellectually assertive, ambitious women who were rarely as sturdy emotionally as they appeared to be on the surface. For Shep, breaking down the arguments of these women was far more important than simply seducing them. There was no greater love than to demolish an argument of some worthy but wayward female foe. This, then, was the road to seduction for Shep Bottomly.

A prodigious Ping-Pong player, Shep Bottomly loved to ever so gently stroke the coarse-to-wavy hairs of his considerable mustache after he had demolished your serve; and during brief respites in the game room in the basement of International House, he would proceed to devastate political and historical arguments as being put to the service of the ideologically incorrect practitioners of wretched statecraft.

There was an apocalypse brewing at every turn of Shep's mind (not all of his data was nourished on the brink of the Cold War, nor imperialism nor racism). For Shep Bottomly there was a certain magnetism to ideological dogma. All who thought counter to his theories were part of a "conspiracy of medieval mischief" that would soon enough go drowning off into the sea from the high mountaintop of "icy hypocrisy." Whenever Shep "minted" a fond phrase that he found particularly delightful, he paid himself a hundred times by tweaking his mustache. When the riots broke out in the cities and the Vietnam protests mounted, he crafted new oracles of despair for the moment, but at the same time, hailed his predictions concerning the latest manifestation of America's destruction. At a particular moment in my dialogue, Shep sprung the logic of his arguments upon my "artistic tendency to read history, backwards and incorrectly—and through the prism of artist-tainted, discolored, and dislocated eyes." At these moments, when obviously Old Shep would have to be the declared winner by any solid-minded slate of jurors, I often thought of this image as I watched Shep stroke his mustache and purr like a Maltese cat over the power of his debater's point victory. I didn't take in 95 percent of his raving rant, which for me was really reactionary.

Shep Bottomly always liked to sit cross-legged (which I thought was like a girl), and in a manner different from any black male I had ever known, as he leaned into those Pall Malls with a hard-down lip-pinching drag; blue-penciling away and underlining key sentences in his studies of Dostoevsky and Tolstoy. The left hand held the cigarette and the right hand held the blue pencil.

Whatever forces of spirituality that possessed the soul of Shep, they branched off into two attributes. First, there was the *appreciation* he had for classical music. Appreciation, not necessarily love, particularly for Beethoven (whose powerful Fifth Symphony often vaulted out of Shep as he listened to FM with a dramatic downbeat fashioned out by that sturdy blue pencil, as if he were not only a maestro but a military commander; particularly the finale, which was a call to arms and his own personal national anthem). With his waving blue-pencil baton in hand, he declared war on the unappreciative illiterates of the world who did not appreciate Beethoven, or Mozart, for that matter.

Shep's meticulous approach to musical values in the classical mode was more in line with that of a diagnostic review; yet, whenever there was a soul and a spirituality in the manner, I reflected, it was called out by certain classical music. Generally speaking, Mendelssohn was a little too delicate; Brahms too romantic; Literature? Too perilously complex. "You writers," he'd start off with, "are too damned hard to pigeonhole."

Then he might give a discourse on the Germanic influences upon W. E. B. DuBois. A few minutes later, Shep would reveal to you exactly why he also loathed the ethos of German genius. He was reading Erich Heller's *The Ironic German* at the time. Mrs. Titlebaum, who enjoyed telling stories on her tenants when they were behind in their rent to those who were consistently on time (or, for heaven's sake, ahead), often described Shep as one who reminded her of the Teutonic spirit.

For all of the shifty-eyed ferocity in his spirit, women found strands of attraction in the turbulence of the scoffing Shep's spirit. "He is so needful," one damsel in distress reported to me. Her statement gave me pause, for I never saw Shep when he wasn't in complete control of a given situation or debate.

I decided to take Shep Bottomly out to the Night Light Lounge to see what he really made of us. I put him up against the barmaids and let them see how bad he is. For to me, most of the women Shep dealt with were pushovers. They'll eat him alive, I thought, particularly Gracie Rae. Although Estella by Starlight, the romantic, would probably fall head over heels in love with his hapless wunderkind. What would Molly Savage *not* do to him?

I started to answer a question he had raised by describing some of the denizens of Eloise's lounge. Shep's question, so scientifically put in a declarative statement: "I want to meet with workers in your aunt's shop."

He seemed oddly fascinated; yet, he was full of irritability as to why I had not tried to awaken their potential for political consciousness and action. You sound like Leonard Foster, I almost said. Initially, he started off laughing in a way that reminded me of one musing at the possibility of going to the carnival to see the clowns do their routines, wearing funny masks; that we were about to be entertained by this slate of lost humanity.

Nothing fascinated him more than did the saga of McGovern Mc-Nabb. The terrible tonnage that was McNabb had been retired from his job as a cook on the railroad years ago.

"You see, Shep, because of McGovern McNabb's great girth, he could not actually hold up his long, blue silk stockings, which he wore because a Negro medical student once upon a time told him to wear these stockings, which would in turn help McNabb with his varicose veins. McNabb tried to find garters to hold up the wiggly-piggly unraveling stockings that kept falling down despite his voluminous thighs."

"Unraveling? How so?"

"Oh yes, because by the time the stockings had actually climbed up the mountainous legs they were stretched beyond serviceable recall or recoil . . . so that new, more substantial garters were needed."

"Joubert, how can you say these words with a straight face?"

"Until recently, McNabb was seen and heard, too, going around to women at the bar trying to solicit some portly woman who would allow him to interrogate her about informal personal details concerning her stocking size and where she 'purchased her garters,' when he was inebriated. Or, at other times, he would seek out advice on the 'stretchable potentiality of garters.' But the garters would always fall short or burst in the thrust of their mission. And Shep, you talking about a straight face! McNabb got his highly polished Asiatic yellow face slapped red-unto-Chinese-red for his brashness and rudeness. Last I heard, he had received some seven slaps per week. 'What size stockings do you wear my lady? Or can you give a history of your garters' durability?' McNabb rendered that all up in that proper low-down tenor of his Mississippi Mud Pie (he likes to refer to as only his) voice range. Whereupon soon enough, his face was wopped, mopped, cracked, and even spat upon.

"Completely ignorant of the rise of the phenomenon of panty hose, McGovern McNabb usually approached women who were more than just portly. Usually, the women were quite large, hippy, and big-legged (although the term 'big stockings' was held forth by certain men at the lounge as complimentary, concerning a lady with much shapely meat fashioned upon her frame . . . gams worthy of games, albeit hugely fashioned in the grand manner).

"One of McNabb's partners was Short-Knocker, another gave himself the name Sir Iliad Browne (self-knighted, of course) because he was denied entry into Williemain's Righteous Rites and Royal Ramblings Club. The others were Talcum Tommie and the trio of Freddy, Flint, and Fly.

"About this time, McNabb's niece, the demure, self-depreciating Drucilla McNabb, had devised the idea (through much contemplation, prayer, and even consultation with faith healers) that her uncle McNabb's only hope for physical and spiritual salvation was through marriage. When she told me this on the telephone I felt doubly shocked, given her pristine voice and the ungovernable soul of her uncle. God help the woman, I almost exclaimed. At one time I had a crush on Drucilla, so I almost wanted to warn her away from undertaking the enterprise she went on to describe: finding a wife for her uncle. But since Drucilla was such a religious person—the vision of McNabb's salvation through marriage had emerged in her imagination through a revelation—I decided to hold my peace.

" 'Since I never set foot in any establishment where spirits are sold, I was wondering if you might have his three closest friends give me a call. I want to beseech their aid,' Drucilla said, in that sweet and lyric voice of hers. To my surprise, Drucilla actually convinced Short-Knocker, Sir Iliad Browne, and Talcum Tommie to support her in this marriage scheme. 'To find a woman worthy of the finer, inner qualities of my uncle.' But what became apparent to me early on were the factors in the friendship of McGovern McNabb and his buddies. His boons were always trying to parley some joke against 'Slaughterhouse' McNabb; this despite their general affection for the towering man who weighed perhaps nearly four hundred pounds and stood six feet, six inches. They simply wanted to help him and test his resolve. They loved his largeness of spirit and appetite, and loathed and even envied his undisciplined ways. And of course, none of the three men had ever been married.

"Whereas his devoted niece Drucilla had fixed her vision on an extremely thin (homely, too) spinster, her three operatives were working on a ruse of their own in keeping with their mischievous ways. Ads were placed by the three (with the wicked Fly leading the way). *Wanted dead or alive: a woman weighing about 89 pounds . . . or, weighing in at at least 299.* Ads of this sort were placed in either the obituary section of the *Forest County Dispatch* or the 'Love Forlorn' column. Also, the woman who weighted eighty-nine pounds soaking wet must have papers to prove that she ate no more than seven times a week. Food stamps did not count. They would have to present a grocery bill from a certified food chain.

"In the local post office box marked XYZ Affair, the McNabb's three buddies received some thirty-three positive reactions to the proposal of meeting a 'truly alive male of towering stature with not a gray hair in his head. He can fulfill all the demands a natural woman is looking for, especially during these days when it's so hard to find a real man, in plain view.' There was a postscript listed that the respondents could meet and reach the delightful man in question, once they answered the ad in a positive manner. Even a little box to be checked was provided."

Then, Shep Bottomly asked a civil question: "Why did they place the ad in the obituary section? Of all places!" Not a bad query but an innocent one.

"First of all, widow women and spinsters often read the obituary column to find out who died, so they could get dressed up in their finery and attend this social occasion—the ritual of a funeral. But second, and most important, a wake and a funeral are the perfect places to celebrate life by finding out who (in this case a male, of course) recently lost a spouse. And their children; how many? And is there any chance for me to catch him on the rebound? I'm telling you, Shep, as Sister Goodpastor is lowered in the grave, Brother Goodpastor had better get his skates humming down the highway or he'll be lowered into the bed of some sister that very day—and by nightfall, the lonely hearts sisters are going to flock to his house before the funeral home returns his living body to this front door, and the obsequies are still hot in the ears of each mourner, and the funeral breads are still warm in the oven."

I decided to take Shep out to the bar on a Blue Monday Chili night. When we arrived at Aunt Eloise's Night Light Lounge, Molly had her hot plate sizzling with Touch-Back Baby Chili, as well as her splendid, highly economic, and artful moves behind the bar as she went about the mixologist craft. Molly was soon polishing off "this yellow-red yallar, mis-educated nigger" with a third bowl of her famous chili, but then she told him to "walk fast. Let me see your coattails flip and do handstands," when he kept driving off her good customers with his "off-the-wall-shit-on-a-shingle-slobbering poor-man's junkie hop-hustle snot-rags for sale cop-out. And what's worse than anything else, he's running out good customers who have a pocket full of money and the knowledge of good whiskey and wine. Two things your B. O. Plenty friend is very short on; short on good manners, too." And when Shep got up to go to the john, Molly howled: "Say there you spoiled sapper sucker. You going the wrong-ass way, the e-x-i-t door is in the front of Joubert's auntie's establishment. Besides, that seat in the john is simply too commodious to accommodate your hard ass. Hurry up and get 'im out of my sight, Joubert, before I come down in a natural puke hemorrhage."

All the time when he wasn't going back and forth to the bathroom, Shep stood perfectly still; taking in good-spirit Molly's lampooning, but steadily chasing off some of her best customers. Even on Blue Monday Chili, everybody usually wanted to make haste and get their taste of Molly's chili before and after drinks. Now they ran from Shep's harangues. Then she finally said:

"You bad news on a slow night buster, with your quick-draw-snuff-brain-slickeyed-shit-yallar-mustard-turds-for-schemes-down-to-the-drain dreamers! Joubert! Where did you find this Robin Hood for scandal, for shame? I know you are the earl of dropouts, probably heading up some secret agency for dropouts; but where did you find this clown prince? This Joker of the pack? At the truant office, when you were in the seventh grade?"

Howling at many of her jokes, Shep Bottomly was truly eating out of Molly's hand (as well as consuming an all-time record of thirteen small cups of her Texas-style chili), and taking her verbal shafting and bombshelling with glad grace. Indeed it crossed my mind: this is probably the best natural fun this man has had in his life. And when we finally left, I thought I saw a tear forming in Shep's left eye. But perhaps it was from too much smoking that tears got into his eyes; those dammed Pall Malls. His face was mustard yellow over screaming brick red after five martinis, thirteen cups of chili, and a pack and a half of Pall Malls. Attempting to survey the whole sweep of the evening, at one point on our way home Shep got wound up and suddenly was speechless, completely lost for words. That was also the night that Shep came into my room for the first time and I was listening to Billie Holiday. To my shock, Shep claimed that he had never listened to a recording of Lady Day's in his life and kept calling her Judy Holiday over and over again.

∎

Still, Molly Savage often asked about Shep, to my surprise, with a grain of spite mixed with pity for his detached, lost soul. "How's your friend Hemorrhoid Bottom's Up? Ain't nothing in this world more pitiful than a frustrated, yallar-red-nigger who ain't composed his peace with his second mind into a whole note tune over this aggravation, spelled down upon us as a people like a plague. That sorry fucker probably can't pour piss out of a jar without dirtying up his drawers . . . or should I say his diapers. Act like he never had anybody's good lovin' chili to say nothing of Molly's. High browns, yellows, and lily-white ladies done spoiled that boy, upsides down."

Old Shep (as he enjoyed being called) always had some woman, girl-friend, or would-be lady friend to do his laundry. Indeed, if a young lady wanted to get over with Shep, the best way to achieve an introduction to his heart was to offer to do his laundry. More important, however, Shep loved to actually watch a lovely young thing scrubbing his dirty linen back into a condition of unstained whiteness. Personally, I hated to see his women friends reduced to this level of courtship, but I had to admit that at least it meant that Shep had a clean change during those weeks he was seeing a given woman. The first time I saw one of Shep's ladies down on her knees scrubbing his dirty drawers with such vigor, I found myself weeping furiously in the corner of my own room. For this image immediately aroused memories of Lucasta Jones, and the saga of how the man she cleaned and scrubbed for was about to leave her the next week for another, before he was sandwiched between two trains in the Santa Fe Railroad yards.

Except for one of two upper-middle-class, sheltered, fair-skinned Negro women (who had never heard of Karl Marx or Lenin until Shep enlightened them), all of Shep's serious ladies were lily-white maidens. Most of this group were Jews, but the most recent woman was the Australian I had gotten to know rather well. Shep and Mary Frances Essault had met in London.

Immediately after I returned to the Avon from dropping Ma Fay Barker off and getting my haircut at Williemain's Barbershop, I started going through my mail. There were seven rejection letters from theater groups, revealing their general lack of interest in my play on Sugar-Groove. They were planning to return my play under separate cover.

Each rejection letter expressed a variation on the theme—that the play was too long, dated, and too ethnic. Then, at the bottom of this heap of cruel missives was a letter from Shep Bottomly's Australian lady. She was trying to get her life sorted out after a brief encounter with the strangely alluring Shep, whom she always referred to as Shepherd (which, after all, was his full name). After flying from London to Forest County and facing Bottomly down about the marital plans "they had crafted" in England, she now wrote me the following:

Joubert, I've thought a few times about that short article about the curious inversions and the implicit comment which informed the coinage of Negro slang. You lent it to me, do you remember? If you get time, could you type me a copy and send it? Did you, incidentally, ever read that book I had, Unless Some Man Show Me? *Was it at all engaging to you? I like the bit about the* Book of Job.

I am currently writing this in Casualty Waiting Room, at Guy's Hospital—possible appendicitis. I've had trouble for years and am slowly getting worse, but in the last week, I had two attacks of severe pain. So I thought of how this investigation was timely, but I hate and loathe the thought of being in a hospital again (all those memories), even if not for long. I've had to come here since I've returned to the neurological clinic to alleviate symptoms caused by stress and anxiety. You remember those pills I had to take for back problems, which, between us, was exacerbated by Shepherd. He is supposed to arrive tomorrow, but this is the third time a date of arrival was sent out, but no one arrives at the airport fitting the description of one Shepherd Bottomly III. And by now, Joubert, it seems useless anyway. He doesn't communicate; as if it were his prerogative to lead my heart or our mismanaged affair out of bondage by the drivel up his nostrils, the whip-chains of his mental superiority, and the mock of his whims.

But then I do get desperate telephone calls from Shepherd (at frightful hours). Finally, he manages to grind out three letters (in nine months)—three very terrible and vicious letters, as spun out by one of those dreadfully mean-spirited characters of Dostoevsky, and in which Shepherd crafts a persona as one of abject cruelty who is compelled by evil. Shepherd responds humanly when he hears my voice, long distance, rasping over the wires, about his flagrant neglect. And he promises to write, and he doesn't, except these sacred three texts of lamentation over race, of spiritual denial and surly torment, beyond hope or belief. Apparently, Shepherd can respond to my voice, but can't face the music (unless it's Beethoven, behind whose masculine voice he hides) when he must look me face-to-face, eyeball out to sea, adrift, with a flag so torn, like one of his undershirts, and mangled so much that none can claim him as one of their native sons. What is to be done? That, too, is also the *question. There are many who can't love another or haven't the time for it (nor perhaps the capacity, either), for they are so in love with their own precious reflection, because, for them, that visage is beyond perfection.*

Dearest Joubert, I miss you very much. If, as I've heard said, it's a miracle the Negro race survived and foolish people like Shepherd and others say it's because of the violent resistance of people like Fulton Armstead, he is terribly wrong. Because it would not have survived with its humanity intact and able to contribute to all other people of this world if it weren't for people like you, Joubert. If I don't marry Shepherd Bottomly, and it seems unlikely, then I haven't deserted you, or Shepherd and family for that matter, because you will always be in my life. I'm part of what happens to you all, because I am related to you all.

Love,
Mary Frances Bacon

P.S. I tried to get that Mahalia Jackson record you've got. (The Billie Holiday I've found and listened to when I can take it, which ain't easy, baby.) I hanker to hear "Oh Didn't It Rain." It reminds me of that night in your room, but I find it is unobtainable here. It's available in the United States of America only. . . . Hope some day to find it.

P.P.S. Invisible Man—*absolutely unbelievable novel. Quite a masterpiece.* Like Crime and Punishment, *one simply couldn't put it down. Thanks, Joubert, for recommending it . . . and never once putting me down.*

From the room next door, I could hear Beethoven's Fifth Symphony reaching yet another crescendo.

I slipped a note beneath Shep's door reminding him about the plan for tonight. We would go out to the Night Light Lounge to close up and then catch a jazz set.

P.P.P.S. Shepherd often talks about going eyeball to eyeball, stone-cold sober, man to woman.

It all looks quite dreadful, Joubert, almost as if Shepherd truly is a schizoid. I have no idea of what expectations, intentions, etc., Shepherd Bottomly has for coming here and I simply can't prepare myself—after all these shivering months through the chills and tortures of our mismatched hearts. As you yourself, Joubert, might say, I'd be a nut to be hopeful. It seems that the conclusions that I came to at Christmas were justified; that there is simply no justice in this affair for Mary Frances Essault Bacon. I am full of foreboding about his ever coming alive to my love for him for any longer than a phase of the moon. At least in Forest County we parted lovingly. And I still care and Shepherd does, too, probably, as much as he is capable of—but it doesn't seem as if Shepherd is capable of anything deep, nor any realistic commitment, over more than twenty-eight days. It's as if somebody had a pair of seamstress scissors (in the long-ago and faraway time of his past) and cunningly snipped away at the outer ring of Shepherd's heart; this bruised heart never healed properly.

Despite all of the bags he comes out of (as you often proclaim it in your engagingly idiomatic way), the heart of the matter is still this: Shepherd blames all of his shortcoming and personal unsuitability on racial disfranchisement. There is little question that the powers and principalities of the White Western World of Capitalism—Spewing—Democracy—for—All sails under false colors. Let me quote to you something Shepherd wrote to me recently. (His letters are rarely what one would call love letters.) "There is a heinous undertow of values below the marketplace (which actually drives the very cultural lifeline of this economy) and there does dwell and thrive those powers who have sold their souls. Here of course I'm not talking about the soul in a spiritual sense, nor surely not from the angle of vision that black America overuses this term. I'm simply talking about the shock that occurred within humankind that happened hundreds of thousands of years ago that makes us capable of being a little higher in mental potential for scientific thought and decency than the animals. But these corrupted sensualists of the marketplace set the price (blood, bondage, and material usurpation) for the very symmetry of those above ground, even as they feed and nourish on the blood, labor, sweat, and profit of the blood pumped from above ground to their awaiting troughs."

Yet all of the imperialistic abominations of this world, Joubert, are not soaked in blood and steeped in the fetters of racial persecution. To be sure there is much of this, particularly from a minority's perspective; and I am surely aware of persecution as a woman, if not being involved with Shepherd has *surely awakened me to a new level of consciousness. I am very unhappy about Shepherd and the shape he is in. He is so dreadfully needful. A shipwreck in the sights of we few (deploying binoculars) and a long way from home, or to the lighthouse.*

Love,
Mary Frances Essault Bacon

Chapter 2

The last time I took Shep Bottomly out to Eloise's Night Light Lounge, it proved to be too much for him. Some of the regulars were roasting McGovern McNabb and it was too terrible for Shep's eyes to behold this six-foot, six-inch, nearly four-hundred-pound McGovern. Once again, McNabb had become virtually ossified and not near a stage of wakefulness yet, although that's what they appeared to be prodding him into. To awaken him into consciousness through tough-edged signifying.

Talcum Tommie, Fat, Gracie Rae Gooden, Freddy, Fly, Flint, and Nighthawk Townsend were participating. They were standing in a semi-circle. Daisy Dawes was perched upon a barstool. The seven customers were standing near each other for drinks over whose most outrageous signifying riffs and dozen playing taunts could and would "awaken" McNabb first, because they believed he was really taking it hard.

Assuming that the remarks were vicious, vital enough, profane, imaginative, and cunning in their species of wit, to call McNabb out of the stew of his nightmare of sleep (because of the power of their evocative voices full of flaming verbal torches). Then the night-enshrouded McNabb would be forced to stand up or go down, dead. But that's when it occurred to me that customers were not using a substitute or even an escapegoat for McNabb. Hell, they were preaching his funeral. And the body-wracked, hypersensitive soul of Shep just couldn't take it, but I'll give him one thing. At least he tried as he soaked up his Budweiser. For the denizens believed in playing a game deeper than his.

"Preaching a sermon over McNabb," I assured him, "in order to astonish the Terrible Tonnage into a state of wakefulness."

"McNabb, I hear tell Lucifer slipped your mammy in the dozens so hard she foamed at the mouth, lay there on that very floor you're lying on now, just a-pleading for more; never to leave her side, never to stop riffing on your profane trumpet no matter what he was saying," cried Talcum Tommie.

"I'd simply say McGovern McNabb's inner parts are rusted out. His outer body is greasy and his soul is gutless. But will you ever look for a day and see how lubricated that head of his glows," offered Nighthawk Townsend to Talcum Tommie.

Gracie Rae said, "Greasy? Yes. Gutless not body and soul. Buttless?"

"McGovern McNabb was always so bad-assed," Fly started up, "thought his piss on a dead tree make the limbs sprout green leaves in January."

"His niece thought of herself as becoming a nun."

"Are you trying to say McNabb's half-ass?"

"Old timer is half past twelve on a yallar man's face clock."

"McNabb's been KO'd so many times himself that down looks like up to him."

Daisy Dawes kept waving her wobbly, cardboard church fan with her preacher's portrait in his face.

"McNabb's one sorry-ass, I'll put it down that way up."

"Old Rib-Roast is one royal rum and pain in the ass," offered Flint.

"But greasy on the surface of his skin and crown, not to the bone?" He was a chef.

"Boneyard, you mean?" Fly said.

"Tub of boiling stewmeat without a crackle of bone. Oh, they say he could really burn that train down, before they railroaded."

"A butt of lard and boatload of chitterlings."

"It is my understanding that the human form contains nine feet of intestines. Terrible Tonnage probably is possessed by thirteen feet and nine inches of wrinkles."

"Rodents of hell gonna have a tall-tale time of 'em. Gonna rip and run and cavort and devour like they on the highway and back road to heaven, and living high on the hog," Gracie Rae said.

"When the butchers cut him down on Fat Tuesday, the ants and worms gonna have a World War Three blitzkrieg through the battlefield of his guts," Flint said.

"But what a head. Lost his crown over at Hedy's once upon a time. Gals over there declared if the circumference of his crown was any indication of his Johnson's radius, gonna put down her habits, pick up a shawl, and join up with nuns; Black Muslims, too."

"Thirteen point nine ahaha inches. Ain't too, too bad. I'd be thrilled to hoooold that in nat-natu-ral hand. Give a heap of ladies loads of loooow-tion and tons of sat-is-faction," Freddy the clean-up man said to everyone's confused delight.

"He's a pistol all right."

"Some broads at Hedy's say he shoots off blanks with that cap pistol; but fires off some most poison airborne farts, and all in the same breath."

"He'd burn down a pure whore to a natural hoe with that detonator of his."

"Mac Mac ain't shit. His chitterlings ain't nothing but puddings," Nighthawk said.

"McNabb got tons of oil tucked away in the pouches of his intestines within the rolls of his belly. Enough to lighten up the wine-dark sea, to spy on the Old Man of the Sea, Proteus doing his magical flip-flops."

"Whales could set up some welfare relief if that went down."

"McNabb's daddy was the devil's understudy."

"Undertaker you mean."

"Underwriter, I say."

"Well, he got drafted. And you know one thing about Uncle Sam; he's the big whore in the whole world; he'll bunk down with any mammy's boy. But even in boot camp they commenced to referring to him by his dog-tag number."

"It's enough to make an atheist crawl from Mississippi to Harlem on both his hands and knees."

"What about his mother?" questioned Flint.

"Who ever-ever ever heard tell Nabby had ever-ever had a mother to-to begin with?" said Gracie Rae.

"Me, myself, and I heard tell his mother was a whale and his daddy a shark (a loan shark)," Nighthawk Townsend said.

"Was a sardine," corrected Fly. "I seed him naked."

Deep down upon the floor, the apparently sleeping McNabb snored grandly and gently offered up a fart: an effluvium of burnished hog's ears.

"This Mac Mac is trying to signify with his bounty horn. I'm gonna get my razor and carve up this turkey for the sharks," said Gracie Rae, who was very drunk.

"Nighthawk, listen up to what Gracie Rae is putting down. Sharks don't want McNabb's foul flanks. They're particular about the types of low-life humans they'll eat these days."

" 'Member that time his niece took him to the doctor about his weight, drinking, falling-out fits, gout, flat feet, fallen arches, crabbed-up toes, arteriosclerosis, angina, arthritis, hemorrhoids, lumbago, farting fumes, and heartburn?"

"Doctor said McGovern McNabb would have to take three boxes of Ex-Lax, six bottles of Black Draught, and nine bottles of Fleet's plunger for a starter-up. You know, to get him cleaned up and cleansed down."

"Why, I could tell her how close them whores over at Hedy's come to reporting to the authorities at Coyote, concerning the length of his farts and his long-legged Johnson."

"As long as his intestines," said Hawk.

"All I know is, plumber's union would have a shit fit if they hear tell of what McGovern McNabb is putting down."

"I recollect that time wherein Mac Mac died; went off to Heaven. But seeing as they only serve honey and milk up there, Nabby allowed as how he has drifted in on the wrong party. Meantime, he commenced to smelling that frying and righteous fumes of catfish just a-stirring, ascending into the skies. Fool became the first soul known in spatial history what begged to be sent to hell in a rocket ship. Thought he could get a job as the devil's head chef," Nighthawk said.

Everybody started cracking up. But I thought of that time we had placed fifty pounds of dirty clothes over his body, full of lice and everything unimaginable, and left him out there in the park. Six hours later, what did he do but transform them filthy rags and tatters into an eight-foot bear's outfit, and scared the holy hell out of some Halloween trick-or-treaters. Shamefaced up behind the masquerades of our so-called civility, or it should have.

At high noon the next day, I was at the desk, working on the transformation of my notes towards an epic play for much of the early afternoon.

Now I noted from my window—looking out to the streets—the cocksman Purvis Cream enter the Avon with one of his special major mollies, Zenobia. It was about 1:30. I remember looking at the clock on the wall and thinking, it is way past my lunch hour.

I continued to work at my writing desk, between scoops of red beans and rice and cups of beer. About 2:45, I reclined across my bed and soon was asleep, coming in and out of layers of dreams.

Then, I was dreaming of that story W. A. D. Ford told of the time he got busted of the treasures he had put up in a crapshoot. For a time, he had worked in a carnival sideshow in order to make pocket money. In his double-sized funhouse fantasy booth, Ford placed one hundred and one mirrors of subtly varied sizes, and at strategic juxtapositions, so that the adults (kiddies, too) would be presented with "fragmented cells," or with various phases of their facial identities, Ford said, which that billboard to the sideshow pregnantly proclaimed.

I woke up about five minutes to three. While fixing a pot of tea, I observed yet another one of Purvis Cream's lady friends—hot-tempered Henrietta—advancing towards the Avon only half a block away. My God, I thought.

I immediately hurried out of the room into the hallway, to make a call on the wall phone adjacent to the landlady's office, and up to Purvis Cream's apartment (before it was too late and where the swift and speedy lover had his own telephone near his bed).

"Man, you'd better get Zenobia out of your room, pronto; piss pronto. Henrietta is picking 'em up and laying 'em down, and she's about to lay her fist on the downstairs doorbell."

"Bear-Meat man, you just crashed my ass out of a mellow shower. Had me a stash of big-fun weed waiting with a jigger of Chivas Regal on the side to warm me between joints."

I could hear Purvis Cream take a long-legged drag on his weed just now, then continue: "Plus, baby-sweets, no reason for H to ring, she's got a key to downstairs, that is. 'Sides, she's on the rag. Dig it! Z left twenty minutes ago, in time to make her gig. Bear-Butt, they clocking in, they clocking out, on time, and according to my stopwatch. You been snoring (and maybe snorting, too) on guard duty, through all the deep-sea diving and the laying cut action, Jackson? Some sorry-assed sentinel. Now get on back to your keyboard, Mr. Typewriter. Try to make the scene on that paper, since you ain't making it on the white sheets with no hot type, if you know what I mean."

Purvis Cream rarely referred to his stockade of ladies when he was talking to others about them by their full names. He'd call them Z or H, or his other affairs might be heralded as X, Y, Z. Soon you could hear the banging too loudly on her lover's door. I turned and headed back to my room. Purvis Cream's got 'em clocked—coming and going, I reflected wearily. All of which got me to thinking back to an earlier birthday party at the Rumpus Room when Purvis suddenly left about 11:45. Left Henrietta with the line that he had to go out south to meet a man at a bar on a surefire deal—to pick up a hot TV, twenty-inch screen, for thirty-five dollars. Set ran originally for one hundred fifty dollars; that he'd join the party at Joy Willoughby's apartment, "later alligator."

Actually, Purvis Cream was rushing off to Forest County Hospital to check on Zenobia, who was giving birth to his baby. He had left her in the early stages of labor on the alibi that he had to clock in early to his gig until he got some relief to take his place, or get fired, before picking up Henrietta. As a male nurse at University Hospital, he had worked across town from the Forest County Hospital. Cream took Zenobia to the Forest County Hospital and stayed with her long enough to get her through the first hour of her labor. He wasn't sure if her labor signs were true or false. He then split, claiming he had to get to his gig at University Hospital, only in point of fact, he had taken the night off to be at my birthday party, and mainly to be with Henrietta, momentarily.

Purvis Cream got back to the ongoing party about 2:45. Henrietta gushed into the arms of Purvis when he entered the apartment. Her long-lost hero was back from the wars. How could he pull it all off, I wondered out loud? Twenty minutes later, Purvis went down in the car and was soon back with a twenty-inch TV, which he proceeded to give to me for a birthday present. The gift was the hit of the party and it sealed the honor of Cream's story. When I got the television home that morning, Shep Bottomly and I discovered that the damn thing didn't work.

Purvis Cream took care of the money for at least three women of so-called independent means that I knew directly of. There was also Yvonne, or Y. Zenobia worked as a medical technician at Mercy Hospital where she mainly did mammograms. Henrietta was a nurse at Forest County Hospital. They would give Purvis Cream their money and he would put it into his bank account, he once explained to me with great sobriety casting its way upon his medium-light-brown complexion.

Keeping each of his ladies' money separate in the economy of his own imaginative pigeonholing, Purvis Cream gave each woman a stipend to live on. That was his word, "stipend." It was actually an allowance. Purvis showed me several elaborate twelve-column worksheets of how he specifically handled and divided their contributions. He had also invested "their money," as "our bread," into several lucrative enterprises through the saving and planning advice of certain physicians and surgeons whom he admired greatly. They were always putting Purvis on to something good.

I thought of these lost-and-found ladies gone (there may well be more than three, I reflected) as I showered and prepared to go to the hospital to see Leonard Foster the next day. For Purvis Cream had devised a kind of pyramid club for handling their "contributions." Yet rather than look like a flagrant, heartless cad, he held the actual numbers down, I reasoned. Whenever they needed money, in addition to their monthly stipend that he gave out on the twenty-eighth day of each and every month, Purvis would immediately go to their account ("not mine but our accounts," he'd always say) and withdraw the money. The interest on the account remained that of Purvis Cream's, of course. But whenever he would break up with any lady, there it was: their bread. He'd go and withdraw the exact amount of money she had given Purvis for his safekeeping. Plus, he'd give each a certain amount of interest on the principle (never the proportion the money had actually earned). After all, it was still Purvis's account; therefore, his generosity in turning his account into their account for the lifetime of their romance. "Their dust and my dust is still commingled," he would submit, for the life of their romance, long after their romance had ended. "Greater love haveth no man. . . . You're a poet, Joubert. You should dig the depths of the shit. Besides, I don't just take in any old average kind of slipshod broad. She has to pass an inspection test that's tougher than any kind of lower G.I.

they give at the Forest County Hospital, I can tell you that, my man."
Purvis had convinced each lady that he had been acting in her interest
in keeping her money in his account in the first place, lest she squander
it all away. This would be a kind of kitty that they had together and
the lady in question would have this memory of Purvis darling—and
how they actually had shared a bank account once upon a time. Then,
you'd find him hovered over a glass of Chivas Regal, reefer in hand,
tears welling up in his eyes, and playing Bird's "Just Friends" over and
over again.

As I reflected, in many ways, Purvis Cream could convince his women
that he was actually taking care of them over and beyond their own
capacities to take care of themselves, despite the fact that each produced
a paycheck (of their very own) at least twice a month. Also, it finally
became clear to me that while the individual woman was under the spell
of Purvis, "the contribution to our account" allowed the lady in question
to forget about money and actually think there was a possibility for the
next step, the big step, down the aisle (as revealed at the birthday party
by the lady-in-waiting, Henrietta). And that combined-bank-account
routine indicated Purvis Cream's marriageable attitude. It could not be
long before "Here Comes the Bride" was heard, and "I'll be the lucky
one," Henrietta said, shortly before she helped blow out the candles on
my birthday cake.

To the

Magical

Memory

of Rain

....

Rain

Evening, a sudden clearing of the mist,
For now a fine, soft rain is sifting down.
It falls, it fell, was falling-surely rain
Is something that always happens in the past.

Hearing it fall, the senses will be led
Back to a blessed time that first disclosed
To the child a flower that was called *the rose*
And an extraordinary color, *red.*
These drops that blind our panes to the world outside
Will brighten the black grapes on a certain trellis
Out in the far, lost suburbs of the town

Where a courtyard was. The dripping afternoon
Brings back the voice, the longed-for voice,
Of my father, who has come home, who hasn't died.

Jorge Luis Borges
translated by Richard Barnes

There was a young woman by the name of Desirée Dobbs, who was quite strange, very beautiful, and easily enchanted by some things and not so enchanted by others; she had been sheltered by a mother who had read nothing but fairy tales to the girl up to the time Desirée was fourteen.

The young woman's father, whom she remembered with keening fondness, had died when Desirée was but nine years old; and because he was killed in a terrible accident, the mother received a monthly allotment, which was sufficient for her and the child to live on, if they lived quite frugally. "Frugal" was one of the words Desirée had learned to spell and think about a lot as a small child growing up. The widow often took in sewing in order to augment the pension she received from the telephone company, which started three months after Desirée's father was killed in a sudden thunderstorm as he descended a telephone pole.

In the heart of Desirée, the arrival each month of the pension check marked another memory of her father's tragic death, echoing through the aching, living presence, even as it recollected his violent death. On many occasions, the father had appeared before Desirée out of a night of tumultuous rain.

But when Desirée had attempted to look closer, he had vanished back into the stormy night. These appearances occurred, often as not, when Desirée had done something to upset her mother. Desirée awoke finding herself screaming: "Take me with you!" But except for his picture on the mantel, the father of Desirée was nowhere to be found. The mother, who was a deep sleeper, heard none of this. They often argued fiercely over precise memories of the dead man's body and soul, in the light of day. Desirée was quite fond of the mother, but there was something missing in their relationship; "I cannot put my finger on it," she often said to herself. The gulf between the two women appeared to be growing. She often wondered if, in fact, she really loved her own mother.

With her nose pressed against the windowpane, when there was a fine and gentle rain to hear inside the gathering beads of precipitation, which made everything clear that was unclear and unclear that was clear, Desirée discovered herself trying to trace seven droplets to their doom with her finger. Thinking one particular one was especially blessed because it got stalled midway down and would not go down dead. Fine flicks of rain upon her windowpane always commanded Desirée to back up in time. . . .

"Take three steps back, then dribble forward. It unveils the beauty of the leaves in the trees, where I take my pictures with the camera Daddy left behind for my hands alone. Summons his voice back to me, though he died out a terrible thunder. But because of rain, when it's as gentle as leaves of springtime, lace, and prayer, he is unveiled to me: undead Daddy in a blessed hour when he unfolded to me the meaning often of the dearest things of nature, in the park, at the zoo . . . the magic and the miracle of how even a camera worked. What didn't he know? That all should be in harmony in nature. . . . The fall-of-the-rain sound on this window is his voice, his step. . . . Fine upon the window it is the perspiration beads upon his face, after doing a heavy work of exercise . . . of building my dollhouse, so that I can come along with a towel so very big to handle and wipe away the gathered perspiration from his temple (where God dwells) and the contours of his princely face, which is also my face to trace, with my fingers, there and now upon this windowpane, so full of grieving rain. When I see the fine and gentle rain, I hear echoes of Daddy dear, nothing that Dreaded Death can never, ever. Dreaded Death has no music to make this echo of his voice and footfall unreal."

As they had sought shelter and refuge from the storms of life, Desirée and the mother had moved from neighborhood to neighborhood over the years, in order to combine modest, affordable, respectable living within the confines of a decent community; and this mode of "migratory" living, as Desirée called it, became increasingly difficult, and a course of constant upheaval to the soul of Desirée. This young woman had transferred schools seven times in the last four years, in the attempt to find a neighborhood that was safe, and where the schools were good. Now she was attending an all-girls Catholic school, Sacred Heart of Jesus. Desirée was an honor student for the most part in school, except for the fact that she shocked her mother, Mother Superior, and the nuns, to the point at which they all stood stock-still, when it was proven beyond a shadow of doubt that Desirée had absolutely no aptitude for geometry.

"You must rein in your many talents," the nun Sister Mary Marie said.

The mother could not but reflect upon the problem of escaping from the woe of turning neighborhoods and second-rate schools, which had plagued her as well. And she remembered how her very own dear and departed mother had persuaded the lovely Jewish couple, for whom she worked as a maid, to allow her daughter, Desirée's mother Felicity, to use their address to attend Brighton High, then ranked as the third-best public school in the state, and fifteenth in the nation.

Desirée had three hobbies: reading, her dollhouse, and photography. Her father had given Desirée a fine camera the week before he was struck down. The camera had been quite advanced for the time. Desirée carried this camera everywhere her heart traveled.

Desirée Dobbs was quite beautiful to look upon, blessed with a fabulous figure and the alluring eyes of a starlet; the young woman stayed in the apartment most of the time when she wasn't out in the park, taking pictures of trees, small children at play on the swings, and strolling lovers. Desirée often read deep into the night, until those bewitching eyes became heavy with sleep (took a last long look at some irresistible but real vision of the most gorgeous guy in the world of magazines); then looked into the seven mirrors, just above her vanity table, in the small cupboard of a room that the mother had converted into a sewing room. Then Desirée would fall asleep. Sometimes she would dream of her father, or of that very attractive medical student whom she had assisted in her senior year in high school.

It was the handsome young med student's job to surgically remove the hearts of live white rats for experimentation. On several occasions, Desirée had been almost struck off her perch upon the high stool in the laboratory by how closely his sleek platinum-blond hair and that of the rat's coat of white fur had become associated in her imagination, until he turned a swift, glacial glare upon Desirée, in order to bring his assistant back to the reality of her (waiting) chores in the laboratory. The young student thought that the transfixed Desirée was so mesmerized by the operation that she had become hypnotized. Then Desirée Dobbs would scurry off into a tiny nook of a room shelter, normally employed as a room for the staff, to avoid not the work but this man's eyes. There she would dote on romantic stories she was reading, or her favorite Greek myths. On one occasion—after banishing herself from his presence— Desirée raced out of the hospital, down the steps, only to discover a rainstorm. The memory of a Nigerian seamstress came streaking across the landscape of her imagination out of the turbulence. And then she heard the African woman's words, rendered up in a chilling laughter not unlike the April rain she found herself in: "Beware of the naked woman who offers you a skintight dress."

In her heart of hearts, it occurred to Desirée Dobbs this very day that what she hungered for most was a man with an excess of spirit who would awaken her floundering imagination through the furor of his magical touch, which would be all steel, robed in deep, dark velvet.

In addition to a sewing machine, Desirée's room also contained a rack for dresses and the rather large dollhouse that Desirée's father had crafted for her—even before she had started to ask for dolls— with his own hands. Desirée had taken the dollhouse everywhere they had moved. (In recent weeks Desirée had lodged some of her growing paperback book collection of the classics of literature in compartments and rooms of the dollhouse.) Once upon a time Desirée had fashioned a nativity scene in this dollhouse, with the figures of Mary and Joseph and the shepherds, and the Babe shaped out of the tinfoil and scraps of materials from out of the mother's sewing basket used for clothing. The hay in the manger, where Desirée had placed the Babe, was formed from brittle bits of straw, broken away from the bottom of the broom in the kitchen pantry. She had determined to do this good deed after hearing the story of how Herod had tried to play a harsh hoax on the three wise men, so that knowledge of the Babe's whereabouts would be delivered into the evil of his devising hands.

Desirée often spoke of the spatial confines of her secret place, a projected dreamhouse fashioned from the slants of the sun. Glances from the rays of the falling stars would provide her with a sturdy baton of brilliance, which she would also use as a warning wand to the world, to ward off evil spirits and to welcome good hearts and souls into the circle of her embrace. Desirée spoke of a white robe spun from the Milky Way, in which she would command, with the wand in her hand, all who crept within her purview with great dispatch and fairness. Yet another side of Desirée believed dearly in the words that she often heard from her favorite priest, Father Fabian. That if you were a true Catholic, then you were in this world but not of this world. . . . At moments like this, the words of Desirée's saintly soul came forth. "The currency by which the world transports its deals, covenants, and bargains is haunted and stained by marked money, dripping with blood. You must remember this," her astonishing father had said to Desirée as he placed a kiss of goodnight upon the temple of his young daughter.

But during those times when her soul soared to the heights, Desirée often said to herself, in an imaginative fling, "Let me scurry off for my camera to capture this world." Desirée rarely spoke to anyone about her great dream of the high-flying, most Gorgeous Guy in the world, who would rescue her just as she was in the throes of a terrible monster and would take her off to a paradise not made by hands but eternal in time and space, forevermore. Desirée longed to do something quite reckless with the man who could and would introduce into her life this excess of energy, amid the proper amount of romantic adventure of the most vaulting kind imaginable.

The widow had said that in order to secure the best possible educational setting for Desirée that she would never purchase a television. Some opera was played on the radio. The story of Carmen was her favorite. Strains of classical music were allowed. The girl had never entered into the darkened theater where motion pictures were projected upon a silver screen in her life.

But there was this unforgettable, strange experience that had drawn her to the sideshow at the carnival, with her mother, when she was twelve. She dreamed often about it, and it was all mixed up with her father, the camera and the binoculars that he had given her, and his beckoning, beckoning, beckoning expression out of an enchantment of smoking rings. . . .

■ ■ ■ ■ ■

At the carnival, Desirée had loved the magicians. And there were seven of them—tall and handsome. Desirée worshiped this team of handsome, guitar-playing magicians. After their performance closed out, she discovered from a woman standing next to her that they all wore masks, Greek, African, Asian, and Nordic masks, so who was to tell what they looked like, truly. But one thing was for sure, each played a most alluring song upon his guitar.

Into the inner sanctum of this carnival world stumbled Desirée. She had finally drifted away from her mother. Lost in her search for the cotton candy booth, she ended up in front of the stage, where a blazing Technicolor sign proclaimed STEP IN-SIDE-OUT OF YOURSELF. FUNHOUSE FANTASIES. And high above this sign, in the most glaring lettering she had ever read:

GETTING TO KNOW THE SECRET FACE:
THE ONE YOU WEAR BEHIND THE MASK

More than anything else Desirée sought a magic wand of words of wonder, which would distill all into a miraculous moment of everlasting ecstasy that would also be a moment of reverie, something akin to a permanently glowing reverie. Yes, and return her father to her. Because for a long time, Desirée could not accept the death, the murderous electrical storm of her father. . . . And thinking she had actually seen the live body of her dead father, she had slipped away from her mother, saying she was going over there for cotton candy, while her mother continued on in idle chatter with some male high school chum she just happened to see in front of the pay booth leading to the Ferris wheel.

And so Desirée slipped off into this tent, where her eyes had last traced the handsome stranger who wore a Dobbs hat just like her father's, and she was so certain, and the heart of Desirée thundered in the chamber of her chest.

But the man who keenly resembled her father, from a distance, was nowhere to be seen inside the carnival sideshow amid the large and unruly crowd. But what did appear out of the sudden eruption of the mob of many colors was the man billed simply as the Worldwide Wizard. And Desirée observed how so many colors composed the complexion of this man upon the improvised stage, which was positioned in the very middle of the enlarged booth, where he could see all. Even though Desirée was some forty feet from the stage, she wished that she had a pair of binoculars about her neck, which would allow her to look deeper into this fascinating man's face. She had the camera her father had given her but wondered if picture taking was permitted. Probably not.

The legendary W. W. W. Ford, as he was also billed, wore a purple smoking jacket; faded, starched, and sharply ironed blue jeans; alligator shoes; a lavender shirt; a high-top lily-white hat, with a red plume set jauntily in the band. He was smoking a long, elegant-looking cigar. In his left hand W.W.W. held something akin to a leathery pointer (or a stuffed snake). Desirée came to believe with all of her heart that the thing in his hand was a wand of some sort. Although she did remember with great delight the pipe and aroma of her father's tobacco, Desirée didn't like the smell of the janitor's cigar, which always "polluted" the first floor after he had run the carpet sweeper in the morning. The smoke curled into being from the lips of the Worldwide Wizard intrigued, allured, and drew Desirée towards the stage. And to her amazement, W.W.W. appeared to be beckoning her towards the stage, through the magic of the smoke rings.

Desirée found herself being ushered forth by some compelling force . . . out of the reverie within the flow from the cigar smoke, she pondered deeply. He must be smoking a very expensive cigar, she reasoned, composed of the finest tobaccos and crafted in some faraway land, this side of paradise. The fleeting memory of seeing the opera *Carmen* (where the furious beauty had worked at a cigar factory) flew past Desirée's imagination so quickly she could not grasp; for just at that moment, the astonishing W. W. W. Ford commenced to send up the most intriguing set of smoke rings; perfected circles, magically crafted swooping upwards circles, which drew the young woman ever closer to the stage. Perhaps if she got closer, she might see her father or see the place where he had drifted off the very face of the earth. Nothing had appeared before her living eyes as stimulating as this W. W. W. Ford, but Desirée for the life of her could not tell exactly what it was that so entranced her about the man who appeared to blow life into magical circles. Of course, her father had often delighted Desirée by blowing nearly perfect rings from the smoke of his pipe. But nothing had intrigued her as much as this W.W.W. since the time when as a girl Desirée had discovered that she had a crush on Mandrake the Magician, and despised Narda for the proximity the woman had to Desirée's hero. Meantime, in her eyes Ford appeared to be beckoning Desirée, and her alone, to come closer, closer, closer to the stage.

■ ■ ■ ■ ■

Desirée had been overwhelmed by the wonderful world of art, particularly when Sacred Heart School engaged the services of the noted playwright Joubert Antoine Jones for a presentation. Mr. Jones gave nine workshops/seminars under the general banner of "My life, as springboard for the creative writing experience."

Desirée kept a Penworthy pad filled with copious notes, recording everything Joubert Jones said. She wrote down on her pad: "Mr. Joubert Antoine Jones led the classroom and taught through example how to use your experiences, and ways we could use our very own memories as the basis for stories and poems, and scenes for plays. The samples out of his laboratory revealed how a well-trained imagination can transform the ordinary into the extraordinary. And this is how he has been able to take his material and round it all out into character sketches for personalities we've come to see and love on the stage in his plays. Or character sketches he is currently 'working up' into roles. He even went so far as to bring in actors who have either appeared in his plays, or who are going to appear in his plays, in the near future.

"The fact that a prizewinning playwright took up this amount of time with us (yes, I realize he was paid, but still in all this project took up time that he could have spent at his writing desk) really speaks volumes about this man's values.

"We were required to write and produce one, one-act play for the class, using our fellow classmates in assigned roles. Yes, employ, because we had to actually pay them a certain amount, which came from the receipts of our different productions, at the school. All of this was great! However, the writing was something else again. I selected my father as my leading man and tried to express how much his building of my dollhouse meant so much to me. In the play I made a crash of lightning kill my father, and when this happens I had the heroine's dollhouse also struck down and broken into smithereens. Then the stage was darkened and the play was over. Everybody wept at the ending, even Mother. I ran into the bathroom and stayed for twenty minutes, crying, vomiting, and wailing over what I had done, what I had created. Finally the Mother Superior came into the bathroom and ordered me out of my confusion and heartache.

"Now I'm wondering if I would like to be a writer, after all, if it causes this much grief."

One the stories out of his life that Joubert Jones told Desirée's class concerned a revival scene that Desirée Dobbs could not get out of her mind. She thought this story continued to intrigue her because it involved factors that were close to her life. Like her, Mr. Jones had been raised as a Catholic. Yet this story involved elements of ritual outside of her upbringing within the faith. It revealed aspects of religion she was only vaguely familiar with. And as it had happened with Mr. Jones, this story broke across her path with fear and trembling and very definitely out of the blue.

On his way to a pickup game of basketball, Joubert Jones came across a place where a huge tent was being erected for a revival. He found the pickup game, perhaps a mile away. But the fascinating thing was that he was drawn back to the revival later that evening, and what he saw and heard apparently had great impact on him, eclipsing the sermon he had heard at the noonday Mass at his home church, rendered up by a German pastor with a most prodigious voice. Jones felt that this event had helped to reshape his life and he described it in his lecture "The Transformation of the Self."

■ ■ ■ ■ ■

Last June, Desirée and her mother had attended a wedding of a third cousin (female), where the couple's best man and maid of honor sang a beautiful love song, shortly after the priest pronounced them man and wife. During the singing, Desirée suddenly discovered a deep crush developing for the best man, within her own heart. Why was it that the very terms "best man" and "maid of honor" were infinitely more enticing than "bride" and "groom"? And more pleasing to the ear. The duet had the most beautiful singing voices, she had whispered to her mother as they (and the five hundred spectators) listened to the duo singing in an especially rounded off and elevated space, just beneath the statue of Jesus and His Sacred Heart there at Blood of the Lamb Cathedral. The best man had a wonderfully rich baritone and his partner a lyrical soprano, and, though not the most gorgeous guy in the world, he would do, this best man, until the real thing came along. Desirée found herself embarrassed over this admission. The bridesmaids all wore sleek and shimmering silver dresses.

But on the train ride home from the wedding, Desirée overheard several of the younger men gossiping, in a matter-of-fact manner, that the bride was two months pregnant, and that the adorable flower girl and ring-bearer were offspring of the married couple. One girl laughed and joked that the bride was lucky to have finally hooked him, even though it took two and a half pregnancies to "reel that sucker in." To her considerable chagrin, Desirée overheard the gossips now deliver reports on the best man and maid of honor, from their seats across the aisle as they played four-hand bid whist, that the best man was only allowed to serve and sing because he was on a recently devised release program for prisoners, and that the maid of honor was a recovering drug addict. She wept a long time to herself, as Felicity slept for nearly all of the six-hour train ride back to Forest County. Finally the words crept across the landscape of her mind—endlessly, "but who will be my maid of honor?"

For nothing up to this time had more shocked Desirée than the news of the private lives behind the wedding party. Nothing had upset her sensibilities so much since the time when a drunken uncle had spilled red paint on her dollhouse (accidentally, no doubt, but the deed was done). The heirloom from her father's hand, defiled.

About forty-five minutes before the train arrived in Forest County, Desirée fell asleep and dreamed of one of her three favorite myths, the story of Orpheus and Eurydice.

■ ■ ■ ■ ■

There were several other Greek myths that caught Desirée's devotion, concerning the lives of the Divinities. When she and her mother returned from the wedding, Desirée determined that she would enter the speech competition at Sacred Heart, in which the students were invited to recite from memory a Greek or Roman myth, and to dramatize the saga in any way they chose, as long as they didn't vulgarize the essential meanings of the story.

Desirée—who liked to dream of herself as a goddess from time to time—loved most of all the tale of Diana, the Virgin (actually, more than she worshiped the story of the Virgin Mary), centered on that time Diana had gone off to bathe and, certain that she had found a safe and sheltered place, gave over the immediate instruments of powers to her serving maidens, the nymphs, her javelin, her quiver, and her bow to one nymph, to another nymph her robe, meantime the third knelt at the feet of the goddess and unstrapped the sandals from her lovely feet. Desirée found her soul soaring out of her body as she retold this awesome tale before the select committee.

Soon other nymphs poured water from urns for Diana to bathe in. Hidden away in a cave, as it were, all of the females felt a degree of safety. But soon a traveling marauder came upon the scene, at the very apron of the cave, and the nymphs, as soon as they saw the young man, ran to hide the nakedness of the bathing huntress queen from the ravishing eyes of this young man. As they attempted to shield the bare body of tall Diana with their bodies, they screamed to warn the chaste huntress of their concern, for the queen was shocked with surprise at the male presence, and she turned many colors of the rainbow. Because of her height, this male could see part of her nakedness not covered by the bodies of the loyal nymphs.

Diana now immediately turned to seize her arrows, but she could not get to them, so she thought to hurl a gush of sparkling water from the fountain where she bathed. Then she screamed out loud to the man with the offending eyes: "Go and tell now, if you are able, that you have set eyes upon the naked goddess, Diana!" Immediately a set of stag's horns emerged from this hunter's head.

Then the voice of Desirée, alarmed with excitement, cried out in ecstasy: "His ears swooped up like saber points; soon, all parts of his once-smooth body—his legs, his feet, his hands—were a forest of hair, and a hairy, spotted hide adorned his body. Now fear consumed the so-called brave hunter and bold intruder (even now, as several of his hunting party sought out his driftwood whereabouts, the dogs leading the way).

"For just as he made up his mind to run away—as if to escape his afflicted condition—his own dogs set upon this hunter. Soon one of his dogs buried his teeth into the stag of a man; yet another seized upon his shoulders. Then the others from the pack were now upon him, setting their teeth into his flesh. Following his dogs were the hunters' companions, for they thought by following their trail, they would soon come upon their ally. They called out his name, at a passageway where the dogs had for some reason stopped, as if for respite. He turned when he heard his name ring out through the leafless trees. But his compatriots could not see what had become of the young hunter amid his dogs. The terrorized Diana, of course, was without pity for this swine, this stag, until his dogs had turned on the intruder and torn his life out of him, and ripped all of his flesh away."

So powerful and eloquent had been Desirée's rendition of the Greek myth of Diana that she was awarded first prize for oration and performance at Sacred Heart High School.

■ ■ ■ ■ ■

On this particular first day of May, after the mother and Desirée had returned from cashing the monthly pension check, the woman found herself looking down at this young woman who was seated before the seven mirrors (her head buried now in Tolstoy's *Anna Karenina*), and Felicity found herself reflecting once again upon how much Desirée favored the deceased husband, a man so very handsome that women would actually turn in the streets to admire him. A solitary star. This gift of the solitary star glanced up at her mother, just now, with tears welling up in those lovely eyes, which were the eyes of her father. Mother and daughter were, more often than not, warring sisters over the actual meaning of the husband/father/sire/lover's legend. Besides, the young woman was about to turn eighteen tomorrow, and there was something Felicity needed to say to her—had needed to say for a long, long time. Yet perhaps today, she would get it all out . . . find her tongue.

There was of course the legend that a boy is blessed or lucky who very much resembles his mother; but what of a girl who greatly favors her father? And they were alike in many other attributes, jealously observed: for example, the role of the secret life. It was as if her dead husband had breathed that aspect of his life—along with his looks into the very fashioning stage behind the jails of Desirée's smile. Yet her smile afforded no key to the locket of Desirée's heart, Felicity thought, as she studied the girl, aided by the illuminating sunlight reflecting upon her face.

As Desirée dressed to go grocery shopping with her mother, she got to thinking of the myth of Vulcan, which for some strange reason always reminded Desirée of her deceased father. Kicked out of heaven because of his lameness, Vulcan was taken in by two sea goddesses, who cared for him for nine years. He became good at his trade. In order to avenge his mother's cruelty, he devised, while working at the very bottom of the sea, a crafty throne, and he sent this attractive seat to the mother. She readily accepted the gift—which she assumed to be a peace offering—but when she sat down on the throne, the mother was immediately made a prisoner by the unseen fetters and chains, which wound about and entrapped her body so that she could no longer rise. One God was able to get Vulcan's attention, to get him to undo what he had done. This was Bacchus (whom Desirée did not generally like yet found herself bewitched by). He was a friend of Vulcan's. He showered Vulcan with wine, led him to Olympus, and talked him into freeing Juno from her fetters.

Several young men, and older ones, too, had sought the daughter out, stalking Desirée down, in many cases. By clever and cunning means, they had so beleaguered this young woman that she had finally beseeched her mother to change their telephone number to an unlisted one in order to elude suitors, street royalty, ministers, vagabonds, pimple-faced imps, punks, professors, and social workers. She had announced to Desirée that all of this would have to stop. Stalkers, yes, anything to avoid them, but suitors with portfolio, young men on the way up, that was as normal as springtime. She had been reluctant to change their telephone number, seven times in the last three years, but she finally went along with the daughter's proposals, because of the rising number of assaults against females in the area. Two weeks before, Desirée's mother had decided to move once more. A shocking rape of an octogenarian had occurred just three doors from their apartment. But the point was, the mother reasoned, where could you hide?

The mother had thought seriously about getting a huge dog and putting him on a chain for the protection of herself and the daughter. But the realtors seemed angry over her proposal.

"A good watchdog would tear an attacker apart," she told Desirée. For her part, Desirée thought of getting a dog that she could call her own and place a nifty rhinestone collar about its throat.

Still Felicity pondered the problem of precisely *why* this beautiful young woman shunned all suitors and callers. Surely there must be some fellow worthy of the brightness in her smile, who would find the key and turn it to a new treasure stone of passion.

"Desirée, you won't be getting any younger," she said, as they now prepared to go shopping. Perhaps it was also because of the beautiful day in May, more than likely it was the very real presence of the pension check on this day, which also marked the anniversary of marriage to Desirée's father, but something else goaded her on.

"What's wrong with all of the fellows at school, or church? Is none swift enough to move your heart? Haven't these guys learned to talk to a girl, in the proper way?"

Perceiving herself as ever the practical romantic, Desirée now thought, *Who decided on naming me Desirée anyway?* Probably she has had a few drinks, after getting my daddy's check cashed. She can be a witch at times.

Placing her hands upon her hips, Desirée declared: "Nothing. Everything."

"All of them can't be sour grapes. Surely there must be one in the bunch with the heart and the passion to command and sustain the little fox's appetite over the course of more than three dates, and a final supper . . . one who can toll the bell to your heart. But what troubles you so? You act like a brokenhearted girl. Yet none have claimed you." Then she went off to the bathroom to finish putting on her makeup, leaving Desirée momentarily to mull over her words.

Immediately Desirée started to weep into the oval cage her hands made about her tearstained, lyrical face.

She thought of that poem Leonard Foster had dedicated to her. He was a wild, crazy poet; and he had tried to get Desirée involved in political activities, but all of his urgent attempts "to turn you around" seemed plotted misadventures to Desirée.

■ ■ ■ ■ ■

As she applied her makeup before the mirror in the bathroom, Felicity thought of Desirée. He who might hold the keys to your heart must play upon the strings of your heart, with the fingers of a talented harpist. Then, thinking about this first day of May, the anniversary, about her own dead husband, whose body and spirit were beloved in her memory and so filled with energy. Oh, the unfairness of life. Struck down in the prime of life. And their great, unbridled passion together (except for that one transgression, or had there been more?), when it suddenly occurred to the woman that perhaps this beautiful Desirée, who cried so easily over plays, and wept upon the pages of great love literature, who so resembled the passionate lover of her very own heart, *was in love with herself, alone* . . . even as she could hear the hypersensitive Desirée weep so profusely just now before her seven mirrors, in the wee sewing room. Was Desirée without heartstrings of her own to pluck? Then this image of a beautiful harp without strings broke upon the landscape of the woman's imagination. Yet with all of her heart, she could not tell this heartless young woman what she had set out to really unveil.

Now she roused the daughter from her tears, unfolded a handkerchief, and allowed the girl to wipe her eyes upon it. Then she put out the frozen cuts of lamb for the evening meal to defrost; it was the last meat they had in the refrigerator. Felicity brought a bright blue dress with long white ballooning sleeves; seven antique white buttons adorned the garment's high collar, which engulfed three-fourths of a neck. Felicity spread the dress that she had made with her own hands the length of her daughter's bed. It was the gloom around Desirée's body and soul that bothered her. Something was terribly wrong with this child. Just how would she take the news of this (despised) *gift?*

Soon the mother and daughter were off to shop on their regular, two-week grocery shopping ritual. It was a beautiful May day and the two women—one almost eighteen, the other thirty-six—hurried out to enjoy this rare spring blush so blessed with the freshness of spring, full of wonder and rare appetite of the elements and powerful with the impending energies of coming summer. And despite the pollution of Forest County, this day seemed swept up with a kind of pristine freshness, Desirée observed; and so perfect for picture taking. She vowed that as soon as they returned from shopping, she would fill her camera with film and dash out into the park to capture the beauty of this day in the eye of her camera.

At the supermarket their basket almost collided with that of the Nigerian seamstress, who had made her mother's wedding gown. They had not spoken in years. Soon Desirée left the women to their gossip over old times, and went into the next aisle to pick up some of the items on the shopping list. But she could not help but overhear the booming voice of the African woman tell a frightening tale to Felicity, about a young prostitute who was found dead in a garden apartment, where, as it turned out, Desirée and her mother had lived only six months before. Police were seeking "her pimp to question him about the murder," the Nigerian seamstress reported, in very matter-of-fact terms.

It appeared that the young prostitute had been strangled to death, with an electrical cord. The mother of Desirée had said only, "Thank God we got out in time. I could tell that building was going to rack and ruin, when they let it go over half black. Realtors just don't care who they let in anymore—after the building becomes half black—as long as they can pay one month's security and the current month's rent."

Then Desirée heard the Nigerian woman tell of having to move out of her apartment because of a drug dealer who had paid six months rent in advance and kept his box booming with drumming music so loud so that he and his customers could run their drug deals undisturbed and silence the rest of his neighbors, who were to figure he just liked to party a lot. "Truly, I couldn't sleep for those booming drums as if they were playing in an open-air stadium. I went to knock at his door to ask him in an exceed-ing-ly neighborly manner to cut that booming phonograph down. But just as I was about to put my knuckles to the door, I could hear, ever so faintly (because of the absolute thunderstorm of the drumming), this black man, this neighbor, this drug dealer winding up one of his savage deals. Now, I understood, Mrs. Dobbs, what he was attempting to protect from the silence of the truth. Necessity demanded that I move immediately. But I did look his number up, and called him, an hour or so later. Asked him, beseeched him to cut the phonograph player down. He virtually spat venom in my face through the telephone wires. Called me a 'black African bitch' and said that I 'should take my black ass back over there with the monkeys and the lions where I belonged.' He then threatened to blow my brains out. I took out a peace bond on the man, Mrs. Dobbs, I tell you, I moved out of my nice, neat apartment the last day of that month, at dawn. . . . My but how your daughter, Desirée, has grown up to be such a lovely looking young lady."

■ ■ ■ ■ ■

But out of the supermarket, on their way home, with three bags full of groceries in their arms, foul weather struck down the day and swept up the loveliness in a monstrous rain. Felicity felt that she had been momentarily prevented from making any revelations to Desirée. They needed to hurry home. The street was quickly evacuated of all human life, except for an occasional speeding car, splashing rain everywhere. There was something terrible, awesome, and even magical about the way the weather had so suddenly turned on itself, Desirée reflected. She doubted whether they would make it home before they were consumed by the drenching downpour; *almost struck down dead*, ran through her mind. Desirée suggested a cab. Her mother said that they couldn't afford one, besides, it would be next to impossible to get a taxi to take them a mere four blocks. They could make it home if only she could get Desirée moving. Well, this was what it meant to live under a tyranny, the young woman thought to herself. She was always using a mask of excuses.

Soon the two unfortunate women were the captives of a shocking thunderstorm, three long blocks from the street where they lived, lightning and furious rain pouring everywhere. Grocery bags were soon so rain-drenched that apples and oranges were falling upon the pavement and produce was flying about. Rain-sopped paper bags were falling apart and completely crumbling in their hands. Racing on their high heels, the women were nearing home a half block or less away when the heel of Desirée's left shoe slipper cracked and came off. She didn't have time to retrieve it. Thanks to her years of ballet lessons, she was able to maintain a semblance of balance and didn't fall, but much of the produce came tumbling onto the street. Vegetables and packages of frozen meats were sucked up in the storm. Her mother was far ahead of her. And Desirée didn't have time or the inclination to retrieve the slipper, but hobbled the twenty-five yards to the door of the old apartment building. Just then the paper bags were swept out of the hands of both women by the powerful grasp of the thunderstorm; as if struck by the wand of cruel magic, the women discovered themselves arriving home empty-handed.

As Desirée took a hurried, last look down the length of the street, she saw, approximately five feet from the doorway, the complete harvest of their two-week's grocery shopping transformed to litter, jetsam, and flotsam, as it were, in the man-overboard-mayhem spun by the windstorm. The brown paper bags whipped about like so much foolish garbage left over from a masquerade carnival scene, and Desirée's high-heeled silver slipper appeared to romp about in the rain. In the distance, an extremely tall figure, a dark stranger of a man, appeared, carrying aloft a huge umbrella, which miraculously enough, seemed undisturbed by the wicked wand of the thunderstorm. The huge, lily-white umbrella appeared to have the power and size of a protective canvas above a circus tent at the freak sideshow. As she dashed upstairs to get in out of the fierce storm, Desirée thought of the unfortunate incident as yet another example of the Dobbs's condemned condition, and why she must get away. Even the last sight, that of the tall figure in the distance with his huge umbrella, seemed yet another manifestation of the madness, which now blew out of the rainstorm. A deranged set of circumstances, which kept her and her mother on the brink of a living unreality . . . forevermore. The mother despaired at the loss of all their groceries to the thunderstorm, simply and bitterly, as being plain bad luck, and not atypical of the reversal of fortunes in weather and in life, Desirée wearily reflected.

Now Desirée was drying the mother off with a series of bath towels; then she gave her a fine cup of pea soup and put her to bed. No sooner had the mother's head collapsed upon the pillow than she fell fast asleep. Just as Desirée turned to the place where she had left off reading *Anna Karenina*, the doorbell rang three times. Shocked by the shrill peel of the bell, the frightened and bewildered Desirée crept to the door. And who could it be out in this terrible rainstorm? Someone beseeching them for shelter and comfort out of some calamity as driven as this terrible thunderstorm?

When Desirée opened the door (but at a safe crack, of course, as was her training, and only to the extent that the six-inch chain would allow), there stood the "most absolutely gorgeous guy in captivity," she heard her heart throb, in her throat. He was so magnificently attired, and yet to her eyes he remained—astonishingly enough—untouched completely by one drop of rain, not even the slightest hint of trickle. . . . Well, of course, he had the gigantic umbrella . . . and oh my God is he forever and a day tall. . . . But the breathless Desirée exclaimed to herself, "Just how had he bounded up the four flights of steps with such accelerated speed? On the wings of a dove? No. An eagle?" Now Desirée unfastened the chain, feeling completely safe in the lyrical lair of his hypnotic, dark, soul-draining eyes. Desirée had never heard her heart pump with such life before, except the times she had tried out for the track team, and almost broke her neck (or so she thought) attempting to vault the hurdles, at breakneck speed. . . . Like the rewinding of hundreds of feet of film, flashing backwards faster than any forward thrust she had ever encountered. . . . Oh, it was . . . he was too much.

Just then the most gorgeous guy in the world said, "I've come for you Desirée, to take you away from all of this," in a rich, deep tenor voice, full of mellifluous melody, honey, rhapsody, gentleness, urgency, and righteousness. Just too marvelous for words, Desirée heard her heart proclaim. At least that's what Desirée thought she had heard him say. Because he was just too gorgeous for words, words, words alone to know what exactly he didn't say, or did say.

If Vronsky looked like this, no wonder Anna lost her sense of reason, Desirée wept to her heart's delight. Just then the most gorgeous guy in captivity took three large military steps backwards in the hallway, completely dominating all the space in time, she thought. But just then he brought forth, in the form of an offering, a huge white umbrella, which contained, for heaven's sake, the four bags of . . . no—it couldn't be . . . but four bags set about in a perfect circle on the outskirts of the gigantic umbrella filled to capacity and untouched by the furious rain in the same condition these items were in when Desirée and her mother had left the store, she now discovered, as she picked her way through each bag, going to and fro, from the door to the kitchen with one bag at a time, as if to savor the miracle. In the kitchen she reexamined the contents with even greater thoroughness, finding her fingers moving over the contents of the bags, as a gifted harpist might touch upon the strings of the instrument while running over a sweeping, lilting version of *The Blue Danube*. Sure enough, all of the selected items from the shopping list that she and her mother had purchased were there (or maddeningly, their equivalents).

Mistrusting her first impression, Desirée reexamined the bags filled with groceries—they were without wrinkle or blemish, though her face virtually wrinkled up looking at the wonder of it all. Her temple was rain-wet and soaked, as if she and her mother had never emerged from the thunderstorm at all. Then she recounted the numbers of all of the fruit, for Desirée had a photographic memory of which she was quite proud and didn't need to consult the grocery list her mother had written out. She said to herself, "I saw with my own eyes these very apples rolling down the street into the mud in the thunderstorm only minutes ago," and shook with terror and awe. Desirée found herself trembling with an untold fire and throbbing delight and desire. She was propelled, like the track star she often dreamed of being, and she vaulted down the hall to capture the most gorgeous guy in the world, who had spun out of some miraculous magic the life back into her shopping bag. "It is but a wonder . . . it is but a wonder . . . it is but a wonder," she howled over and over again, until she was back at the front door and facing her miracle worker with her face tilted back as far as possible to encounter the reality of the most gorgeous guy in the world.

When Desirée returned to the door, the most gorgeous guy in the world simply said, "I've come to take you away with me, but you must hurry, because we cannot afford to let this beautiful night escape from our grasp." He reached into a secret compartment within his jacket pocket—just beneath his heart—and the dazzling stranger said, "But how can you hurry along without this?" He then produced from his pocket the fine slipper that Desirée had lost, with the heel pounded securely into place. Now the slipper shone with a brightly polished glaze.

Captivated by the mere glance of the most gorgeous guy in the world (who was so magnificently attired in various phases of the color purple), Desirée was momentarily speechless before this presence. *I'll not put my complete heart under your hammer*, Desirée said to herself over and over again, as in a self-fashioned litany. The material of his clothing appeared spun from silkworms. He wore a smoke-colored leather jacket. A fox's tail was drawn through each shoulder strap.

Finally Desirée found a portion of the power of her tongue: "Tell me . . . tell me, just what is your name?"

"I have been called to the name of Reign," he answered.

Reign was tall and thin and regal in his handsomeness. His complexion was a lyrical blend of deep rich bronze, a meshing of many burnished browns. The vision of an immense chocolate bar filled Desirée's imagination. No blemish had ever dared visit his face, or so did the visage of the most gorgeous guy in the world appear to Desirée. No barber's razor had ever touched down upon such a face, she thought. The pronounced Indian-Caucasian features, pitched to beauty in his African American, bronze burnished face, were discovered in the gaze Desirée affixed upon the beautiful specimen shimmering before her. Just then Reign fell to his knees and placed the repaired slipper upon the unshod left foot, a perfect fit. She gave it back to Reign, ran barefooted back to the sewing room, found the other high heel shoe, and as soon as she allowed Reign to help her to put both shoes on, discovered that she stood a full two inches beneath his armpits.

Now in an attempt to help the girl find her tongue, the most gorgeous guy in the world opened his mouth and said, "You will need little clothing, either, other than that which you have on your back. Where we will be going, you'll be dressed and redressed to kill from crown to sole. Notice how a rhinestone diamond has already been placed on the outer instep of your shoe."

Hearing her exhausted mother snoring away, Desirée asked, "But-but, what of my mother?"

"We are going on a great migration."

As Desirée appeared to ponder the meaning of his invitation, the most gorgeous guy in the world took off the handsome, brilliantly alive rhinestone belt he was wearing and gave it to her and said, "Leave my champion belt of priceless value at the foot of your mother's bed, along with whatever note you feel you need to quiet her concerns, as my gift not so much to you but to her. It was a relic of Ashante royalty in my family, from way back when. But now, hurry, Desirée, and sweep up whatever you need for our marvelous journey (we must not disturb your mummy's slumber) into space and time. I'm going to show you a world, higher than any mountain, deeper than any valley."

"But you hardly know me. . . . And anyway, how exactly, Reign, did you know my name?"

"There is little that I don't know about the divine Desirée."

"*Oh*," she said. Desirée appeared now to try to outrace her heart, and fled to her mother's room with this unbelievable belt. How will Reign keep his pants up without it? she found herself whimsically musing; then, shocked over these stirrings, she blushed in her embarrassment. The deeply snoring Felicity remained undisturbed by the high-heeled footfall of her daughter's step into her room. Nor did she waken when the daughter placed the worshipful Reign's belt upon the foot of her bed; or even when Desirée placed a kiss upon her mother's temple. Desirée scrawled a quickly conceived note, with her eyebrow pencil, upon an envelope from the IRS. But the note contained no pertinent information, for Desirée could not say for certain exactly where she was going. Let me hurry for my binoculars to see this unknown world, and my camera to capture this unseen universe, Desirée said to her pounding heart, which seemed to drum with the beat of the rain as it struck down upon the roof.

■ ■ ■ ■ ■

Felicity had a secret that she needed to unburden to someone—preferably to Desirée—concerning the deceased husband of her bed. Yet how would Desirée take to any suggestion about her father that did not further celebrate her vision of his perfection? Theirs had been an ideal marriage in so many ways (sprinkled with only a few imperfect aspects), and yet there was that one troubling tunnel of darkness. The only place wherein the reality of Felicity's mysterious unsettlement could be unveiled was through her perpetual dream (which truly had nightmarish implications). And indeed the mesmerizing memory haunted her dreams with ever-expanding power: like a bloody dagger hovering over the brain.

Hardly had her head fallen upon the gentle pillow when the saga reappeared with the growing power and manifestation of a haunting dream. Yet why did she also delight in these venomous visitations? Felicity wondered.

When she married, Felicity had full confidence in her homemaking skills, and her crafts never failed her. Yet there was one arena where Felicity knew she was a failure—ironing. A craft of dubious worth for a modern women, she fretfully told herself, and yet the practice of the art to perfection could also be another way of subduing her man to her powers. So, from the beginning of their marriage, Felicity had taken her handsome husband's soiled shirts to be laundered and ironed by the hand of one Lucasta Jones. Felicity had learned of Lucasta's transforming powers through the Nigerian seamstress.

Although she could not regard Lucasta Jones, who lived in the basement just off Prairie Avenue in a decrepit neighborhood, as anything more than a laundress, Felicity was forced to admit that the way this woman Jones turned out her man's shirts was nothing short of magical. Why, even the way she sprinkled the clothes before her, with a flick of a wrist, reminded Felicity of the manner in which a priest joyously sprinkles his congregation as he comes down the aisle for High Mass. Where had she, this lowly Lucasta Jones, picked up this form of ritual-like adoration for the awakening of the litter of shirts at her elbow?

Now, Felicity's handsome young husband looked gorgeous in these beautifully turned-out shirts. He was immensely pleased with, and proud of, his bright new wife, and to find her so unexpectedly talented in this area of their union. Twice a month (and completely unknown to her groom) Felicity would take the shirts, in a sack, to the wee basement room, just off Prairie Avenue, at Thirty-third Street, and engage the services of Lucasta Jones. When she went down the steps into the tunnel leading to Lucasta's dwelling, Felicity always felt as if she were entering a rabbit hole.

Meantime, Felicity's husband continued to brag to all of his coworkers just how talented and loving was his young wife—Yes, *we can see*, one and all exclaimed, *look at the adoration she puts into the pressed-out shape of your shirts*. It's almost as if she had put her brand on her husband's shirts, making doubly sure that no woman would dare to lay claim to that which Felicity's alone deigned to have and to hold. That was the essence of the office gossip when he would come to get his assignments, or during those times when he wasn't wearing his uniform and was doing his paperwork. The confident young husband even conveyed a revised portion of this lighthearted office gossip to Felicity's ears. They both had a long laugh over the story, in their breakfast nook, but he laughed louder and longer.

Felicity did not become pregnant until the fifth year of their marriage, and by then. . . .

■ ■ ■ ■ ■

To the eyes of Felicity Dobbs, this Lucasta Jones was a primitive, a rustic. She always wore an old, greasy head-rag; her mouth often looked as if her teeth had just discovered a sour apple. Often, this Lucasta Jones was still in her tattered purple bathrobe when Felicity arrived with the dirty laundry. She was still stretching her limbs and yawning at high noon. Perhaps she needs a new mattress, Felicity speculated, wildly.

The laundress always kept her eyes cast down (as if there were some treasures beneath, in the deep blue sea, that she, and she alone, could see) when she spoke during their bargaining encounter. And as for speaking, Felicity was tempted to say, "*Cat got your tongue?*" This Lucasta Jones always gave you (her customer, so to speak, for in plain sight, as far as Felicity was concerned, this laundress had absolutely no business sense) a two-inch square paper cut-out slip, from an old wrinkled brown paper bag, with a number scrawled on it, and Felicity's last name. Asking too often Felicity's last name in not an altogether speculative manner, Lucasta would say, "Now your name and how do you spell it, ma'am?"

"Dobbs. *D-o-b-b-s.*" She dared not get Lucasta involved in the actual spelling of her first name. There was a placard in red print, in the shape of a heart, just above the ironing board, that read:

LET NOT YOUR HEART BE TROUBLED.

When Felicity would return to pick up the shirts (always placed in a large brown shopping bag), she would not accept the bags provided by Lucasta, fearing the basement dwelling was infested by cockroaches in secret recesses. Instead she placed them in the sack she brought. Lucasta always washed, and even ran an iron over this sack, too. Felicity then paid her in nickels, dimes, and quarters, plunking down each coin and explaining to Lucasta the marketplace value of each coin (as one might train a small child by dint of rote repetition the times table, or what power each coin has at the candy counter). Felicity never deigned to pay off this sleepy-faced yet self-possessed woman in folding money.

As to the barter between the two Negro women over an actual sum for service and trade? (Even though Felicity always presented the same number of shirts to the laundress's hand, upon each occasion.)

"What's it worth to you, Miss?"

"It's Mrs. Dobbs. *D-o-b-b-s.*"

"Yes."

No wonder Negroes have such problems mounting an actual business enterprise, and really making a go of it, Felicity often thought at this moment of their encounter as she smartly turned on her heels and removed herself from this odd and foolish woman's premises. And so, Felicity Dobbs would pay her what she wanted to shell out, not daring to allow herself (nor to ring down upon the counter, where Lucasta actually took in the laundry) any admission of the woman's question, nor of the dominion this strangely magnetic, talented to be sure, almost loathsome, surly dark-brown-skinned woman had over her life, and of the anointing hand she had unknowingly laid as a sheet over Felicity's marriage bed.

Upon certain occasions, Lucasta would be listening to recordings on her small, battered-looking phonograph, which stood on a rickety deal table in the corner of the room. Lucasta seemed remarkably enchanted, Felicity observed, by the tortured soul of Billie Holiday's voice, particularly as Lady Day sang "No Good Man," or "Good Morning Heartache." After hearing this despondent, depressing voice, so full of stormy weather, Felicity was glad for the shelter of a good man's arms to avenge this kind of sentiment about love.

Other times when Felicity went to pick up the shirts, she discovered Lucasta was playing—over and over again—Mahalia Jackson, singing "Didn't It Rain." On these occasions, Lucasta seemed brimming over with zeal, as if she had been visited by trance. Felicity could not tell if the laundress was drunk or coming through some form of hallucination.

Supply and demand continued to go just fine under Felicity's controlling hand, during the early months of her pregnancy. But the last time she visited this laundress, Felicity received something of a shock wave from the sharply transformed appearance of Lucasta Jones.

In the seventh month of pregnancy, Felicity became too large to go out unattended. She was vexed not only over the burdensomeness of her condition (even as she had dearly dreamed of having a baby of her own) and that she could not tie her own shoelaces but that she would have to inform her handsome husband about where she had obtained the service for his shirts, and most woefully, that it was not she, Felicity, who performed this wifely service for him. But Felicity did unfold the truth about whose talented hand was actually doing the intricately artful ironing of his shirts as her dutiful husband knelt at her swollen feet to lace up shoes. Facing this moment and measuring up to the truth was important to her sense of honesty and well-being, Felicity proclaimed to herself, over and over again, as she bowed her head in prayer, just before lights out.

Although Felicity had feared her husband's response, he had not shown any anger, nor had he revealed any of the shrillness, or slightly surly demeanor, which had surprisingly marked this latter stage of his wife's confinement—right along with his euphoria over her impending delivery. Indeed, Victor Dobbs seemed simply beguiled by the clean, un-folded fabric of Lucasta Jones's relationship to his glowing shirts. Felicity felt wiser and clearer about the unfurling of her pent-up situation—of the false currency of her previous tale concerning her powers to emboss his shirts with such magic, when in point of fact those powers were in the hands of another woman (and for God's sake why not give her credit for the talent our Heavenly Father had given her).

The husband of Felicity Dobbs would have to go over on Prairie Avenue and pick up his own shirts, until she could return to her old walking stride, after the baby came. Ah, the coming of the baby, perhaps that is why he accepted the story of the ruse with such grace. But then, in one of the many varying phases of her easily soured temperament during her pregnancy, Felicity speculated that he was so leisurely with her over this story because he actually wanted to loop her in with a species of possession, *Because I forgave you, when you lied to me for years, I therefore have dominion over you, and will make you pay for my forgiveness. . . .* Ah, but that was being black and evil, and unworthy of their joyous marriage and the marvelous little stranger in her stomach.

Felicity gave her husband this woman's address and the ticket slip with their name scrawled out in the hand of a third-grader with the number Lucasta Jones had assigned—369—marked down in the corner. "She knows precisely the right proportion of starch to use," Victor Dobbs said of Lucasta's perfected craft, after he returned home with the shirts.

■ ■ ■ ■ ■

In her dreams, Felicity was revisited, as always, by that moment late in her sixth month of pregnancy (actually, it was the last time she was to ever lay eyes upon Lucasta Jones), when she was initially met at the basement door not by Lucasta Jones but by a fully romping rat with a fury to get to some big cheese as it scurried across her feet as if she didn't exist. Felicity's heart nearly vaulted out of her body. Surely her baby was marked by this encounter. Just then Felicity was shocked again by the appearance of Lucasta Jones, who was leading her into and down a dark tunnel-like hallway to her small room. Gone was the greasy blue head-rag. Lucasta's hair was hanging down to her shoulders. This must be a full-length wig, Felicity immediately thought. Her hair was beautifully dressed, as if talented hands, like those that transformed her husband's shirts, had accomplished this feat of style upon this laundress's hair. But on this occasion Lucasta Jones looked her dead in the eye as they conversed.

Felicity discovered that this woman was "possessed by crazy quilt, slitting hazel eyes, as a cat in the dark." Lucasta wore a red dress so breathlessly bold and tight to the backbone, you wondered how she could ever exhale. In the room where Lucasta apparently did everything, Felicity's eyes met those of Lucasta's nigger man, lounging about on the couch in the room, with his right leg dangling over the rickety arm of the rancid, yellow couch. Vulgarly handsome, this nigger of Lucasta's could not, and would not, take his slaughterhouse eyes off her legs (as he sucked upon a toothpick dipped in gold). Felicity observed, out of the corners of her eyes, those shaving-razor evil eyes upon her, angled to strip her nylons away, even though she was swollen with child. At this moment, Felicity would have loved to use the iron as a wand to press out the burning eyes of Lucasta's "No Good Man." Because his searching, deep, dark eyes were so despicable and so devouring of her pregnant form, Felicity cried for a power to transform his eyes out of his head into seashells loaded with self-destroying nerve gas. He had the longest eyelashes. Were they false? Lucasta referred tenderly to this surly brute by the name of Tucson. It was Felicity's view that people like Lucasta and her lover lived in an eternal body of emotional waves.

"You got folding greenbacks this time, Miss, ur, Dobbs? Too many coins rings up holes in my pockets," Lucasta had laughed gingerly. Her man, this Tucson, made a loudly snorting noise, as if to cough up, That'll be the day I die, so it seemed to Felicity.

Why, that black bitch, thought Felicity, when she got to her car; she thought that I had paid her off in coins because that was all I could afford. She thinks she read me out.

Even after the baby was born, the husband of Felicity went twice a month (as far as she knew) over to the basement apartment on Thirty-third and Prairie to deliver and then to pick up the sixteen, no longer twelve, shirts that Lucasta Jones did so beautifully. Felicity could detect nothing, but Victor Dobbs looked even more stunningly turned out than ever before in her envious eyes. There was a very heavy halo, Felicity thought, about his aura, which was utterly unspeakable, as she played solitaire during the last weeks of her confinement. She wiped out this thought immediately, but couldn't help wondering if Lucasta's self-styled laundry was a cover for a cathouse.

Victor Dobbs always insisted that he could deliver the shirts and pick them up because it was all on his way to and from work. What could Felicity say other than to despise Lucasta Jones and loathe the artful power she possessed with her iron. In one of her dreams, during the last stages of her pregnancy, Felicity had dreamed of bashing Lucasta's brains out with that very ancient-looking iron. During the years that followed, she merely wanted to tear that lover's tongue from out of Lucasta's mouth. For until the week before he was killed in a rainstorm, her husband had continued to deliver his soiled shirts and pick up the transformed ones out of the basement on Thirty-third and Prairie Avenue. A perfectionist, Victor Dobbs seemed to be paying his wife back, in Felicity's eyes, for not being all that "I had purported to be," by routing his path to Prairie Avenue. But he accused Felicity of nothing. Had the core of her soul been sacked by the heart of her heart? she wondered.

Three months before his death, Felicity visited a clairvoyant to find out, for fact, what her heart told her was truth—that her man was seeing another woman. The clairvoyant has said, "There are people in this world, my good woman, who operate on a sphere beyond logic, love, and morality. They climb high, but they are ultimately brought low." She never answered directly, just enough to break your heart, Felicity confided to the diary she had recently started. And yet there were never any lipstick traces about the collars of Victor Dobbs. Their lovemaking, though less frequent, had lost none of its fervor. In the dark, Felicity did not find the brand of Lucasta upon the lips of her only lover. Yet there was something so profoundly splendid, special, untouchable, alluring, and not to be arrested about Victor Dobbs. He gave you everything or nothing with that same enchanting or withering glance. You were always a glance away from Paradise or the poverty of nothingness in his bewitching, glacier eyes. Did this apparently not-so-lackluster Lucasta glean similar lush-leaf lyricism, dripping with dew, or the distance of desolation from his eyes, as well? she wondered out loud, as her pen sailed ahead, upon the pages of her diary. Although she absolutely loathed what she assumed to be truth about her husband and Lucasta, Felicity also found herself praying, down on her knees, that the evil Tucson would not catch them in bed and come between them with a razor as penetrating as his eyes.

Two weeks after her husband's death in the electrical storm, Felicity had another encounter that shook her to the very foundation of her mournful state of grieving. On her way home from the telephone company, where she had received a top executive's guarantee that she would start getting a solid monthly stipend for the rest of her life, Felicity ran into the loquacious Nigerian seamstress coming out of a currency exchange. It was then that she told Felicity, in midflight, "The terrible thing that adds to my grief for your burdensome woe, Mrs. Dobbs, is that you know, of course, how it was me who gave introduction to you concerning Lucasta Jones, who can do such wonder work with laundry and in particular with men's shirts. I know you used her services regularly for your late and highly esteemed husband's shirts. But do you know, Mrs. Dobbs, that poor woman's man was smashed to death when two trains collided in the Santa Fe freight yards, backed right up into each other, just as it began to rain. The wreckage occurred. . . . It was upon the very day of your beloved husband's demise."

Finding herself panting breathlessly, Felicity asked: "What did he look like? Lucasta's man?"

The Nigerian seamstress went on to describe Lucasta's man in great detail. Immediately Felicity remembered seeing such a lounging, flirtatious fucker eyeing her from that rancid yellow couch, where he no doubt bedded down the lascivious Lucasta Jones.

But as always, this Nigerian seamstress—dressed as she was in some kind of loud, purple tribal array—had more to unravel: "And it was a common-law misarrangement, don't you know. So, she, Lucasta, gets absolutely nothing. Besides, Mrs. Dobbs, I'm told that her man, Tucson Barlow was his name, was about to leave poor Lucasta, high and coinless, the very next week, for some swift gal up in Detroit. Here's my hand to God Almighty, but aren't men (not your dear and well-revered late husband), most of them, pure, low-down horse shit on a stick, when all is said and done?"

Felicity took the Nigerian's hand, shook it, and took a completely different walking direction. She felt no pity for the shameless Lucasta for obvious reasons, she now reflected. Also remembering, too, that she had to buy a new shirt for her husband's burial. His unironed sixteen shirts had remained in rough-dry condition, as far as she knew, at Lucasta's dwelling. Victor Dobbs was to pick up those shirts on the day he was killed. She, of course, would do nothing to reclaim her dead husband's shirts from the "house of Lucasta," Felicity said aloud in the wind.

■ ■ ■ ■ ■

"I'll not allow . . . I'll not allow . . . my heart to be under any man's hammer," Desirée said aloud, and almost completely out of breath, just now, as she affixed the straps of the binoculars and then placed her gift from her father into the camera case. Soon the most handsome couple the world has ever set eyes upon were downstairs, and onto the streets. Now Desirée—who considered herself tall for a woman—discovered that she barely reached the elbows of Reign. The rain had completely ceased, and there was a rainbow in the heavens; then Desirée saw at the curbside that there was a purple stretch limousine, with smoke-colored, ultraviolet windows. When the most gorgeous guy in the world scooped Desirée up into his arms, she was completely breathless as they entered

the limo. The chauffeur was dressed in black, and when he turned to greet his passengers, Desirée observed the driver was wearing a ski mask with only shocking blue eyes showing through; he had a red carnation in his lapel.

The limo took off in a cruising manner, like a plane, or a gigantic bird about to ascend the heavens, Desirée thought. Though she had never been in an airplane in her life, she could only imagine that this was it, this zenith of overdrive. She had been in a limousine once before when Desirée and her mother had left the funeral for her father in a car, similar to this one, but not nearly as well appointed, Desirée now reflected. The driver of that limousine was also a part-time blues singer and steel guitarist, Lightning Chord Rodgers.

By pressing a small blue button the most gorgeous guy in the world was able to present an extended, bright bar of worldly delights. A variety of liquors, candies, mints, miniatures of the best bourbons, scotches, vodkas . . . caviar . . . pates. . . . More than anything Desirée was stunned by the wonderful glass mirror that reflected the beautiful image of this fabulous couple before her eyes: Reign and Desirée Dobbs. She wondered if he had a last name. Well of course he did. But he was too gorgeous to need a last name. Still, Reign seemed something akin to a stage name a renowned entertainer might carry.

Soon the most gorgeous guy in the world took a small pouch out of his jacket pocket. He took a beautiful shard of a reflecting glass, with an oval-shaped golden border, and then from the pouch Reign poured something that looked like snow (Oh, it isn't, silly girl, she laughed to herself) or confectionery of some sort. Now deploying a barber's razor—that he plucked from the lapel of his smoke-colored jacket— Reign pressed a button on the handle and a glistening, six-inch blade shot out. Then the most gorgeous guy in the world commenced to segregate the fine powder before him into columns, and now, out of a receptacle containing glistening gold paper—wrapped straw, Reign selected one and proceeded to inhale several columns of the white powder before him through this golden straw. Turning on occasion to Desirée, between moments after inhaling, Reign exclaimed, in a beautiful, whispered, throaty manner, that this experience was "more wondrous than the breath of an angel."

Upon another glance, when, after the breathless awe she felt when he looked into her eyes, she looked in the mirror before her, at them, Desirée thought that she might explode with glee. For the mirror *now* revealed a man, this Reign, as the most gorgeous guy in the whole universe. Yet the power of the mirror's perfection, rendering up everything in such exact detail, suddenly afforded her another slant upon the eyes of Reign that she had not noticed before. There appeared just the slightest discoloration, as if a tiny dapply brush stroke had been touched up, in the very corners of those divine eyes, reminding her of a doll's eyes that she often had touched up with Mercurochrome. What a wild crazy thought, she laughed. He made an offering to Desirée upon a small tin plate, of Russian caviar, and a half glass of champagne. His face was still that of a prince, but since he had inhaled three columns of the white powder, Desirée noted how Reign looked cold, brilliant, not as sweet, yet perhaps even more enchanting and awesome than ever. In the mirror before them, this couple, thought Desirée, could surely take Hollywood by storm. Reign had uncommonly long eyelashes and Desirée could not tell, for the life of her, whether the eyes of Reign were velvet emerald or velvet and streaked with the color of purple. Perfectly guileless, she thought. Now the tiny flicks of red in the corners of his eyes had evaporated from her view.

As the limo floated down the Drive, her guide lifted a small portion of the white substance that looked like confectioners' sugar, as she peered down into the pouch offered to her by the most gorgeous guy in the world. With a wry smile, the most gorgeous guy in the world gave voice to his wildest dreams, by revealing to her the paradise that awaited her as Desirée took part in the ritual initiated by the most gorgeous guy in the world; and soon Desirée was in paradise as she followed in close imitation of his every word, inhaling the white powder through the golden straw.

Meantime, up front, the driver spoke in a gruff voice through his ski mask, upon the car telephone, barking out orders to a series of command centers, or so it appeared to Desirée.

But she did not dwell upon all of this for very long, because she was now enraptured in the arms of Reign.

■ ■ ■ ■ ■

By the time they arrived at the high-rise apartment building on the other side of town, Desirée was breathless and seeing visions. Soon she was up into the arms of Reign as they came to the door. (Like a bride, she thought.) They received an uneasy salute from the doorman. As they entered the lobby of the building, an aged parrot who was perched upon the five-foot-high ashtray stand leading to the elevator, started croaking:

Do an about face young fox. . . .
You can't stand the paradox. . . .

Soon the elevator was exploding upwards, but Desirée thought that she was about to fall down the quite visible airshaft (was this the *paradox* the aged parrot had referred to?), and she found herself screaming and weeping all at the same time as they entered a vast apartment in the arms of the most gorgeous guy in the universe, and now he closed the door. The lights were quite low. Soon the light was turned on full blast, and Desirée saw signs unseen by her eyes before.

All about the vast room Desirée was shocked to see young languishing and lounging women naked or nearly nude. Some were in cages. In other cages she observed *adorable* baby lions. Soon Desirée was asleep and she found herself dreaming of Leonard Foster, and the words to the poem he had dedicated to her came charging forth in the imagination of her total recall:

A WOMAN NAMED AUTUMN, TO DESIRÉE DOBBS
Yet Autumn still wields a switchblade within my shadow
Troubled existence as I recall her soul labors in
Crackling chords of my soul, as drawn rosary beads of denial;
I vault . . . as her tossed slippers, silks, stockings
Golden as a flaming ghost sailing upon the plumage
of a peacock's feathers; transformed in the lightning
of my days as sudden rainbow amid the poisonous
atmosphere, that brings me no peace, only shattering
Solitude: where I can go mad mooning over the memory of
Lucasta, called mother by all but me. . . .
Break and go down in the valley to break upon the bones

of my fractured bones, weave and skip farewell, as any
Deadly leaves break a heartthrob, as the sea made to
Tremble. . . . And upon this magical lily-white altar-sheet
We float and ride as before the sticks and bones aflame
In the grievous valley below/before the fiery Sea. . . .
Mother, who are not called, Autumn and me.
Desirée is pristine perfection, without guile,
she became as a God sent, little child.
My heart thrust as the rhythm shaped by Autumn's lips
as a pure dove: the joke of the blood is the very mud-making
Mansion castles to paradise we ourselves make of love. . . . Upon
the apex of the hill of destruction and sacrifice, I hold a
pearl in my hand; oh bruised-blood goddess upon the pregnant
Eve, clawing at the straightjacket of interning death
(The role of lovers in die of death's dice, as bony
Tomb slabs afire to the sea's sucking breath; oh sew up my
bleary, profitless, grainless soul in rice paper;
the brooding bones behind my eyes are as pearls turned
backwards upon the holocaust of the seas to see the fathomless
depths down the tolling hours without numbers where the chalk-
flaked bones of my fathers lie beyond numbers and the blood
of their voices weep out to me for revenge not of redemption
my iced eyes unable to focus upon my bespectacled grief, in
the many thousands devoured by the alabaster sharks; and
the layered folds of the sea's transformations of my
Layered and lost soul, in the liquidating sea) . . . and the
seas aflame, alive as devouring tolling tongues with
redemption (with teeth in it) forever and ever world with
being and beginning; and an icy, alabaster-bastard-God.
Ill-colored riding the tides down the length of distance,
with Ahab upon his charred-challenging shoulders. . . .
His left hand as a dreamer's filled with covenants of bribes
as chains; his right hand with slippery iniquities as the
millions of losses . . . spoon-fashioned and spoon-fed to
death with faith. . . . To strap our souls up in chains. . . .
Desirée dearest: I believe in all things visible but
Mainly the invisible ingrained within the indivisible
blotted-out marginality of our bones, and our mothers'
bones. . . . Oh mother they never allowed me to know, as

mother. . . . Oh wayward mother, Lucasta . . . Miz Lu . . . Auntie
Luz . . . but never mother. . . . Even unto her (Autumn, lost-
found sister of the storm) . . . "never call me mother
but Lucasta" because you see she read it in a lily-
white folks magazine, in a straightening-hair parlor,
that it was sophisticated to have your children call you
by your first name to break down barriers to the heart. . . .
My fathers flew as host flakes of flesh flung holocaust.
We as partakers of their divinity . . . oh bread and wine,
wine and bread . . . no remembrance chalice cup can behold
the possessions and properties of their souls beyond number.
Jesus were you there in the wave, and the water, the light,
and the horror of their bruised blood beginning on the way
here to nowhere. The magician who walked upon water, as
We held our breath, enshrouded in the miracle of His Freedom march.
Desirée: I must confess this to you (you with your figure
akin to an hourglass): I ripped backwards Autumn's peach-blazed
Throat to find the devouring wand within her wine, only to discover
the shape of madness there, trembling in my hands. . . .
Bones more fragile than my own, as smashed twigs in the valley linking me
to below and the fragile lightning cord throat of the tumultuous,
TIME melting sea of horrors beyond breath, cocaine, kindling,
and the Host, high upon the Hill . . . the Sacred Heart of Jesus.
"You're mine," I wept; "HE'S yours," she faded, as I then heard
a cry divine, little Desirée of the Spirits: "This is my
body, and this is my Blood." My very touch appears as a
Blight across the earth as a lightning chord . . . carrying
Horrific news of our tragedy and their calamity . . . without
Grave markers engraved upon our national consciousness, world without
end. . . . Beyond the Grave's soul-plucked harp and violin.
Dearest Desirée: You must remember this from my diary
Autumn supped Chivas Regal, devoured apples for dinner,
read everything, without markers, worshiped Leadbelly and
Mendelssohn and lost her mind grieving, eyeing away at me never
quite losing my own, cultivated and therefore corrupted as
Weedless garden—refined Lawd beyond feeling, because she
had to know it, who knew nothing at all, but despair, dis-
Location, and desolation . . . oh autumn, without tears of thee i spin. . . .
As before this altar place we float, as numbered coffins,

spirits of sacrifice to the Sacred Heart of Jesus aflame, in a
windstorm . . . avenging arms beyond the soulless. Possessed
By heartless men without souls to proclaim as their own.
Sea change of calamitous violations, magicians on both sides
Who tricked us (almost) out of our species for a profit beyond
the Soul, beyond numbers, Autumn, with you in the arms of your
Accursed fugitive, wanton, wanderer, lost in the corridors of a
Thousand-faced cells and the hapless houseless, fiendish chambers
of the Souls' wreckage, homeless forever and ever—oh
cherished World without—. My very face: a disguise
Through my fault, through my fault, through my fault. . . . Therefore I. . . .
Flung out upon the avenging music of the Holy Ghost

Oh Desirée, hear this: join me, in the struggle to buoy
Me up, with your pristine majesty, your perfect soul sings
Out to me down the tumbled down world of havoc, hate,
and peckerwoods without number. . . . Into the bright and morning
star of death, I fly fearing no good within the
cherishing of all evil, as the way of the human condition,
unless, unless . . . unless we, as a people . . . when in the
accursed course of human events . . . and all that jazz. . . .
Into the valley of my art I etch out the fetus of god
like the wrinkles of Time frozen in the ghastly valley
of bones upon bones, as chalk markers in the rising tide
aflame with our sacrificial bodies. Oh Sacred Heart in a sack-cloth.
When Autumn's violin rasps under the icy fingers of Death
I recall that first frenzied bloodburning making mansion
of lovemaking the torrid moon mad-mud of summer's
wolf-howling Blues. Sailing down that pearl from heart
to hand as limbs to ashes, as bones to skeleton to the
burial (seeded with Our essences rite) in the valley below
Then out to the sea aflame—as a victory garden—grieving
past Original Sin in the very breath of the wind's
breathing Being-Becoming; sucking us out to the inferno
Riding the tides, as a fiery pale rider, beyond this
Imperfect Hell: cursed from the groundswell of land, man,
and God, who art Almighty to the last light spewed of
Howling grief, forever and ever world without end, amen.
Love—sweetest Desirée—like Death is but a shadow a
mothering body creates from within the oscillating

Moon's rays oh mother mary in the sweet bye and bye
We poor banished children of Eve in flush, flood, and
jettison of . . . and Lucasta, now I lay me down to die
for Freedom. . . . Dearest Desirée come ring-out the news
and ride this freedom/Gospel train with me . . . before it's
too, too, too much, and much much too late. . . . Upon the Avenging
Arms of Jesus I ride out to the monstrous sea.

■ ■ ■ ■ ■

Desirée was awakened by the sound of a prodigious crash, as if someone
had broken a window with a two-ton wrecking ball from a crane. Just
then, miraculously enough, the most gorgeous guy in the world was at
her side—reassuring Desirée that all was in proper form. Then, in a
matter-of-fact manner, he told the story of what had happened in the
apartment just next door. Desirée was shaking her head in tune with
the early morning airing out of the apartment and wondering about her
dream of Leonard Foster's poem during Reign's revelation of what had
gone down next door.

It was simply put, the story of a man who had thrown the chair
out of his fiancée's front room window, after he discovered that his
lover had been having an off and on affair with his brother during the
times he was at work as a pilot for Eastern Airlines, the "Wings of
Man." After his explanation, Desirée's Adonis, that was Reign, said that
he had to "scurry off to work." He now replaced his gold felt house
slippers with his alligator shoes. There was to be a fashion show in this
apartment's extension starting at 8:00, Reign informed Desirée. It was
now about 6:15.

All of the nude women were gone. Desirée had a splitting headache,
completely different from anything she had felt before. She felt extremely depressed and all alone in the world; yet there was everything
to keep her content. Soon she found herself longing for the fine white
grains of confectionery that the most gorgeous guy in the universe had
floated beneath her nose, upon the hour when he had redeemed her, as
he put it, from the street where she lived.

The next day the most gorgeous guy in the universe announced that
he "must go out to work and capture the essences of this world." When

he closed the door, leaving Desirée alone in this huge room, she thought to herself, but I thought that Reign had said he was going to work yesterday. She believed she had heard, just then, a strange noise in the hallway. Perhaps it was the man who had thrown the chair out of the window, returned now to hurl the young woman out of the window. Soon the sound disappeared.

Desirée passed most of the morning and afternoon trying on the grand stack of dresses and robes that she had selected at the fashion show the day before and that Reign had paid for, by dint of a mysterious credit card that was pure white, like his huge umbrella. But she longed for his presence and just as important, the strange confection-looking substance he had given her to sniff the night before.

Desirée heard that eerie noise in the hallway again. Soon a key was twisting in the lock of the door with a sound akin to that of someone trying to get out, not in, it seemed to the frightened Desirée. Now the door opened, and in came this huge snake with his tongue licking about. He placed his head into her lap and declared in a voice that was full of authority, rich and rather familiar: "Now you must search my head for lice." Desirée found many horrible things growing there, which also seemed to grow or expand, even as she killed them with a knitting needle. But amid the abominable field of lice and other insects, she soon found a steady supply of what looked like the confection-like substance the most gorgeous guy in the world had given her the day before. She sniffed the substance, the snake left, and soon the most gorgeous guy in the universe returned.

He said to Desirée, "Were you afraid of me when I came in a little while ago?" And Desirée said, without particularly grasping the portent of his question, "No." Then Reign went about the business of his all-consuming work.

Now Desirée decided to go downstairs to call her mother in order to inform her that all was well. But in the elevator, on the way down, she encountered on the twenty-first, fourteenth, seventh, and first floors a vast snake. At each stop, these serpents entered just like a natural man. Desirée thought to herself that perhaps she needed some fresh air. Yet, as was the case when the snake entered her apartment and placed his head in her lap the day before, Desirée believed that nothing could harm her, as long as she was lodged in the apartment of the magical Reign. Between Reign and the beautiful substance, so like snow, or confectioners' sugar (that she blew up her nostrils with the golden wrapped straw), Desirée believed that nothing could harm her. As the ritual was repeated over and over again each evening, Desirée and the most gorgeous guy in the universe would sniff and snort "the white avenger against death," as Reign called this magical substance; then the snake would come in. Then the stranger would return, who appeared now to resemble, in the imagination of Desirée, Reign himself. It could not be, yet the tenor of the voice of the snake, and that of Reign, had a similar resonance within an echo chamber of sound and authority. It was almost as if they were working shifts, Desirée thought. The fact that Reign had referred to the confectionery material as the "white lady avenger of death" now took another turn in her imagination, for initially he had explained his meaning in the following terms, in a princely voice: "I called the white lady the white angel of death also, before our encounter with her, because she guides us through the portal of life into death and out to the other side into paradise." This reminded Desirée somewhat of the strange way Leonard Foster had dedicated the poem called "A Woman Named Autumn" to her, yet the verse had been more about this haunting Autumn than it had been about her.

In the apartment, Reign wore only his silver and gold felt house slippers. In the streets, when he left the apartment, he wore one of his seven pairs of alligator shoes and the smoke-colored leather jackets. Desirée decided that she had to get out of this place. She could never get the most gorgeous Reign to ever speak about the meaning of the snake that always came in just after her prince went off to work. And to where? to work? Nor could she get Reign to talk about the white lady avenger of death that she found in the serpent's head amid the rank rot and the lice; and he would say nothing of the individual snakes that appeared at the four stops, when the elevator carried her downstairs to get some air. Meantime the wardrobe he purchased for Desirée grew more and more gorgeous: very masculine, or extremely dainty in its fashion, by twists and turns. She had not thought of her dearest guide, her dead father. Perhaps with the power of his avenging arms, she could remove herself from this place. At this point, Desirée recalled that time when she was at the circus and followed after the man she thought was her father into the circus sideshow, only to encounter W. W. W. Ford and the seven alluring mirrors of enchantment that never reflected the man who so strongly resembled her father. Desirée commanded herself, just now, to get out of this place. Simon says, "Stand up," she laughed.

Finally, when she came to the front door of the apartment building, she encountered the same doorman she had seen in the beginning when she first came into this building. The name ELDERBERRY was embossed on his golden nameplate affixed to his dark blue uniform. Desirée told the doorman that she wanted to pick up a pizza. Then she started crying, and asked him to step aside. Then she confessed what was going on about the snakes she encountered in the elevator, but said nothing against the most gorgeous guy in the world, even as she did invoke the name of Reign. Desirée also said nothing of the avenger white lady of death in the snake's head, nor of the white powder she and Reign drew up through the golden straws each night.

But the kindly looking, middle-aged gentleman Elderberry said now in a voice that sounded like an echo called up from a man twenty years his senior, "Young lady you are in deep, deep trouble. The man you are involved with is one of seven brothers; they are all magicians of various stripes. And most of their magic is evil, particularly your man, who has got you by the nose, as I can righteously see. *His heart is not included in his body!* He is one of seven who was born without a complete soul. Do you know what this all means, young lady?" His voice was full and grieved well upon Desirée's hearing, with urgency and dread.

Desirée discovered how much her body was trembling from the mirrorlike glint she gleaned off the bold-faced purpled-colored horn-rimmed glasses the doorman wore. But without a heart? And was this possible?

Then with a twinkle in his eye, the doorman's voice sounded off in a different way: "But there is hope in all of this. I mean, you can just split the scene, but that solves little or nothing. Look, highly desirable one, there is a collection of hearts in a great big bag under the bed, in the master bedroom, dripping with blood. Child, you must go get that bag and bring the contents down here and then we'll—you'll go from there. But you've been sucked up by the seventh son of a seventh son and number seven in this tribe of bag-men-bad-men-trickster demons. . . . Go!"

Desirée trembled all the way upstairs, for she decided to walk rather than ride the elevator in order to give herself some time to think over what had happened to her and what she must now do. She climbed up to the twenty-eighth floor where she lived with Reign, for she also feared taking the elevator because the snakes might manifest on the twenty-first, fourteenth, or seventh floor. But born without a heart, which existed outside of his gorgeous body? Nor even a soul? "Oh, my God," Desirée screamed. "How can he be soulless when he is so gorgeous and filled with heart? Has so touched my heart." Desirée had already thought of herself as Narda and the most gorgeous guy in the world as Mandrake. Yet the doorman Elderberry's words, coupled with the visitor snake and the emerging serpents on the elevator, and the white powder he gave her, kept Desirée excited or vastly depressed. . . .

Finally, Desirée reached the twenty-eighth floor. Though completely exhausted, she entered quickly and immediately fled to the master bedroom to retrieve the sack of hearts. She went straight to the gigantic bed and looked beneath it and found the soggy, bloody bag inside a huge washpan (which reminded Desirée of the kind of basin that the mother had often used to wash her feet in). Now Desirée peered into the bag and found seven actual hearts pumping furiously on their own steam, or so it appeared. Amid her howls and screams, she raced out of Reign's vast apartment with the blood-dripping bag in her left hand ("Oh my God, my father's binoculars and the gift of his camera," and so she raced back into the apartment to retrieve these properties, with her heart pounding like a drumming hammer). But it appeared as if her detour to retrieve her binoculars and camera was a mistake that would trip up her needed flight from this place of her captivity. For all of a sudden Desirée heard a voice so familiar, warm, thrilling, and sexy: "Stop! You think you can trip me up baby, but I've got front-page news for you." It was the voice of Reign himself.

Then as she hurried to the stairwell, to race out of his world, she thought, "If it is true that he has no heart in his body, then he'll not be able to race me down the stairs of twenty-eight flights."

Then in a voice she had not heard before, he said, "I'm reclaiming your heart now." So, off they went and around and around did they spin, race, and swing down the stairwell. . . .

Desirée never knew that she could fly in a circle, in whirlwind with such speed, even as Reign took long strides in these alligator shoes of his. Besides, Desirée was so breathless from climbing up the steps that soon he was about to overtake her. Apparently the doorman, Reverend Elderberry, was wrong, she thought, about the most gorgeous guy in the world, who had stolen her heart. A ruse finally came to Desirée, and she swiftly dropped the huge heart-shaped bag, three steps behind her, just as Reign—in seven long strides—would overtake her.

But because of the smoke-colored glasses, which adorned the eyes of Reign, the most gorgeous guy in the universe had missed seeing the bag of bloody dripping hearts. It was just at this moment that the girl heard the voice of the doorman screaming to her to duck into the elevator (Desirée thought he had sent it up to her just in the nick of time), and as gorgeous Reign lunged for the body of Desirée, he tripped over the bags of hearts and went tumbling head over heels down the passageway fourteen stories below, letting out a shriek like a pig being slaughtered. Reign landed on the concrete floor, facedown, but no blood was spilt.

Meantime, Desirée continued to fly down the stairs, at breakneck speed, because when she actually got to the bottom step and onto the lobby floor, several people were crowding around the Reign; and a doctor was down on both knees trying to examine him. Suddenly his face turned ashen. The doorman, Reverend Elderberry, leaned over him and said, "You are wasting your time, Doc, looking for a heart."

Greatly irritated by this intruder, the physician said, "Get out of here, he is still breathing." But then he stammered a bit. "I can't seem to find his pulse . . . or his heart."

The young woman was heard now laughing hysterically, and none could hush her. "Somebody slap some sense into that bitch," the serious and grim-faced young platinum-blond doctor said. His hair was now on end, as if he had been hit by an electrical shock. Finally, after five minutes of her rollicking and bitter laughter, as if somebody had given Desirée a shock of laughing gas, the doctor proclaimed that the most gorgeous guy in the world was dead—for all eyes, if not ears, to see. The doorman appeared to be shedding tears into a huge colored handkerchief. Soon, the kindly Reverend Elderberry was fulfilling Desirée's request and flagging a Yellow Cab at the entryway to the apartment building.

"Such . . . such a wonderful man, that Reverend Elderberry," Desirée said, feeling lucky to be alive.

"Smooth ole dude all right. But you should see his sons. They are a real treat and a trip, too," the bright-eyed cabbie said.

"Sons?"

"Yeah. Right smart lot of successful sons. Ladies' men so I hear tell. All seven of them."

By Dawn's Early Light: The Meteor in the Madhouse

C h a p t e r   I

Coming out of the Greyhound Bus Terminal at 2:45 P.M., I was vulnerable to the first solicitous and available cabbie.

I was also faced with how to confront this November air, which was in a mournful mood, full of pensiveness and delivering pulverized punches from the Hawk set up for winter. Some gloom always attached to November for me because it was this month of the year (November 21, 1975) when my dear aunt Eloise died.

Just then, I encountered a powerful urgency in the form of a short, stocky, dark-brown-skinned woman with close-cropped hair, tanned down and sleeked back with the aid of Royal Crown pomade. In her tough but worn black leather jacket and her blue-black turtleneck sweater, the stubby cabbie barked directions to me, a seemingly aimless gentleman, to take her cab, a dust-caked, ramshackle taxi—Fleet Lines—as if she were representing central casting and I was slightly out of it and she needed to pick me up out of my listlessness. Forest County had become a center for filmmaking recently. By now, the Hawk seemed to play its own variation of the blues, which was wrung out of the underbelly of a whale.

The cabbie wore a brightly shining tin-silver badge for a name tag: GEORGIA C. J. GLOVER. Behind the smile of her great toothy grin, there was an overall mask with a pugnacious imprint, which she could flash on and off like an engraver's neon sign.

Flexing through the well-creased ebony leather jacket were the arms and biceps of a muscular middle-weight boxer and the quick gesturing hands of one deft at duking it out if necessary, as she swiftly removed my luggage to the trunk. "Where to, mister?" she queried in a fight baritone, which was not displeasing to an inner ear pitched for listening to the saw and bleat of songs tuned for outrageous telling and lying. Almost before I could get the suburban address of the university out of my mouth, C. J. Glover had my big bag in her arc-swinging right hand. When she opened the rear cab door for me to enter, the still awakening, sleepy eyes of this playwright fell upon two other travelers inside the vehicle. A blond female with a pug nose, wearing too much purple-streaked mascara, was seated on the front seat passenger's side. Blessed-cursed with a Kewpie-doll countenance for a face, she was dressed in a Chinese red pantsuit. In the rear was a hovering and trembling young scrawny male—Asian?—no more than twenty.

I immediately balked, "What the hell's this shit? You can only take on one customer at a time! There are laws." There was the immediate voice of rap music barking forth in unknown tongues from the radio.

Stern, unhurried, and full of certainty, C. J. Glover alerted, "Yeah, knows all rags and regs backwards, forwards, sideways, too. Probably rewrote a few of 'em, too. No inconvenience meant to you, sir. Been driving for twenty years. Tell him, Martha Hopper."

"Hell yes! C.J.'s one of the best. Book on it," the blond cried out like a cheerleader and in a voice that offered me no tranquillity. Her bobbing head did not miss a beat to the barking auctioneer's voice of the rap singers. Her diction cracked out of a West Virginian large rock hurling down a West Virginian tributary.

Then, the cabbie's dark mask for a face cracked into a benign beseeching grin. "Just let me run this refuge—whatever—over to Chinatown, and we will be on your merry ways, mister, in three shakes of a lamb's fanny," C.J. lustily coughed up through her crackling baritone, which descended to barrelhouse voice sounds and then became an approximation of Armstrong singing "Mack the Knife."

Glover took an unhurried look at the scrawled-up note in the young man's hand (as if turning it up for a quick exam). There were a few greenbacks pinned to the schoolboy's notepad paper. Returning it all to his palm, C.J. pronounced to her hack "Hit the road, Jack" as she accelerated east, and the emerging Asian face attempted to make heard some utterances about "Dullards, I—"

"And now Glover old girl, should I stand this inconvenience against your tips?" She smiled broadly.

Situating my body into the rear of the cab and out of the nippy November and chilly wet bite, I found myself doing an imitation of a famous Forest County scribe who was telling me how a cabbie got Dan Rather lost in the city.

"Drop his lost puppy butt off under the El tracks, near there. He'll make it just fine. Close 'nough to Kingdom Come. Is this the year of the dog or the rat? He could pass for either," the blond said in a shrill, streaking tenor voice (full of purple ice) as her head kept dipping and bopping off in time to the best of the rap music charging from the battered radio one moment and threatening to fade away the next. Then, Martha Hopper would proceed to give the radio a swift kick-in-the-butt motion with the right heel of her trendy black boots.

For me the crazy rap maze of cackling voices and unknown tongues would return from the underworld kingdom of cackling and crackling, to howl into disjointed knee-jerking jargon, and then clucking up near English. Others were bewailing and bemoaning, exhorting and extorting black English in a vainglorious search to uncover the Mother Tongue behind the veil thousands of miles away in "the Motherland." It wasted a lot of Washington down the sink bubble-bath-babble-scrabble over what is or is not the Mother Tongue, and getting it all mixed up with Mother Nature and the Natural Mother. Meanwhile, now million-mile mansions in the new frontiers of the skies are being discovered, pitched out of the fiery, thunderous mouth of Mother Nature.

Cousin Phillipa was teaching ghetto kids how to think and write in order to soar past a dunk. Always a new project for her washed-out foundlings, not translated in ghetto languages.

Lyrics from the rap burst forth with such crackling tongue speed that it reminded me of a foreigner trying to imitate the spiel of a tobacco auctioneer, or the lashing bid 'em in voice of a slave auctioneer in the not-too-distant past, proclaiming the wonders and satanic qualities of black flesh—particularly female—and pitched to the savage palate of the lascivious marketplace. Merchandise for any price: "Bid 'em in . . . boys . . . bid 'em in."

Observing how the Chinese youth had a lather of sweat about his temple and held tightly to a crumpled-up note, I felt my own nostrils twinge over the peculiar odor of the Asian; repulsive and dislocated out of time, this heart-pounding, breathing skeleton (don't call him Queequeg) seemed at once full of energy and decrepitude. Faced with this eerie stranger, I found my own imagination flickering back to the profiles of "guests" (prior to Vatican II) at Mass who knew not the Latin ordering nor the ongoing ritual performance before their eyes. He'll not be tongueless for long. What the hell, he'll be calling me a "nigger" soon enough, I thought, with the aid of "his kind," and the horror of horrors: the rapper's raking rape, as well. (Even now, he was trying to untie some words—at intervals—with "dullars I got" leading the way.) With his jabbering, exposed, long yellowish teeth, I wondered at some point in his sojourn had he been eating cabbage?

His tatters for clothes were patched up from the cheapest materials, like those hawked by summerwear hustlers around the world and especially over on the Maxwell Street of my childhood. His bloodstained, grayish-white socks were somehow stuffed or shoved into his rope-soled shoes. With a red scarf (infested with dead bugs) whipped about his throat, this wiped-out Chinese lad presented a profile for candidacy to the carnival or circus sideshow. About his grab-bag garb was the stench of old cabbage. From where had this buried child emerged? A Kabuki version of *The Pit and the Pendulum*! Were those mourning waters upon his temple? Had he emerged from the mainland fully clothed? Could he use some camphor oil or was he poled and pooled out of the piss of existence by some boatman's rod and reel? Who was the somebody ready to welcome him into the perils of Chinatown? Was it some dragon ready to devour him whole, body and soul?

"C.J., who do you think you supposed to be, Mr. Confucius? Hell, this piss-poor punk don't the fuck know what you say, up from down, any shit-faced how. By, up-under, near, or beneath the El. Chink-eyed sapsucker don't know your black English from my honky black-and-blue English. 'Sides, baby, I'm hungry as a hound dog's tongue."

"Martha, you love to spread confusion, don't you, gal? 'Cause soon as he sees faces in the streets of his own kind and all them little cells of Chinese chicken scratch, he'll embrace. He'll lighten up. Ain't that right, mister? A glowworm will let go-a-go-go on the insides of his temple."

"Me, too, after I get what you promised to put into my mouth three hours ago, and this dear bitch ain't taken care of business yet."

"Watch your mouth (and your lips), Martha, we got gentlemens of class in this cab," C. J. Glover said, with a sentimental whisper.

The cab sped away, and the head of the blond bopped and nipped with the driven beat of an infuriated drummer as she was consumed by the rhythm of the songs and the rapper's rhymes. Martha Hopper seemed to know each syllable as some wanton but talented revealer and reveler of unknown untempered tongues (buried in the desert veins of a valley from yesteryear). Hurried back to life by some puppeteer's art, the blond's whipped-up, hip-hopped, tongue-twister talents found delight in (no matter the tastelessness of the words she spewed forth), all of which apparently delighted her translator's palate for heterodoxy and hieroglyphics. Her head beating and neck snapping was so fierce, as if bent on self-punishment, while at the same time giving some invisible puppets (or dolls) a good, old-fashioned head cracking with her own noggin. She was one rag-doll rapper, I laughed. Certainly not a paper doll to call on. Perhaps this Martha Hopper had dreamed of playing with black dolls and had ended up playing black rap. But there she was an American original; her whiteness pitched into the shadows of blackness.

Sounding off as if I had been recently released from the grave after a thousand years of being buried in the valley so low, I now dared to offer up, "Could you cut that down a trifle?" But my words were no match for the amplified onslaught and backbeat of the singer's imitation of life—jawboned and crackling thunder. Maybe my grandson, the actor, would continue his lessons with Professor Joubert Antoine Jones's course packet titled "Rappers 99."

"Yeah, I can see for myself. What you do, mister? Lawyer for royalty? The syndicate? You got some sweetheart deal up in the 'burbs? Hope you ain't no overcultivated ass," Martha said with a whispery, wicked laugh. Then she gave a flirtatious wink.

"I teach creative writing and literature," I said, in a silvery whisper. "Mainly, I coach kids who want to be playwrights," I said in a weary voice.

After taking it all in and sizing me up, "You sure 'nough got a sugarplum of a sweetheart deal," Martha Hopper laughed.

Turning her head quickly to me, C.J. said softly, "Martha could teach a course or two on spreading confusion. Spreading shit, too."

Martha continued to bob her head and then snapped her fingers and jabbered to the pitch and spiel of the rapper. She was truly jammin' now!

Then in a voice of sweet prodding, C.J. said, "Gentlemen probably prefer Pavarotti to your ghetto-box gang-banging."

Martha flicked the radio tuner down a fainthearted fraction. At a long stoplight C. J. Glover declared, "Well one thing's sure, you can come to the right place for lies. I get a thousand and one stories a month right in this very cab, mister. Some lies better than Satan can conjure up on a holiday, if he takes one. Why just two Sunday mornings back, sky-high sucker told me his soul was in such a worse-off condition, devil himself can't auction it at any price, even to a fire sale. So, he was on the way to the Apple. Flying out there to see if he couldn't find himself a publisher to peddle souls or his story to. Knew he could, too. Coke high and still flying, probably pitched so high he didn't need no plane to wing his way to the Big Apple."

Martha howled, "C.J. mix mound of Jack Rabbit shit and horse manure into more lies than you can shake a stick at. Don't know the difference between Chinese and Siamese."

"Now look Miss Fur Pants of 1978, I know what I saw and I saw what I read."

" 'Cause you can't tell who's lying, who's flying, who's facting, who's backtracking, and who's simply crackin'."

"A priest may be humping little altar boys and sending part of his monthly check back home to support his sister's hongry children. A gang-banging pimp may be running for mayor. I don't know these days—do you, mister? Another fare from the airport was coming from the reception following a fabulous wedding where the groom suddenly ups and puts down some ill crazy shit before he lifts a toast. Told all his guests to look beneath the bottom of their chairs. Open the envelope they finds there. No, it was not Academy Awards game show. What's inside? His bride and his best man hot into the act! Ballroom got overheated. Folks was fainting. Priest what married 'em upchucks all over the place. Groom raises up a toast to the bride and best man: 'Fuck both of you.' He splits the scene. Groom's mother starts bleeding from the nostrils. Ten batches of medics arrives, then the manager of the hotel and catering folks flies in out of nowhere. Bride's father comes at the best man with the cook's butcher knife. World's gone stone-cold crazy, mister."

I started to say, Yeah, and are you two partners tag-team wrestling? But I held my tongue.

The Chinese lad continued to tremble as if caught up in the early stages of some big, bad fever leading to a breakout of a new, deadly strain of Hong Kong flu.

Pointing over her shoulder, C.J. said, "He be somebody's little, shivering, snot running, Angel-chile. I don't care how fucked up and crazy, too, this old world is, Georgie, C. J. Glover knows right from wrong. Whosoever scrawled a number on that Chinese laundry ticket pinned some bread to this note. This boy meant something to them back over there."

All of this now sparked something in me: "I know what you mean on both counts, too. World's mad and sleek and greasy, and God help the innocent without sufficient mother wit. God help the perishable needy and the greasy greedy, panting for the needy. And save the needy from the greedy from within. Ah, it's all so crazy.

"I've got this wonderful but terribly needy younger cousin, Phillipa, who teaches third grade in the ghetto, where the kids are greedy for— hell, they are starved for affection; hungry for some form of uplift, a boost. Then she's trying to help out with the problems in the high school, too.

"Not long ago, through secret passageways, beloved but gullible Phillipa had brought in one dozen cartons of Trojans for the upper-grade dudes and placed them in a small cove of a room. Her best girlfriend Jacquil (who teaches part-time chemistry in the adjacent high school and algebra in the upper-grade center) was to dispense some of this treasure trove the following week when she returned from Las Vegas, where she had gone on sick leave to recuperate.

"Phillipa had purchased the Trojans at bargain-basement prices, because of the large lot. On her return, when she flipped on the light switch, Jacquil discovered their enterprise had been ripped off. Apparently, this was not so secret a storage place and was now being used by upper-grade kids to make out and lay-up atop the boxes of acquisitions. Now, 'hot rubbers' are selling on a black-market scheme by some cunning young Johnny-come-lately, prince of the apple-sap-seed."

"Mister, you speak so proper, even when you tell a funny story. Problem is, how to get these steamy young dudes to pull up those Trojans before it starts raining, before they starts to fumbling, feeling, and fucking in the dark," Martha said, her wrathful voice coming from some place on high.

"Yeah, 'cause these young stud horses just won't keep their hot dicks in their pants. Hot to leap into some sis-tuh's box. So pantin' to pull down the first hot young nasty's pants. Frantic-panic studs ain't got time to pull up a cold Trojan. Think they triple-time hip. Bloodless dudes so ripe they don't hold you; can't be a natural-born man lest you boning up your trim-swimmin' freestyle and comin' clean to the bone. Sis-tuhs be sapsuckers for a riff rap by any riffraff. Breadless brothers don't have to have no hang, just be hung. Nine months later . . . ," trailed off the voice of the reflective C. J. Glover.

"Dullars, ah got. Dullars, ah got," the Chinese youth finally unraveled his words. Then I found myself remembering that time when Aunt Eloise, two months before her own death, had visited Haiti, bursting plumage of pastoral paintings. There were beggars in the streets of Port-au-Prince where blood was being sold (as in a bank). "Blood for bread"; youths, kids, begging adults, pregnant girls crying out and striking their breasts as if invoking some weird penance and voodoo beads about their necks. Tatter-flagged beggars crying, "Blood for bread." A litany of utterances from the ill-formed, zigzag line leading to the boxed-off portable latrine painted in red, white, and blue, which stood as a makeshift receiving chamber. Puny natives offering up their arms in a most unbloody manner for the body and soul of bread; some to buy wine, others to buy drugs. Those in the middle praying to Damaballah, and farther down the line several right hands going up and down, over and across the upper body in a whipping-style motion. Sign of the Cross, again and again, praying and hoping the door to the sanctuary of a latrine would not suddenly be locked: boxing off the day's service for blood into bread. Hypodermic needles pitched to the wasting-away veins. Man does not live by bread alone, yes, but Haitian art depicted none of this. A nation in need of a fix to leverage its fixation over voodoo and Catholicism, unending in the pimpish Papa for starters.

"Georgia, I just hope he means something to somebody over here and not some bloodless, greedy creature. Obviously, this kid is a natural-born needy sucker," I said.

"Best be saying dollars you got ain't yours to give away. Best be having something to sell over here that don't cost you an arm and a leg," C. J. Glover said in a sweet-self baritone voice, yet almost as a litany to herself. As if to bring the direction of the conversation back on track, I heard her listening just now to Prince's "When Doves Cry," but as a message in the interlude.

A few blocks later and suddenly coming out of a mean interrogator's mode, Martha Hopper said, "Mister, what could you do for a boy like this?"

"Don't fuck with my fare, Martha Hopper. Could use some class in this cab," C. J. Glover said, even as she winked at the lady with the long blond hair, and their eyes met for a fleeting moment.

"He'd have to learn my language in order to become an American, first of all," I said dryly.

C. J. Glover continued to delight at how, apparently, the blond knew with almost too much precision the way rap songs jangled forth out of the radio that needed a kick or slam every few minutes to get the sound back on track. Martha was like a drummer kicking the pedal. Between songs, she didn't like any of the disc jockey jabber, or the commercials.

Now Martha had C.J. buried over the wheel in convulsions of laughter for pithy vignettes of her flights and car chases with gangs and cops in the last three days. And I thought, "C.J., I know what I could do for a girl like this—send her to a cuisine school. Teach her some refinement. Let her read *Pygmalion* to settle her pugnacious baseness."

They were a hapless, half-hip duo. And yet, they were also a scream and a lark. Where had they met? A newly renovated Kitty-Cat Club up on the North Side?

Georgia C. J. Glover drove her hack with the unhurried sensibility of an artist in a lounge chair before an easel. Making her turns, stroking away in her own rhythms and time, she even made up faces celebrating her craft of avoiding near encounters in traffic; turned it all into either interior monologues, brief dialogues, or spats with Martha.

When C. J. Glover maneuvered her cab into Chinatown, the lad's face went incandescent, and he gave a "bulletin" for all to hear, "Chinatown," tolling three times. C.J. winked at me and howled. The youth gave her all of his "dullars." Quickly, she was out of the cab and shepherding him to the corner and around it.

Wasn't it crazy, the circuitous routes life took you on? Was this the man's fate, too? How the hell did I end up over here in Chinatown?

C. J. Glover had parked alongside an antique white Buick, while Martha Hopper and I waited in the cab. The blond observed, "Whomsoever did this wild, weird, work gotta be dyslexic." She was pointing to the oddly fashioned, backwards scrawl and printout of gang names, signs, and slogans that made the auto look like a carnival for high jinks of all kinds, I meditated.

It was a morning full of pensive moods, blue streaks, as if you were lost in a chill, and fog was on the way but doing a slow crawl, a killing dance of an octopus in motion. The question was, When was it going to rain? "How did he get from over there to over here?" I wondered out loud.

"Well, Mr. Playwright Coach, or is it 'professor'? You know the story about catching the fish that swallowed the queer queen's ring? Now I'd like to see that inside one of them fortune cookies. Near the fucking river. Maybe he swam over for all I know."

"Martha, you're a trip and a voyeur, an Easter bunny made up of a half loaf of butternut bread. That's probably what your fortune cookie would reveal." Martha was not amused.

"Hey dude, don't try to strip, don't scope me, and please don't try to script me," she said, as if preparing her tongue to untie a scheme of rap curses and cutting verses. But the slight shift in the chaff of her tone was mainly playful. Then Martha Hopper got back to her most pressing needs.

"C.J. should cop some Chinese carryouts. She never thinks about nobody but her own big black butt. Nobody. Other than that she is boo-too-ful people. As a matter of fact, they oughta give C.J. a half dozen carryouts for delivering up this lost-found yelping little orphan puppy. Wonder how much ass he peddled to get to America," Martha mumbled to herself. "You know, mister, C.J. has her a heart bigger than the whole state of Texas."

"You do appear to hold contradictory ideas about C.J."

"Not to my mind, I don't. C.J.'s family hails from some lost African tribe that landed in Jamaica before Plymouth Rock. Each of 'em could outfight anybody. She's probably a third cousin to Jack Johnson. (Looks like him, too, though Georgia is squat built.) Point is: nobody but nobody was goin' pick that poor piss pot up. (Could you smell—how could you not smell him, less you suffer from a hugely stopped-up nose?) Nobody but C.J. would of done it for love or money—period. Do you know—course you don't—exactly how long he'd been waiting for a cab? How many wouldn't pick him up! And her talking about his kind would know him. That's shit. They can be heartless to their own, too. His kind didn't care enough to take that Chinaman the last dog-shed miles to his destination. This all might be a set up for what we know."

"Now I'm descending deeper into the dark about your regard for C.J."

"Ain't got nothing to do with my regard. Georgia like and care for many down-and-outs, but she don't love nobody. Her heart belongs to the state of Georgia. Period!

"I had had so many jobs. One of them had me strutting my stuff 'round the boxing ring between rounds with a red, white, and blue placard carried aloft announcing the next round, no matter how much blood was split between the two fighters in the last round. Ain't it crazy how you get into things. I figured I could do all what these dudes did without getting cut 'cause they don't allow razors inside of boxing gloves. I'd run and jog with these dudes. Meantime, too, I'm building up my biceps at the gym. Hey mister, want to actually feel of my muscles? My right arm is royal."

"I don't think so," I demurred, defensively.

"I've got a real righteous left jab. C.J. herself said it."

"I can believe it. How did you two meet?"

"At a cockfight. Not too far from where we gonna drop you off, in the 'burbs. C.J. was part-time driver for a distinguished, silver-haired-looking cracker, who smoked a cigar longer than an elephant's dick with a hard-on; called himself the Lone Ranger. He was a freak for cockfights. Would only appear at those cockfights wearing a mask and his white Stetson hat."

"Oh," I smiled and let out a wicked scream.

"C.J. is my trainer. She's done everything, too. For a time, she passed herself off as a man in order to get work as a grave digger. 'Time after time, times is tougher than an Eskimo's titty,' C.J. will say. As for me, I got energy to burn off, if she'll just fucking feed me. Want to know something else about her, Mr. Gentleman? C.J. has two sets of false teeth. If I'm lying, I'm flying."

When C.J. got back into the taxi, she immediately prevailed on Martha to switch radio stations. "Them raps most probably racked the brain of this gentlemen of distinction to seeds. You all right back there, mister?" Soon they were listening to another musical sphere. This station was playing "Never Let Me Go," by Luther Vandross. Georgia and Martha hummed a duet to the music. For a minute or two, they were lost in each other's glances and whispers, grooving touches and soft laughs over old jokes. C.J. headed for the Drive. I thought of the manipulation of the needy. And the neediness of the greedy. Hell, everybody was needy.

Take A.M.-P.M., who called my office at the university the week before. I would get calls from A.M.-P.M. (who now claimed himself to be a cinematographer) from a variety of telephone sources, booths, or, when it was turned on, from the hookup in his cell of a room concerning a film he was "putting together."

He always wanted to "make a place for me before it was too late." Apparently, A.M.-P.M. (he came by this name because he might call you at any hour of the day or night) was conjuring up a movie pitched to epic proportions. And yet, concretely, it was difficult to say specifically what the projected footage was all about, or, for that matter, how much actual film had been shot.

Sometimes in the dark of night, I would get calls from him enraptured within the snuggle of his hammock, which was hung up from wall to wall in a tiny room of a shoddy hotel on East Forty-seventh. Most often, he was about to run out of coins (and would soon enough run out of nickels) when he called from one of the few telephones left in the slums that was not torn from its moorings. On many occasions, his voice had the quality of a rusty nail scraped over a fossil. I wondered if this wretch, wheezing and retching wretch (who had evidenced potential as a poet, once upon a time), would not be better off in the quarantined section of Forest County Hospital for those suffering from tuberculosis. But soon enough, perhaps in three weeks, I'd get another call in which it was revealed that A.M.-P.M. was back in his hammock (the power restored), swinging away and making these "key telephone calls" to potential backers for a film that either did not exist or would never be made. Or, was there actual footage in the can? Yet his ideas about a film-in-progress intrigued me. (I was always ready to stop whatever I was doing in order to be engaged by yet another story from: madman, fool, banker, intellectual, cop, clown, tramp, rouge, priest, baker, whore, or politician.) He never actually made a formal request for any specific amount, which was either very cunning or yet another manifestation of his innocence; probably a little of both.

A.M.-P.M. had a scroll of potential contributors. But how many had actually sent in "donations"? I was aware of five "participants" who had expressed interest in the enterprise. Mainly, they considered themselves "donors" not to his project but to keep him from drifting off into the growing community of street people. Yet, they were always ready to offer some mythical rationalization about the creative powers of A.M.-P.M., as if creativity were a faucet that one turned off and on. Because he had taught in certain black studies departments in the early days of their formations, A.M.-P.M. had contacts around the country and would call on some of the leading black academics in this country. Actually, a few of these men had been his former students. They remembered him with great sentiment and would send along a few dollars to support his "cause" on occasion. Always remember the fallen brethren. "Brother has lived the life and we all know how creative he is," call went out. He was not without pedigree in their imaginations nor in their memories of him when he was a poet out of the beatnik era, then into the civil rights, Black Power period. Some of these backers were quite successful men and had gone to school with him. Now, out of a sense of guilt or nobility, they would "lay a little bread on the brother before he is buried underground over on Wacker," as one executive of the Urban League had told me at a famous soul food restaurant over lunch one afternoon.

There was also the feeling that A.M.-P.M. had fallen through the cracks mainly because of the evil value system of white supremacy. For he had always evidenced a "racial vision and lived a vagabond, bohemian life," as an associate provost for minority affairs at the state college had informed me at a South Side bar at closing time.

Describing himself as a "get-down brother, who still loved to boogie," this associate provost declared, "Let me run it down for you, Joubert. My man was passed over so as to raise up some of these sistuh artists. Bourgeoisie B's, well educated and talented, sure 'nough. But raised up by The Man all the same to keep the truly radical brother in check, down, and running. And none of them have my man's grit, shit, or wit. These new, young, fine creative sistuhs ain't paid no firing-line dues, Joubert. We both can agree on that. This nigguh's bad, Joubert, get down, bad."

"Mad, too."

"Your response shocks me. Tell me the true artist who ain't mad to the bone . . . to the nines . . . Bird, Monk, Billie, the list is endless."

As we headed for the door, I said, "But the question must be: 'At the end of the day,' as you big time executives are so fond of saying, where's the beef? How much actual footage does A.M. have in the can?"

"Joubert, you harder than a heart attack. Don't have any pity in your heart for your brother artist. Now you been writing all your days. How much stuff you got hidden away nobody's read? What about that painter, what's his face? Van Gogh. Crazy, too. Cut off his ear and gave it to a whore. Look at all the canvases he left behind."

I started to say, Why doesn't he? We should all give up the ghost about A.M.-P.M. and admit that he's a charity-ward case and how he's faked himself out of his own jockey strap.

As if he had overheard my thoughts, the associate provost declared, "See, Joubert, that's the problem with us, as a people. We give up on our folks. You got to lay in the cut. Pull up the fallen brother, as much as you can."

"Thanks for the Cliff Notes on the saga of the Fallen Brother. However, I think I'll keep my hands in my pockets."

A week later I received a call at midnight from A.M.-P.M.

"I want to save a slot for you. Let's see. I've got you down at 135. No, that's Wilson Pickett. Number 129? I can hardly pick up this book it's so—oh no, that's Armstrong's."

"He's dead." Ah! The ghost payroll of Forest County.

"Oh, I know, 128! That's you baby. On the money."

"How much bread, A.M.? An arm and a leg?"

"See how your change going. Practically anything welcomed."

"Oh."

"So look, Joubert. Oh, did I inform you about Wesley?"

"Not the—?"

"Did I say 128's open with your name? Cool. Yeah. Wes is looking into it. I'll get back to you about Backer's Row. Lay low. Later."

The sweet musical essences didn't completely bring quiet to Martha's appetite. For soon she was saying, "I'm hungry! And when Martha Hopper gets hungry, C.J. (hello, world), she gets fistfighting evil! How I'm going to keep in prizefighting shape without getting my proper nourishing? You must want me to go out this world backwards or something. See, C.J., your problem is you don't take care of your own. You always helping some others."

"Don't I ever know how hongry you can get when you gets evil! (Now, imagine a white blond gal with that word even waxing on her lips, voodoo red. I'll leave all of that alone.) But Gawd help the world, when you say you are starved."

"C.J., you should have copped us some Chinese takeout. Do I have to tell you everything, while you over there playing Miss Fucking Care Package—Travelers' Aid—Mother Teresa—Jesus Lover of My Soul!"

"Basically, Martha (Don't worry mister, this here is just friendly fire), basically, you don't think before you leapfrog talk. That's all what's wrong with—. I got a very patient fare back there and could not expect this extra-special Mr. Gentlemens to wait no longer. 'Sides, after the way you showed out prejudice to that poor Chinese boy, I'm truly surprise to learn how Martha Hopper will eat their pecks in a pinch."

"I want to go to Popeye's," Martha proclaimed.

"Nothing in the world like Popeye's chicken. Lawd knows. (Don't worry mister, you just caught up in friendly fire, but you'll survive Martha and Georgia.)"

"Colonel's chicks ain't spiked with poison either. C.J., we could hit one of 'em on the way back from dropping off Prof Writing Coach, here. But I prefer Popeye's night and day."

"Or, you prefer, you pretty pug you. Mister, don't you just love this girl? She knows something 'bout almost anything. But basically, she don't understand shit from shinola. However, she's in training. No seriously, I am training her (in all kinds of ways). Since Martha was (still does, too) all the time getting into fistfights, I'm telling you, mister, by me getting this baby into prizefighting, I probably saved her from getting killed. Calm down," she said to Martha, "next you'll be crying and wantin' your bottle."

"Yeah, and I'm fighting mad right now, and my stomach's about to beat my brain's out."

"You see, mister, I joined Martha up with Ring Plasterers. All women pugs. She's had ten fights. Won all by TKOs. Now the problem is she don't know when to move in for the kill. I just bet that's what you think. Basically, the dear little Martha here likes to punish up on her opponents. Behind this pug's cute face is a hard-nosed killer instinct, for blood, baby, blood."

I reflected that there was something about Martha that one might define as possessing an incendiary soul.

"Martha keeps good time on the small bag."

Then C.J. cleared her throat and settled in with "Mister, you might could help us out here. We trying to come up with a pure name for Martha, a kind of sportin' nickname. Help me pin a tag on this pug. We ain't hardly hit on one proper to propel her pug power yet."

I started to open my mouth to say, Why don't you call her Raging Bull. No, alas and alack. Let the dead past bury the dead. (Oh, there goes the spirit of Aunt Lucasta just now.) Somehow Blond Bombshell was not quite proper, nor very original.

As C.J. drove her cab the final mile to my destination on the campus, I thought about the kind of tip I would add to the fare. It would have to possess a flair that would not appear nor sound antiseptic.

"What about Deep Purple Ice? Or, since you like rap so much, why not just Purple Ice?"

"Sounds like a death warrant to me," Martha said.

"I kinda like it. Somewhat! Maybe Ice-Water Martha would be good, too, and not too cold either. Deep Ice is righteous to a heartache."

"Are you signifying with me, grave digger?"

"White girl, if I ever slips you into the dozens, you'll know it. (More friendly fire.) Why you ain't laced up yet."

A nickname for C.J., too? River-of-No-Return. Another kind of tip for Martha? Obviously, the girls had enjoyed my company, somewhat. Perhaps I'd suggest they call the trainer Mother Goose. They were quite an "entanglement," I laughed. A mischievous idea formed within my imagination.

With my direction, C.J. negotiated the cab through the narrow entrance to the campus, leading to the building where my office was housed. Martha turned the radio off and C.J. turned on the inner light of the cab. She put on a pair of heavy-duty spectacles and proceeded to look up the rate from the Greyhound station to this suburb in a blue-gray book that appeared in the condition of a battered text to my eyes. "Wishes to be exact, Brother Prof," she said in a deeply reflective voice. "Wants to be fair, too. Deduct something for the time we took off your time, so as to drop that kid off in Chinatown, mister." Her pronounced bill was fair and square, I mused.

An old line came unleashed from within my soul as I mulled over the proper tip and C.J. made out my receipt for the trip.

"I'm like big bear's daughter. Ain't got the better parts of a quarter." And so in a voice of one copping a plea, I demurred (as I handed C.J. the exact change for the fare) the old folk line. With a bolt of surprise, Martha howled; a chuckle from the deep bass drum of C.J.'s voice box.

Then Georgia said with a merry twinkle in her eyes, "Mister, just what is your name?"

As the driver bounded out of the cab to retrieve my luggage from the trunk, I unfolded seven dollars, which I placed in her hand. We walked to the front of the cab, and I placed my right foot up on the front bumper on the passenger's side. Martha rolled her window down completely. C.J. stood at the driver's side with the door ajar. I said, "C.J., I'll make this quick and smart, because it's nippy out here in the November dark; campus security might roll around and wonder if we weren't playing Three Pigs in a Blanket. I'm going to tell you my name in the form of a rap and a tip for Martha, too. I'll verse you but I won't curse you." I steadied myself for a moment and said, "Now let me select my rhymes."

As I worked up an effective treble-tone sound, a flood of rhymes emerged as babbling waters of unknown tongues—untapped before. Then I spat forth:

"Just because I'm a so-phis-ti-cate (having known the great and near great), don't get faked out by my balding pate. Don't contemplate; you can't re-pu-di-ate. Or try to up-date, low-rate nor con-tam-i-nate, or even com-pli-cate. This bad-ass-prime-mate's fate. Don't try to negotiate nor perpetuate a crate of tales; they predicate out of their power-intoxicated-state. Yes, and don't try to commiserate (since I sure 'nough don't equivocate). Just you get your own soul straight. 'Cause this cat-of-nine tales can adjudicate, coolly interpret and renegotiate. Now please get this straight—my soul condition, through any evil State of perdition—and previous condition. So turn your cab 'round. Go straight back downtown. Interrogate and turn all around those clowns and clones, heed the 'pealing tones. Who would complicate the fate— Who would slay the estate of this man—Joubert Jones!"

The gleeful women screamed, but each in her own way.

"Sir, can I have your autograph?" C.J. said, and extending one of her cards for me to write on.

As I was giving my autograph, Martha said, "Well, Mr. Jones. You simply got to create a name, a punch line, a tag for me. You're a riot, Mr. Jew-Bear Jones." Her arm extended across C.J.'s torso and out the window with one of C.J.'s cards in her fingertip.

C. J. Glover just shook her head in disbelief. A great wall of amusement turned her dark mask of a face into yet another countenance not observed before. It was as if she had just seen and heard General Colin Powell suddenly rise up from his chair before the Joint Chiefs and not give his prepared speech, but rather launch into a rap before this distinguished gathering.

Now, as I picked up my luggage, I watched Martha and C.J. embrace wildly; two bodies grafted as one and conjuring up in my mind an image of a couple who have come upon a specialty shop of unique and even relic intrigue, while out strolling on a pleasurable excursion in part of the city they had not seen before. And the paradoxical fun of the discovery hurls them into a fun-filled embrace after leaving the curiosity shop. Quaint and, yes, a little delightfully queer, they both proclaimed.

As I started to ascend the steps leading into the building, a cold chill came across me as one who has emerged from a swim into unknown waters, who can't get the iron water liquids wrapped about his tongue and circulating about his gums, out of his mouth and off his tongue to depart from his soul.

For five minutes, I tried to spit out the easy come, easy go rhyme-rap out of my mouth, in the men's room. Was the spirit of Aunt Eloise about and haunting me with a verse-curse of her own? These waters kept reemerging in my mouth and became juicy slush about my body and soul. "Aunt Eloise's curse!" I cried aloud. I felt ill and washed out by the spiel of those words, words, and more words. I felt the penance from my aunt as a cruel stepmother. (And much tougher then, when as a kid she would say, "Go wash your mouth out with a lot of soap and water" after I had spat forth curse words.)

I thought now of Leonard Foster, of his constant disdain of my perceived "frivolous actions." Amid the spectator's put-down of the show-out, there was much truth in the poet's assessment of this playwright's passion to create a set piece and to act the role of cut-up.

As the elevator slowly ascended to my office in the tower, I recalled reading fragments of Cousin Epistolla's diaries at the summer home at the Pier. I had decided to write the Pope and spill all of the beans about the nun. I had started to get it all down using Aunt Eloise's Esterbrook fountain pens, which I found in a hidden compartment of an old desk. There was enough ink discovered in seven bottles for me to pour off and compose one of blue-black ink. I found myself incorporating many quotes from Cousin Epistolla's diaries. Her own riff on Free Will was a howl and a relic smasher; and all of it got my playwright's imagination to ripping and rambling, flying and flinging forth. For her memoirs contained some fabulous materials—lovable and lascivious, lyrical and rowdy-bawdy and taboo-breaking all over the place.

There was more than enough material here to springboard a play. I decided to, first of all, nominate the lowly nun for a station higher and more elevated in the hindsight of the Creator, if not Almighty God himself, and ecclesiastical Roma. Yes, more elevated than sainthood and more real, albeit more fantastical, too. What shall we call it? Wizardry Untold or Divine Wizardry? (Too much Faust? Too much bourbon?)

I had been well into the thirteenth page of my petition, when I was hit with an attack of the hiccups, which lasted for sixty-seven minutes before it subsided.

It was at the height of the hiccup attack that it occurred to me I had been visited by Aunt Eloise's hit squad from the other side of the grave for the grievous gall of writing the Pope this BULL. Specifically, the assault had started at the exact moment when I had conveyed in writing (and quoting from Cousin Epistolla's text) how she had dressed herself up as a priest and heard confessions and lowered her voice in order to know firsthand more about God's purpose and man's mischievous or evil deeds. A priest at the parish church had aided and abetted her in some mysterious ways (perhaps revealed elsewhere). He later renounced Holy Orders and sent her heated love letter epistles. In one, he thanked Epistolla for allowing him to return the compliment by giving him "a close shave and providing me with the garments to live amongst the nuns of your order and to learn of their habits."

Now as I entered the front office of the department, I scoffed. Could the Holy See take this without vaulting the petition to elevate my cousin from the condition of *blessed* to that of *saint—From See to Shining Sea?*

Flipping on the light in my office, I immediately turned on the coffeepot, added some Colombian coffee, and smiled at the impending aroma. Atop my desk, I discovered a virtual mound of papers, but in neat stacks of mail: newspapers; students' graduate work, naturally; and requests for reference letters, eternally.

Chapter 2

Now, as I stirred the cream and sugar into half of the cup of black Colombian coffee, I thought, "Well, let's tackle the *New York Times* for starters." Suddenly I glimpsed a subheadline from the *New York Post,* just to the left of the *Times:*

DRUGGED-OUT POET ROBBED

LEFT FOR DEAD IN THE GUTTER

I quickly delved into the story of a personally shocking account, published in the edition two days ago. It was to my angst a story of Leonard Foster's downfall.

His badly beaten body revealed that he was in critical condition. Discovered in the rainswept streets of a New York slum, near a drug den, with a packet of cocaine stashed away in his purple beret inside the thin inner lining (which one?) of his tattered and muddied topcoat. Ah, that same old green and orange great coat, no doubt, with ripped-open and sewn-over patches for pockets. The poor bastard! Beloved and howling against and lamenting over—bought it from the Catholic Salvage, late November 1965. I reached into the bottom drawer of my desk and poured off about a jigger of Maker's Mark into the coffee cup.

A narco car of undercover cops had discovered Leonard Foster in the snow, called the medics, and they had rushed him to a local (unnamed) hospital. Listed in critical. . . . My God.

It was revealed in the article, from the word of his live-in-lady, that Foster had depleted the total cash limit his bankcard allowed in order to deal for the four packets of cocaine. A robber had brutally assaulted him, left Leonard Foster for dead, and taken three of the four packets. Leonard's unnamed lady friend—"a junkie and a prostitute"—told the police of the "hobby" she and Leonard shared: "freebasing." I took a swig from the bottle of Maker's Mark. I'll have to fly out to New York, or get in contact with Shirley and see. The rush of bourbon through my body braced me for the moment, but I felt terrified for Leonard Foster and guilty as hell for abandoning him.

DRUGGED-OUT POET ROBBED

LEFT FOR DEAD IN THE GUTTER

What a headline, I cried, finally sipping from the cup of coffee, my caffeine mixture, Gem of the Ocean.

Why the robber(s) had left one packet of cocaine was unclear, as best I could glean from this story. Maybe some not-too-distant cruising cop car had frightened the robber(s) away. Or, I speculated, had some undercover detectives leaped out of an unmarked car—earlier—beaten Leonard, and, the marketplace bidding, stripped the "monstrous merchandise" off the body of this tormented, lost poet left to freeze to death in the snow? *Oh, God, that it would come to this—the lyrical, ruinous Leonard, who had made a riot of his life. His soul had been on a rack for a long time. Luckless, hapless Leonard, the loser. A murderous morbidity coursed through his veins. Abandoned by all but particularly by me, especially me,* I grieved. Me abandoning him, too, the pledge to Aunt Eloise, Cuz Lucasta, and Granny Gram Gussie to watch over this child of the storm. Shirley Polyneices, too. I had promised her.

Something out of Welling's production at Stratford, Canada, of *A Midsummer Night's Dream*, out of Theseus's mouth, about the mix of wild poet and lover. . . . Yet why should I grieve so totally over Leonard, after the letters of denunciation I had received from my would-be kinsman? He had accused me of stealing our magazine, *The Dark Tower*, and not accounting for the five hundred dollars the poet had contributed. Twelve issues had been published. Now only seven copies of each number were in my possession.

Not surprisingly, *The Dark Tower* had not made a profit. At three dollars and fifty cents the magazine was overpriced for the early seventies, when it finally emerged as a biannual (not a monthly). But the magazine had profited yours truly plenty, Leonard had contended. When the director for an Off-Broadway company, the Sky Loft Players, read a severely cut version of *The Roof, the People, and the Steeple* in *The Dark Tower*, I was contacted and the work was eventually performed. Later it was nominated for a Tony Award. Honors and prizes, university appointments and honorary degrees, and money for one-acts had followed.

Deeply agitated over what he perceived to be my success, Leonard soon discovered that his partner had sent several copies of the magazine (the second number) to different theater people, with the hope that one would show some interest in the drama. "The tails of your tales possess many tongues, with the razor's edge of deceit crafted away in their tattling and tolling," the pissed-off poet wrote me.

Spilling some of the cup of Colombian coffee, I murmured through my conflicted memories of Leonard some words of religious incantation (long since forgotten until this moment) for Leonard's physical and mental rehabilitation—*To thee we cry, poor banished children of Eve. To thee do we cry, poor banished children of Eve. . . . To thee do we send up our sighs, mournings, weeping into the valley of tears. Turn then, most gracious advocate, thine eyes of mercy upon us, show us the fruit of thy womb.*

Maybe Leonard thought this shit up his nose to his brain would bring a poetic exaltation, never heard before this side of paradise: jump-starting the powers of his imagination. Ah, need-based Leonard, freebasing into the new enslavement. But here Cato is wrong about buy not what you want but what you need. Leonard was so needy (always peddling in the wrong market for a spiritual high and comfort, in order not to deal with the horrors of abandonment) with his own river-deep vulnerabilities and callous insecurities. Pity poor Leonard, with no name in the street other than junkie. Yet I also felt now as a pirate and not a friend. Only Cousin Lu stood up as a mother.

I immediately started to make phone calls awakening the dead. Shirley, first of all.

The last time I saw Leonard Foster was under a peculiar set of circumstances, touched by the wand of strange, smokinghouse madness.

After appointments at several universities and colleges—where I taught either playwriting or literature courses—I finally settled down at my current post, in 1987, with a chair in creative writing and literature. This position doesn't intellectually circumscribe me into extolling any of the foolish literary theories abounding in most contemporary English departments; nor is there any attempt to edge me off into embracing the "patty-cake, patty-cake baker's man, roll 'em in the oven just as fast as you can," programmed *theories* of M.F.A. writing program chefs or cooks. No, I don't have to serve on committees, and I can pretty much come and go as I please, as long as I teach three courses a year, scheduled for the quarter system. Sometimes I'll double up and get the spring quarter, or the fall, off. I can devise any kind of course my imagination conjures.

Around the time of my appointment to this chair, our family started going out twice a month to a most delightful brunch at, of all places, the local Holiday Inn. Often time Phillipa—the cousin I helped to support through college—joins us at these Sunday brunches and provides us with the latest intelligence report on life at the ghetto school where she teaches. We end up crying one moment and laughing the next, high jinks and then howling in horror over the administrative absurdity, amid our tears, in the next breath.

Our family came to enjoy the variety of the cuisine, and the general treatment of the staff, so much, that we planned a small graduation party for our grandson, Xavier, upstairs (in this very place, which was to become the scene, pouring forth with smoke, and providing this quite shocking encounter, and what proved to be my last memory of seeing Leonard Foster alive).

I particularly enjoy those brunches where catfish, oysters Rockefeller, and eggs served over lightly are part of the fare, and topped off with a glass of champagne. Now I suspect all of this reminds me of my dear, deceased aunt Eloise and her fun-filled, innovative brunches, at which dozens of people from the *Forest County Dispatch*, the Altar and Rosary society, and her gang from up at the pier arrived at 12:30 and left at 3:00—half of their number loaded down with Aunt Eloise's marvelous gumbo, oysters Rockefeller, and Möet champagne. And on certain occasions she would devise, stir up, and serve her varied blend of eggs and lobsters. Even now, many years after her death, I can't hide the tears when I start thinking about my aunt/stepmother, Eloise: divine and devilish, even as I have read her letters over and over again.

It was during this phase of my life that I started to develop the midlife male woe of having to rush off to the toilet—desperately seeking a urinal. Unfortunately, the designers or architects of this Holiday Inn placed the men's toilet on the second floor. (You can, of course, wait for the elevator, if you can, in point of fact, hold out.) On the second floor there is not only to be found the johns but a variety of sounds of eloquence and bartering, too, going on in the spaces and sites of the formal rooms used for small banquets (like the one our family engaged for Xavier) but also public events of enterprise or those with a religious format.

In some rooms there are antique shows going on, or puppet performances. In one room, with slide shows through another scene, there was an ongoing discussion of uterine fibroids.

Once upon a Sunday a gaggle of twelve-year-old boys and their dads were in heated discussion over which player would garner the most prestige and money in the baseball card racket market: Joe DiMaggio or Willie Mays. With the nerve of the devil, I would actually open up the doors of these rooms (the length of a boot), when eavesdropping wasn't supplying me with what I needed, for say a seven- to ten-second once-over-lightly viewing and listening in. Well, I'm a playwright, so what do you expect! Especially from one who is bound to seeing set scene possibilities.

Then there are often religious groups of an itinerant source: floating faith crapshooters, you might say.

I might hear bellows or belches of a religiously vocal spirit bursting from these rooms just before starting my descent back to a fine brunch (when some toddler opens the heavy doors, with the help of her big sister, in order to tiptoe off to the washroom).

I have a great love for rhetorical patterns of eloquence in sermons and sermonettes—which I transform and project into the body and soul of my plays, in the form of monologues—as all the drama critics have noted, and not always in tribute to my play either. They often speak of *how* these sermons go on and on. Meantime there is some necessary point of the play to be considered, and my characters appear to go off on some tangent—I say to hell with these notorious critics.

Not a few times have I found myself three or four steps on the way down, descending to the brunch on the first floor, when a door opens and such a burst of eloquence or furor emerges, and with the attraction of a magnet I am drawn back upstairs to this very door, having to contain myself from catching the door before it closes out the highly charged octane: a verbal call to the Light. For I am always looking for an oracle-like nugget to transform into the ongoing sweep and swim of a monologue wailing out of some preacher. So given to the creation of preaching monologues, this playwright got his fingers meanly pinched as the door closed on his right hand. From somewhere inside a baritone male voice clamped down: "This ain't naw peep show, for naw creeping and crawling daddy longlegs." Embarrassed now to the quick of pain in my book-signing right paw, I eased back downstairs to the brunch table.

Bounding up the steps at my best speed, without forcing a sudden leak, I was on my way to the men's room—and my physical booth/urinal of relief—when all of a sudden a door opened: I didn't have the time to crank my neck to the left. (The swirl and swim of a very wondrous, powerful, and alluring pipe tobacco charmed my olfactory glands, even as the aroma all but overwhelmed my nostrils.) What I did hear was a voice—in the form of chants and utterances, which were still immediately recognizable: a high-pitched tenor, with laminated layers of Leonard Foster's voice. It was him, all right, I was perfectly sure, and I would rush back to the door of that room as soon as I. . . . So I stumbled now into the john and swiftly swept down my zipper—in time, I hoped—and whipped out the old bronzed goldenrod, but this time my fumbling fingers (not moving with my normal bumblebee fleeting dexterity) failed me, didn't flip the old pickle out soon enough, in rhythm with the beat of my body's urgency; ergo, a goodly shot of urine now covered my underwear and my pants, by the time I had my gentleman properly aimed for the walls of the urinal.

What now to do with these telltale trousers?

How in the world would I ever cover myself up enough to shield yours truly so that my wet drawers and pants would not be noted nor observed by the party of twelve people attending my grandson's barbecue banquet below? That was Leonard Foster's voice chanting, I kept repeating to myself (with half of my brain trying to concentrate on the implications of sudden outbursts of the operation at hand).

Leonard's voice was leading the way, in the forest of fiery tongues—filled with the Holy Ghost and oh, the smoke pouring forth. When I arrived at the door, a certain tranquillity was momentarily achieved. Leonard was revealing something about Yoruba culture. A new turn in his philosophical bent? "Ah, ah divination," he proclaimed, as both climax and transition, in the "structure" of his spiel.

When I actually opened the door by no more than the length of a boot, in full nerve (and not even for a fleeting moment allowing myself to think of this pissy patch on my pants), there indeed was Leonard Foster, with that expensive pipe going in and out of his mouth, as he spoke in tongues and babbled out of his mind, as he had been speaking in unknown tongues earlier, when I had passed the room on the way to the john, but then as I came ambling down the hallway, with the sobriety of a lecturer:

"You have heard of, been John-*baptized*, as it were, in the idea of three persons in the one God; but let me inform you, school you, my dearly beloveds, of another tradition out of West Africa, from whence came your forebears, my forebears. We are speaking of two gods. Let me speak of Orunmila. For he is known for his capacity for bringing order out of chaos; he also possesses a judicious angle of vision, when it comes to the seeking out of truth. He is one blessed with the capacity for knowing the most profound secrets of humans and the gods. He conveys all of this in a language as rich as anything in the Bible, or the Koran.

"We piss-poor humans can't get to him in a straight way. We need a go-between and this intermediary is one called *Esu*. Esu is something else again, my sisters and brothers. He is male and female, cop and crook, healer and trickster, too. Esu can stand for chaos, or the happenstance of coincidence, or high-minded principle. You can dance in this faith and indeed you must, if you are to reach true divination exploration. Knock yourself out with the dance in order to dance the devil out of you and to communicate with the gods." Then he started dancing about. Leonard never was much for innovation on the dance floor.

My mouth dropped open, at Leonard's words and his actions. At the left side of him there were six females, dressed in white, and to his right, six males dressed in antique white. They nodded away in an attempt to keep up with Leonard.

The atmosphere within the room was wild, odd, and alluring, with the rich tobacco aroma, the strange movements of the dancers, and the musical vibrations. I recognized this smoking effluvium of high essences because I had given Leonard a pouch of this very brand some twenty years before (after I purchased this tobacco, an admixture, proclaimed as Hummingbird's Wings 007, while in London, to see a series of plays and review them for a new magazine out of New York). How was I to dare speculate or even guess that one day this admixture would come to the aid of Leonard and be used as an instrument to evoke ghosts? Spirits? Tongues of fire by a former poet, turned firebrand civil rights leader, turned wild letter writer, turned Black Power advocate, turned, I don't know what—cult healer; but there he was kith, if not kin—his pipe full of himself and looking wild, sated, and daft. Leonard Foster's eyes were turning "otherworldly" just now. His head was rolling about his neck, and I thought it was about to reel and roll right off of his very shoulder. The men in the audience dressed in sober black; the women in bright red colors.

Meantime, the women on one side of Minister Foster, the men on the other, were reeling and rolling back and forth, ever so gently and smoothly, as if combining a holy beat with a quiet grace that was sensual in a peculiar way because of an Indian pulse and soul beneath. This music was conveyed by the dexterity of an Indian guitarist, standing far to the left of the men. He was draped down and out in a beautiful maroon Nehru suit. The room was about forty by forty feet and loaded down with the aromatic power from Foster's tobacco-smoking pipe.

Although it was impossible to detect what was going on within Leonard's eyes, because of the mask the goggle-dark shades provided, the handsome honey-brown skin seemed to tremble from time to time. His cheeks were sunken. I had the fleeting, eerie feeling that Leonard had hit the skid of bad times since our last encounter, some years before in the hospital. Now the Indian guitarist was playing certain refrains from "The Death of a Princess."

There were forty people—mainly well-dressed black women—in the room. Many appeared high on some form of ecstasy-driven spirits, listening intently to the weird babble in tongues of Leonard Foster. His babble was pitched forth and in some strange way connected with the lyrical yet strange Indian musical strains. Leonard has not observed me, wet pants and all, and I was beginning to think, "They are going to start missing me back at Xavier's small celebration."

Recalling certain jazz-gospel-preachers trying to climb their way up a slippery slope of self-invention (and yet this audience was undemanding, so he continued to fly by the seat of his pants, which was always one of the main problems with Leonard), he seemed stimulated by sustained drags, deep drawing in snorts, and then extended withdrawals upon his pipe. Oh, hell, I thought, there must be more than just simply Hummingbird's Wings 007 stuffed away in that pipe. Just then one of his sexy attendants lighted his pipe with a crackle of a long-stemmed match. A wicket-picket-woman, I called her, of fire to fire. But Leonard Foster was too drugged out of his mind, I perceived, to even take much note of them. But drugged out on what? Not simply the pipe tobacco!

We had called Leonard Foster the bejeweled-player when he had the pipe in his mouth in the old days, for he had glued a glitter of many mock tiny rhinestone glass bits about the outside of the pipe's bowl. What would the church people think of this—if they knew? Leonard had developed a glint in his eye for power then, if they could see behind those dark glasses. I imagined that I could see there. Before I could get a good speculation going, didn't Leonard sweep away those glasses? He had his sights barreled down and razor glistening on me. Yes, because, you see, he had suddenly seen me through the shades and was not unmasking me. His eyes seemed to be angrily saying, "Joubert, you always did piss me off royally. Now look what happened to you." Or, perhaps it was my paranoia of being found out, when I had just found him out, up there high upon the improvised stage, bloodshot eyes and all.

What Leonard proceeded to do (after he pointed me out with the Indian-head pipe to his flock) was something else; for he cried out in a call-to-arms voice: "*There*, my beloved, is the epitome of that which I have warned you against. The Lucifer gone *out* of the Light. Dare ye come into the Holy Presence with much devilment to dispense? Yet beloved, I have evoked him all right, this Lucifer Longstreet. Behold the One who moves against the Light. I want him out of my sight." And when Leonard Foster said this—as if upon commandment—the faithful came charging after me, so I ran soon, hobbling in a hurry (if that's possible) back down the steps; out of breath, but breathing hard; moving three steps at a time, with the high heels and the screaming rush of Foster's overwrought harpies behind me: venomous vamps with wicked, dissembled tongues, tolling away claims of righteous loathing for their prey. God, if they ever get to me, they'll tear me asunder, I wailed in my plight—tear me apart body and soul.

I tricked them by employing an Elgin Baylor head fake, and they went one way like a herd of cattle, rushing right into a young bellman with a stack of luggage on a cart. At last glimpse, Foster's posse all went splattering, and I saw the upended bags, the bellman's hat rolling with a tiny twinkling bell attached, and I heard several women screeching over their wrenched ankles, as I headed—all wet down the front—off to the garage.

I had parked under the building and it occurred to me (as I took after my old 1963 green Lincoln Continental, in leaps and gulps) that there was a black eye-patch mask that I had used at a masquerade party many years before, in the trunk, along with a white pompadour hair piece. I got these set-piece properties out and donned them immediately. I had also used these disguises in my playwriting course from time to time. Hell, my pursuers would think they were suddenly confronted by a drag queen driving this ancient green model, polished into splendor, I thought as I drove out of the underground, pissy wet. And as I wheeled around the block, I thought I saw a trio of Foster's sistern tipping down the street going the other way. Parking two blocks away, under a tree, I got out and took from the trunk the old pair of blue pants, which I often used for odd jobs. They weren't dirty, because, you see, the very idea of my doing odd jobs is something of a ruse I play out on myself and family members.

But rather than enter the small party celebrating my Xavier's party, hailing his acceptance into one of the major universities—all wet—I remembered that the local market of a drugstore did handle a line of Fruit of the Loom underwear, eight blocks from this Holiday Inn.

I drove there, purchased one three-pack of shorts, used the men's room, ripped open the cellophane from the pack, put on a pair of the briefs, and pulled on the workman's trousers. Fortunately, the pants were dark blue, so with the black eye patch and the white pompadour headpiece, I just knew I would throw off that posse of pursuers sent out to bring me down by that low-down Foster. By Leonard Foster of all people, whom I had shown the greatest kindness, love and attention, devotion supreme. The ole "bejeweled-player," indeed, and driving his flock on me in vile terms. "*There,* my beloved, is the epitome of that which I have warned you against. The Lucifer gone *out* of the Light."

And yet it was but a wonder that he had not tried to get me to send him along some money to bankroll this "church" of his. His money to be sure. But what was I to do with his bank account, if he spat me out of his soul's path with such loathing, if he thought this ill of me, his kinsman? This enterprise of his was obviously out there on a wing and prayer and a huff of smoke. What of Granny Gram Gussie and Lucasta Jones and the others who bound me to him? Had he forgotten all of this? Or, in his embracing of some species of Yoruba faith, had it got it all mixed up with talking in tongues and the stories I had told him on many occasions about W. A. D. Ford, and his wild rituals, and manipulation of his flock? Had some of my telling taken an obverse turn within his soul? Just as I thought it provided jokes aplenty, food for folly, and warning paths not to embrace, had some of the pus and poison of Ford taken root in Leonard and grown up as a demonic knowledge of evil?

I decided to really test these disguises and parked a block away and didn't use the ground-level garage.

When I walked over to the Holiday Inn, the disguises worked well by throwing off several of Leonard's female operatives: for when they were twenty feet from me, they crossed the street, thinking I must be some crazy actor performing in a play, or drag queen, and therefore perilous to the purity of the mission inherent in their found cult. Whatever this cult stood for.

This will provide stagehand fodder for costume properties, to say nothing of a wealth of wild properties for my grandson's imagination. Studying acting as he is, he'll absolutely love this getup, I thought. But what will the other kids say, his friends, his new girlfriend? Full of questions, as always, I am certain. (Perhaps I'll just wear the black eye patch, I reasoned, and I did.) I would quietly state, "Well, I thought I saw a half a dozen former students who had received D's from me in the not-too-distant past, so I elected to don this outfit and throw them off. But no, that would sound somewhat chicken shit. More important, Xavier will continue to think that I am the coolest. (I recently got him interested in reading *The Great Gatsby,* which he loved. He's even thinking about how he can stage some of it.) Indeed I would enter the banquet room by coming through the kitchen—what a sense of drama. Xavier will give me the latest word, which is the equivalent of *the living end, Grandda*. And so I entered, having avoided Leonard's crowd, and was heralded by my grandson immediately—as the "coolest McDaddy this side of paradise."

Aroused by the lavish way I was greeted by Xavier, his stunning new girlfriend from Chattanooga, and their theater pals—I had been away only about forty-five minutes, and had forgotten about, or put aside, the more pressing question of Leonard Foster for the moment, and that I had pissed in my pants—once again—perhaps I had better see a urologist, after all. Even as they were greeting me like a long-lost conquering hero.

After I dropped my grandson and his friends off and took a long route home, which is often my wont when seeking to communicate with some higher oracle of thought, I started immediately back to thinking of Leonard Foster and feeling guilty. For, yes, why not admit it, confess it, even: I had talked too much about my wild days with the wanton W. A. D. Ford, and the rituals that went down at his temple known as DIVINE DAYS, for the good of the hypersensitive soul of Leonard. And that, yes, he had ended up not only absorbing it all but taking in a species of the Ford philosophy of soul mastery, or the mastery of souls— ALL SOULS even, no doubt at the very point when he, Leonard, was condemning me most for having "sold your soul to the devil in the hideous form of that wanton W. A. D. Ford." Leonard was taken in the fever and fervor, albeit by proxy, through the power of my recapture of things past, filtered into his living present and into the imagination of his own idea for a wandering cult of unquestioning devotees and worshipers.

Could it be, for example, that my telling Foster of Ford's legendary project of presenting *Paradise Lost* in drag got to Leonard in an obverse manner, in the solar plexus of his soul, as it were? And yet Leonard had his own impact upon me. His idea, for example, that there are people born without souls in this world was a continual power evolving within me, over me, through me, surging, swelling until I found myself gradually accepting the idea.

And, of course, his old flame from days of lore and yore, Shirley Polyneices (who had followed Leonard all through the South, during Civil Rights marches), was nowhere to be seen in his cult of crazies.

Some of the sistern wore fine perfume (and wicked pink hats) strong enough to hang out on the periphery of the tobacco-cast aroma. All of this would have greatly offended Shirley's sense of the dangers of "conspicuous consumption." On the other hand, I wondered out loud if one of the chosen sistern of Foster's wasn't bankrolling his ship enterprise. I had never envisioned Leonard as a ladies' man. Masquerading as, masking for a ladies' man.

Chapter 3

Turning off the Outer Drive now, and on into the downtown area, I elevated the sound on public radio's tribute to the blues tradition. I had taught the music of some of these artists, whom the experts were discussing at this moment, for example, Howling Wolf. I had met him on at least two occasions. An up-tempo white student (from behind dark glasses and wearing his blond-headed version of an Afro, with a ponytail like the patriots—some latter-day saint) had asked me after class, "Hey, Prof, you really meant it? You knew the Wolf?"

"I didn't know him. I did encounter him, once or twice." Then a whispered word, "We were using the latrine—station to station, or stall to stall—we exchanged a few words. How much I dug his soul-compelling music. Not exactly how I phrased it, but what I tried to convey."

"Oh, wow, you mean you pissed with the Wolf?" turning red and full of awe and envy, a natural-born brash-ass.

Ah, youth! Black students would have called me a "hip-McDaddie." I probably received a "Good" or an A from the hip white kid on the student evaluation forms. Shaggy-headed blond, threatening to become a rapper, or even a blues singer. Maybe he was a music major, or a theater person. (My grandson, Xavier, doubtlessly knew the fellow.) This blond, who always wore a big Afro comb stuck up in his back pocket, was humming "California Dreamin'" in class, got onto the rumored word that I am a great Feliciano fan. If he's a radio, TV, and film major, he might just do an updated version of *Black Like Me*. Win an Oscar. Become a millionaire. Get himself a shoe-shine boy and endow a chair in the name of the Beatles.

The streets were bad; snow was melting quickly. It would be slippery, or slushy, almost everywhere you walked. On public radio they were finishing up a discussion on the significance of Little Walter's music and his personal friendship with B. B. King. Continuing the tribute, they were now playing some of Little Milton's work, which I admired. (Most engaging and ironically tragic that Granny Gram Gussie never liked me to bring any blues records over for them to listen to. Only Mahalia!) One of my favorites now, Little Milton's "We Gonna Make It."

> We may not have a cent to pay the rent,
> but we gonna make it, I know we will.
> And if a job is hard to find and we have
> to stand in the welfare line, I got your love,
> and you know you got mine

Some of the power of "we people on the pavement, looked at him."

Hard to think of the Little Dreamer in the past tense. Still, Leonard had appreciation for the blues. He was always getting involved in yet another cycle of political pipe dreams (where cultural energies were debased as being "not relevant to the needs of the revolution; or, worthy only if they were refueling the resources of ruthless rebellion"). The Little Dreamer had believed that spirituals, gospel singing, and the blues represented perilous nostrums and opiates. All of these forms were perceived as celebrating the actual nightmare of our previous condition, from which we must be awakened, by any means necessary, according to the late Leonard Foster. All of this music kept blacks "sheltered from reality and blinded, even providing psychological disclaimers," concerning the "true nature of the police state and the reign of terror African Americans truly lived under," as the Little Dreamer had often stated his position.

> We may not have a home to call our own
> but we gonna make it, I know we will.

Our car may be old, our two rooms cold,
but we gonna make it. . . .

No, no, not any of this kind of music for Leonard Foster, as he would have insisted that you turn off the blues as you might turn off a faucet. Yet on this morning, his presence was so much felt in this old Lincoln, I thought. On this day of my discovery of Leonard's death, I could not cut away from the singing of Little Milton's husky voice, as I turned now to find a parking lot near La Salle Street, where the Cold-Standard Bank was located. Why not park in the underground provided for the bank's customers? Oh well, too late, driftwood, driftwood, driftwood. My usual term for missing a traffic connection. Off in space. Must be something in the DNA. My grandmother Daphne's sense of direction had been the worse. Going now 'round in circle after circle—and no place to land the old craft—up the parking lot rungs, where would it end? "Up, up, up, you got me spinning," Garner's romping and roaming "Red Top." Finally, there was sufficient space on the top rung, before you had to find your way out on the rooftop parking. Launched the old green Lincoln Continental's wide body in shelter enough: room on both sides.

Now I just sat there, amid my tears, over the hypersensitive Leonard Foster. For in all truth, he would have believed in the overall sentiment expressed in Little Milton's song, even as he despaired over the form of the blues on record or in person. Yet finding delight in the line "And if I have to carry around a sign, / Help the deaf, the dumb, and the blind. . . ."

Little Milton's slice of humane humor created a smile on my lips:

We may not can spare a roach a crumb
But we gonna make it,
I know we will
And if I have to carry around a sign,
Help the deaf, the dumb, and the blind,
I've got your love, and you know you've got mine. . . .

I sat there for a time, thinking of my former student Kingsley Gaines III, now a vice president at the bank, *and* what a pleasure it would be to see him this morning. Perhaps I might give him a call, and he could come down and have a quick coffee with me. I could try anyway, but V.P. for Community Affairs Kingsley was probably already busy. I'd try anyway.

With the elevator descending to the ground level, I wondered how Leonard Foster would have dealt with the fact that his money had been transferred to a white downtown bank. I felt certain that the Little Dreamer had not heard the fate of the African American bank: Liquid and Solid. This black-owned bank had folded. What was I to do, find another black bank, and yet another? There was only one remaining, and the course of its fortunes appeared hopelessly flawed. Here we were in 1992, and what was I to do, keep the money hidden in my mattress, or locked away in a wall safe, rather than "go dead downtown, to Whitey"?

Man in a tattered winter coat peddling *Street Wise*, all up in my face. "I think not." I swiftly turned up the collar of my topcoat to the Hawk, and folded into the bank's revolving doors.

Moving into the interior of Cold-Standard—the bank was not crowded, it was 9:15—I had settled on a cashier's check, set for ten thousand dollars and paid to the order of Memphis Raven-Snow's Funeral Home. They had pledged to handle everything. Now I needed to get over to a teller who took care of cashier's checks.

I wasn't rushed, but I needed to get this check into their hands today and sign a few papers. This amount of ten thousand dollars would cover the following: purchase of the coffin, the airfare, flowers, preparation of the body for burial, one limo to the grave site at Lincoln Cemetery. I would write an announcement for the *Forest County Dispatch* and do a two-page obituary for those who might attend the funeral.

With the remaining portion of the money, I thought of trying to convince the university to start up a minority lectureship in Leonard Foster's honor, in the form of a reading by a rising poet, or there could be a lecture on contemporary black poetry.

Chapter 4

W*hy Was I Born?* It had been a simple enough task: return to Williemain's Barbershop; retrieve the eyeglass case with my reading spectacles inside. I would go the absentminded playwright's nut role route. The barbers would love it!

Discovered I had misplaced the reading glasses when I had gone to Memphis Raven-Snow's Funeral Home to give the secretary the cashier's check so that we might commence the process of bringing the dead body of my kinsman Leonard Foster back from New York (where he had died of crack cocaine). Found near death in the streets, at the apron of a drug den.

No doubt, I had dropped the case at Williemain's. The secretary had found a pair of glasses off a dead man's body, which I used as a substitute for reading and signing the prescribed document of release. (I still had them in the lapel pocket of my jacket.)

Now just as I was leaving, three long-legged lads—draped in bright colors—entered, almost knocked me down, and immediately took seats in the rear of the shop.

My right hand was on the doorknob of Williemain's Barbershop (feeling in self-possession now that I had secured my own gold-rimmed glasses and no longer depended on the glasses of a dead man).

Just as I was turning the doorknob, Galloway Wheeler revisited his rage and trembling over "those belligerent black punks" in the shop, earlier that morning. Then he said in Latin (as if to throw the youthful newcomers off), "Can such anger dwell in heavenly minds?" My tutor over forty years ago, when the very best high schools still offered four years of Latin . . . if I commenced a series of recollections over the honored, now lost, Past, I'd never get out of here.

"*What is this world of ours coming to!*" Wheeler now bewailed. The promised end, he warned, by making the scissors sound off as mock sabers clashing, just above the head of the choirboy in his chair from Pilgrim United.

I felt my hand start to turn the doorknob, for I knew Mr. Wheeler sought an extended run of amen arpeggios (in Latin, or in English) in order to affirm his dour state of mind.

One of the ministers, who once upon a time had derived a monthly stipend from the mayor's slush fund for certain politically supportive Negro preachers, was clearing out his throat. Then, Reverend Alfred Belton declared: "Mr. Wheeler, let's not forget how before the ranting, licentious mob of homosexuals, Lot was ready to compromise the flesh and blood of his females: 'I have two daughters, both virgins; let me bring them out to you, and you can do what you like with them, but do not touch these men.' I say this to say that Almighty Gawd has a divine plan, beyond the scan of man!"

Outside a white Bronco drew up to a sudden pause, in the early dusk of the November day.

Someone in a ski mask hanging out of the window. Sudden hailstorm of rifle fire. Bursts of charged lightning crashing the shop's windows. I was hit twice: high right shoulder and left leg. Fell to my knees, with the doorknob in my right hand. Plaster, shards, and fragments of shattered glass everywhere. Framed pictures of famous black legends, athletes, and entertainers came tumbling down, wall to floor.

I saw Galloway Wheeler collapse in a pool of blood.

Craig Cratwell was hit in the left thigh. I saw him hobble over to his colleague's side to aid Mr. Wheeler.

Seemingly unharmed, Reverend Belton was screaming for help. (The frame from DuBois's portrait over his shoulders.)

Before my bleary-eyed vision the three newcomers, in their silver slippers, *somersaulted* into talented hurdlers: they vaulted over me as lodestars. I felt staggered in violent pain from head to toe. Then my body fell forward. . . . Too long, so soon, the medics were placing us upon white slabs and we were rolled away and elevated up, up, UP. A fire alarm hailed our way; we zoomed and snaked through the late afternoon streets; the ambulance truck swirled, twisted its way in and around homebound traffic. Was I going into a state of shock?

A young blond female medic asked: "Where were you hit?" Then a black medic was loosening my sports jacket and shirt. He sent his stethoscope to my chest. She was doing my pulse. "What is your name?" I felt damp and dislocated, back and blue, with the blood of my body everywhere. All I could think was: the wicked wounds were over there and back down here and the absurdity. . . . So I said: "Lucifer Wrongstreet, lady." Then the imminence of death. "Where are *my* eyeglasses?"

Despite the fiercely pulsating pain in my shoulder and my blazing left lower thigh, my right hand retained its strength. Both medics kept trying to get the doorknob out of my right hand; I kept pumping it like the trigger of a gun.

I heard the words come and upon my unclean lips I started to mumble, "Hail Holy Queen, Mother of Mercy, our life, our sweetness, and our hope—to thee do we cry, poor, banished children of Eve. . . ." Was I going to lose my life or a limb? And then I faded into a brilliant spider's web of oblivion and light.

Sometimes, when as a high-flying child, I would bear witness to a swift, ghastly yet gloriously lucid Light. Then a sheath or cone would skyrocket out of itself upon this road of darkest night. A Light so real, royal, and raw keeningly dreadful, majestically turbulent and perilous to behold that I thought my world—even the World—was about to consummate the Promised End. The first expression out of my mouth was, *My Lord and my God, why hast thou forsaken me?* And before I would have time to reach my long white bed: Almighty God was about to strike me down, dead.

Suddenly from the tips of my toes to the temple of my being I came to feel why my path is astonishingly blessed (out of captivity, this profoundly accusatory moment, even as I still felt the shock in my kneecaps). And across the way, the light in the tower of the darkened church, where runaway slaves—out of the alabaster South—had hidden one hundred fifty years before.

Crossing my way—just now as I moved on tiptoe out of Terror and flung my way home—my satchel full of books, rocks, slingshots, marbles, comic books, a tambourine, a homemade crucifix, and a string of crystal rosary beads, the color of bruised blood. What if I had gone the other way? Not the long way home.

Illuminated initially down this long road homeward ever so high-flying in the distance: an anointing moon, in solo song ascendancy. So that I would almost proclaim aloud, in the beautiful tranquillity of spiritual symmetry cast out by a moon's soprano sax sliver of a silvery lucidity on a bending note, "Here God, Himself, must live, and this lyrical spectacle of beauty is His reflecting Eye."

Light of His Body is spangled out of the Eye. A stellar Beauty of moon and a furnace of stars of such supreme magnificence I thought I heard strains of Bach's "Jesu, Joy of Man's Desiring," out of Aunt Eloise's old stucco blond Philco, down in the basement, where we had clustered about in an unbroken, unbowed circle to hear the rung-by-rung exploits of our secular savior Joe Louis, the Brown Bomber, in fifteen rounds of boxing or less. We didn't need to be told this soldier was "a credit to his race."

This illumination of God's visage cast out of the moon's roaming, rambling eye and then the clusters of stars. Ahahah yes, but if all of this is true, then understanding God Almighty, His nature and His mysterious purposes will always plunge me back before myself to the question: What isn't a manifestation of His creation, if Blake was right? "Whatever it is that Lives is Holy." Too much to bear witness to the terrible Light of this "truth." I was shocked just now down to the sockets of my kneecaps. Not in submission, nor surrender, for I would always be condemned to the Hellish Quest Search down some solitary road—I seemed to have known that from Jump—and without Diogenes's lamp. But where did this mysterious road lead? I was furious as a harp-threaded, Coltrane soprano sax, blistering the flickering, last dying wick of candlelight tongue of Being out of a church of ashes. Unless and until—world without end—the arch Ancestral experience took me over, and "God Struck me Dead!"

Yet the beauty of this expanse of night—at first Light—was in its way as van Gogh's *Starry Night*, Aunt Eloise and I had seen it at the Art Institute. Had the painter seen beyond blinding sight and then his fingertips touched by the Thunder-Head of this God-Head unfolding the power of the Holy Ghost to the daft genius's temple, topped by a crown of candlelights?

Time and again, until I came to tearfully expect it, I stood there in the fabulous shock of what this suddenly enraptured moment meant, leading me into, conducting me out of this apron of Holy Light onto a stage of sudden naked blackness, and then thirty paces into pitched night: this bolt of a terror bathing of Light-streaked-labyrinths. Make me try to dance my way out of the reaches of its mad Beauty, yet essay to recognize the power it had over me (as nine cone-piercing points of ultimate conviction, judgment, and accusatory searchlights), through me, beneath me, as one moved to a Holy Roller dance of dervish, defiance, and deliverance. Yet not unlike a sizzling and brilliant razor nearing your body, if you didn't strip your pockets and unfold all of your belongings to the heady figure, in ski mask, before you: that robber on the wrong-way-road home, years before. Called simply the Mother Goose, with his sharkskin jacket (black laces stitched about the sweep of the garb's circumference at hem's bottom) draped in a rogue's manner over his broad shoulders, as if he wore a rainbow. Oh, his royal stiletto polished into some eerie and evil tool, burnished beauty of a luminous road, not taken by any fool, the Mother Goose sliced a sinister music in three Zorro slashes of the torrid air, just above my head. Now at the hour of my death, I thought, as I handed over my pouch of marbles and my quarters. Once again, I had lost my way.

Searchlights—as ray guns—stripped out the last lights of pristine, bright sparkling in our eyes. Seized. "Niggers don't blow a breath," the cop cried; two squad cars jammed us. Slammed up against the graffiti-splashed wall. Spread-eagle to the nines and raked up, over and out like weeds, with their nightsticks. Nape, backbone, tailbone, thighs, balls, nuts, shinbone, anklebone. Pickpocketed by the *Po*-lice state. Revolvers at the ready. Spittle for eyes, their haggard jowls were the color of purple pigs' feet. As we young reckless, partying lions came leaping and crashing out of Hyde Park, by dawn's early light. We were high. Thought we were excruciatingly cool. Sober now. "You apes, take your heads out of your asses. You deader than doornails." BLAZER was on his nameplate. After someone handed the Watch Commander his tinted glasses, we were released on his word. "Wrong niggers," he whispered, in a hoarse, whiskey-tranquilized voice as we flung over each other to see who could get out of that door feet-free-first.

But now I was being rolled in upon a long white table, in the waiting room to death? I knew not operation salvation. (Granny Gram Gussie knew the story of Lazarus better than I.) At the apron of the swept-about partition I could see scores of shoes coming and going in a frenzy, a babble of tongues. Remove the bullets and pluck out the eyes of my assailants. Then I thought, "*No.* Not an eye for an eye. Punks weren't aiming for me. Kids in the orange and red jackets. Vengeance is mine, sayeth."

Rolled away again and again, world without end. Hypodermic to the arm: an explosion of Light occurred. Soon I was gone, in tune to a last sudden visage of Light over Jordan in my drifting-away eyes! I was truly long gone into the twilight.

In the long dream it was revealed to me how this shaft of light enfolded me, as a gift of God Almighty: new robe, new shoes, new crown, even spangled starched wings. New tongue, rainbow about my shoulders, as a long-gone-academic garland would be, could be—if I should learn somehow or other to convert it: this dervish of firelight with a scarlet of voodoo for lipstick, in Mardi Gras madness; seven flaming faces of chaos did whirl me to hypnotic madness and enchantment, upon the seventh time of turbulent appearance.

You see it was all something akin to when as a twelve-year-old you are warned time out of mind not to go over into the area where the bad folks live: "the Sizzling Skillet." And so as soon as possible, you bound breathlessly over there, out of your familiar darkness, with a rabbit's foot—hopping speed, into the brimstone blackness. Not only because in putting "the Sizzling Skillet" down with such scorching and imaginative (also lying) intensity, coupled with the Light illumination of mythical experience, the admonishing adults have unwittingly transmuted the area—in perfect pitch—into a beguiling place called *Lucifer's Haunts.* Meanwhile, five minutes and twenty-seven seconds later—hurdling down another road—they are celebrating their folk wisdom, spun up from brutalizing experience, with the retainer: "You see you got to go there to know there."

Lucifer's Haunts, indeed. For this was not my first time in this hospital bed, under uncanny circumstances, but that other time, at the razor's edge of floodlights. On my way "home" to the Gypsy-faced woman of havoc and heaven, armed with "A Love Supreme" for me; triple-extra-strength Tylenol for Gertie; and picture puzzles for the girls.

At the razor's edge of a flaming Lucifer. And when I almost got hung up in the nude to tell the naked-butt truth (up up up and out of Gertie's bounteous bed).

I could catch a glimpse of her ex. His well-strapped razor held aloft and glinting in his huge ham-bone of a right hand (his left pitched to choke out a flame). A new kind of sweat burst across my temple. Past the john, twenty-one steps from the bedroom door cracked open the length of a boot. Screaming on each other in the hallway. Murder-mouthing beyond a series of bitter venomous arias. The fireman's voice: a belching exhaust pipe of carbon monoxide. Her voice full of vipers, fangs, acid, and ashes. Would I be consumed body and soul in the pitch of their asphyxiating gas? Thought Gertie had changed those damnable locks. Firefighter had not changed his mind. The devil's in the tumblers. Whipping the only two things I saw in reach, her red negligee about my loins (we'd burned up the bedsheets in tumbles and twists). Donned a puffy, white, beltless robe. Heard Gertie hit the floor. Down for the long count? I was up at the window's ledge, ripped up the shabby green window shade in a gulp. Thank God, we had opened the window all the way, before things got steamy. Heard pounding steps of the fireman's wrath trampling forth to carry me? So, with a Hail Mary and a Geronimo *I went Flying!* like Batman, in the midsummer morning, or was it as a bat out of hell?

Crash-landed into the alley below. Did I break my kneecaps? Found there an hour later by scavengers, who turned me over (red negligee, white robe, and all) to the ambulance drivers. Probably thought I was a dropout from a haunt of hermaphrodites. Yours truly ended up at this Forest County Hospital, where I was born. Coming in and out of consciousness. Then I was asking Cuz Lucasta, "Is my leg broken? My kneecaps? My arm? Oh, my aching head! And it hurts down here and *especially* back down there. Am I going to lose a limb?"

"Wonder you didn't lose your natural short-arm, boy," Cuz Lu said. Her next strapping? "How many times you think you got to die? Don't need to puzzle that out, chile! How many times I warn you, time out of mind, 'bout stirring up still-glowing coals in other men's hot beds?"

She was weeping into a strawberry-colored handkerchief. I was glad to be alive to get to see her weeping. I could not straighten up, nor turn from side to side—forget all about flying right or left. Then Cuz Lu said, " 'Spose I was to tell you that long, white robe was the fireman's? Would that put some fat meat on your rock-hard head? Or, turn a light inside your dim-witted brain? Joubert Antoine, you ain't hardly constitute for this kind of action."

Drifted away again by a ringing, blaring red light and descending back down, I could hear strains of Louis Armstrong's "Mahogany Hall." Dreaming of stories, leaping house scandals: thundering mouths of my great-grandaunt's brothel, a celebrated, bric-a-brac broad of a Madam. Had a street named for her in the Crescent City. Talked to Aunt Eloise about that time Bishop L. Moon visited her establishment—dressed in a Santa Claus getup—and passed out packages of toy dolls from his sack of plenty to the inmates: picture puzzle of the Vatican for the Madam; and tiny tobacco pouches of cocaine for the caged parrots in the parlor.

Then I saw a burnished-bronze miniature coffin being elevated onto a conveyor belt—and now running 'round and 'round a track ("Run to Heaven and run right back"). Until just as I thought my loping head would drop off of my neck, I realized how the thimble-size fustic-colored coffin was hooked on to my choo-choo train that Daddy had set up for me on the basement floor, decades back into the quarries of memory. The long runaway train was *smoking* at breakneck swiftness, in the incandescence of its Terribleness. The red, white, and blue window curtains were streaked with soot and Black tears. And as now I lay me down to sleep, I pray the Lord my Soul to keep, if I die. . . . I dreamed the question: Was the soul of Mr. Lincoln, or the fabled runaway Mr. Frederick Douglass, locked away in a weary land inside? Exactly who was the conductor or the engineer heading up this service to nowhere and yet a bridge to Heaven? Was this train bound for Glory?

Suddenly there was the sound of Light and the long Sabbath song chanting, which emerged out of unfolded rockets, upon the night and underneath that. I thought I heard the stellar serenity: awakening to the unquestioned bliss of Donald Byrd's "Christ, the Redeemer." Beneath this, an unveiling out of weaponry: shimmering silver into golden hoops of other voices crashing at the crescendo of foils and swords, yet into a brazen luminosity of dissonant golden whole notes, in which a trumpeter led the crescent shape by holding the stellar tone, seemingly without breathing: my secular redemption. Our New Jerusalem. A dividing Light could multiply into many pigmentations. Sound clothed in Light and meteors of madness; lyricism of such supreme Lightning wrapped me up, unfolded, and stripped down my bed. Rolled away. Breathless before the Word and the surgeon's scalpel and now I lay me down to. . . .

Captured essence of Falstaff's raw belly-laughter of a crack-up call. Brooding Hamlet's royal eloquence. Trapped between those two in a final sprocket of life-span-time. To Falstaff do I roundly proclaim through the bell-ringing golden trumpet of Armstrong: "When I die I want you to dress me / In straight-laced shoes, box-back coat and a Stetson hat. Put a twenty dollar gold piece on my watch chain—So the boys'll know I died standing pat." And to the grief-stricken eyes of the Melancholy Dane, daft and roaring over dehydrated Ophelia, I heard my voice echoing old Dipper-Mouth's grainy voice: "I went down to St. James Infirmary, / Saw my baby there, / Stretched out on a long white table, / So sweet, so cold, so fair . . . let her go, let her go, God bless her, wherever she may be; she can look this wide world over, but she's never find a sweet man like me." Lord, my mind clothed in the righteousness of Crescent City sounds of profane beauty behind ornate grillwork, labyrinths of jade; jokes behind the masks of the Zulu Kings. Hoodoo out of Voodoo.

When as a child you sucked up too much summer fun—on Armstrong's birthday—and hours of enchanting reading, and you fell fast asleep beneath a tree in the surrounding garden on the Fourth of July, with your mouth wide open, as you doze, and yes, you do snore and then quite by accident, a gnat flies past your twittering lips. And you realize you are still clothed in your Sunday best, because of the tribute at the Tomb of the Unknown Soldier. And you awaken to the celebration down by the lakefront and all the evening through you are taken up by the spectacle of the fireworks, the rocket shelling, reaffirming *this* tribunal, *this* sacred, pistol-whipped, scarred, bloody, diced document, too troubled to read, and too rare not to behold, study, cherish, challenge, and change. Daddy turning the ribs on the grill and whistling through his teeth, Armstrong's "Struttin' with Some Barbecue." Aunt Eloise's very own self-styled sauce at the ready, which she simply called Vamping with Venus.

Heaps of potato salad, spooned away in mason jars, tumblers of lemonade, Fox-Head-Four-Hundred beer, and one small tub of chitter-lings, and several canisters of string beans; Cuz Lucasta brought catfish, and sweet potato pies. The ever-unfurling flag, now heaving for breath, then in curt, snapping salutes to the wind. Or, later, when you dared to wrestle with the harness of the sacred words of scripture, out of Daddy's mouth; the Thirteenth, Fourteenth, and Fifteenth Amendments—so loaded with the portent of light to our drinking fountain, so parched for the waters of Redemption, within our cast out into the darkness. Down freedom's road, and told "to make it, or don't make it, best way you can shake it," was the way Grandpa Forester had explained. Then there were the fiery tongues of our bursting in air liberation—many murdering magnificos out of tune—who questioned why we should be here, even as they played the gathering crowd like jugglers at the carnival. . . .

LEONARD FOSTER in a coffin appeared before my eyes just now. What could I do in this bed to bury him, when I might be . . . my gown-stripped body may be . . . this attachment to my Johnson . . . upon this bed, or another they may be shipping me over to Memphis Raven-Snow's Funeral Home, by high noon? But what of my soul condition? All of that time I spent with W. A. D. Ford, which must have cultivated something rotten: a cancer within—not far from the bullet holes. In the clutches of death words spelled out in my longhand: there are people in this world—there must be thousands of them—who are born with all of their body parts and their marbles, too, and they may even come forth like a flower, but they exist without souls (perhaps they have lost their souls, like kids who lose their mittens in the snow, forevermore, in the whirlwind of some wintry galaxy) even unto the night when they flee into the shadow of death and see their light consumed in ashes. But did Ford have not a soul? Well, he surely had one hell of a spirit, quite a codpiece, too. Deep-sleeping Peter bound to the bodies of his two sleeping watchdog sentinels was suddenly illuminated by some tremendous, long-legged light, at the crack of dawn, an escaped slave, escaped out the darkness, once again through the cavelike labyrinths. Was there hope for me, oh Lord, lying, in the need of prayer?

And just then, pitched to the meteoric cry of an improvising blues harmonica, consecrated someplace within my soul:

"As He died to make men holy, let us die to make men and women free-to-be-free."

In the terror and turbulence at that point in the road, lightninglike and beautiful to bedlam, I beheld again a glimpse of His breath, a remnant of His Righteousness, His mayhem bellowing, His styx and stones, the spatial hideousness of the mask of Creation behind the hound of Heaven edict: *Let There Be Light!* A fragment of the transforming light knocked down Saul's condition, on the road to Damascus. Pitched against the Light.

From the corruption and the contagion of this world, would I ever find rest, sleep, and soar past the shadow of death, surrounded by lilacs, in the awakening door, next to the chamber of the Little Dreamer? Out of life's nightmare, just east of the Euphrates and Eden?

If I could but scoop it all up like a cup of some sacred fiery drink, that would save my spiritually dehydrated state, while destroying the thousand and one shocks and impurities shackling my constitution. I shuddered so much with the image that water leaped from my soul: the last liquids there. Out of my mouth a thunder's heat uttered: *There, too, God Almighty Does Dwell.* Then I was hearing Blake's words: "Whatever it is that lives is Holy." So, *was this* then a visit from the Holy Ghost and His flaming tongues of sound: crackling Light bursting through the insufficient air? And yet *you* go figure the Old Man out: Why David? Why Job? Why Peter? And especially why Paul? Which was of course the point: the content of their character gave Him yet another measure of the human narrative. But that wasn't quite it, either.

The emerging question, from the long walk home, there in the sacred moonlight gone mad, with the rings of light seen about the moon: *Why Was I Born?* encircled the quartered crescent of my lips. Where and just who is God Almighty, if He can create this spectacle? And do nothing for the starving millions but provide them with foul oxygen the breath of life. What constituted His very Being? The backbone of His spirituality. Oh, had God gone to sleep on us? Oh, if only I could purloin some of this Imperfect righteousness and horrifying by wondrous Light and never, never let it go, but it was all entangled in my mind with "Gold, silver and gold / All that you can hold / Is in the moonbeams." Pocket this cone of Light within the vestment of my Soul for safe-harbor-keeping as a runaway slave hounded by the bestial chains to be reclaimed by dogs, before Dawn's early light, anchored in the meteoric light of affliction's furnace. Then I heard the pealing voice of the pearl-eyed Little Dreamer's "to seek out a sea change in the depths of our American grief, our wanton lasciviousness, our hideous squalor, our luxurious avarice. Oh let that sea goddess arise out of the cloaca-low slime of the Father of Waters." Oh, to drink deeply of Democracy and to not go down dead and be swallowed up whole. Our "to be or not to be. . . ."

The insatiable Being of lightning burned through my very Soul to the chambers of Judgment: black-robed night, with a white collar of the moon's sliver. And I heard the telling voice of my aunt Eloise whipping through my bewitched, entranced, and bedraggled teens: "the tempest pot of paradise. Though the steam heat'll threaten to blow your top, young man." My mandrake's pole pitched up a tent to hike the too gorgeous gamey gals and goose them up royally. To strip the breath out of panting, luxury of my school sweetheart's searching and seizing tongue. There we were breathless in Washington Park, out of breath, soon humming to the merry ole soul, King Cole's "A Blossom Fell, Beneath a Perfect Tree to Heaven." What's this: a rustle high in the limbs? Some squire up a tree (many branches of the human family) sent up to stake out my stiff? Stiff finger and third finger and she knows too the power of my limbs could kill a thief, or a snake-up-the-tree. Oh, to ram the Trojan shield in this rubber volume. Can of cracked-open sardines in our luncheon. Smells me out; I'd rather ride her than capture a whale. . . . Said something (drowning in her seed) that she meant the moon to me to be or not to be born. . . . (Pitched to the sticky rung of her panties.) In the forever gasping death lock of sugar-love loaf. Her eyes drifting me apart beneath the Tree to Heaven, where we were drugged and strung out on intoxicating romance, when suddenly careening through the leaves a gift sent down to us from on high in the heavens? A streaky turd, climaxing upon the starched white blouse of my heart's band only.

Down on both knees with only Aunt Eloise's old coal-oil lamp on a nightstand to light the railroad man's way to his avocation, I see my father Jerry Jones so well. His tumbler of bourbon and a glass of eggnog at the ready.

I was real gone in the darkened basement; struck down upon my hands and knees, with only the headlight at the engine's beam for duty and illumination of a boy's way: this new gift, elevating me out of childish ways (as some special anointing ceremony) and so sleek, swimming, slick, and wondrously swirling around, with my spirit-stripped body and soul pitched to its enchanting, swift-sweeping rhythm, enclosing my spirit, my breath gulping in the miracle, as if this train and its furious route were bound up with a glory beyond any secular light; a gift from God Almighty: dark as Sugar-Groove, with his silver, smoke-gray eyes. The Lionel train had power to revive my father's spirit to a childhood he had never possessed and to take me into the environs of a world of childhood, where responsibility and magic were one.

Streaking black and silver train commenced to take circuitous paths: new switchback reroutes and detours had been suddenly set up at various invisible but real stations, to throw it asunder. (Throw me asunder, too.)

From upstairs I could hear Aunt Eloise dancing slowly, softly, on the linoleum kitchen floor to the voices of the Ink Spots singing "Street of Dreams," with Kenney in the lead:

Dreams broken in two
Can be made like new
On the street of dreams. . . .

When Aunt Eloise finally descended the steps into the basement and cast her gray eyes on Daddy down on his knees, and both of us so obsessed within the all-consuming circle that the train made, she just arched her hands high upon her hips and shook her head in bemusement and chauvinism. Meantime, Daddy truly didn't realize that there was a fourth presence in the basement of Eloise's estate, for he was so captivated by my Lionel train, and he kept squeezing the black pump of the rubber value, which when "played" with the right touches imitated, or gave off, forms of railroad warnings, howls, blaring and bleating sounds, and cries that sounded very close to the echoes of animal wails amplified to eloquence. After about fifteen minutes, Daddy started into giving imitations out of his own mouth of those sounds: hooting, honking, whooing, whooping, and offered up in a spiritual ecstasy, which also sounded off as the wailing and blaring, low-down voice of a jazz-blues harmonica. Finally, Aunt Eloise said, "Well, once a man, three times a little boy. However, it does occur to me that the actual sovereign, boss-man, engineer, and conductor isn't getting very much direct fun out of his ownership, or even partnership—in this railroad system. (Perhaps he's like the prince in exile.)

"Why it appears to my journalist eyes as if a great train robbery has occurred, right here on my very own basement floor. Why has the Masked Man of the Plains flicked from good guy to outlaw before our very eyes? Or, is Prince Joubert being prepared for a speaking role in graceless Daddy's religious train worshiping service? Closer to the truth? A nonspeaking role, as altar boy acolyte? Now I haven't heard a grunt, hoot, nor howl, Jerry, out of this child's mouth! Miss Eloise would be a fool and not just a foolish hausfrau, if I'd ever expect *a man*, who spends half his time on trains, not to spend the rest of his holidays down on both knees, imitating choo-choo sounds with the worshipful fanatical eyes of a seven-year-old, during his Christmas layover.

"My marriage is railroaded! Might as well go up in the diner and dish up dinner," Aunt Eloise said. Then she let out three wails, which sounded like the pure horns emitted at train crossing designations, in order to show the *boys* in her life who was sovereign over space, time, and distance, in this earthly house. She wasn't through with us yet. For soon Aunt Eloise would be off to a meeting of the Altar and Rosary Society, or the Foresters Society, or one of her half a dozen social clubs, or covering a story for the *Dispatch*.

Meanwhile Daddy was hooting and honking like he was chasing a hound of heaven 'round and 'round a mountain with the train, the switch at his fingertips. He had the world in a jug and the stopper in his hands. He hadn't heard a word that wife of his had said, I speculated. As the train climbed the uplift and Daddy was in the catbird seat (but before Aunt Eloise let the door slam), all of a sudden who should arrive in our very midst but my aunt-stepmother's parrot, *Franklin Roosevelt*. That bird got drunk from a seven-second whirl atop the caboose, flew, and dropped the note my aunt had attached for her husband (right off into

Daddy's eggnog), which read: "Hot dogs on the stove. Ready in ten minutes." Then we heard the front door slam.

"The many layered pedigrees of my Eloise," Daddy was saying.

Now Daddy was revealing the place where the Jim Crow car appeared, going south or coming north until "we got to the nation's capital." The color curtain of separation. Daddy spoke of Mr. Randolph in reverential terms. Aunt Eloise had interviewed him; came home that night with stars in her eyes.

Breathing back in time through a masquerade learned to play with Light, blazing off a machete, Lucifer loaded. As a boy, I learned to play Light off mirrors and mirrors pitched against the Light. How to blind with Light by bouncing it off reflecting mirrors to toy with long-legged Light to blind a batter, or lost drifter, or Jehovah's Witnesses out fishing for lost souls. To make Light a killer angel angling a glistening razor slit to the throat.

Splendor of Loathsome Light, purloined out of the wonder Light polished to a blustery brilliance. Then a gutsy and grainy, cunning voice came to me and said, "Boy, what you suiting up to do: pickpocket the Redeemer? 'Son of God loves pure light.' You got to die to the Light of this world's Lusts, royal rags, poisonous and polluted traps to start to know that kind of lyrical Light you so breathless to wear and to know. You must be stripped to be undressed to be redressed. Oh, yes, mirrors do steal souls!"

Now I was taken to a higher place and dropped off to make it home on my own out of the pitched blackness of darkness. I looked for a church, and there was no hiding place for me, over there. There I saw a six-foot skeleton, stripped of all flesh, even unto tissue, dangling from a scaffold, with a black high-top hat, intricately interlocked to the phalanges of the right hand. The bones were polished so finely that the skeleton appeared as polished white gold. I heard Lady Day singing "Strange Fruit."

I saw the halos about the heads of saints in church paintings. Or, climbing up to the rooftop after the rain to see miracles come alive as rockets, constellations crazy with God's luminosity of vision. When night undressed herself, only to bare her body parts. Skin and skeleton stripped naked to shudder and shimmer, no more jokes, nor adornments, no more reigning duplicity: stuffed, breathless Democracy.

Candlelight march: did I hear a requiem Mass commencing? Plenty with bagpipes, tenor saxophones, kettle drums, harps pitched to Paradise at daybreak, for a supreme love; and wailing in the no-longer-tranquil reflecting pool of lucidity. *Then*, before the memorial to the Redeemer, in marching protest down a road to wash away the sins of segregation. Walking, wailing, trampling till our feet got sore, blistered, and then that other time, we bathed them in the waters by the baptizing shore, on the Fourth—transformed by the secular charged scripture of the Word made flesh. *Then*, Look and Listen: a tall man, with a rich deep-mahogany-brown complexion and a face recalling the Redeemer's read the declaration-document, in down-home preacher's accented breathing: a high-pitched tenor, and furious with crackling light at the upper registers. Made the North Star's accusatory July Fourth speech—the rhetoric glow—as spun gold, out of the furnace of Affliction: ah Freedom and Independence. Carrying a huge, six-by-six-foot burnished wooden cross—as he uttered forth—plucked out of the fires at Downs Chapel, a Negro church in Forrest County, Mississippi. Our Stations of the Cross.

Now became a transfixing, troubling halo of censure, nightmare, and responsibility, with the music troubling the air, the dawn, the water, the rainbow, the vision, the Dream, the Light, the icy slippery sacred papers, the smoking-hot-ice *breath* of our Constitution, to be or not to be. That we thought we saw and beheld at razor's edge, at fingertips, and tongue, so that we fairly stopped breathing. That we might, could, and would now walk, talk, sing, clap hands, and shout and allowed our rhythm to drum out the contradictions and weaknesses of our own Constitution. To be or not to be into a blazing Light, anchored in our agony—*but of course*, and lost our way, once again, in the light of the American labyrinth/laboratory, even as we thought we had found our way in a new, meteoric dawning. Out of that rugged, mean old, long-legged, shifty-eyed road, full of switchback connections. *Oh wasn't that a wide river, river over Jordan, Lord.* That would be Marian's voice and Mahalia's baptizing zeal over and over again: "Jesus say you must be newborn again . . . you must be newborn . . . again." And now you think you can dance your way out of Death's path forevermore. Then out of the last Light ablaze from cast-out-chaos, I thought I saw the silhouette of God in the Reflecting pool—giving a counter call sound; and I did hear Mahalia humming over and over again: "One More River to Cross," until I thought I might die of exhaustion. *Hold on. Hold on.*

Hold on. . . . As before me now emerges my cousin, Phillipa, at my bedside (with a rosary in her hand). She, who teaches third-grade ghetto but ends up being wet nurse, babysitter, mother, bitch, yellow hoe, auntie, dietitian, tutor, truant officer, cop, big-sister-girlfriend, psychiatrist, coach for a mainly stunted classroom of the new malnutrition (nearly half of whom are crack babies weaned out to half past seven) in the darkly despised and out-of-the-loop light of destitution. Puking and pooting (and panting) and snotty all about your unofficial nurse's apron. Maligned, lined-up, lined-out. Chalked-up, crossed-out, branded, tied-off, and marked-down. Crabbed and snail-slow: Phillipa tries to save their segregated imaginations from melting into the thin air of isolation, a walled-in nursery without rhymes, only riddles on the coatrack.

Phillipa, this I do remember: the night of your first day there, you had enough pipe dreams to awaken the dead. Hold up, Phillipa. Breathe and blow, as you stoop down to lift up these least of these, as you dare to go down dead to find some remnant in the rake and scrape and scraps and ashes and embers of leftovers, as you try to invent a tomorrow. But don't sentimentalize these love-starved addicts, the babes of isolated adolescents. Oh, steal them away from the deadly slumber of the slums. Oh, tomorrow's tough-titty, but you got to suck it, splattered across the graffiti of the ghetto world's walled-out imagination, drugged day into night, night into day by the boob tube's bankrupt auctioneers of hypnosis; and the rascality of the rapper's raking in markup of plunder, mayhem, and rape.

For you, precious and hopelessly idealistic and bloated Phillipa, no one is poor, on the street of dreams. You cannot be parsimonious towards these starvelings with your disproportionate love, duty, imagination, excellence hung upon the shingle of your soul's pursuit. For crack babies—appearing as still-life forms of babes in Toyland. Pitched away on maypoles of madness in their mood swings. And others lethargic as those of another day, banished to stoops and addled by summer's sunstrokes. Tribe of the inner-chamber holocaust and nothing good can emerge out of there. But you, Phillipa, believed it not, in the wide web of accepted wisdom: a pitched dragnet to keep the niggers haunted and hooded down dead, as so many hammered down coffin nail heads. Picture puzzles by the score to trigger the rifles of their imaginations. You see grist and grain in the grief of their papers. How intimately they live with the reigning hollow Holy Ghost of the dehydrated life, amid their cool swagger.

Their marked-up papers, their drawings stuffed with puzzles of peacocks for pimps, razorbacks for daddies, and arched pipes stocked with gold out of their shackled dreams. How to breathe and blow new wind over the western horizons. How to baptize them out of their nodding away to nothingness, without chanting and swindling them to a deeper sleep slumber party: drugged on Afrocentric palm wine and juju beads, and hammer-headed rappers.

Phillipa, you nervy zealot, who once upon a recent time incorporated the backbone of black Moses into your lesson plan at high noon, hidden away in an old lunch pail atop teacher's desk. When suddenly you placed a gun to the head of a diamond-studded chieftain of the Conquerors, when he came to auction your children out of this world, backwards, out of the arms of your classroom, in order to chalk them up as chattel for the new disciples, to tattoo them up with the branding iron of Brotherhood. And how that very night you were strip-searched by three white cops on your way home from a school conference: "How to Reshape What's Left Over." Always the long-legged plight of the Negro. Reconstitute the night. Give backbone to the crushed vertebra. How do you grow a flower in the muddy matrix of their apathy (which they already define as being cool) and deal with the malignancy of the insufficient spiritual funds of the school's official nodding-away snores of nothingness, drunk on the tepid tears of the despised waifs? Boarded up czars iced away in a martini palace: oh, go teach the children upon a purse string made of tattered shoelaces, they proclaim in their nostrums of financial tie-ups. They are our future, our very own cross to bear of tied-up gold. You teach them well and you lead the way, marching with the torchlight of your discipline. "Whatever it is that lives is Holy," yes, but it also can be astonishing in the terror of its unattended Lightning.

In the Let There Be Light pronunciation across the troubling rivers of time, the curving crescent path of a star fragmenting every hour on the hour, it now appeared in the hideously lost paths of hope. Yet another star curving up the slope of the Freedom Train omits way home to where once upon a time our mothers were peddled by the pound of flesh only seven blocks from the White House. Oh, His Light divining rod and resuscitator answers not to this charge so odious to Humanity and Freedom's Holy Light. Had I been shafted by this imperfect Light? Pitched to madness? The fabric of our sacred taper of papers wrapped not in sackcloth but mothballs. Drugged on Democracy in this vain, wasting, antiquated laboratory, I fly up a ghostly ladder, which looks like down to me: soldier of an endless cross. Strung up with my mind fixed on Freedom, time out of mind. Yet baby, who can kick this DEMOCRACY habit cold turkey—and call it a day? Oh, the citizens of Pandemonium on the now burning river and I am overcome, stripped without a gas mask, no oxygen of relief in this runaway Republic?

Phillipa, I could see some of these things—which will not pass away—when I visited your school, in February of last year. Oh, high-charged, deeply vexed Phillipa, called out of your name, "bright-skinned mis-shapen heifer," and runner-up for a Golden Apple for teaching your kids how to be and not be and how they might learn to untie their tongues, as they learn to tie their shoestrings. Flowers you purchased for the seven funerals of your kids, blasted away before the eyes of their kin on stoops. Oh, out of the swallowing scum of their existence, you, Phillipa, try to craft a garden of hyacinths. Oh, Phillipa, don't you weep, don't you mourn, Pharaoh's army got drowned. Don't think you're alone. Lazarus can be called out of the Lightning! Even as you look to find God's love and Christ's mercy in the hopelessness of their chaos.

Oh resuscitator, beware of love's yoke—you can't live on breadcrumbs sopped up and their hapless, strapped-down condition. You cry out, Phillipa: "How long, oh Lord? How long, oh Lord?" And I, your cantor, chorus in with you: "Too long / too long. . . . So long." You will not be vanquished. They are your rhapsody in black and blue; but you remain childless and manless. Imprisoned to your obsession for their nutrition of body, mind, and soul, you, Phillipa, have starved yourself, even as I see your bloated cheeks before me allowed day into night out to McDonald's to become your Midnight Special—night out.

Your prologue of an introduction of me to them (in the Uplift Series that you conjured up) proclaimed: "Now I want to present to you my dear and famous cousin professor and playwright. . . ." And you went on and on—too long.

Now I was suddenly hurled into frozen space.

Chapter 5

Back to myself, now I remembered the story about Hopkins Golightly at Reverend Elderberry's party. Golightly, whom I first saw in the dunking cage at Riverview Park, had really come up in the world. Now he was an associate of Reverend Elderberry, preacher, politico, and president of one of the leading black men's social clubs.

Well now, by some arrangement, the host signaled Hopkins Golightly to filter throughout and gather certain select effete politicos, supposedly to take them to another room where they could talk politics and see this kingdom of his welfare war chest. Soon after, Golightly took a party of twenty off to the side, then down yet another space of gloomy corridors—he held a torch aloft in his right hand to light the way. Snowden T. R. Barker, the aged opera buff and singer of lieder, columnist, and a wonderfully delightful sated gay, turned to me and said, "Baby-Bear, let's follow on this way. I'll be your cover. Party that Elderberry's about to fling down too corrupt for the nephew of dear Eloise." Then, from out of a box, Hopkins Golightly gave each of us a small, pencil-thin flashlight. We were going down several flights of steps, moving out of the darkness made fleetingly light by a weaving and shifting brightness pitched out of the slender sprockets of light we threw in order to guide our steps, lest we trip and fall. It seemed as if we were descending the swift slope of a mountain at midnight with weak flashlights instead of flares to kindle our way. We had gone down, it appeared, into the basement. Then, we followed Hopkins Golightly into this room which was about thirty feet by thirty feet, and it was here that this sublevel operative for the administration opened us up to another world.

That President Elderberry (who always wore a black eye patch through these proceedings, or so I was told) also owned this building was one thing, but that he partied down over here was something else again. Just then, we took a sharp turn to the right. President Elderberry, his blond, and now one who proved to be Hopkins Golightly led the way. Elderberry opened us up to a huge, gigantic room the size of a spacious apartment, which was fabulously appointed, as the magazine tells us, and the doors of the well-stocked bars were hurled wide open. There was a large fireplace and a swelling wooden deck composed of three rosewood dining room tables jammed with all kinds of foods: roasts, turkeys, and swelling platters of fruits and vegetables with chefs ready to do carving and serving. A majestic Egyptian rug adorned the floor. The spirit of the partygoers was constantly staggered by the surprise arrival of the famous and notorious from all walks of life (as if to say, "How did *you* know about 'this throw down jam'?"). There was a trio playing a kind of imitation style one heard from the Jazz Messengers, and in another corner of the room there was a South American juggler, a holdover from the masquerade ball, who was delighting a fragment of the crowd by keeping aloft seven plates. "What was this Elderberry trying to do—outdo Ed Sullivan?" I wondered out loud.

I discovered or was a part of the uncovering of this secret cache, quite by accident, early one morning at an after-hours masquerade party for charity. This affair filtered down to about twenty people, then it built up again. We went from a downtown hotel to a building on the South Side. We found ourselves moving along intoxicated, feeling our way breathlessly out of a side door and down along a darkened corridor in this building (now a part of the slum) and led by our host with a candelabra. The light was held high by Elderberry and his after-hours blond, who had by now, of course, taken off her black high-heeled pumps and was "wearing" a tiny white kitten over her left shoulder. It was dark, as dark as when you enter a movie house, the film already started, and all you can see are the flicks from the screen lighting the way and the usher's flashlight; but here the light was the flare from President Elderberry's candelabra leading the way and his broad's blond hair. Then I heard her howl out, "Let's get really funky and see if we can't discover some ghosts in this man's haunted house. See if we can't fuck 'em back into life. Let's go on a pilgrimage."

During the 1960s when I worked as a reporter for the *Forest County Dispatch*, I would spot Golightly on the Far South Side going in and out of the Soul Restaurant, taverns, greasy spoons, beauty parlors, package goods liquor stores, cleaning establishments, at the back door of storefront churches, and dipping into barber shops. He was busy raking in the quarters, dollars, and fives from his clientele, who were playing their gigs in the policy wheel, known as the Clearinghouse Book. Each time I would make clear certain cultural references or refinements, he made a special effort to acknowledge the lads, and made specific eye contact with each of them.

I'm telling you that enterprising Hopkins Golightly developed quite a successful route as a numbers runner. He was always neatly attired, sporting a blue beret in order to cover his lost hair. You might see him at the better watering holes at night with his steady lady, a winsome barmaid, with a throng of followers. A blond wig was snuggled atop the deep mahogany of her ebony-colored face and she had sharp features.

In early 1964, I saw another turn in Hopkins's life. Now, he waited tables for the lunch and dinner crowd at a popular restaurant on Twenty-third Street three days a week, and also worked as an assistant precinct captain.

A principal chore of his assigned operation was to build up the stockpile of various "goodies" for "those in need," based on their loyalty and his power of persuasion within the community at election time. Why, by the time for spring primaries or when the "nervous days of early November" rolled around, the dependable citizens of the slums were rewarded with what was later referred to satirically as "matching grants."

Hopkins Golightly had a virtual war chest in a hideaway cellar swarming with towering bookshelves of toilet paper, Kotex, hundreds of paper plates (left over from the Machine-sponsored barbecues, banquets, and picnics), scores of Asian wigs, hot irons, thousands of cigarettes by the carton, seventy-five cans of Agar hams, pint bottles by the hundreds of cheap bourbon and Wild Irish Rose, new Maxwell Street sports jackets from old fences, TV sets of all makes, and cheap lines of panty hose piled on high. And, of course, there were shoeboxes, lined with greenbacks, stashed away in an old safe, which had survived a fire in a Mafia-owned restaurant. For when all is said and undone, money is still the mother's milk of illicit political salvation.

And all of these things were to prod those asleep from their chains of apathy to awaken and vote, thereby drawing them off into a deeper nostrum. As well as rewards for those who aided Golightly by driving folks to the polls, goodies for others were needed for a little booster, a little handout, handstand to make it to the polls on time, because the liquor stores were closed until six.

I didn't know him well at all. My father had known him and spoken with him when Williemain had the old barbershop over on Forty-seventh Street. There was one unforgettable scene after a masquerade ball when I walked down a corridor where that treasury was revealed to me.

With the evolution of the Civil Rights Movement—which rolled right into the Black Power thrust—Hopkins Golightly was soon observed right in the swarm of things. The late 1960s and early 1970s found Golightly completely bald, so in order to stay current he had to purchase and don a high-arching Afro wig (his arc of triumph), which was so immensely powerful to look upon that he became known around the barbershop as "old Woolworth." (And I mockingly thought to myself, "Ah! Old Golightly is indeed blackening up—but now on his own terms. But was he?")

Through his political contacts, Golightly was now an assistant director at one of the Urban Progress Centers, yet another special flooring within the possibilities for the momentarily bottomed-out hustler on the make. He wore his purple and dark blue bellbottoms and high platform shoes, and in his midfifties, Golightly stayed so fit and trim that he appeared as a man of thirty-five. He also wore a sharply clipped goatee and was dearly draped in a Nehru wine-colored or blue suit on the weekends, when he was seen with his black blond at lunch or with his white blond at night, rapping away at one of the high-powered Rush Street watering holes.

In 1972, I made a discovery while covering a protest rally around City Hall, where two hundred or so marchers were condemning the arrest of two black youths who were accused of murdering a white child in Hyde Park. To my surprise, who should be at the very center of the dissenters but Hopkins Golightly, complete with dungarees, brogans, a farmer's red handkerchief swept about his neck, and a purple and red dashiki bloused about his torso. Soon he appeared at the microphone, giving the police department hell for arresting the high school students on the basis of the most flimsy evidence. Sounding off as an invigorated race man, Golightly's speech was such a stirring cry from the soul, I fully expected him to produce a harmonica and wail away about the troubles visited upon these "innocent youths." Then rifling, "Let us die to make men free!" The boys were sentenced to one hundred ninety-nine years in prison; four years later, the convictions were overturned by the Supreme Court.

During the rest of the 1970s, I would see Hopkins Golightly on a regular basis before his vendor stall painted in green, red, and black outside of Operation PUSH on Saturday mornings. As a working journalist, I would go to the former Jewish synagogue to cover meetings for local newspapers. Golightly's was one of the larger tables selling books, proclaiming the universal soul of BLACKNESS, and the growing Afrocentric mood of that day. Two-thirds of the three deal tables were loaded down with imitation African jewelry, and a rainbow of dashikis made from cheap linen was also for sale. Dressed in one of the scores of dashikis he owned (and adorned with a medallion sculpture piece of Africa), Golightly could even outhawk the Black Muslims declaiming the white man and proclaiming, *Muhammad Speaks* all up in your face! Shaking a fistful of beads in one hand and palming one of the books with the other, Golightly then proceeded to give out one of his fine business cards with each sale. His studio, where he now made jewelry, was located on the top floor of the same building where he had at one time kept his political war chest in the basement.

One of the most popular bars during the Harold Washington campaign for mayor in 1983 was a handsome-looking establishment in Hyde Park called Butler's. Campaign workers, journalists, "double-agents" for the riddled machine, BUPPIES on the make and on the way up, and just plain black folk drawn collectively to Harold's charisma gathered at this large bar where one could also get a meal. Usually, the gossip circulated around the room over Harold's political possibilities and his personal life, and was far more appetizing than the dishes of food served to the clientele. As the evolving campaign started to sizzle, one could expect to see everyone who was anyone, with even the most rickety skeleton of credentials in the black community, now herded forth to rattle on Harold and to hail him as our secular savior.

Defunct now, Butler's was a perfect watering hole for this spectacular, path-blazing campaign devoted to an expression of growing black political sophistication and a solidarity previously unheard of in Chicago. For not only could you discuss Harold's chances of becoming Chicago's first black mayor, you could make your wildest predictions in a black-owned (safe) establishment, where sophistication meets sophistry (and even stuffiness) and with a standardized dress code unheard of in Hyde Park. Where the black bourgeoisie was guaranteed that a policy of "no entry" for riffraff (pitched to bar downtrodden, ill-kept, or rowdy blacks in the main) was enforced. Through a myriad of conversations at different tables over a three-month period, I became aware of many middle-class blacks (who had been prohibited from the power lines of jobs and influence at virtually all strata of mainstream economic life during the years of Da Mayor's democracy) who were now ready to claim a piece of Chicago's action.

On a slushy January night, I arrived late but spotted Hopkins Golightly midway into deep conversation with five fairly well known PR types concerning the public relations firm he had set up in "order to ensure Harold's victory," and soon damning the way Jane Byrne had "sold out black people." Hopkins was sporting a new "do"; he wore an Asian wig. (Perhaps one of those left over in the basement from his Daley days.) Hopkins wore a purple dashiki, an imitation gold Black Power medallion, and a handsome, Italian-cut, wine-colored three-piece suit.

Like the hard-driving compulsion beneath the Harold Washington campaign and the tenor of his years in office, the blues had evolved out of an underground freedom movement of its own. Rooted in the Delta, rerouted out of Memphis, and retooled in St. Louis, the blues hit Chi-town with the power of a train howling down the tracks at midnight and in rhythm with the great sweeping masses of black migration from Mississippi and other southern places. But I didn't realize until the summer of 1987 that Golightly himself had taken the route of the blues to Chicago via Highway 61.

Attending blues sets on both sides of town, I happened into a newly formed club not far from Rush Street one blue Monday. Out of the sweltering night and into the lavish intensity of heat at every heartbeat, the power of this Delta original, a three-piece band with a wailing guitarist as lead, was charged and soul-slamming. Ninety-five percent of the spectators were young whites. For now, the blues forged one of the soul-stirring secular standards of Forest County artistic consciousness.

The two large droning fans seemed to form a fourth force of the heat waving off from the voices and instruments of the Delta-born bluesmen: life imitating art. Then, towards the end of the first set, Old Fox Foster, as he was called then, made a pronouncement: he wanted to bring to the stage an "old backwater boon-buddy of mine, from the heart-of-home. We came packin' and screamin' out of the Delta in a pickup truck and onto Highway 61 together. My buddy's been out of wailin' onstage a few years, now, but deep into all kinds of troublin' waters in this year man's town, so he knows blues up, down, and sideways. Old Fox Foster here will tell yawl how this stud blows breath into all them tiny cells in a harmonica, so bad, you think some woman was inside each one of them lying, grieving, cursing, cutting her man or getting some deep-down groovin' and lovin', and make a blind man see the dawn with that silver harmonica of his'n. Welcome to the stage my main-man, brother-man, Hopkins Golightly."

As the audience gave a hardy applause, I sat there in a sweating spell of surprise bordering on shock, and yet. . . . Soon Golightly emerged from the back dressed in patched-up overalls and an unbuttoned blue blouse of a shirt, which revealed the white streaks of hair on his powerfully built chest. Then he was wailing and twanging on that harmonica, performing feats of magic; Delta songs and Chicago-brand streaks, hawk-haunted rambling and gagging. He led the way for three songs. Between the third and last offering, the guitarist asked that the hat be passed "to help reencourage my man to keep on keeping on." The audience responded generously, as a huge farmer's hat was circled aloft around the room.

Golightly had a new/old hustle going for him, I howled to myself, and as the audience called for him to sing some of their favorites by other performers, I suddenly found myself standing on a chair with my arms upraised, protesting over and over again, "Golightly, something out of 'The Battle Hymn of the Republic.' "

The audience turned a loathsome face upon me as if I were a damnable buffoon, an unhip outsider. I was as out of place here with my cry for this song, as an unkempt drifter who happened out of the cold into Butler's, not wearing sports jacket or tie.

Finally the bouncer (and part-time owner), who took your three dollars at the entrance, came to grab my elbow and warned me that he would have to ask me to leave. "No way! If you don't cool it, no way can you stay here!"

But exactly that moment Golightly cried out, "Nowhere you may roam, there is always some fat-meat from your own used-to-be-home. That voice out there—I can't make the face out—knows something out of my past, trying to put some fat-meat on my head and not no wig hat either. Important to me, been running from it, embracing it, and then again denying it. So, yes, I'll respond. Hell yes! I'll wail on down 'The Battle Hymn of the Republic.'"

Obviously, my request had sounded uncouth to the cool of blues tradition by calling for something so unattached ("no way"). But the captivating Golightly had redeemed me with the audience. And as I listened to him cry, wail, pray, yodel, criticize, and bemoan on that harmonica with tears streaming down his face, I realized that he was not simply tuning "The Battle Hymn" upside down and upon its head, Golightly was trying to breathe the breath of jokes, heartaches, agony, duplicity, hustles of all kinds, triumphs, and failures, and blasting out his life's laboratory into the ruptured, rowdy, no-holds-barred, cruel saga of this country. Pouring it all into "The Battle Hymn" was this most essential American outlawed spirit. So my request had helped him to retrieve, if not redeem, himself, at least momentarily. But Lawd today, Golightly had to turn back to the blues and its potential for rifling an unearthing saga about all the lies concerning the self and the state of the Republic. The wonderful irreverence of the blues pitched through the silver instrument at his lips helped old Golightly in his attempt to re-create a new consciousness about this tragic, embattled Republic so constantly in need of a wailing-on-down-blues-hymn.

Back to the old Divine Question *Why Was I Born?* which was so grievous within my very tormented Soul. And the Light of divided ways. Night from Day, Day from Night, Black from White, White from Black. Now being returned to the Actor's Studio of Forest County, early this singular day-into-night, where they were rehearsing this new material to be inserted into my play of 1987, *Towards Jerusalem by This Lamplight in My Hand.* The two voices I heard were from the major characters in this play, which tore so at the central issues of my day. I was hoping and praying that this new infusion would bring up the agony of my Soul, in divining ways for *Lamplight,* before more of this troubling yet life-throbbing blood was spilt.

Lamplight was an attempt at a verse play. These actors had played the two major roles in the original. One was a pastor of a church, God's Golden Leaves, Pompey C. J. Browne, and part-time actor. So, he was playing out the words I had slated for him, but he was adding his own improvisation as we went along, in the reading. The actress was a new beauty whose very soul sprang from the ethos of old Forest County. I hoped that the light I saw in their eyes would prove to be sustained light, upon reflection. I listened to their comments and noted them and headed out south to Williemain's Barbershop. In this rehearsal I played the role of Reverend Eli Elderberry.

REVEREND POMPEY C. J. BROWNE: Sadie-Sue, why so gloomy, on the eve of your stellar day? What a gifted dawn when Clay Cratwell lifts your veil. Sisters throughout Forest County would love to don your wedding gown and the veil you'll be donning tomorrow morning. A wedding gown weaved out of history. Many a miss would be Breathless with bliss and the mystery of a new unfolding.

SADIE-SUE: Granny O was supple and clever, as she was wise and kind, Granny O left the wedding dress (that now wrings out my Soul, as an affliction) to the first of her two granddaughters, who married. She left a bed quilt fashioned by Her own hand to the granddaughter who did not marry first. Then she left this sly postscript, "Lucky girl, number one, You'll have a warm body—this granny-stitched quilt will keep you warm, truly, too."

REVEREND POMPEY C. J. BROWNE: A gown riddled by history; stitched in folds of mystery. Or, as the hunters say, a hit is history, a miss is mystery. Though how a miss becomes history Is surely no old maid's mystery. Sounds as if there was Wizardry to this granny that you hold so dear, Sadie-Sue.

SADIE-SUE: Well, why a miss remains a miss is both ancient history and a mystery. Perhaps she miscalculated her firepower, Out of the mythical lines of family lore, it appeared that Wretched Marvella, my jealous-hearted, evil, elder sister Would wear this wedding gown. Then her lover was lost to Marvella forevermore on a rain-sleeked southern road. Like a rabbit plucked out of a high hat, her catch-as-catch man had swooped out of Marvella's life, before his truck vaulted into wreckage and flames. I pity her, too, because Marvella grew precious when the man she worshiped Loved her, or so she thought (which he did in the orchard Time and the gathering up season, before her Paul called it a night on the eve of Marvella's impending wedding day). My sister Marvella was clueless to the midnight action This bogus Paul was weaving (now you see me, now you don't). As if the heart were a pair of loaded dice. Playing musical chairs with some of the most shapely sisters southwest of Paradise.

REVEREND POMPEY C. J. BROWNE: Marvella's continual obsession (before she spat her rue into My face and told me what I could do with my white man's religion) was this: the collusion of Sadie-Sue, with one Milton Beefeater Barnes, Clay Cratwell, and the racist state *Conjured* her Paul down the road to his untimely fate.

SADIE-SUE: We loved the dude when he was *down* and righteous; not Duplicitous and long-gone wrong. Who tampered with the Transmission of his truck? We never revealed to Marvella How her beloved Paul unveiled a scheme in a bar the night Before: to sack this dizzy broad Marvella for a less Troublesome paramour, a shapely Crescent City Creole babe. Now Marvella has slipped some weird fix on the fragile Harmony of my heart; and stalks the day to seize any happiness I might have the luck to capture, in this lonely world.

REVEREND POMPEY C. J. BROWNE: Sadie-Sue, estrangement of sisters is not new. No matter the yeast, the garb, or the bile. What appears new is Stripped from older barrels, cloth, or guile.

SADIE-SUE: Will my gorgeous mate be damned to lift a bloodstained veil? Cursed to embrace blood-smeared lines streaking Down a grievous face, revealing his bride's accursed fate.

REVEREND POMPEY C. J. BROWNE: Come clean with me, as you have upon a few occasions Sadie-Sue. Maybe I can help you before it's too late. I don't need to know your plans. I want to know the shape of your dreams.

SADIE-SUE: So then Reverend Pompey know the woe, if you are to know my Dreams (shaped up without symmetry) you must learn the new nightmares. Ride me so low down, as a hound bent to Hell. Then you'll tremble over the trouble I've seen out of the Shattered light of my eyes, behind the mask I wear before a world gone mad, for me and Clay Cratwell.

REVEREND POMPEY C. J. BROWNE: Don't slip behind a world of words wrapped in wrinkled veils.

SADIE-SUE: Are you sure you're with me, Reverend Pompey? Nothing sounds me out, not even the peal of the church bell's altar call.

REVEREND POMPEY C. J. BROWNE: What? Didn't I see you through your drug addiction? Must I enumerate?

SADIE-SUE: In the last seven days, the nightmare of my bridal room oozing with blood. My soul soaked up in seven *shuttering* veils.

REVEREND POMPEY C. J. BROWNE: Is this some dream gone mad? Out of whose body does this Blood pour forth? Clay's? Marvella's?

SADIE-SUE: Are you still with me? Or against me, like Marvella? Even If my Soul's skidded down a road of Nothingness in my Utter despair.

REVEREND POMPEY C. J. BROWNE: Don't be foolish. Of course I'm with you, even unto death. I'm with you beyond hearing. I'm ready as always to listen to the mystery of your heart. Wasn't I there to pull you up from the Drug scene? My heart travels wherever your Floundering spirit flies. Sadie-Sue, you are as my own Flesh and blood. As long as your flight into Nothingness Is stripped of guile and lies.

SADIE-SUE: If Clay knew what awaited him at the altar rail, Would he lift a hand to raise my bridal veil?

REVEREND POMPEY C. J. BROWNE: Did you hear, smell, or see a raving apparition Fixed as a drug dealer's paradise spread out across the length and breath of your imaginative brain? That drew you like a magnet to believe a bloody plot Unraveled the lace of your knitted wedding train?

SADIE-SUE: I'm down on my knees: a scullion at prayer (or so it appears). Then as a scrubwoman soaking up the blood flowing and me wringing it through the sleeves of my soul's impaled redemption.

Everywhere to Nothingness.
Pouring, throbbing, bursting forth
Now through the floor of my bridal room
Transformed (like my dreams). . . .
Back in time to the very room where I was born. Abandoned. Then raised upon a star of faith by my Halo of a Grandmother's guiding hand and Odessa's Heartbeat to the very dust and clay of my being. Yes, and trained to soar beyond the limitations of the powers and principalities of this world. To Soar an octave higher to ascend the altar call.

REVEREND POMPEY C. J. BROWNE: But not always beyond the temptations of the things of this world. Yet I can't see Clay in all of this. Nor the—. But go on. My lips are sealed.

SADIE-SUE: Now stripped down naked, soaking up blood. Reverend Pompey, at first my sight was sealed off to see just what I was Deploying to soak up this blood. Seeing only these hands Before me, scrubbing, when suddenly, as one who is shocked Out of her breath by heart failure in the last lap home, In the marathon race to embrace prizewinning ecstasy, at the finishing line—at long last—I discovered it is My dove white wedding gown handed down in bliss That I am defiling. WHY? That I am soaking, sponging, Wringing out this blood—into a huge bucket. (Oh, the very breath of my life shocked out of my body.) Deploring the act, as if in the beginning, I was defiling the substance of my heirloom's reverence. Lord, Reverend Pompey, a bucket consumed by blood, wrung out of my wedding gown, wrung out by these hands, as a witch's fingers, given new power to defile, as an abomination. But I can't stop the flow. No. Whose blood? Whose body? Throbbing blood. For now Reverend Pompey, I hear pulsating: the blood, the blood droplets wrung from *her* wedding gown, But of those beads stitched there by the Sewing Sisters Of the Mending Ways. Blood wrung down from my wedding gown by this bitch—Sadie-Sue's hands. (The mask of her face Wedding veil.) Granny O's gift of a gown to this scullion Granddaughter, unworthy of the name, the acclaim, to That of scrubwoman. For it was this scrubwoman Odessa-of-the-Spirits I came to acclaim her, whose collected nickels, dimes, quarters, and dollars put me through, through all Pulled me up to everything made available to me.

REVEREND POMPEY C. J. BROWNE: Some evil has engulfed your mind; hooked the very threads Of your bliss; and threatens to unravel fabric Almighty God has bound together. Sadie-Sue, don't allow midnight's Nightmare to hang your paradise on the edge of a precipice. Hurl *All* evil hauntings out of the landscape of your mind. These hauntings lead you back to Nothingness, which projected you into total wreckage, even as your commercial Star flamed brightest: did this malignancy grieve its way Into your unraveling soul, in another form during your Drugged-out days? Now returned in the guise of a new, outrageous, flamboyant knitting. Listen, Sadie-Sue, There are scores of spirits (not simply two) contending For the crown of your vulgar and refined natures and the Myriad membranes of those hidden mysteries raging beneath your gown, your brain, your soul, your crown. Look out for tomorrow. And all of untold tomorrows You and the gifted Clay are destined for to embrace each Other in wedlock of God's showering stellar Light. Don't let this nightmare ride you, as if its sleek destiny Were prophetic, Is prophetic, and held for your fate in the pale Rider's gloves of its funeral immoral grasp. I say bliss and Christ *not* gloom and Lucifer control the Reins of your outraged soul. Has that evil-spewing sister Marvella hounded you with some contraptions of the mind? With some of her jealousy-inspired loathsome curses? Marvella no doubt dreams she could trip up some man before It's too late to even try. Envious because you've pulled your life up out of the depths of drugged dregs and despair; Hers is still married to chaos, wasting away, unraveled by Reckless living. Still this desolation troubles me beyond Veils the illusion you are allowing to fall away. I can't Stand to see your Soul fly backwards to the Nothingness Which opened you up to a life of self-destruction. Weaved you to waves of wicked madness to a point where you rarely Recognized your name, your destiny, your face, your blood.

Hurled you to the precipice of Nothingness. But continue, surely this is the end of the nightmare, Time out Of mind. It can't follow? How can all of this be? Think Logically! Granny Odessa loved you beyond living. Her soul Was an inspiration (Is an inspiration) that was renewed By your achievements. If anything, she gave up her soul, Hung out her soul on the spirits of your ambitions. Miss Odessa would never have dreamed a double cross, A way of dividing you from yours. No, some wicked Divination threatens an eclipse of havoc and horror, Lies and wreckage, I can see it in your eyes, Sadie-Sue. This calamitous anticipation.

SADIE-SUE: It starts all over and over again—each night—this hideous Ritual: soaking up and wringing out. I can hear the aged Creaking, rocking chair of Granny O's. Clocked to foreboding Death, too? I don't know. Do you? I don't know. Moving in rhythm within my hands and the throbbing gasp of the sponged-up blood. Wrung out precisely by these hands Now trembling before me. Clay's to have and to hold from This day forward? Those of the cocaine addict, who once Laid claim to the body and soul of Sadie-Sue. And if all this were not enraging enough, Reverend Pompey, this Sadie-Sue in my nightmare goes about her task as driven as a scullion without a care, which shocks me all the more, as if she were Not sponging up blood, but a thick red juice tumbled by Chance upon somebody else's floor. Wringing out my soul to the core.

REVEREND POMPEY C. J. BROWNE: Hurdling up a false-faced ecstasy ladder behind the back Of Almighty God? Flinging you into an ecstasy of Nothing, Then and now.

SADIE-SUE: But no. It starts all over and over again, World without end. This hideous ritual: soaking up and wringing out. Wedding dress robed in blood. Is it me? Or is This ghost of Sadie-Sue? Hung up. Haunted. Strung out. Hung out to dry in a windstorm, high upon the precipice Of cocaine glaze. Penalized for all the hell she has raised.

REVEREND POMPEY C. J. BROWNE: I told you if you would come clean with Almighty God, He would not hold your dreams in ransom. Would not allow The Lucifer of spiritual Death to sack your soul. Question becomes this: have you sold the immortal Soul God weaved and grieved into the very shape of your being? Have you totally driven out the Deadly Lucifer, Hurled him out of your life, where he had taken you up The precipice? Come clean. Has he hooked his way back Into your life? Sacked the Spiritual breath out of your Soul?

SADIE-SUE: A new hell, Reverend Pompey. A new flourishing, flooding Hell. Payment for the old downfall? I can hear that Ancient creaking, rocking chair clocked now to foreboding Death, moving rhythm with

the throbbing hands of a clock as I sponge up blood wrung out of me
so fitfully by these Brown hands before me.

A wicked horror of a nightmare besieging, hooking body and soul,
and engulfing my wedding gown. My soul soaked up in This blood,
now as voices, Reverend Pompey in this gown, that Speaks to me
not of love but in dumb-mouthings, Babbling (with every breath I
breathe) pitched to break my heart. Gasps of unarticulated but ever
so compelling moans and sobs and gasps and trembles pitched from
the Floor, from *where and when*, I don't seem to know.

REVEREND POMPEY C. J. BROWNE: Sadie-Sue, Clay will step off with you,
as you romantic Dreamers grace the measure of your resounding days
By the pitch of Almighty God's sacred music.

SADIE-SUE: Then will Clay lift a bloodstained veil to Death riddled and
streaked across this mask I wear for a face? And then call it a day?
Or find ecstasy there? In the arms of a blood-soaked scullion? No,
Reverend Pompey. Blood keeps oozing, pouring upwards From this
floor. Like a wounded body blasted in a combat Zone. (I can't help
but see the life Clay left behind, In the 'Nam, where he got shot
down, received a Purple Heart over there, but almost embraced the
final breath.) Reverend Pompey, rocking away in measured heartbeat
is Grandmother Odessa, endlessly rocking in her creaking chair,
Where she once upon a time had cradled me in her loving Arms,
saddled with the curse, the sin, the heritage of My affliction, as
her burden in the afterlife? Cradled me in her loving arms, in this
room where we once upon a Time played musical chairs. Now my
neck cranks my face to Granny's visage: Bruised blood in patches;
etched out Testimonials: I told you so, I warned you of the woe,
Sadie-Sue, of turning your precious head and heart away from my
Redeemer, your Redeemer. This marriage cannot Be pitched to eternity. Warning me when, as a child, Granny O's forebodings forever
and a day proved me Grievously wrong, wrung out of tune, again
and again Suddenly. Granny O turned out to be Odessa, Prophetess.
My wedding gown—hers originally—now pitched to this savagely
insulting enterprise! Frayed and worn in time Needful of the Sisters
of The Mending Ways caring craft; A raveled sleeve, and a bit of
basting here and there, Glistening new beads, Bleeding beads just
now of woe.

[SADIE-SUE *leaves and* REVEREND ELI ELDERBERRY *enters.*]

REVEREND POMPEY C. J. BROWNE: Suffer the little children up to me. Harm them not, for such is God's Kingdom made. I've known these kids since they were children. I presided Over the wedding of Clay's parents: Lily-Beth and Joe Barry. Tried to pray Lily-Beth through the horror of the comas. Tried to help her weave her way back to Almighty God. When her very soul was placed upon a fiery rack, when the baby girl expired. Sound Sister Odessa was one of the original leaders of this church, when my old church, God's Golden Leaves, burned to the ground. Oh, now God there's that old accusatory voice, from within, blessed with the power to relentlessly signify and antagonize. "Reason why Pompey never falls on his knees to God Almighty, *in private*, in prayerful submission is not that he believes in atheism, But rather the common complaint of skepticism, which comes in the *comforting* form of *oh, my rheumatism.*" Unfolding of our predicament allows God to know He reigns over a lost-found tribe; but not *why* in His wanderlust He rules (without a yardstick, known to man, that's the trick). *This* they don't teach you in church, nor school, Because He's Almighty, Fool. He can just about play it hot or Cool, at any climate, without fretting over something called blood Pressure. Can present a cruel face of a gargoyle Or, one that's totally righteous and royal. Make you believe you were born to toil. When He blows His cool in the Old Testament in form of his wrath, who's to call Him to heel, in His magnificence? "And Pompey, just to think of it: down over Here you rule out any broadcast of your pessimism, your dour doubting would sour faith, would jar the light out of the candles of faith in hundreds of temples of the mind. And what would poor little Sadie-Sue say: Drive her to a sanitarium, if you blew your cool." But perhaps it's a sign of irreverence not to Question God Almighty. You fall on your knees to lay a decrepit role, before God, man (and sistern). That when you fall on your knees, ultimately, you don't know why.

REVEREND ELI ELDERBERRY: But you can't admit that you might as well die. No, not die, but be dead. You lie! Why do you stigmatize in order to dramatize, what should simply be looked upon as a faltering of faith. Or, Pompey, to admit that either you are wheezing to death, spiritually, inside, or that you've been judged unfit to stand naked before God Almighty, though you've cracked some deal with your Savior, which allows you to continue your performance on the outside, indoors, upon the stage at your temple (which used to be a movie house once upon a time, or so I've been told). For you to cry, Stigmatize, Hell! You fall on your knees with your eyes closed (amid the sisters' sighs) to avoid truth winking out before the audience's witness as illuminated in men's eyes.

REVEREND POMPEY C. J. BROWNE: Reverend Pompey C. J. Browne judged unfit to stand? Me, you had better get behind. . . . *You* stand in Mortal danger of losing your soul.

REVEREND ELI ELDERBERRY: *I* don't have one, remember. We are in this thing together, Brother. It's an enterprise. Something like sibling rivalry, but a deal is cracked: between us, as brothers. You suppress your turbulence. I, knowing you better than you are willing to admit, threaten to pull down the grandiose garb you wear before the world, and show out the underbelly of your unbelief; the effluvium of your farty drawers, The shitty silk of your soap opera rhetoric. Getting a vaudevillian shuffle all mixed up with something called the Divine Plan. The old fake like I'm dying (you know that part in your sermons, Pompey), when all the sisters howl out for Mercy and you pretend Like you are dying, just for forty-five seconds (I've Timed out this stuffings, you see). And then, Miracle of miracles, you are suddenly reborn to an old-time, new-time Magisterial Profundity.

REVEREND POMPEY C. J. BROWNE: Get out of my house, my life, my word! Oh, what proportion in the measure Of man's soul is adjudicated as immortal? Has a chance in the ultimate crack-up into tiny puzzle pieces, to live, eternally? Fragments of toylike pieces that twang and Twist, hurl and bang in time and space, to be saved; then trip off the stage out of the blinding sight of time, to be not saved, not engraved and flake away to splotches upon flying saucers, but go and on. No not You.

REVEREND ELI ELDERBERRY: Now, You are dealing more to the point. Let's see now: You, Pompey, end up preparing to crack up some egg plucked from the fridge, into a frying pan, Into the fire, only to discover it's hard-boiled; But it's too late, you've already started, tapping about the circumference. Who played the joke (laid an egg on your faith) before you expired? You see, Pompey, if I can continue to get you to think, before You act, I can come out of the shadow, and shore up Your soul, before you turn to a rotten apple, before you really stink.

Now I hear the voices of angels cry: NOW BREATHE. You may breathe again and out of an alto voice emerged: Coltrane. His spiritual fluidity beyond a sermon's tongue, though he preached in stem-winding velocity. Orchestrated circles beyond encyclicals of the rowdy and the soulful. Then, even the most long-winded mouthpiece for the Maker brought to the sessions of sweet, staggering, imaginative, and jamming gigs, *Ascension* beyond harmonies supreme, clairvoyant and wild. Crystal sounds of the soprano could take the damnedest routes and reinvent a beauty-boss-blitzkrieg and madness from a fragment flint of sound. Amid the abundance: cunning riffs and redundant ripples played out of scraps and scrabble, which flicked from his horn of plenty out of a sky-high squall and scream to know out of the avalanche to be and not to be: strung up, strung out, redeemed out the Light. Then at Stage Center, 'Trane rode the wind with wings shaped out of an isolation, Pristine, yet rowdy, Soprano to the Heavenly female voice on the right-hand side of the Creator. Tenor What didn't this lightning rod have up his sleeve? Confidence supreme, pitched to power the madness of his endurance. The meteor in the madhouse and the madhouse in the meteor. Whatever it is that lives is hellish, holy, and whorish. An endurance steeplechase. A thousand uplifts/Fifty takes. Teach me, preach me how not to . . . take me there. How to love and be loved in return. At Down Center there is only Chaos to order us to God. A jugular throbbing beat to God to head off rushing to judgment what heroin cannot deliver. A deliverance beyond the syncopation of heroin.

An outlaw Angel hurled to earth to uncover this furious and fabulous Coltrane serving at the pleasure of this carnivorous God-Head of Chaos, Discovered the ranges of freedom's changes (and long-divisions) amid life's redundancies, his yoke, and the idiocy of the joke enshrined in the word "nigger." Explorer beyond any far-flung Bird, charged to discover: *a design in the furnace of affliction. Yes and a remnant.* I say a supreme blown out of the chaos of burning tongues. Knew that *you* were always knee-deep in the middle of the overflowing river of Styx and shit. Where mayhem scored melodies, time beyond recorded time. The fractured whole noted: train-cars sweeping in a thousand and one directions and always, *always*, ALWAYS the territory beyond. His nerve endings PITCHED to terror and tenderness.

A righteous stud; a thousand lift-offs out of rhapsody and this one more river and the meteor-madness and the maladies mirroring the Age, and try, try, and oh, cry, grieve to shake Him, drowsy God-Head, loose by each Almighty shoulder blade till He becomes Undone and awakens and twists His body and soul to become One with our accusatory Agony, within the labyrinth, the cross, the turbulence of our passage, our furnace, and give back the shape of our manhood—amid the nothingness of a promised end, in the promised land but a tree to life lynching—as we give unto Him, now in the beginning, word without end, the tongue to His Voice, the meaning of His long-gone music. Until He, God, recovers *lost time*, recuperates, by dis-covering and finding His split tongue reconstructed, in the millionth time made music: our mouths bloody with song. Then He, still, only can try to read the new chord progression there knee-deep in the river beyond Styx; where many thousand were dropped off, chained at the collarbone and black corpses in the Father of Waters yet weep in flooding upheaval. Yet I was suspended above in the air looking for Mr. Lovejoy's printing press in that river running with blood and the blue-black ink.

But then I was drowning and gasping for breath now out of the man from Hamlet's last dying plateaus of righteous reaching-grieving riffs.

And I heard myself—before a mask-streaked oracle—in the trans-fusion of liquids and long-legged Light, "Jesus told me that the world would hate me if He changed my name."

High above and someplace with the twilight, I perceived a winging-off crescent, a golden note, now sealed in a boxed covenant. Soon I was beginning to recognize why some god had struck me down dead, ahahah to awaken, newborn, to see with new eyes, renewed tongue, ears pitched to the pulse of day into night, feet to outdance David. Yet tied down within this hospital bed, for I was so uproarious of Spirit. Refined not like silver but in a furnace of affliction. Not to be totally astonished by the Creator, or man. Somehow I felt no more at home with Isaac than I did with Ishmael. Awakened now by the meteor of *that* first Light and dawn's early light. No wonder I had to go down dead in this madhouse—in order to breathe upon the righteous and rowdy riffs of existence again. Oh, yes, and now to wail with a horn full of plenty: LET THERE BE LIGHT, Baby, LET THERE BE LIGHT.

LET THERE BE LIGHT, BABY, LET THERE BE LIGHT. But then as I let my eyes filter across the room, they fell upon the tear-drenched eyes of my nurses. I could feel no evil for the Lord is with me, His staff is with me, and then I could feel a swoop of angelic voices beneath my gown as I sailed out to other voices and other democratic chambers and other spheres into the distances of time.

Editors'
Appendix

The World of Forest County

John G. Cawelti

Many of the characters in *Meteor in the Madhouse*, including the narrating voice of Joubert Jones, appeared in Forrest's previous novel *Divine Days*. That novel described a week in 1966 during which Joubert Jones began his serious life commitment as a writer by moving out of his family's house and into the Avon, a colorful rooming house near the University of Chicago.[1] In 1972, the major period that Joubert remembers in *Meteor in the Madhouse*, he was still living at the Avon. Many aspects of character and motivation in *Meteor in the Madhouse* reflect *Divine Days*, though Forrest is usually careful to reintroduce his major figures. Other important elements of *Meteor in the Madhouse* relate to Forrest's Witherspoon trilogy, consisting of his first three novels. The character of Leonard Foster resembles in some ways Nathaniel Witherspoon, the narrative character of those earlier novels.[2] For example, Foster's poems, two of which are quoted at length, are similar to the stream-of-consciousness narrative of *There Is a Tree More Ancient Than Eden*, the first of the Witherspoon novels. However, Forrest has not simply repeated things from these earlier works but has transformed them into a new tapestry presenting the world of Forest County (his fictional version of Chicago).[3]

Meteor in the Madhouse opens with the novella *Lucasta Jones, in Solitude: Lives Left in Her Wake*. *Lucasta* opens with a section titled "November 1992—I," which frames the work along with a corresponding section from the fifth novella, *By Dawn's Early Light: The Meteor in the Madhouse*, called "November 1992—II."

The year 1992 is twenty-six years after the events of *Divine Days*, and this framing narrative presents the last days of the protagonist and narrator of *Divine Days*, Joubert Antoine Jones. Now a successful playwright, Joubert returns late at night from a lecture engagement and drops into a fitful sleep. He dreams of a day twenty years earlier, in 1972, when he visited his grandfather and grandmother Gussie and Forester Jones at their home and went on to see his adoptive cousin Leonard Foster in a psychiatric hospital, where he discussed Foster's situation with the latter's girlfriend, Shirley Polyneices. Joubert's ultimately unsuccessful visit with Leonard takes place during the second novella, *Live! At Fountain's House of the Dead*. The third novella, *All Floundering Oratorio of Souls*, consists largely of memories from Joubert's young manhood, evoked by the experiences of the present. *To the Magical Memory of Rain*, the fourth novella, does not involve Joubert directly, though his relation to this mythical fantasy is really quite complex. Finally, in *By Dawn's Early Light: The Meteor in the Madhouse*, we return to the night of November 1992 and follow Joubert as he takes a taxi home from the bus station. He wakes to a day of many errands, including a fateful haircut. When he returns to Williemain's Barbershop to retrieve his misplaced reading glasses, Joubert is mortally wounded in a gang-related shooting.

Lucasta Jones, in Solitude: Lives Left in Her Wake

This novella is appropriately named after Joubert's great-aunt. The memory of Lucasta Jones not only haunts Joubert but is suggestively present throughout *Meteor in the Madhouse*. Lucasta's significance springs from the different things she represents to the people who knew her, which gives this seemingly obscure woman a profound importance in many lives. As a foster mother for Leonard Foster and a surrogate mother for Joubert, Lucasta played an important role in the raising of the two young men. Lucasta has also been a symbol of erotic excitement for Joubert. One of his most powerful early sexual memories is of seeing Lucasta's legs when she dug into her stocking to get money from her favorite hiding place. In fact, Joubert often thinks of Lucasta when he is attracted to another woman, such as Leonard Foster's lover Shirley Polyneices, with whom Joubert visits Leonard at the hospital.

Although Lucasta had a powerful influence on many people who enjoyed her extraordinary dancing as well as her skillful ironing, this talented woman was unable to fulfill her remarkable aesthetic and erotic potential. In fact, Lucasta's is a story of repeated giving and loss. She has lost children, including Arthur Witherspoon and Leonard Foster, both of whom were taken from her, and lovers, who have invariably walked out on her. In many ways, Lucasta is the living incarnation of the blues, a character whose life carried out on a different level some of the patterns of her idol, Billie Holiday. Lucasta's complex symbolic significance is strikingly summed up by her sometime occupation of washing, dressing, and beautifying corpses for morticians. This vocation dramatically symbolizes her human fate of trying to give love and care to those she is doomed to lose.

Born in 1890 on Dahomey Plantation in Forrest County, Mississippi, Lucasta Jones left there at the age of twelve to begin her voyage north. After a year in Memphis working for the Memphis Raven-Snow's Funeral Home, she moved north to Forest County, arriving there in 1903. In 1905 she had a baby by the legendary Judge Jericho Witherspoon, who took the child from her because he believed her "too young, too wild, and ill prepared" to raise a child. This is the first of Lucasta's many losses.

As a young woman Lucasta was a dancer but supported herself by her work at the Memphis Raven-Snow's Funeral Home. When she quit that job, angry at the way her employer cooperated with Judge Witherspoon in taking her child, she worked for a time at a much more difficult job at Fountain's House of the Dead. Finally, Lucasta was reduced to washing and ironing shirts, into which she poured the grace and rhythm she had shown earlier as a dancer. Some of Forrest's descriptions of Lucasta's movements are among the most lyrically entrancing passages he ever wrote. Lucasta appears again in *To the Magical Memory of Rain* in connection with her final occupation as a washerwoman whose beautifully ironed shirts are the only way in which she can still express her artistry.

Like many artistically talented African American women, Lucasta was doomed to disappointment and poverty in her later life. She is analogous to the brilliant writer Zora Neale Hurston, who was forced to spend her last years in obscurity working as a domestic servant.

In the late 1930s and 1940s Lucasta was a foster mother for the doomed Leonard Foster and a kind of surrogate mother for Joubert. Her influence on the two boys, especially in terms of art, was clearly very deep in spite of the many tragedies of her life and her failure to establish any kind of permanent relationship. Both boys became writers, Leonard an unsuccessful poet and Joubert a playwright.

Two of Joubert's most powerful memories of his childhood involve Lucasta. One is of a mysterious funeral, the first he had ever attended, at Fountain's House of the Dead, when Lucasta worked there. Joubert never does find out who the corpse was, but he never forgets his first encounter with death. The other memory is of a dark day in November when Lucasta's lover Tucson telephoned to tell her he would not marry her and was leaving her forever. Joubert instinctively responded to the seemingly inextricable relationship between Lucasta's remarkable and beautiful grace, the erotic feelings she aroused in him, and the pattern of death and loss that seemed to follow her until her death in 1966.

The novella is divided into three chapters. In the first, the haunting bluesy sadness of Lucasta's life is set against the wonderfully sparkling and comic vitality of Lucasta's sister, Gussie, and her husband, Forester. These characters were modeled to some extent on Forrest's own beloved great-aunt and great-uncle, whom he regularly visited at their little house in the Woodlawn—Sixty-third Street area of Chicago's South Side. Adamantly refusing to move as the neighborhood deteriorated, this amazing couple continued to raise a garden that brought a little flavor of the Old South to the urban wasteland. Wonderful Granny Gram Gussie, who even in old age dominates her powerful but adoring husband, is one of Forrest's great older women. She has the vitality and the vivacity of Sweetie Reed of *Two Wings to Veil My Face*, the woman who actually raises Arthur Witherspoon. But Gussie is much less devout than the deeply religious Sweetie. Even at her advanced age, she has enough human vanity that she rushes to put on fresh makeup when she imagines that her idol, Walter Cronkite, might appear to report a local fracas on television.

Granny Gram Gussie's irrepressible zest for life and her down-to-earth common sense (except when Walter Cronkite is involved) are also juxtaposed with the craziness of Marvella Gooseberry, a Forest County poetess who is standing off the police on a nearby roof by threatening to kill herself. Like Leonard Foster, Marvella has been traumatized by the violence that accompanied the civil rights struggle. In Marvella's case, her lover Paul was killed down in Mississippi, and Marvella believes he was betrayed by others in the Movement. Eventually Joubert is able to calm Marvella by promising her that he will arrange a confrontation between her and Milton Beefeater Barnes, a local character who is one of those blamed by Marvella for her lover's death. Later, in novella 5, we discover that Marvella's beloved Paul was about to leave her for another woman before his "accident."

This chapter also provides us with some important material about the background of the Jones family and its relationship to the white Bloodworth clan, plantation owners in Forrest County, Mississippi, and sexual exploiters of the black women whose destinies they control.

In the second chapter, Joubert's dreaming reminiscences shift to his close friend and adoptive brother, Leonard Foster, who, like his foster mother, Lucasta, has somehow never been able to find an outlet for his manifold talents and is driven to madness by his failure. Joubert's troubled relationship with Leonard is complex, and this pair in some ways resembles the pairing of the tragic Lucasta and the comic Gussie. In the next novella, *Live! At Fountain's House of the Dead*, Joubert attempts to bring Leonard out of his madness by reminding him of some of the earlier experiences that they shared. Eventually, instead of calming him, Joubert's comic reminiscences bring on a renewed attack of Leonard's madness. After this, the two kinsmen lose touch. Later, in *By Dawn's Early Light*, when Joubert reads a newspaper account of Leonard's death from exposure and a drug overdose, he remembers sadly how little he had seen of Leonard in the twenty years between 1972 and 1992.

The final chapter of *Lucasta Jones* takes us back to another, still earlier, November, remembered by Joubert as a traumatic time in which he saw Lucasta plunged from the height of joy into the depths of despair. This is the moment when Lucasta received a phone call telling her that her beloved Tucson, whom she expected to marry that very day, was leaving her. This terrible moment is associated in Joubert's mind with another early memory of a visit with Tucson and Lucasta to Riverview Amusement Park (an actual amusement park in Chicago).

There they watched Lucasta's friend Hopkins Golightly sitting in a cage and taunting white men to throw baseballs at a target connected to the cage. A bull's-eye on the target dunks the black man in a pit of water. This spectacle with its horrifying racist symbolism is one of Joubert's introductions to the reality of white hatred and racism and is also the background or undercurrent of Lucasta's failure. Racism is a major reason that Lucasta could not fulfill her potential as a dancer. Moreover, Lucasta's lover, Tucson, is transfixed by the significance of these black men suspended in cages to amuse whites. They make him aware of the fundamental vulnerability of his life and unwillingness to commit himself to anything for long. Joubert remembers this episode and other visits he made to Riverview to see and think about the dunking cages. It is with this in mind that he now approaches his visit with Leonard, another traumatized black man deeply vulnerable to white abuse and having difficulty dealing with his life. The dunking cages and the character of Hopkins Golightly are important motifs that will recur in later novellas, particularly in *By Dawn's Early Light*.

Live! At Fountain's House of the Dead

Considerably shorter and less complex than *Lucasta Jones*, the novella *Live! At Fountain's House of the Dead* continues Joubert's dream-memory of that same November in 1972 by portraying Joubert's visit with Leonard Foster and Leonard's further breakdown in spite of Joubert's best efforts to amuse him with humorous reminders of their childhood and youth. Leaving the hospital, Joubert encounters Jessie Ma Fay Battle Barker, another powerful older woman. Ma Fay's life has been a constant battle against the effects of racism and her own debilitating illness, but she has never given up the struggle or let her troubles keep her from helping others. Unlike Leonard Foster, Ma Fay has an inner strength that inspires Joubert to seek her counsel for some of his own troubles.

The action in this shorter novella is quite subtle because it consists largely of Joubert's telling stories in hopes of restoring Leonard Foster to sanity. The real center of the novella is the strange double nature of Fountain's House of the Dead and its proprietor, Thurston Fountain. A funeral home by day, Fountain's was the setting of the mysterious funeral that Joubert remembers attending with Leonard as a child. However, Fountain's is reputed to be a brothel by night, and Grandpa Forester, who does night janitorial work at another brothel, knows about it. Fountain himself is a cadaverously thin man who dresses himself up for funeral ceremonies in a costume that makes him appear as if he has just risen from the dead himself. In fact, this novella is full of images of life in death and death in life. These images relate to the condition of Leonard Foster, whose response to the trauma of the struggle for civil rights has been to bury himself alive in madness. Joubert hopes to help him resurrect himself by telling humorous stories of such transformations, but Leonard finds it nearly impossible to adopt a comic perspective on what are to him matters of life and death.

Related to the theme of blurred boundaries between life and death is the motif of cross-dressing and ambiguous sexuality, which also plays an important role in this novella. Grandpa Forester takes on extra night work at a fancy brothel patronized by whites mainly so that he can buy fancy hats to dress up his beloved Gussie. However, Gussie generally refuses to wear them just as she tries to keep knowledge of Grandpa's work at the brothel a secret from the boys and even from herself. To disguise the brothel, Grandpa has come to refer to it by a secret name: the Doo-Doo-Drop Inn.

Joubert has heard many stories about this place from Grandpa, but the most striking is one he overhears Forester telling a reluctant Gussie one night. A white Southerner regularly comes to the Doo-Doo-Drop Inn and chooses a prostitute not to have sex with but to allow him to dress up in women's clothes and parade in front of. When he leaves, he not only pays for the girl's services but also gives her the fancy gowns he has worn for her. The girls are very eager to be employed by such a client and have even been known to sell their gowns to Thurston Fountain for dressing up the dead. Now Joubert thinks that the mysterious funeral he saw at Fountain's may have been that of a person who was gay or a transvestite and that the community did not want to openly acknowledge this transgression.

Joubert mistakenly thinks that he has made some progress in bringing Leonard back to life, and he begins to reminisce about a hilarious episode early in Leonard's career as a civil rights agitator. This involved a demonstration against a grocery store known as the Red Rooster, which sold adulterated meat to residents of the ghetto. However, to his surprise, Leonard seems to regress to this earlier time and begins to rant in the manner of a sidewalk speaker, finally lapsing into such a fit that the attendants are forced to sedate him. It is clear that Leonard's suffering has been too much for him and that he may never again rise out of the death in life of his madness.

All Floundering Oratorio of Souls

As the second novella centers on themes of life, death, and transformation, the third novella deals with the pursuit and the failure of love. It focuses on three characters, two of whom are Joubert's fellow residents at the wonderfully diverse Avon. The other character, McGovern McNabb, is one of the regular customers at the bar operated by Joubert's aunt Eloise, the site of much of *Divine Days*'s action.

Shep Bottomly, a would-be intellectual and off-and-on student, hangs around the university and its International House looking for political arguments with all comers. He is one of what Joubert calls the Deep Brown Study Eggheads, who would rather win an argument than actually get anything done and would rather argue than anything else. Shep's father, the only African American professor at the local junior college, is a conservative economist. (Shep claims he became a conservative because liberal journals would not print his work. In rebellion, Shep considers himself a radical Marxist and a disciple of W. E. B. DuBois.) Though women are often attracted to him in spite of his political obsessions, Shep is only interested in white women but cannot establish permanent relations with them either, as Joubert realizes from a pathetic letter he receives from an Australian woman who had a brief fling with Bottomly in London.

Though Shep represents a totally different world, when Joubert takes this Deep Brown Study Egghead to Eloise's Night Light Lounge, Shep is fascinated by the four-hundred-pound "terrible tonnage" of McGovern McNabb, who often comically enacts the life-death motif by drinking himself into insensibility on the floor of the lounge. But it turns out that there is a strange connection between these two very different characters. McGovern McNabb is equally unable to establish a lasting relationship with a woman despite his daughter, Drucilla's, best efforts to find him a wife. In the end, McNabb is back on the floor of the Night Light Lounge, where we are treated to an amazing roasting and "signifying" over the comatose body of the inert McNabb by the barmaids and some of the regulars.

The last "oratorio" is the brief tale of Purvis Cream, another Avon inhabitant, who is so successful in his love life that he has women coming to his apartment in shifts.

To the Magical Memory of Rain

The fourth novella is quite different in style and atmosphere from the rest of *Meteor in the Madhouse*. To use a musical analogy, it is like the slow movement of a sonata or symphony. In a drastic change of pace from the complex development of *Lucasta Jones* and the scherzolike wit, satire, and sparkle of *Live! At Fountain's House of the Dead* and *All Floundering Oratorio of Souls*, *To the Magical Memory of Rain* reads like a myth or fairy tale. A dark version of the Cinderella story with touches of *Alice in Wonderland* and Greek mythology, it takes place in a magical world quite different from what is found in Forrest's other work. Only the more mythical sections of *The Bloodworth Orphans* or some of the tales of W. A. D. Ford in *Divine Days* have a similar aura.

At first this novella seems disconnected from the other parts of *Meteor in the Madhouse*. However, Desirée Dobbs, the heroine of the novella, is briefly Joubert's student. Her adventure begins when she goes to a carnival where she encounters a man who seems to resemble her dead father. Instead, he is apparently one of the many avatars of W. A. D. Ford, the demonic trickster of *Divine Days*. Later on, the haunting Lucasta Jones appears as the laundress who ironed the shirts of Desirée's father before his death. Moreover, it seems that Leonard Foster was once in love with Desirée and wrote her a poem that is quoted toward the end of the novella.

The magical world that Desirée enters seems to exist alongside the real world of Forest County, and Desirée steps into it, like Alice in Wonderland, as if she is stepping through a mirror. The story itself is a tale of love, enchantment, and deception, which, viewed from the other side of the mirror, is a story of the terrible seduction and corruption of drugs, for Desirée's dream prince turns out to be a drug lord as well as a magician and a serpent. Desirée's narrow escape at the end symbolizes her passage from the dreamy romances and dreams of girlhood into the colder but ultimately less destructive world of a young woman. Forrest powerfully evokes the seductive enchantment of the world of drugs that has destroyed so many African Americans and nearly hooks Desirée forever.

By Dawn's Early Light: The Meteor in the Madhouse

The date of November 1992 indicates that this is a continuation of the framing narrative that began in the first novella. It is divided into five chapters.

By Dawn's Early Light shares certain features with *Lucasta Jones*. Both novellas have a playlike dramatic scene at the center. At the end of *Lucasta Jones*, Joubert is on his way to visit Leonard Foster at the psychiatric hospital, while in *By Dawn's Early Light* he reads about Leonard's death from a drug overdose on the streets of New York City. Characters like Lucasta Jones, Marvella Gooseberry, and Hopkins Golightly, who appear in *Lucasta Jones*, return in important ways in *By Dawn's Early Light*. Finally, while *Lucasta Jones* deals with the beginnings and some of the important sources of Joubert's art, Joubert's life comes to a sudden and tragic end in the course of *By Dawn's Early Light*.

In chapter 1, Joubert rides home from the bus station in a taxi driven by a black woman. He is taken to his office at the university, where he plans to grade some overdue student papers. There are two other passengers in the cab: the driver C. J. Glover's white lesbian girlfriend, Martha, and a bewildered young Chinese boy who is on his way to Chinatown. The wonderful conversation between Joubert and the two women is one of Forrest's great comic passages and illustrates his remarkable ear for speech rhythms. Their discussion ranges widely over the contemporary scene and is suggestive of the new kind of multicultural and multiracial America beginning to develop in the late twentieth century. (This incident is based on an actual cab ride that Leon Forrest took in the mid-1990s on his return from a lecture to his home base at Northwestern University in Evanston, Illinois.) Joubert also comments on two kinds of literary creation: the con games played by an aspiring filmmaker he nicknames A.M.-P.M. for his unfortunate habit of calling his friends for help at all hours of the day and night and the diaries of his cousin Epistolla, a devout nun with a remarkable fantasy life. A high point of this chapter is the rap that Joubert improvises in place of a tip for his taxi ride.

In chapter 2, Joubert is going through the mail in his office and comes across a two-day-old edition of the *New York Post* with a headline announcing Leonard Foster's death: DRUGGED-OUT POET ROBBED / LEFT FOR DEAD IN THE GUTTER. The shocked Joubert thinks about his growing alienation from Leonard and remembers the last time he accidentally ran into his cousin, at a Holiday Inn where Leonard was preaching to a group of his followers. Recognized vaguely by Leonard as his enemy, Joubert is pursued by some of Leonard's followers, and in a hilarious chase sequence disguises himself to sneak back into the Holiday Inn, where a party celebrating his grandson's acceptance at a major university is in progress.

In the third chapter, which takes place on the day following the evening of his return from the lecture tour and his discovery of Leonard's death, Joubert goes to Williemain's Barbershop, his old stomping grounds from *Divine Days,* and then to a downtown bank. Here he gets a check made out to pay Memphis Raven-Snow's Funeral Home for taking care of Leonard's body. He thinks more about Leonard's death and its meaning.

In chapter 4, Joubert returns to Williemain's Barbershop, where he has left his reading glasses. There he is caught in an apparently gang-related shooting and is mortally wounded. The rest of *By Dawn's Early Light* represents fantasies, visions, and memories of the dying Joubert in his last hours.

First there is a kaleidoscopic section of flowing visions centering on the theme of light somewhat in the style of the stream-of-consciousness passages of *There Is a Tree More Ancient Than Eden* but more controlled and less diffuse than some of the wilder sections of that novel. Joubert apparently undergoes a sort of near-death experience in which his consciousness is flooded with light, which also manifests itself in sounds like the flowing lyric improvisations of the great jazz saxophonist John Coltrane. The motif of light leads Joubert from an otherworldly vision to a series of memories of his childhood. He thinks of the light in a church steeple that led runaway slaves to freedom and then of his delight in seeing van Gogh's *Starry Night* at the Art Institute with his aunt Eloise, Joubert's stepmother and aunt. But he also feels his childhood fear when he sees the light reflecting off a razor held by a street robber known as the Mother Goose. This is also associated with the searchlights on a police car that stopped Joubert and his teenage friends one night, until the watch commander realized he had the "wrong niggers." Next, he remembers the red light of an ambulance taking him to a hospital after he has jumped out of a window to escape from the irate ex-boyfriend of a woman he was making love to. Finally, he goes back to the headlight of a Lionel electric train that he and his father played with in the basement, to the disdain of the more sophisticated aunt Eloise. The toy train, like the symbolic train in *There Is a Tree*, becomes a gospel train and a funeral train as well as the train to freedom. This leads Joubert to a larger vision of the social and political hopes and terrors of his time and the impact of these struggles on the great tradition of African American women singers like Billie Holiday, Marian Anderson, and Mahalia Jackson.

As if through association with these powerful women, Joubert thinks of his cousin Phillipa, the ghetto teacher who has apparently come to visit him in the hospital. Phillipa symbolizes the continued struggle for redemption against hopeless odds, for "making a way out of no way," which Joubert has tried to celebrate in his plays and which has destroyed the unfortunate Leonard Foster and has now risen up to claim Joubert, himself. At this point Joubert seems to lose consciousness.

In chapter 5, Joubert recovers consciousness and has two extended memory experiences; one is of meeting again the remarkable character of Hopkins Golightly, the man he first saw as one of the "nigger" targets in the dunking cages at Riverview Park. Golightly has reinvented himself through several different avatars and is now a figure of some importance in the world of Forest County. The second and last memory is of a recent rehearsal of a section of Joubert's revised 1987 play, *Towards Jerusalem by This Lamplight in My Hand*, which Joubert apparently attended a few weeks before this final scene.

Years ago on one of his visits to Riverview Park, Joubert had seen Hopkins Golightly arrested near the dunking cages when he engaged in a one-man protest by singing a blues version of "The Battle Hymn of the Republic." What Joubert now remembers is having attended a performance by Golightly at a blues club full of young whites, an affair connected with a big party in honor of a man who would soon be elected Chicago's first black mayor. Golightly had carried the blues up from the South with him and had never forgotten his roots in spite of his many transformations. He is asked to put on a blues performance, in the course of which Joubert asks him to sing "The Battle Hymn of the Republic," reaffirming their long connection and the theme of Christ's transfiguring of "you and me."

Golightly is a fascinating character a little bit like Forrest's wonderful vignette of Meedmoxy Spears, the archetypal Chicago hipster whose transformations symbolized the changing African American culture of Chicago. Forrest created this character for a *Chicago Tribune* series of essays on Chicago culture by writers like Saul Bellow, Sara Paretsky, and Forrest. But Golightly is also in this context a Charon figure who becomes Joubert's guide to the underworld. At the beginning of chapter 5, Joubert remembers when Golightly, now the chief henchman of one of Forest County's leading preachers and politicians, led a select group of supporters into an underground hideaway where "a majestic Egyptian rug adorned the floor." In this strange cellar one encounters "the surprise arrival of the famous and notorious from all walks of life" and other features representing Hades and the underworld. Symbolically, Golightly is a mythical figure, like Charon, beckoning Joubert toward the next world. Significantly, his final gift to Joubert is a commingling of the great African American blues tradition with the vision of Christianity, a combination that Forrest believed to be the greatest strength of the African American cultural tradition.

The final episode before the powerful brief valedictory, in which Forrest writes the apotheosis of his protagonist and himself, is a section from Joubert's play representing a dialogue between the preacher Pompey C. J. Browne and Sadie-Sue Gooseberry (the younger sister of the mad poetess Marvella) on the eve of Sadie-Sue's wedding with Clay Cratwell, one of the barbers later shot along with Joubert at Williemain's Barbershop.

Sadie-Sue is a recovering drug addict, and Pompey C. J. Browne is a highly successful man of the cloth who is often criticized for his overly dramatic sermons. He is an important character in *Divine Days* and in the section Forrest later added to his first novel, *There Is a Tree*, where Browne preaches a memorial sermon for Martin Luther King in the after-hours Crossroads Rooster Tavern. Forrest sees the kind of mingling of the sacred and the secular that Browne represents as a great strength of African American religion, but he is also aware of the ambiguities that can arise with such a combination.

In this scene, Sadie-Sue asks Pompey's help in dealing with a recurring dream she has been having in which she wakes up in her bridal room to find it oozing with blood, which she desperately but unsuccessfully tries to wipe up with the bridal gown inherited from her grandmother. Sadie-Sue evidently feels great guilt about her past as an addict and also some concern that she is going to be married while her older sister, Marvella, seems doomed to loneliness and madness. She fears that when Clay Cratwell lifts her bridal veil he will discover her face stained with blood. Pompey tries to assuage Sadie-Sue's fears by reassuring her of God's love and questioning whether she has truly freed herself from her sinful past, but he is not very successful and even begins to doubt his own belief. Finally, Eli Elderberry, a highly cynical but successful preacher and politician, enters, and he, too, raises serious questions about the power of Pompey's faith.

Finally, these doubting voices give way to the voice of the hospital nurse, which becomes Joubert's final vision of angels crying "NOW BREATHE." The sound of Coltrane's soaring melodies return to become a tragic but triumphant valedictory along with the vision of transcendent light as Joubert is launched on his journey "out to other voices and other democratic chambers and other spheres into the distances of time."

Notes

1. Forrest refers to "the university" both in the narrative present and in Joubert's memories. However, he probably means two different universities, though he does not differentiate between them. In the earlier period, the university is clearly the University of Chicago, at which Forrest took some classes and near which he lived as a young man. The University of Chicago is located on Chicago's South Side. In the narrative present, the university where Joubert has his office is presumably Northwestern University, located in Evanston, Illinois. Forrest himself taught at Northwestern during the last part of his life.

2. An introductory summary of Forrest's first four novels can be found in "Leon Forrest: The Labyrinth of Luminosity," in *Leon Forrest: Introductions and Interpretations*, edited by John Cawelti (Bowling Green, Ohio: Bowling Green State University Popular Press, 1997).

3. In some sections of this final novella, which were among the last things Forrest wrote, he did not translate "Chicago" and some other local terms into the symbolic guise of Forest County, as he did in most of his earlier works. Though Forrest would probably have changed these in the course of revising the work, we, as editors, have decided to leave them unchanged.

Genealogies in

Meteor in the Madhouse

Merle Drown

JOUBERT ANTOINE JONES (1937–92) is the narrator and central figure of
Meteor in the Madhouse. His mother, AGNES TOBIAS, was born in 1920 and
died in 1940, after which her sister, ELOISE TOBIAS, married Joubert's father,
JERRY JONES (1917–49). After Jerry Jones's death, Eloise married HUGH
HICKLES. Eloise raised Joubert.

Jerry Jones is the son of GUSSIE JONES, who was born in 1900 and is also
known as Granny Gram Gussie. Gussie Jones is Joubert's grandmother. Although Jerry Jones's father was the white man CURLEW BLOODWORTH,
it is FORESTER JONES, married to Gussie Jones, whom Joubert treats as his
grandfather.

LUCASTA JONES (1890–1966) is Gussie Jones's older sister. She is the
mother of ARTHUR WITHERSPOON, by JUDGE JERICHO WITH-
ERSPOON. (Arthur Witherspoon, and his son NATHANIEL WITHER-
SPOON, appear in Leon Forrest's other works.) Lucasta is also the foster
mother of LEONARD FOSTER (1932 or 1934–92). Both boys are taken from
her.

Leonard Foster is Joubert's foster cousin and is often called the Little Dreamer.
His father, ROLAND LUKE FOSTER, was fathered by a white Bloodworth
and an unnamed black woman.

About the Author

Leon Forrest was born in Chicago in 1937 and is one of the most important African American writers of his generation. He taught English and African American studies at Northwestern University until his death in 1997. His novels include *There Is a Tree More Ancient Than Eden*, *The Bloodworth Orphans*, *Two Wings to Veil My Face*, and *Divine Days*.